Dreams of Decadence
haunt me through the ages, blood
my only relief.

*The Best of
Dreams of Decadence*

From Angela Kessler, editor and publisher of the pre-
mier vampire magazine, *Dreams of Decadence,*
comes an elite selection of prose and poetry as eerie
and immortal as the undead themselves. Collected for
the first time in one volume, these dark dreams bring
to life the irresistible lures and longings of the vampire experience—from the gothic to the modern, the
fanciful to the fierce, the icy-veined to the hot-
blooded.

The Best of
Dreams of
Decadence

EDITED BY
ANGELA KESSLER

A ROC BOOK

ROC

Published by New American Library, a division of
Penguin Putnam Inc., 375 Hudson Street,
New York, New York 10014, U.S.A.
Penguin Books Ltd, 80 Strand,
London WC2R 0RL, England
Penguin Books Australia Ltd, 250 Camberwell Road,
Camberwell, Victoria 3124, Australia
Penguin Books Canada Ltd, 10 Alcorn Avenue,
Toronto, Ontario, Canada M4V 3B2
Penguin Books (N.Z.) Ltd, 182–190 Wairau Road,
Auckland 10, New Zealand

Penguin Books Ltd, Registered Offices:
Harmondsworth, Middlesex, England

First published by Roc, an imprint of New American Library,
a division of Penguin Putnam Inc.

First Printing, March 2003
10   9   8   7   6   5   4   3   2   1

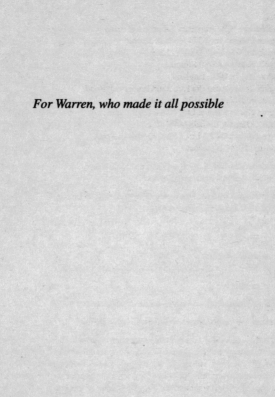

For Warren, who made it all possible

Dreams of decadence
haunt me through the ages, blood
my only relief.

—Warren Lapine

CONTENTS

INTRODUCTION

I admit it: I fell in love with vampires at the age of sixteen, when two of my friends talked me into reading *The Vampire Lestat.*

I never dreamed, though, that I would edit a vampire magazine. When I met Warren Lapine at a science fiction convention in 1993, he mentioned that he had been thinking of starting a vampire magazine. The title would be *Dreams of Decadence,* from a haiku he had written:

> *Dreams of decadence*
> *haunt me through the ages, blood*
> *my only relief.*

A neat idea, I thought, and a great title.

Warren and I became better acquainted; I began working as an associate editor for his magazine *Absolute Magnitude,* and he came to know and trust my taste in fiction and poetry. In 1994 he came to the conclusion that he was never going to get around to editing *Dreams of Decadence,* and asked if I would like to give it a shot. Sure, I said, full of trepidation and bravado; it should be fun.

I had no idea what I was getting into.

I sent out a call for submissions, and was surprised by both the volume and the quantity of submissions. I put together a good, solid issue, including the final story in this

anthology, "Under the Tangible Myrrh of the Resonant
Stars" by Charlee Jacob, which is still one of my favorite
stories I've ever published. *Absolute Magnitude* was always
full-size with a color cover, but the first issue of *Dreams,*
published in October 1995, was digest-size, photocopied at
Staples, and had a plain red cardstock cover. After all,
Dreams was only a side project, and anyway, we weren't
sure how much of a market there was for a vampire magazine, so we didn't know if it would sell.

It sold. We sold out of the first run of twenty-five copies
in one day at the first convention we took it to, and eventually that issue sold over 1,500 copies. The next issue had a
cover with red line art printed on white cardstock; it, too,
sold over 1,500 copies. Chain store Hot Topic picked up the
first two issues, and sales were good enough that they ordered the third issue, as well. By now we had the idea that
yes indeed there was a market for a vampire magazine, so
the third issue was printed on an offset press, with a slick
three-color cover. Sales exploded from there; with issue 5
we went to a full-color cover, and issue 6 (with a dreamy
cover by Beryl Bush, which we also used on the 2002 collection *Dreams of Decadence Presents: Tippi N. Blevins
and Wendy Rathbone*) had a print run of four thousand
copies and sold out in two weeks flat, with Hot Topic begging us to send them a thousand more. With issue 8 we
went to full-size.

Our immediate success drove some people in the field
crazy. "You haven't paid your dues," they sniffed. "Horror
is dying," others moaned, some adding, "and vampire fiction is part of what's killing the field." The reports of the
death of Horror are greatly exaggerated; in fact, horror and
dark fantasy have enjoyed a resurgence in the past few
years, and it was the revenue from *Dreams of Decadence*
that allowed DNA Publications to buy *Weird Tales* (which
at the time had lost the rights to the name and was known
as *Worlds of Fantasy and Horror*) and rejuvenate the oldest
genre magazine so that it is once again a force in the field.

Others scoffed, "Vampires are a passing fad." As Warren

says, "Tell that to Bram Stoker." While vampires may not always be the hottest trend of the month (witness the fact that Hot Topic ceased carrying it even though it was still selling extremely well because "Goth is passé"), there are still plenty of readers who love vampires. *Dreams of Decadence* is now available nationwide at stores such as Barnes & Noble, Books-A-Million, and Tower Records. The *Washington Post* did an article on us in August 2001, and it was picked up by newspapers across the country. Vampire novels, too, are thriving, in the capable hands of writers such as Laurell K. Hamilton and Chelsea Quinn Yarbro.

A more legitimate question that is often raised is, "Don't stories about vampires get boring and repetitious after a while?" As this anthology proves, the answer to that is a resounding *No!* The writers' guidelines for *Dreams of Decadence* state, "We want to see original ideas and story concepts, not rehashes. I like stories that take the traditional concept of the vampire into new territory, or offer a new perspective." If one defined vampire fiction narrowly as traditional stories where the vampires are the bad guys and the good guys have to stake them, or the more currently popular stories where the vampires are the good guys and they have to avoid the bad guys who are out to kill them (or both), then it could potentially get boring rather quickly. But as I often say on panels at conventions, many of the stories in *Dreams* are not "about" vampires; they are about interesting characters leading interesting lives (and undeaths). It just so happens that some or all of the characters are vampires.

The stories in this anthology feature vampires who are muses and artists, club kids and bouncers, soldiers and gangbangers, and even one who is just a baby. Some of them work with the police (at least sometimes). The vampires in these stories are both protagonists and antagonists; they feel love and hate, joy and remorse. The settings range from the eighteenth century through the present to the future; some are set in worlds very much like our everyday reality—others are set in worlds much more . . . interesting.

Altogether, they give a glimpse of the enormous range of possibilities for good, fresh vampire fiction.

Dreams also puts a lot of emphasis on poetry, which is dear to my heart. The poetry in *Dreams* can cover a nearly infinite range of perspectives, feelings, and images (while avoiding rotting corpses and too many conventional love poems). The poems in this anthology include Anne Sheldon's poems based on vampire folklore of other cultures, and selections ranging from the romantic to the venomous, from the whimsical to the melancholy, and the quiet dread of Laurel Robertson's "To See You Again." I have tried to pick the best of the best for this anthology, and though it is difficult because poetry is such a subjective art form that I probably could have picked an entirely different set of poems and justified them for different reasons, I do think that these show the range and depth of the poetry that I am privileged to publish.

It is with immense pride that I present this anthology, and I invite you to join us on a journey down the crimson path into the heart of eternal darkness, as we explore eternity.

                                        Angela Kessler
                                        Editor

The Best of
Dreams of
Decadence

Passionato

SHARON LEE

The blood palls, over time. I believe this is the reason why so few of us exist beyond the 150th year of our making.

Over time, the blood palls. Feeding oneself becomes, first, a chore; then an agony; finally, for some—for most—a hell. Anything becomes preferable to the anguish of taking one more sup, so one fasts. And one dies.

Those who survive this crisis of sensibility—those who evolve—are . . . formidable.

Formidable.

I am two hundred forty-seven years undead. Before my making, I lived fifteen years in Philadelphia, the son of a textile merchant. I bear the face and form of a boy in the first beauty of his manhood, as perfect as the night she created me.

My mother named me Evelyn James Farrington. My colleagues know me as Jim Faring. I am a painter. I do badly, which is all I expect. The others who work and live in this building—they take interest in my efforts, squandering hours of their short lifetimes to show me thus of perspective, this trick of capturing the light and this other thing regarding shadows.

My colleagues—young humans. So earnest. So full of life. Of—passion.

Understand that I am not human. I am—formerly human. In fact, I am a predator. But I spoke of evolution. The blood is not, entirely, necessary.

When one is new to the undead state, there is no draught headier, no nourishment more seductive, than a sup of that sweet claret. We drink from the artery in the throat—rich, full heart's blood, sparkling with the passion of life.

Yet, what nourishes us is not so much the blood, but that which the blood carries.

Passion.

Humans have—such—passion.

And artists have so much more.

Above all else, I am careful. When the great thirst comes upon me, as it does one moon in six, I do not drink here. I go away—uptown, to the bars and the music clubs. Most often, I take a singer, though any who play from their soul will slake me. There was a flutist, some years back—vibrant, seductive burgundy! But that vintage is rare.

At home, here in the Abingdale Artists Loft, I husband my resources and watch over my flock most tenderly. It would not do for one of my young colleagues to experience that languor which is the result of receiving the fullness of my Kiss. No. No, they must remain whole, awake, passionately involved in their art, producing that aura of lusty life energy so necessary to my own survival.

There are risks.

Artists are . . . notoriously . . . unstable. The least thing may with equal possibility fling them into a fever of creation or a black despair.

Years ago, I kept poets. The food was hot and wholesome when they were creating, but their passions consumed them even as I was nourished. It was a rare moon passed without a suicide.

Writers of prose are every bit as unsatisfactory as a reliable source of nourishment.

Visual artists are another matter. Perhaps because their work is concrete, perhaps because they work so intimately with the balances of shadow and light, weakness and strength . . . I find painters most satisfactory, though yet inclined to those deadly swings of mood. Rock-steady reliability is most often found in sculptors, but that food is never more than bland.

For a time I kept only painters. Recently, I find the stabilizing benefit of an eclectic herd—painters, potters, sculptors—outweighs my preference for the painterly passions.

Of this current herd, my favorite is Nikita. She paints in vibrant primaries: splashes of bold crimson, thick puddles of yellow, emerald arabesques . . . Ambitious, sensuous Nikita. Really, I am quite fond of her—almost too fond. I must be stern with myself, or I should be with her every day. It would not do to lose Nikita too soon.

Of the others, I especially enjoy Michael, who pots, and Sula, who does woodcuts. Jon is my sculptor, stolid and uninteresting; and the newer ones: Amy, Chris, Fortnay and Quill.

I find eight a good number, though I should perhaps look about me for another sculptor; Jon seems a bit fagged of late.

Contrary to Sula, to whom I go this evening.

I find it best to take myself to their studios, rather than Calling them to me. I find that the peculiar aura of the artist's own place adds a depth and piquancy to the nourishment that is entirely absent from a feeding taken in another part of the house.

Sula's studio smells of wood shavings, of beeswax, of sweat and of yesterday's coffee. Sula also smells of these things, and a salty, overripe femaleness. I believe she has many lovers.

Her back is to me as I enter the room. She is lighting the candelabra atop the battered chest of drawers that serves as her supply cabinet. I see her downturned face in the mirror behind the candles, dark skin waxy in the hot light. Behind her, in the mirror, the studio shows twilit and empty.

I wait until she has lit her last candle; until she has shaken out the match and pushed it, headfirst, into the sand-filled pottery cup that sits beside the candelabra. It is one of Michael's pots, glazed with stripes of sunset orange.

She turns at last from the bureau, heavy breasts swinging

under her loose shirt. I breathe across her eyes and she pauses, the momentary confusion of trance misting her face before she smiles, beatific, her nipples hardening into spears of ecstasy. She moves to her worktable, and I with her. She stands there, staring down—at nothing, save the scarred, stained surface—and in her mind, Sula dreams.

She dreams the most poignant piece of wood she has ever held. In her mind, she shapes it, with the strength of her will, into subtlety beyond mere beauty. Sula dreams with intensity, with pure savage power, and I stand over her, one hand above her heart, one hand cradling her forehead, drinking, drinking, drinking, as much a captive of her passion as she, of my trance.

Feeding of Sula can span objective hours, such is her vitality. Often, it is I who pull away, sated, and she who clings to trance and the dream-thing she is making. Tonight, I barely touched my peak, her lust coursing and lighting my veins, when I felt her—falter.

Shiver.

Against me, as never before, she . . . moaned, vitality spent, heart pounding, but with something other than passion.

Full, yet not yet satisfied, I stepped aside. She slumped against her work table, braced against her flattened palms, breathing in great gulps, as if she had been running, hard and long.

Alarmed that she might be sickening—that she might, indeed, have already passed her sickness to one or more of the others—I let the glamour go, extended a gentle hand and touched her shoulder.

"Sula?"

She started, the remains of trance shattering, shook herself and with an effort straightened.

"Hey, Jimmy." Her usual greeting, but without her usual verve.

"Are you well, Sula?" I asked, and she smiled a dazed smile and shook her head, pulling at the loose collar of her shirt.

"Tired," she said. "Hope I ain't caught that flu's going round."

I smiled and said I hoped so, too. She nodded and turned away, toward the candlelight, and it was then that I saw the cause of Sula's illness.

Just above her collar, dark against the dark skin, just over the luscious vein that runs from heart to throat, nestled two tiny, neat scars of a kind I had reason to know well.

I placed the Sleep upon her, which was a risk. Should the interloper return, Sula would be helpless to ward off the Kiss. But human defenses against us are paltry in any case, and she might actually take benefit from the trance, if the thief did *not* return.

Having done what I might for this one of my own, I went to check on the others.

Michael was locking his door as I came by; he waved cheerily and jangled his keys. "Hot date tonight, man! Don't wait up." He slapped me on the shoulder and would have gone on by, had I not Spoken.

"Michael." Humans are particularly vulnerable to the Speaking of their names. He paused, grin fading, eyes fogged; I pulled his collar wide.

Michael's skin is ivory, shadowed with indigo along the sweetly defined muscles, absolutely without blemish. Whoever had drunk of Sula had not tasted Michael. I straightened his collar and stepped back.

"Hot date tonight, Michael?"

Pale blue eyes blinked, focused. The grin flicked on like a blare of demon sunshine. "Hot is *not* the word," he said with a laugh, and strode on past, wiggling his fingers at me as he went. "Don't wait up!"

"I won't," I murmured, and continued down the hall.

Amy and Chris were in Amy's studio, a tangle of sweat-gilded limbs atop the spring-shot daybed. I Spoke their names, stroked them apart to search, then released them to their exercise.

Quill was before his easel, so concentrated upon the

work that I need do nothing but part his collar, search, and leave.

I met Fortnay on my way upstairs and lay the trance upon him before he had a chance to speak. No marks of the Kiss here.

It would begin to seem that Sula had met her misfortune during one of her frequent trips away. This did not mean my herd was secure, given the ability of my kind to trace any human one has tasted. However, I might not be in such immediate peril as I had at first feared.

I stepped away from Fortnay, who smiled in his vague way and pushed his glasses up on his nose.

"Going for something to eat," he said, looking just beyond my shoulder, which is Fortnay's way with his fellow humans, also. "Want to come along?"

"Another time," I said softly. "I've just now eaten."

"Right." He nodded at the wall behind my shoulder and continued downstairs, walking heavily in his spattered tennis shoes.

In the hallway upstairs, I found Nikita's door locked, the studio beyond dark. I stood just inside, breathing in the smell of turpentine, oils and Nikita's own scent, then went to the end of the hall and into Jon's studio.

He was lying in the center of the floor, the slab of dressed granite that had been his latest project a wonderworks of stone shrapnel, scattered all about. He had been dead a very little while; I could smell the effluvia of fresh blood over the dust in the air.

Jon himself was dry as dust, white as dust. Drunk dry and with casual violence thrown away, much as a human boy will smash a soda bottle when he's finished his treat, and for the same joy of wanton destruction.

I looked at him, my sculptor, dead and drained among the broken bits of his passion, and I was angry. How dare some interloper—some new-made, blood-crazed Visigoth—come into my place, take food from *me*, destroy what *was mine?*

The thief would pay for this outrage. I had not existed for

more than two centuries without knowing how to answer impertinence.

I searched the room and found what I expected to find—no sign of an intruder. Vampires are subtle; our powers many. Jon may never have seen his doom; he doubtless died in a dream of such rapture he barely noticed his own passing.

There were mundane tasks to attend to, then. I have found that the death of one distresses the balance of the herd, even if the one who has died was not especially beloved of his fellows. It were best that all trace of Jon be gone before the morrow, which bit of housecleaning consumed most of my nighttime hours.

I then visited my remaining artists and lay briefly with each, whispering into their dream-minds until I was satisfied that Jon was shrouded in the fog of faraway memory. Likewise, I persuaded each to believe that the studio at the end of the top hallway was a storeroom. That it had never been anything else.

Each, I should say, but Nikita, who did not return to her rooms until sunrise forced me back to mine.

It was to her door I went first, when twilight released me: It was locked, the room dim, the enormous window Nikita prized so highly muffled in yards of sable fleece. I fingered the soft stuff, then stepped round to the easel.

A painting was in progress—a sweep of orange bisecting a dagger of sea-glass green against the stark white canvas ground. The oils were dry, the swirls upon the palette board blots of crusty color. Nikita had not painted today. It seemed that she had not painted yesterday. And Nikita painted every day. It was not unusual for her to paint through the night and into the next day, when the passion was upon her.

I searched the rest of the studio, but found nothing further to alarm me: Her clothes, her completed works, her meager cash were all in place. The tiny refrigerator held a quart of milk, four eggs, half a loaf of bread, a depleted bottle of red wine. All precisely as it should be, lacking only Nikita herself.

On the point of quitting her apartment, I paused, frowning at a blank space on the cluttered wall.

Nikita had done a self-portrait at the beginning of the summer—a radical departure from her modernistic style. It had hung in this spot, now vacant, among the other paintings she considered worthy of being framed.

A short search discovered it, stashed behind six much-despised abstracts, near the edge of the shrouded window. Framed in stark stainless steel, the canvas showed a wire-thin woman in paint-spangled jeans wearing a man's white shirt, untucked, like a smock, the sleeves rolled to her elbows. Her face was a study in the simple power of line and shadow, her eyes great and dark beneath thick eyebrows. She stood at an easel, of course, paintbrush in hand, poised on the balls of her feet. The impression of the whole was of power, of intensely focused, *living* passion.

Carefully, I lifted the painting, carried it across the room and hung it in its place.

Then I went to tend the others.

Michael's door was ajar, but Michael was not within. Chris and Amy were with Quill, coaxing him to call it a day and lend his enthusiasm to a threesome destined for Amy's daybed. As I left, he allowed himself to be convinced, and began hurriedly to put his brushes by.

As last evening, I met Fortnay on his way to dine. As last evening, I refused an invitation to join him and turned the corner, on my way to Sula's studio.

Michael knelt in the center of the hallway, blond head thrown back, a rigor of ecstasy upon his features. The ivory column of his throat glowed in the silver dimness; his naked chest ran sweat.

The figure standing behind his right shoulder, jeweled and painted fingers stroking his sweat-slick skin while pressing its lips to that place where the sweet blood ran swiftest, raised its head and snarled.

It was an admirable face for snarling—pinched and

paper-white, a bare stain of claret across the stark cheek-bones, the lips glistening dark.

"That human is mine," I said, and stood forward. The other licked her lips, slowly and with satisfaction.

"He showed no mark. He came willing." She ran her skinny fingers along the sweet curve of his rib cage. "Didn't you, Michael?"

"Yes," he gasped, hoarse and trance-locked. "Oh, *God*, yes!"

She smiled and bent her head to tongue the place, tantalizing herself.

"Have you no more for me, Michael? Shall I stop?" Her voice was velvet, warm and suffocating, resonant with power. A human could no more stand against it than a dog against its master's command.

"No!" Michael gasped. "Take me. I'm yours . . . all yours . . ." He was groaning, back arched in passion, his manhood straining against the prison of his jeans.

She smiled. "All mine," she murmured, and fastened again upon the heart vein. Michael cried out, sobbing in his frenzy, the passion roiling off of him in sweet, delicious waves. . . .

In my desire to ensure the safety of my household, I had not yet taken nourishment. Here before me lay a feast. I went forward and wrapped him in my embrace, drinking his rapture as the other drank his heart's blood, riding the rising tide of his passion until, at the pinnacle, while I clung, drunk with him and able to do nothing else, save drink more—at the peak of this ecstatic experience, Michael—was gone.

Besotted, bewildered, I staggered upright and stood staring at the other, the drained, white body between us, quiet, as dead to passion as we are.

"You did not have to drink him dry," I said then, the words thick on my tongue.

She shrugged, rosy-faced now, and plump with blood. "There are more," she replied, and waved a ringed hand casually toward the wall. "So many more that all of us together couldn't drink them dry, if we drank three times each evening." She smiled, slyly.

"Why blame me, when you fed, too?"

But my feeding had not slain him. Michael had been very good: satisfying, resilient, strong. I had hopes of a breeding pair, between himself and Nikita, but had put the project off—too late now. I frowned at the other and raised my hand.

"This is my place," I said, and the words were not thick now, but laden with full power. "These are my humans. If I find you here again, I shall break you into bits and bury the bits at four separate crossroads."

A potent enough threat, though she met it with a stare. But I am old and she, I considered, had not yet seen her first hundred years. Her eyes dropped first.

"All right," she agreed sulkily and moved her foot to touch that which had been Michael before she looked to me again. "He was sweet."

"So he was," I said. "Did you find the other sweet, as well?"

She frowned, puzzlement plain. "Other?"

"Were you not here last night to feed?"

"Oh." She smiled, showing malice. "That wasn't me. That was the new one."

"Which new—," I began, but she was done with questions and simply turned and walked away.

After a moment, I entered Sula's room.

It was no real surprise to find she was dead.

It was nearly dawn when I returned to her room, having used the hours between to set a different order of frenzy upon those remaining, so that they packed their belongings in panic and fled into the fading night, scattered and, thereby, safe.

I did not know where they ran to—I had no need. When the present crisis was retired, I would Call. And they would come.

Nikita, now.

Nikita.

She stood before her easel, jeans spattered with the jewels of past passions, wearing a man's white shirt untucked, like a smock, sleeves rolled to her elbows. She held a paintbrush in one hand, but she was not painting.

She was weeping.

Weeping is a human thing. I have not wept in two hundred years.

She looked up as I entered, eyes brilliant, cheeks rosy red. Suffused with blood.

"He said I would live forever," she said with the air of answering a question. "He said I would always be just as I was at the moment of—change."

Superficially true—one *looks* precisely as one looked at the moment of one's making—for as long as one remains undead. But change is—change. We sacrifice to embrace evolution.

"I thought," Nikita said, rather breathlessly. "I thought that if I lived forever—kept painting, learning, *growing*—that one day I would be the—the world's greatest painter." She groped on the table beside her, located a rag and carefully wiped her brush.

"I've always wanted to be the world's greatest painter," she whispered, and slipped the brush into the cleaning jar. She turned from the easel and came toward me—extended a thin hand and lay it against my chest.

"You're one of them," she said. "One of *us*."

"Yes."

Her eyes widened, spilling more tears.

"I can't paint." Her voice was cold. "It's—gone."

"Humans are of passion," I said. "We are—the next level. Reason. Power."

"Power." Her gaze wandered over my shoulder, to the self-portrait I had rehung. "Right." She looked back.

"What do you live on? Not . . . blood . . ."

"A little blood. I live on—human passion. But I am—old. At first, the blood is—necessary."

"It's horrible," she whispered. "Like getting drunk and

high at the same time. Jon. Poor Jon—he was gone so quickly. . . ."

Her eyes were back on my face. "I'm so stupid, I don't even know—I guess I'm . . . invincible, right? I mean, nothing kills the undead."

"Some things do," I told her. "The old ways: a stake through the heart, molten silver poured into the head. Sunlight."

She blinked. "Sunlight?"

"You must be very wary, especially at first. Sunlight will annihilate you, young as you are. When you are as old as I, you may risk a few moments in full sun. We are not of the light."

"Humans are of the light," Nikita said, and her eyes moved again, seeking the painting beyond my shoulder. "Painting is of light and shadow. . . . No wonder you never caught on, as hard as we tried to teach you. . . ."

"Nikita, who made you?"

She frowned. "Made—? Oh. A guy I met at one of the clubs. He said he was eighty years old. He looked seventeen—like you, no lines in his face. Said he was on a . . . mission. . . . All I had to do was trust him." She shook her head. "I don't remember too much about it—he kissed me, I think. I went back the next night. And the next. The fourth night he told me he was going to make me immortal, so I'd always be just like I am now. . . ." Her voice broke.

"He should have trained you more fully," I said. "My own maker trained me carefully, so I would not make a foolish mistake, like going out into the sunlight or attempting to cross running water. . . ." Nikita wasn't listening. She was staring at the makeshift curtain she had drawn across her window.

"I put that up because the sun—made me sick. . . ."

She looked back to me.

"You're old, you said. How old?"

"Two hundred forty-seven years."

"That's old," she said. "And you still can't paint."

"I will never paint," I told her. "Humans paint. And even among humans a true artist is rare."

She nodded then, very slowly, and took my arm and turned me toward the wall. She pointed at the portrait of the human girl, poised before her easel.

"That's yours," she said. "Send the rest of them to my mother, OK? Her name's Sandra Elmwick—she's in my address book. She always said I'd kill myself."

She dropped my arm and went toward the door, her stride firm, her thin back straight.

"Nikita . . ."

She opened the door, looked at me over her shoulder.

"I'm going for a walk," she said. "It's going to be a beautiful morning."

She went, and nothing I might do to stop her, who was impervious now to my Speaking of her name. From the threshold of her room, I heard the front door open and close.

Four seconds later, I heard her scream.

All Things Being Not Quite Equal

DIANA PHARAOH FRANCIS

An ugly vampire with a frizzy perm isn't exactly effective, not even at closing time at the sluttiest bar in the city. There didn't seem to be a man or woman among the drunk and leering desperate enough to take Esther up on her too obvious invitation. Not even when she was wearing a blouse unbuttoned nearly to her navel, tight leather pants and four-inch heels. Not that she didn't have a reasonably good body—a little straight up and down, maybe, but not repulsive. It just wasn't enough to overcome her face. There had been that one guy whose friends had dragged him off in evident pity before he could make a terrible mistake. Oh, it would have been a mistake, all right, just not the one they anticipated.

Truth be told, Esther looked foolish at best, downright bizarre at worst. She knew it the way she knew this entire scheme had been a bust. And she was hungry.

It looked like it would have to be another neck-breaker, though. And if she made many more of those, she'd be forced to move on before long. The whole serial killer frenzy would develop and it would be just too much of a hassle to try to dine around the schedules of the marauding cops and reporters. And this time she'd more than likely have to go abroad—the U.S. was getting a bit small for a neck-breaking serial vampire. Course, if she could get the hang of the overwhelming strength that had come along with becoming a vampire, then she might manage to just knock her victim out.

Esther glanced toward the door and sighed. She'd have split hours ago if it weren't for Desiree. Desiree. Now, she was your stereotypical beautiful vampire. Men and women fawned all over her wherever she went—from the Circle K to The Ritz and back again. With the sex appeal of a goddess she could and did take her pick from whomever appealed on any given night. And she rarely had to kill. Course, serial-killing wouldn't have bothered her much. She got along abroad as well as she got along at home. A breeze. Whereas Esther hardly survived the rare personal interaction of her elevator clerk, much less tonight's bar crowd or a cabdriver in Paris. She could picture herself on the verge of dawn trying to get some drunk Parisian to give her the time of day. It would be humiliating and she'd kill him and then the whole serial killer thing would begin all over again.

She yawned and rubbed her eyes. Desiree was taken care of for the night, and it wasn't as if leaving her here would subject her to any danger she wasn't looking for. In fact, she liked on occasion to mess with these overmuscled construction-worker types.

Esther glanced once more at her watch. It was getting on to closing time and she'd better get moving. She didn't like to mess in her own backyard, as it were, and the farther away she could get from here, the better. It might take longer to hook her up to the murder. Yeah, fat chance. She had the luck of a hooker in a monastery and either she cut it too close and left still hungry, or the thing was witnessed and she had to kill another two or three people just to keep her identity a secret and then the whole thing disintegrated from there.

"Hey!" It was Desiree's sultry voice, and Esther swung around, her brows raised.

"It isn't working. And I'm hungry." She wasn't in the mood to be polite. But Desiree never expected it of her and ignored the acid in the other woman's voice.

"It might have, if you'd even tried to look helpless and easy. But no, you look like, well, like you, but in sleazy clothes."

"Well, you know what they say about cats changing their spots. Look, I have to find something to eat. Catch you tomorrow at Vanity?" She didn't wait for Desiree's nod before she was out of the door.

In the end, it turned out much better than she had expected. She found a guy who'd been mugged in an alley. His blood alcohol was tolerably low and he didn't taste anything like heroin or coke. So she got off easy.

The next night she didn't bother with the slut clothing. That getup and the horrific perm had been Desiree's idea and a pretty bad one at that. This time Esther dressed in her traditional blue jeans and black blazer over a man's white V-neck undershirt. She pulled her hair back into a tight ponytail, hooking it with a silver clasp in the shape of a dragon. It had always been her totem. Even Jeremy didn't know about the tribal dragon tattoo she sported along the length of her left calf. She glanced at herself in the mirror before heading out. Too bad that the myth about vampires not having reflections was just that. She didn't look nearly so bad as the night before, but not even makeup could help the face.

Esther stuck her tongue out at herself and headed for the door. She'd been at this for nearly a year now and she just didn't seem to be getting the hang of it. She just didn't seem to be like any of the other vamps, not even Jeremy, who had sired her. She had developed incredible strength; she could shapeshift fairly well, although she really needed more practice. She was faster than any other vampire she'd met so far, and she'd developed a grace and agility that she'd never even imagined before.

On the other hand, she was still damned plain—okay, ugly would be more accurate, she thought sardonically, but some women underestimated their weight or overestimated their height, so why couldn't she put a kinder spin on her looks? Even if no one else could.

Esther also couldn't hear Jeremy when he mind-called her. That was bad. You're supposed to be able to hear your sire, and all his relations—the family brood. She couldn't hear a single one. Actually, as far as she was concerned it was a perk because for the most part she didn't think she wanted to hear a bunch of idiotic babbling in her head. But what was probably worse was she really hadn't lost her human personality foibles. She still ate chocolate and Chinese food. Well she didn't swallow either of them, but she still liked the taste. More than blood. Which was completely beyond the pale for a vampire and which was why she hadn't mentioned it to anybody but Jeremy. But then he'd been in on the experiment from the first. In fact, it had been his idea.

They'd become friends when she was working nights as a janitor in a clinic. They were a blood bank, too, and Jeremy had liked the irony of working there, though he, like any other respectable vampire, despised dead blood and wouldn't have touched it to save his skin. Esther concurred wholeheartedly with him on that point. Anyhow, he'd been a medic or something like that years ago, before he'd been introduced to the walking dead, and so he worked as a nurse at the clinic. For some strangely odd reason he'd taken a liking to her. A real liking, which was also out of vampiric character and so maybe it was his fault that she wasn't quite up to specs.

Esther had been her usual self to him, which is why she worked as a night janitor where she wouldn't come into contact with the public. Her few coworkers avoided her like the plague. But Jeremy had taken to spending her breaks with her, bringing her bits of gossip and egging her on in her tirades against stupidity.

When the subject of her looks came up, and she had begun to bitch and moan about men and their fixation on big breasts and big hair, Jeremy had listened and laughed at her. And then he had proceeded to introduce her to the world of the vampire. He had thought, and with pretty good evidence (Esther had to admit that, since she'd gone along with the scheme), that if he made her into a vampire, then she'd develop an animal attraction that no man could resist, her face wouldn't break out anymore, plus all the other little perks.

Clearly, he'd been wrong.

Now she'd become some sort of sideshow freak of the vampiric kind. It turned out her genes were stronger than any power of magic. Such was life. Except now she was going to be ugly for a whole lot longer than she'd originally planned. The upside was there was a certain amount of fun to be had being a vampire, not the least of which she could stay out all night in the worst part of town and not have to worry about getting mugged or raped, or whatever. In fact, at first she had courted such "dangers" since they were often the best opportunity she had to eat.

Now she was back to the hungry thing. Vampires liked to eat as often as regular folk and the sex appeal thing was the usual way of luring in likely victims, which is why you find so many of them hanging out in bars. And Esther had to admit that the one time she'd tried eating of the animal kingdom, she'd about gagged. That was not an option. She'd refused brussels sprouts, lima beans and liver as a human, and she wasn't going to dine on anything less than human as a vampire.

Esther jogged up the three flights of stairs to Vanity, where she now worked as a bouncer. It was mostly a hangout for vamps, but it had developed the reputation of a hot spot in town, and so attracted normals like flies. It was pretty much the cliché—vampires hanging out in bars. But if the shoe fits and all that crap, and it was pretty much the equivalent of fast food, or 7-Eleven. But since the various bloodsucking broods were always squabbling about something, it was necessary to have someone on hand who could deal with them. Esther's weird natural resistance to their mind commands combined with her speed and strength made her the ultimate bouncer, and Carmen was happy to keep her on the payroll, even if she was paying an arm and a leg for the privilege.

Now Esther pushed her way through the line and made her way up to the bar. Behind the tide of mahogany, Quentin nodded at her and pointed toward the stage. A makeshift mosh pit had sprung up and Marcus and Benjamin were in the process of trying to clear it out. Most of the vamps involved were willing to back down and drift away, but several were battling with the two dead bouncers. And the two idiots were losing, because they'd always had more muscle than brains, and from the looks of it, the malcontents were of Lucien's brood. Which meant trouble, any way you sliced it.

Esther shouldered her way through the rubberneckers—vamps and humans were all alike in that respect—until she arrived at pitside, as it were. When Marcus fell in her direction, she reached forward and grabbed him by the collar and yanked him from the fray. He spun around, the long nails on his fingers turning his hand into a formidable claw. Esther lifted her finger and shook her head at him before turning back to the fight. Lucien's four had not yet realized that another party was involved and now were shoving a bleeding Benjamin back and forth between them.

Esther sized up her opponents. All of them were about six feet, with slick hair, decked out in understated yet expensive jewelry and wearing your basic designer suits in godawful shades of flower pastels—clearly they had too much time on their hands. And they were damned full of themselves. She sighed. She hadn't been at this bloodsucking biz for long, but had discovered that there were as many arrogant jackasses in this crowd as in the human crowd. She undid the buttons of her blazer and walked into the group, grabbing Benjamin as she had Marcus and tossing him into the crowd. The four looked at her with undisguised amusement and irritation.

"I think it's time for you boys to leave." She liked saying that. It was straight out of some bad fifties movie, but it was still fun. The one to her right crossed his arms and shook his head.

"I disagree. We were just beginning to enjoy ourselves. Get lost." It was the cornflower blue jacket.

"Can't do that. Actually, to tell the truth, I could, but I don't feel like it." Esther propped herself against the stage and waited for the inevitable. Well, it wasn't much. It never was. They tried to bend her mind and of course she couldn't hear them—even though *everyone* could hear Lucien's brood, he being the lord and master of all the vamps. She'd only ever encountered his blood—never him, but they were arrogant as all hell and they had to get it from somewhere. Since she couldn't hear them, she had to wait until they looked at each other in bewilderment before she knew they were through. For a moment she contemplated pretending her brain was melting, but that really would have been over the top.

Esther held up her hands, the nails hardening into wickedly curved eagle talons. That was a trick she'd been playing with for a while—and minuscule shape changes. With a quick movement she slashed the front of the golden-rod and key-lime jackets, raising thin streaks of nearly black blood beneath the ribbons of cloth. Both of them looked stunned and faintly unnerved. They fell back, joined in a moment by the pink gladiola jacket. That left the blue boy. It was Esther's own pack-animal theory for dealing with her fellow vampires. There was always a ringleader in a group, an alpha, and if you let his or her friends know you, too, were an alpha, they would always get out of the way and let the strong sort out the problem.

"Time for you to go," Esther said, letting her hands return to their normal shape.

Her adversary rolled his eyes and shook his head. "Not on your life, bitch. We're not going anywhere."

He had that whole "make me" attitude of a twelve-year-old bully facing down the neighborhood whipping boy. Not very original, and although there were several people in the crowd hooting and egging him on, Esther was coming to the decision that this was getting boring, and she did not get paid to be the floor show.

Her speed surprised him. That and the fact that she did a shape change at the same time so that the pincer grip on his neck was enhanced by the eagle claws digging a half an inch into his flesh. He began to jerk away but Esther gripped harder and he froze. It wouldn't take much to snap his neck. She shoved him toward the back door, gesturing at Marcus and Benjamin to bring his buddies. Beneath her fingers she felt him going vampiral on her. His eyes were beginning to glow yellow and blood ran down his chin from where his teeth had punctured his lip. It always happened like that, which is why Carmen had her toss any misbehaving vamps out the back. Humans tended to get queasy at the sight of blood, and then there was every chance that a pissed-off vampire would get a bit rabid and go hog-wild on the crowd. Very bad for business, and bad for the rest of bloodsucking community.

Esther wasn't very gentle with this one. She pushed through the kitchen and out to the freight elevator, bouncing him against the walls as she went. She twisted her key in the lock and when the doors opened, slung him across to the other side, where his head careened off the wall. Oops. His friends followed behind more meekly.

"You can request readmittance in six months. You didn't do any structural damage, so your chances are good. But don't think of coming back before."

Blue boy was back on his feet, wiping the blood from his lip with his knuckles, though his shirt and jacket were sodden with the stuff that had run from the holes she'd made in his neck. It smelled good. Esther's nostrils flared and she felt that deep hunger stir in her veins. Her lips curled in a snarl and she stepped back, pushing Marcus and Benjamin behind her. Their control was limited and she dearly hoped they'd fed before coming in like they were supposed to. Blue boy would have to handle his buddies whose eyes were beginning to glitter. Esther hit the down button.

"Lucien is going to hear about you," he said hoarsely as the doors began to close.

Esther ignored him and turned around. Neither of the

rubber-headed bouncers appeared to have been too affected by the blood, which meant they must have fed. Good boys. She sent them back to make sure that things were flowing smoothly and returned to the bar. Desiree was there.

"I don't know if you should have done that," she said as soon as Esther appeared.

"What? Them?" She made a face and shrugged. "That's the job."

"Yeah, but couldn't you have handled it a little more . . . delicately?"

"What for?"

"*Fucking A,* Es. Don't you know who they were?"

"Assholes with big teeth?" Esther hooked a stool with her foot and perched on it beside her friend.

"Yeah, well that, too. But those were *Lucien's.*"

"We get a lot of his in here. So what."

"Not like these. The one in blue? That's Lucien's *own.* Rumor is the great one is grooming him for bigger things, if you know what I mean. Pissing the twerp off will only bring Lucien down on your head."

Esther glanced over at the other woman. She didn't sound all that concerned, but probably as concerned as any vampire ever was. Whatever.

"Who wants to live forever?" she asked philosophically as she stood up, noting the irony of her question with a slight grimace. "Better make the rounds. See ya in a while."

There wasn't any more trouble for the rest of the night other than the usual drunken spats, and everyone maintained a safe and respectable distance from Esther. Desiree disappeared before the band made its appearance. That didn't bother Esther. She'd be back if she got bored. It all depended on whom she'd picked up.

Esther hadn't followed her own rules and had not fed before coming in. So that left her less than an hour before dawn to find something or go hungry until nightfall. The thought wasn't appealing. She skimmed down the front stairs, leaving the cleanup crew wiping down the tables and sweeping the floors. The night was overcast and the streets gleamed with a soft film of rain. Esther paused at the bottom of the steps and tipped her head back as she sniffed the air. The air was crisp, although neither heat nor cold bothered her. That was another benefit of being a vampire. She used to swelter in the summer and freeze her ass off in the winter. Now she didn't need special wardrobes for different times of the year, didn't need an air conditioner, a heater or a humidifier.

There wasn't any likely lunch food hanging around or lying in the gutter passed out. Bummer. She didn't have time to do a lot of hunting, and the fracas with blue boy and his friends had sharpened her hunger. She felt her body tense at just the thought of rich warm blood. She licked her lips as her insides began to turn to hot liquid. Her skin prickled and a tremble ran the length of her body. She knew her eyes had begun to take on the glow of an aroused vampire. Only hers went this sort of dusky purple color rather than the typical yellow or green.

"I've been waiting for you."

Esther spun around, her teeth bared. She didn't even try to quell the changes in her body sparked by rising appetite. She didn't know him. He was dressed very much like she was, in black jeans, a black turtleneck, and a black blazer. His long hair was the color of dark mahogany and was clubbed behind his head. Like all vampires—or rather most, because she was certainly the exception—he was beautiful, with a Greek nose, a sculpted face and a tall, muscular body. Esther wanted him, and she was pretty sure he knew it so she didn't bother to hide the fact.

"Who the hell are you?" she demanded, her voice gone husky and deep as her arousal grew.

"My name is Lucien," he said. "Perhaps you've heard of me."

"Oh, yes. Some of yours tore up Vanity tonight. But that isn't why you're here."

"As a matter of fact, it is." He stepped closer and Esther's eyes narrowed. He was stalking her, and she wouldn't be surprised if he were trying to pry into her mind. Only he couldn't. She didn't think he'd like that.

"Well, get to the point, because I want to feed before dawn."

"Yes, I can see that," he said, and Esther bristled. He was mocking her. "I hadn't believed what Andre said about you, but it would appear that he is correct. I can't touch your mind, and I can touch *every* vampire's mind. This is very disturbing to me. You understand."

Esther did. Lucien maintained his power in the vampiric world by his and his brood's abilities to screw with everybody else's minds. So, what if she started populating the world with a brood he couldn't control? She'd thought it through a couple of times since she'd gone to work for Carmen and found out how the system worked. It was just a matter of time until the great man himself turned up.

"You can't kill me," she said bluntly. "At least not tonight. I can take you. I promise." She wasn't bragging and she wasn't bullshitting. He knew it. But her next words surprised him. "Bring some friends tomorrow, same time. You'll lose a few, but you can afford it."

"You're a cool one. Are there more of you?"

Of course he'd want to know that. "No. Not unless my sire threw more accidents."

"Who is your sire?"

The fire in her veins was burning hotter and Esther was itching to feed, and . . . other things. Things that Lucien was not going to be interested in doing with her. She shook her head, her lips curling.

"You can find that out for yourself. I'll not send him your kind of trouble. Are we through?"

"Oh, no. We are most definitely not through. But perhaps this is not the time—" He looked her up and down, and while normally that would have pissed her off, tonight it inflamed her more. He saw the flare in her eyes and smiled. "You'd better feed. Come."

He held a hand out to her and she looked at it. What the hell? She put her fingers in his. He led her to a dark green

Porsche with dark tinted windows and helped her in. Esther tapped her fingers restlessly on her knees as he drove. He pulled up in the parking garage of a hospital. When she looked at him he shrugged.

"People come and go all night. Nurses, doctors, other staff. Easy pickings. Come on."

Once again he took her hand, and Esther wondered if he was trying to keep her from going on a bloodthirsty rampage. She felt like telling him she had a bit more control than that, but a red stain was spreading across her vision as she caught the scent of prey.

"Easy now. Wait until we get some privacy."

He pulled her between a couple of minivans near an entrance. When a lone man came walking up Lucien grabbed him, gripping his throat until the man hung unconscious. He passed the body to Esther. She cradled the man, tilting his head back so that the length of his tan throat was exposed. The hunger was almost overwhelming and she bit deeply into artery at his neck. She preferred the oxygen-rich blood of the artery rather than the bitter-tasting juice in veins.

It ran down her throat like sweet syrup and she moaned aloud. But then she remembered her companion and her eyes flashed open and she watched him sharply as she fed. Lucien leaned against one of the vans, his arms crossed, watching Esther sate herself. As she continued to feed he finally stepped forward and pulled her up.

"Don't drink him dry. You can have another."

Esther let him pull the body away in spite of the sarcasm. He snared her gaze now as he deliberately bent and flicked his tongue over the oozing bruise where she'd bitten the man's neck. The wound closed instantly and the dark stain beneath the man's skin faded to nothing. Lucien dropped the body behind him, running the tip of his tongue over his lips. In the end Esther fed twice more before returning to Lucien's car.

"Where are we going?" she asked when he peeled out.

"To my place."

"No."

"Where, then?"

Esther looked over at him for a silent moment and then gave him her address. If they didn't get under cover soon, they would be in the car until the sun went down. That wouldn't be a whole lot better than his place. Jay, the third-shift elevator guy, gave them a faintly stunned look as he took them up to her apartment. It was hard to be offended. She couldn't recall ever bringing another man up here. She hadn't even brought Jeremy. And to show up with a speci-men like Lucien. It was like Quasimodo taking home Cindy Crawford.

The elevator opened on the top floor—her entry. They stepped into a polished wood foyer carpeted with thick hand-woven wool rugs—money was another perk of being a vampire. Esther waved Lucien into her living room through an arched opening on the right and motioned for him to take a seat on the couch while she switched on a light. Not that either one of them needed it. The room's floor-to-ceiling windows were shrouded in dark curtains that she always left closed before leaving for Vanity. Lucien lounged on the cream-colored suede of the couch while Es-ther leaned against a bookcase opposite.

"Okay. Now what," she said.

Lucien tucked his hands behind his head. "Blunt and to the point. Very well. Let's talk about you."

"What about me?"

"You're a danger to me. You must know that." Esther didn't answer and he continued. "At the same time, you could be very valuable."

"Do stop. You'll make me blush." Her sarcasm wasn't lost on him but his smile held no hint of apology. He was watching her and his gaze was unnerving. Suddenly Esther was very tired of this fencing. She'd never been particularly adept at the social graces, and to be honest, had never really seen the point. She felt tired, tired in the way she used to before she'd been born a vampire and needed never sleep again. She sank down on her haunches and tilted her head back against the blond wood of the bookcase, never taking her gaze from Lucien's.

"Tell me what you want. What fate you've decided for me."

Her words startled him and he sat forward, his elbows on his knees. He scrutinized the flat planes of her face for a moment and then sat back.

"All right. I came here tonight to ask you to come live with me. In my compound. I wanted you to come to work for me."

Esther's eyebrows shot up, but that was all the surprise she showed. Slowly she shook her head. "I have a job," was all she said.

"That's all right. Because I'm not interested in making that offer any more."

So. He'd decided she was too great a liability. Well, if he thought she was going to try to run and hide, he was mistaken. "You know where to find me."

"I don't think you understand," he said slowly, standing and pacing around the back of the couch. "I do not intend to kill you."

"Why not?" It was out of her mouth before she could prevent it, and clearly it caught Lucien off guard. A wry grin spread across his face and he rubbed a hand over his chin.

"Do you know how old I am?" he asked suddenly. Then he waved her answer away. "No, let's not go there. It's a cliché waiting to happen. Let me just say that I no longer believe you to be a threat to me. At least not personally. Perhaps those whom you sire may in time prove so, but that will be a challenge to deal with later. To answer your question—" He came around the end of the low oval table in front of the couch and crouched before her. He picked up one of her hands and turned it over in his, idly turning the carved silver band on her middle finger.

"The fact is that the cliché is true. Longevity gets boring. There are few surprises left. But you are most definitely surprising."

"Yeah, in that fascinatingly repulsive way of an accident on the highway." Esther pulled her hand from his and stood. "You need to get out more."

Lucien rose to his feet slowly, watching her as she strode across the room. "I've offended you."

Esther came to a halt across the room, turning to lean back against the bar. "Let's just say that I find this scene a bit less than believable."

Lucien gave her a hard look and then smiled a faintly menacing smile. It sent a ripple of craving over Esther's skin. He paced across the room then, like a lion stalking his prey with arrogant grace. He placed his hands flat on the smooth maple wood of the bar, trapping her within his seductive embrace as he brought his lips close to her ear. She felt the stir of his breath in her hair and a frisson of desire shot down her spine. Her stomach clenched with hunger, but not for food. "Believe that I want you. Believe that I have eyes that tell me your face does not belong on the cover of a fashion magazine." The tip of his tongue flicked along the curve of her ear. Esther shifted uneasily and turned her head away as slick heat curled deep in her belly. But Lucien was not deterred. The points of his teeth scraped the tendons of her neck lightly, raising the hair on her arms. "I've had those faces. Believe that you excite me like none has in many years."

His teeth closed on the flesh above her collarbone and Esther went rigid. She hadn't experienced lovemaking as a vampire and when she felt the hot draw of his mouth on her vein, her body went up in flames. But then he stepped back, wiping the back of his hand across his lips.

"Change your mind?" It was the only thing that Esther could think to say. The look he gave her was incredulous.

"You never lose that edge, do you?" he said finally.

"Once or twice. Are you done here?" Her tone was only slightly less than belligerent. The predatory desire he'd stirred up was raging through her body like a firestorm. It was not a comfortable feeling.

Lucien reached for her hand again, rubbing the palm with his thumb.

"Oh no, I'm not through with you. But we've got plenty of time." He lifted her hand and pressed his lips against her fingers. Her hand bunched into a fist beneath his touch. He glanced up at her, his dark brows raised, mocking.

"You're way out of my league."

"That's where you're wrong. I *am* your league. Don't you know power draws power? There's never been anyone as desirable as you for me." His hand tightened on hers and he drew her close, his mouth but a whisper from her own. His voice, when he spoke, was whiskey-rough. "Whoever sired you, however you came to be, you're *mine*."

"I don't belong to anyone." Esther's voice was disgustingly breathy.

"Wrong again. Taste of me, feed, and let me—"

Esther pressed her lips to his, sliding her hands up to grip his shoulders. He responded with a deep thrust of his tongue, molding her against his hard length. His blood was thick, bittersweet and rich as nothing she'd ever tasted. As it ran over her tongue and filled her mouth, her body shook. He moaned and held her head between his hands. He let her taste freely of him, and then when he could hold back no more, he breached her tender flesh. She tasted their mingling life and she swayed. Lucien swung her up in his arms, pulling his head back. A thin ribbon of red trickled from the corner of his mouth as he gazed down at her.

"Mine," he said. The look in his eyes was faintly questioning and more than a little arrogant.

Esther reached up a finger and swiped at the blood on his chin and then stuck it in her mouth, sucking. Lucien made a sound in the back of his throat, his eyes glowing a lucent green. Esther nodded.

"Mine," she said.

Mona Lisa

WARREN LAPINE

Terrence Gregor lifted the nine millimeter from his desk. It was a cold, stark thing of unearthly, wicked beauty. He put the pistol to his head and smiled. He wasn't going to shoot himself, not yet. There was one more night of work to be done on his final painting. Then, perhaps, he *would* pull the trigger.

He had a vision of them finding his body slumped over his easel, just a bit of blood on what would be his greatest triumph. "And this small brown spot is actually the artist's blood," he could hear a museum guide say. "Upon completing this painting, Terrence Gregor despaired; he realized that he would never again be able to achieve such a mastery of vision and form. Rather than go on, he killed himself." It wasn't all that far from the truth.

He put the pistol back on the desk. It was a nice fantasy, but if the wrong person found him, the painting might never be seen. The idea of dying frightened Terrence, but not nearly so much as the idea of living. It wasn't fair; it just wasn't fair. He had struggled all his life to master his art, and now that his skills were such that his art could match his ambition, he was through. What a cruel joke. He wanted to scream at the universe—curse the day that he had been born. No one should be born with such a desire to create and then have the ability stripped from him. And in such a gradual manner.

Terrence stood and walked over to his painting. He let out a deep breath. Looking on what he had created, it was impossible to remain in despair. Surely this would earn him some degree of immortality. Could anyone look at this and be unmoved? For the hundredth time he wondered who the woman in the painting really was. He knew little about her. Every night she came shortly after dusk and left just before dawn. He'd tried to explain to her that if she'd just let him photograph her, he could complete the painting without her having to pose for such extended periods of time. She'd flat-out refused. "I'd rather be here when you're painting. It lets me pretend that I'm part of the creative process." Strange woman.

Without her he would have given in to despair; some days she was all that stood between him and the dark abyss. His muse. Until he had met her, he'd never really believed in muses. One either had the fire or one didn't. Terrence Gregor had always had the fire.

In thirty-five years nothing had slowed him down. Not until the morning that he had woken up with numb fingertips. It was then that he heard the words that ended his life.

Multiple sclerosis.

Two words.

The doctors had tried to comfort him, but what could they say? The disease was already fairly advanced. He'd lose fine motor control quickly. Eventually he'd be a prisoner trapped within his own body, depending on others for even the most basic bodily functions. He couldn't live with that. He'd been born for one reason, to create, and if he couldn't create, it would be better that he not live.

He'd purchased a nine-millimeter pistol and a single bullet. After he used the first bullet, he wouldn't need another one, not ever. Terrence loaded the pistol and took it home only to find that he couldn't bring himself to use it. He stared at the gun in his hand for more than an hour, but he just couldn't pull the damn trigger. He put the gun down and cursed. "I've got to be able to do this. I can't let this thing run its course. I won't spend my last days in a nursing home."

"Oh, look, the poor dear is drooling on himself," he could almost hear a nurse say as she wiped spittle from his face. "Do you think he *really* was a famous painter?"

"That's just talk. From the looks of him, I'm sure he never painted anything more ambitious than a paint-by-number clown set."

"You shouldn't talk like that in front of him. They can understand, you know."

"So what? He'll never complain. Once they get this bad off, there's no coming back."

Terrence pulled himself from the image. He couldn't let it happen. "I need to get drunk, that's all; then I'll be able to do it."

He grabbed a jacket and rushed out of his studio. Outside, the early evening spring air helped him collect his thoughts. There was still plenty of time to do what *must* be done. He pulled the keys to his Porsche 911 from his pocket and then put them back. There was a bar just down the street, and the walk would do him good.

Terrence had never been to this bar before; it wasn't up-scale enough for him. But tonight that would be just fine. He really didn't want to take the chance of running into someone that he might know. What would he say? "Oh, hi, good to see you, I'm planning to get drunk and blow my brains out." That would be a real conversation starter.

As it turned out, the bar was a blue-collar pub. It was dimly lit, and through the smoke-filled air, Terrence could see couples playing pool and even a group shooting darts. After finding that the bar didn't serve Bass ale, Terrence ordered a Rolling Rock; it was the closest thing to a passable beer in the place. Once the bartender gave him the bottle, he took it and sat down at an empty table in the corner. The mood of the bar was perfect; there wasn't any loud music or bright lights, and what little laughter that found its way to his table all sounded forced and subdued. It was just the right kind of place to sit, drink, and contemplate oblivion.

And that's exactly what he would have done if she hadn't walked into the bar. He noticed her immediately; she didn't belong in this bar. She was like a swath of bright red on a gray landscape, a spring flower in December. Long, jet-black hair streamed over her shoulders and halfway down her back; her blue eyes, nestled within a delicate face, flashed with life and vitality. Terrence had never seen anyone so captivating. Strength, wisdom, and power all emanated from her. He had to paint her. If he could capture half of what he saw in this magnificent woman he would be remembered forever. She could be his Mona Lisa. Surely he had enough time to complete one last painting before the disease disabled him.

He picked up his drink and walked over to where she sat alone. "May I join you?" he asked.

"Certainly," she said, motioning to a chair across from her.

Terrence caught a slight accent, but couldn't quite place it. "Your accent, it's European, isn't it?"

"You have a good ear. It's Romanian. I've been in this country since I was a little girl—very few people notice it."

"I've spent some time in Europe. I'm Terrence Gregor."

"The painter?"

"You're familiar with my work?" Terrence was surprised; despite being very successful, he didn't run into a lot of people outside of the art community who knew who he was.

"Oh, yes, your work is marvelous. I love your use of color, and your lighting techniques are second to none. I've often wished I could afford one of your paintings."

"How would you like to model for one?"

"Me?"

"Yes, I'd love to use you in a painting. That's why I came over here. You have a great deal of character. I think you could be my Mona Lisa."

"Oh, come now, your Mona Lisa?"

"I mean it. There's something about you that I've got to capture on canvas."

She smiled. "I'd like to be your Mona Lisa. Yes, I'd like that very much."

Terrence pulled out one of his cards and handed it to her. "Could you start tomorrow?"

"I work during the day, but I'd be happy to stop by during the evening."

"I do most of my painting at night, so that would be fine. What I really need to do is photograph you, and then I can work from the photos. You don't have to pose the entire time."

"I don't like photographs. If you want me to be your Mona Lisa, I'll have to sit for you."

"It's really not necessary."

"I insist."

There was something about the way that she said it that brooked no argument. "If you insist."

She nodded. "Is this one of your regular haunts? Uncle Gus's bar doesn't seem to suit you."

"No, this is my first time here. One of your regular haunts?"

"I like a change of scenery," she smiled, showing white teeth. "What brings you here?"

"I needed to get drunk, it's been a rough day, and this bar is close to my studio."

"I'm sorry about your day. Would you like to talk about it?"

Terrence started to say no but found that he couldn't. He told her the entire story almost as if he had been compelled to. When he'd finished she nodded and said, "It must be frightening knowing that you're going to die."

"It's not frightening, it's just hard to overcome my instinct to live. I love life. I love being able to create. I don't want to let go of the passion, but I know that I don't have a choice. I think I was twelve when I realized that I was going to die just like everyone else. It didn't frighten me—it made me angry. I mean, how dare the universe do this to me. Give me such ambition and then only seventy years or so in which to realize my dreams."

"It doesn't seem fair, does it?"

"No, no, it doesn't. I have so much I want to share with the world, so many great paintings left within me. And now, now I'll have time to paint only one more of them. And then my life might just as well be over."

"It must take a lot of courage to decide to end it."

Terrence laughed. "To make the decision, no, I've done that. I just haven't been able to follow through on it yet. It's just as well. If I'd been able to pull the trigger, I wouldn't have met you."

She smiled again. "You flatter me."

Suddenly Terrence realized that he didn't know this woman's name. "By the way, what's your name?"

"Mona."

"As in Mona Lisa?"

"Perhaps."

"Well, Mona, if we are to start tomorrow, I have some preparations to make."

"Until tomorrow, then."

Thinking back on it, Terrence had to admit that it seemed a bit strange. It was almost as if she'd been looking for him. Of course, that didn't make any sense. She couldn't have known what his reaction to her would be, and she definitely wasn't a groupie.

The bell rang and Terrence went to the door and let Mona in. She smiled. "Ah, Terrence, it's good to see you."

Terrence breathed in the smell of her. "It's always good to see you. I can't believe that I'll be finished tonight."

"Do you really think so?"

He nodded. "I'm afraid so. I'm usually really excited when I finish a painting, but knowing that this is my last— well, I don't want it to end. I want to go on painting it for eternity. Of course, I can't."

Mona walked over to the painting and gazed at it. "Do I really look that majestic?"

"More so, my dear."

She smiled up at Terrence. "Thank you."

"For what?"

"For capturing me this way. You're the greatest artist of your age, and to think, I'm your Mona Lisa."

"Only history will be able to decide where I'll stand. We don't have the perspective. Maybe I'll be remembered. I certainly hope so, but one can only hope."

"Trust me, you'll be remembered," Mona said, taking her place on the couch.

Terrence went to work. His fingers were a bit more numb than he would have liked, but if he concentrated, he could still get the sharpness of line that he demanded. It was a frightening thing to realize that this would indeed be his last painting. His fingers were much more stiff now than they had been three weeks ago when he'd begun the painting. He continued through sheer force of will, losing himself in the radiance and magnificence of creating.

Finally he realized that the painting was complete. He'd captured the essence of Mona. She was like some pale immortal goddess, an ageless enchantress defying the universe. Strength and wisdom fairly leapt off the canvas. It was so magnificent that he started to cry.

Mona moved off the couch and over to Terrence. She put her arms around him, comforting him. "It'll be all right, Terrence. The painting is brilliant. You have nothing to worry about. This will make you immortal."

"But I'll never paint again."

"Terrence, look at what you've created. Most mortals never leave behind this kind of legacy."

Terrence looked up at his masterpiece. Mona was right. With this painting he'd accomplished greatness. What more could he want? Eternity, that was what he really wanted. "Mona," he whispered, "I'm not sure if I can pull the trigger. Will you stay with me until I do?"

Terrence had expected her to be shocked, but if she was, she showed no sign of it. "I'll do better than that, Terrence."

"Better?"

She pulled him close and began kissing his neck. Terrence felt the thrill of desire course through his body. He wanted Mona more than he had ever wanted anyone. "Mona, I think I'm in love with you." Suddenly, Mona bit into his neck. Blood burst forth, splashing them and the painting. Part of Terrence was horrified, but that part was small and far away. Ecstasy like nothing that he had ever experienced before exploded through his senses. He became one with Mona. He could feel her desire for him, her thirst. It ached to be quenched. "I'm yours, Mona." The ecstasy went on and on. Finally she pulled her mouth away from Terrence's throat. He was weak and dazed and would have fallen had Mona not supported him.

"Terrence, listen to me," Mona said, blood dripping down her chin. "I'm a vampire, a creature of the night. I live forever. Nothing is held back from me, nothing but the sun—that is all I am denied. I prey on mortals, I drain them of their life force, but I live forever. No disease can touch me. Think of what you could do with your art if you had immortality. You can have it, but you have to *really* want it. You have to have the fire—without it, immortality is more a curse than a gift. If you would live forever, drink my blood. Do you have the fire, Terrence?"

He smiled, brought his lips to Mona's throat, and began to feed. Terrence Gregor had always had the fire.

Presumed Icarus

TIPPI N. BLEVINS

Alex dreamed of the cathedrals of his youth. The memory was so vivid that he could smell the lit candles as he walked toward the altar. He loved the smoky smell of the flame drifting up like ghosts toward the vaulted ceiling. Dour saints peered down at him with their dark, sensuously drawn eyes from the soot-darkened stained glass windows. How long had it been since he'd gone to church? A hundred years? Two? He rolled over in bed and thought that perhaps he would go again someday, and that he would bring the rest of the tribe with him. It would be lovely to smell the candles again.

Now, however, he smelled gasoline.

His eyes opened at the same instant several pairs of hands grabbed hold of his body. Fingers dug into the sensitive flesh of his upper arms, his wrists, his thighs and ankles. The vision above him was chaotic, filled with faces and fire, grins intermingled with ribbons of flame. These were not the morose, lovely faces of the saints he remembered—oh, no. He was looking into the maniacal masks of hunters.

He thrashed against his captors, but they only laughed. One of them—a young girl with a shock of yellow hair and braces on her teeth—overturned her candle and let a stream of red wax fall onto his belly. He clenched his teeth against the pain. Didn't the fool know how delicate vampiric skin was? Didn't she know how the slightest touch of heat burned? Well, of course she knew. Hunters were notorious sadists, the beasts.

He called out to the others of his tribe who lived within the catacomb-like basement of the old warehouse. This close to dawn, everyone should have been home. Alex called out to each of them by name, but none answered. The horrible thought came to him that they were all burned to ashes, and he hadn't heard their pleas for help. Daniel, Olivia, Sasha, all of them dead, and he was next.

He screamed.

Something cold was poured into his open mouth and over his face and chest. He reflexively coughed and tasted gasoline. The liquid slipped into his throat. He screamed and flailed. This time, his captors released him.

He blinked fuel out of his eyes, but his vision remained blurred. The scene before him looked like a Munch painting, streaked with oily colors and openmouthed screams. Were the hunters leaving his abode, or was he seeing things? Their distorted faces grew smaller, the caverns of their laughing mouths more distant. Then, almost in unison, they all moved, and half a dozen halos of light came hurtling toward him.

As the candles hit him, his body went up in flames. The hunters laughed even as he screamed. The heat was agony. Flesh turned to ash on the bone.

He clawed his way out of bed. Like some Midas with fire for fingers, he turned everything he touched to flame, from the silk brocade wall coverings to the velvet chair he toppled in his frenzy to escape. As he lunged toward the door, the hunters scattered before him. He stumbled into the corridor outside his chamber, but more hunters awaited him there. They formed a crescent around him and, tightening their ranks, backed him toward the stairs. He had nowhere to go but up.

As the blaze engulfed his fuel-soaked eyes, he could no longer see. He ran blindly, maneuvering by instinct up the Madeline stairwell, and burst onto the roof of the building.

There, the sun was waiting for him, and ignited what little remained of his flesh.

In desperation, he launched himself off the roof into the air, and fell, burning, from the sky.

He wasn't dead. He knew this because he was in too much pain. Every nerve in his body wailed and his breath tasted like gasoline and ash. Of course, the thought did occur to him that he was in hell, but he didn't believe in that kind of thing any more than he believed in stained glass saints.

Beyond the pain, he became aware of the cool damp cloths that covered his charred body from head to toe. He could see his surroundings through the thin layer of gauze that obscured his eyes. He was lying in what looked like an old office or storeroom, now a makeshift bedroom. The bed beneath him with its coarse sheets felt rough as concrete. Thick ropes of ivy cascaded out of hanging pots, and the air smelled faintly of . . . gardenias? And of dirt, and old newspapers, and of the mortal smells of sweat and decay.

He was not alone.

Someone hummed an idle tune and shuffled about the room somewhere beyond his peripheral vision.

He stirred, and at once the humming stopped. For a moment, everything was silent; then the shuffling moved toward him.

"You're awake!"

Alex struggled to sit up from beneath the damp rags, but his body refused to cooperate. He'd never felt this weak even during his mortal years. Every effort exhausted him. He lay, gasping for breath, unable to move.

A white-bearded face appeared above him.

Alex again fought to sit up—he remembered all too well the last time he'd wakened to unfamiliar faces—but the old man took his shoulders and eased him back down. "Calm yourself," the stranger said. "You shouldn't try to move just yet."

He didn't have the strength to put up a fight even against this elderly mortal; it annoyed him, but there was nothing he could do about it. With a sigh, he forced his body to relax.

"How did you find me?" Alex asked. His voice sounded rough; judging by the pain in his throat, the flesh had been burned rather badly there, too. "*Where* did you find me?"

"You tumbled from the sun in flames," the old man said. He glanced upward with a smile; Alex followed his line of vision but saw only the ivy plant. "I looked up from my garden, and there you were."

"And where exactly would that be?"

"Home." The old man sobbed. "After all these years, my son Icarus has returned home to me."

Alex laughed. The laughter bubbled up out of him despite the horrible pain in his chest. This must surely be a sign of madness, he thought, this inane laughing. But he had little time to ponder the matter as he exhausted himself and tumbled into unconsciousness.

Vampires lived by certain rules, and Alex, although he'd been something of a scoundrel and a thief in his mortal life, had always tried to obey them. There were practical rules concerning the night-to-night matters of hunting and the disposal of one's kills, how not to get caught out in the open just before dawn, and so on. Then there were those rules that were more esoteric, perhaps, but as fundamental to their being as blood and darkness. The most important of these was Loyalty to the Tribe.

Daniel had told him once, "Nothing is more important than your tribe. It defines who you are, how you live, how you die." Alex had come to learn that, though members might be scattered over the globe, they would always have a home.

He wasn't home, though. As he peered down the length of his body, he saw he was wearing another man's scratchy cotton robe. At least he was alive. Daniel and the others were most likely dead, and he was certainly to blame for that. If only he'd been more alert. If only he hadn't allowed himself to become so enraptured by his mortal memories, the tribe would still be alive. He groaned miserably.

Within moments the old man was at his side. "Are you in pain?" he asked. "Perhaps it's time to change your bandages. Just lie still and I'll take care of you."

At first he recoiled at the mortal's touch, but the fingers that unwound the rags from his arms proved to be not so rough and bumbling as Alex expected. Still, he admonished himself not to let his guard down. Daniel had also told him that sometimes the gentlest touch of a mortal hand was merely a prelude to a slap.

"You're healing quite well," the old man said. "Much better than I'd hoped, even. Can you move your arms? Careful, now."

Alex lifted his left arm and gasped sharply at the pain. The skin was tight and sore, and it felt as though embers of flame still remained under the skin.

"That's enough now," the old man said. "Don't overdo it, son."

Alex held out his hands and allowed them to be wrapped in fresh gauze. "You called me by a name yesterday. What was it?"

"You're my Icarus," came the answer. "You're my beloved son."

Alex managed a chuckle despite the pain. "And who are you supposed to be? Daedalus, perhaps?"

"You remember me, then!"

Alex started to laugh again, but he caught a glimpse of the old man's face and realized he was serious. He struggled to sit up. "Is this some kind of trick? Are you insane?"

"Please, Icarus—"

"That's not my name!"

"—you've been through a terrible ordeal. You'll remember what happened to you in time."

"I was set on fire!" Alex winced at the pain in his throat and lowered his voice. "It's not the kind of thing you forget."

The old man shook his head. "The wax in your wings

melted," he said. "I pulled bits of cold wax from your body after I brought you inside."

Alex gave a wave of his hand. "That was how the hunters set me on fire. Gasoline. Candles. It was really horribly painful."

"It must have been a dream," the old man said. His eyes looked wet; was he crying? Not that Alex cared; the mortal was either a fool or playing tricks on him. "You flew too high, too far. I didn't make your wings strong enough, and you fell from the sun."

With that, the old man gave a great, shaky sob and got to his feet. He said something about having to tend his gardenias and shuffled away, and Alex found himself in the company of silence.

As the days went by, Alex continued to heal. The old man returned with apparently no memory of his prior agitation and would spend most of every day in the tiny room, reading or simply sitting and doing nothing. At first Alex wished the mortal would leave him alone, but he came to dread the solitary nights. He told himself it was a symptom of missing his tribe, nothing more. He longed only for the company of his brethren, and in their absence, had begun to look to the old man for companionship. His need embarrassed him, but the shame was more tolerable than solitude.

The old man changed his bandages without fail, always while chattering on about his garden or recounting tales of ancient Greece so detailed as to have come only from memory or books.

And always Alex would tell him, "I'm not your son, you know."

And always the old man would only smile, and pat his hand, and go on with his stories.

Moving still caused him a little pain, but the flesh along his arms was barely pink. Encouraged by the progress of his healing, he removed the bandages from his face, but when he reached up to touch his cheek, the skin felt leathery and convoluted. He ran the tips of his fingers over his lips and nearly wept at the thinness of the once-plump flesh.

He could heal only so much without nourishment, and he had not fed since the morning of the hunters' attack. He knew he would have to leave this place.

One day when left alone, he searched the little bedroom and found clothes: tweed trousers and clean white shirt, a brown felt fedora, shoes and socks. He discarded the cotton robes and dressed hurriedly. The hat was a little too big, but served its purpose in shadowing his face. After he listened at the door and heard no sign of the old man, he left the bedroom.

He ventured out into what he now realized must have been a factory at one time, judging by the enormous conveyor belts and now-silent machinery. His gaze followed a path along the walls of exposed brick and up across the high ceiling to three rows of windows that spanned the width of one wall. Most of the glass was broken, boarded or painted over, but enough of it remained intact that Alex could see a small rooftop garden just outside. Across the street, the old warehouse that had once been his home reflected the molten orange light of sunset.

He looked hard at the building. Windows on the first floor were broken where they had been whole before. Glass still littered the concrete. Hope seized his heart.

Perhaps the others had made their escape, after all. His mind played out the possible scenario where they had escaped from the building, tearing through the ceiling to the first floor and breaking the windows to freedom. They could still be alive, safe.

No. That wasn't possible. They would have tried to save him. They would not have left him. Would they?

He moved toward the windows for a better look, but a piano in the corner of the factory caught his eye. Drawn to the framed photographs that occupied the top of the piano, he moved closer and saw the black-and-white images of a young man. His clothes and hair hailed from an era decades gone. He had a sturdy build, pale hair, and a tanned, smiling face. One of the photos showed the young man in a pilot's uniform, standing in front of his plane. Alex could see nothing of himself in the photo. His own hair was darker, his nose bigger. Even in his fittest day, no one had ever called him "sturdy."

By the time he set the picture down, the sky beyond the windows had grown dark. He could venture out into the night. Someone in one of the clubs would know whether the rest of his tribe had survived. Someone would be able to tell him whether he still had a home or not.

He paused at the door on his way out. The old man would return to an empty home. For a moment, the thought tugged at him. He wondered if he should make some sort of farewell gesture, a note perhaps, and then chastised himself. After all, he wasn't really the old man's son. He couldn't give the mortal anything that memory wouldn't take away.

The music throbbed through his bones even before he walked into the club. He stood in the alley before the riveted metal door and found himself wincing at the sound of the pounding drums and wailing guitars. After the pervasive quiet of the old factory, the music seemed an intrusive noise.

He reached up and knocked on the door. An instant later, a small panel opened in the metal and a pair of eyes peered down at him.

"Alex?"

"It's me, Bernard."

"Holy shit!" A pause, then, "I thought you were dead."

"Well, I'm back," Alex said. "Let me in."

The panel closed and a moment later the door slid open. The bouncer stood nearly as wide as the threshold.

"You look awful," Bernard remarked, and looked him up and down. He didn't do a very good job of hiding his amazement and disgust; his lips twisted as though the tongue behind them had just tasted a bit of bad blood. "Where have you been? Hell?"

Alex pulled the hat lower over his face. "In an old factory, actually. Now, are you going to let me in or not?"

Bernard stepped to one side and Alex slipped past him into a small, unadorned room with matte black walls. The second door leading into the club was nearly invisible in the darkness.

"Everyone thought you were dead." Bernard opened the door. Music flooded the tiny room. "You should probably let Daniel know we were wrong."

Alex felt his heart leap with hope as he had when he first saw the broken windows at the old factory. Daniel wasn't dead. His legs threatened to buckle beneath him. He nearly collapsed from the sudden joy and relief.

Then, just as quickly, confusion replaced happiness. Daniel. Alive. And yet, Alex had not sensed any of them looking for him. No one had called out to him in the night as he had when the hunters attacked. Anger replaced confusion.

Bernard nodded toward the rear of the club. "He's back there."

Alex was already stepping into the club, pushing his way through its fashionably dressed denizens. Their gazes followed him. He moved without feeling his steps. Even the noise of the music seemed to grow distant. He could make out the pale oval of Daniel's face in the darkness. His fingers were like the pinfeathers of a white dove as he lifted a cup to his red-stained lips. When Alex finally reached the table, he could only stand there wordlessly. Waiting.

Daniel looked up. For the bill breadth of a moment, his expression remained blank. Then, recognition was accompanied by a wince. "Alex?" The tribe leader's gaze slipped down the length of Alex's body, then floated back up to his face. Daniel's eyes glittered and he shook his head. "Oh, my poor, poor Alex. You look dreadful."

Alex had too many questions, too many things to say. Everything came out at once. "Did everyone make it out—? Is everyone alive? The hunters—they tried— Where were you? I called out to you— Why didn't you answer me?"

"Alex, Alex," Daniel cooed. He got up and took him by the elbows. Alex allowed himself to be guided into a seat. "All that matters is you're alive, and so are we."

"I thought you were dead," Alex said, the words an accusation. "I blamed myself."

Daniel reached across the table and took hold of his hands. Alex felt the anger begin to melt away. The placid expression of the tribe leader's face soothed him. All that remained was confusion. He bowed his head.

Daniel touched his chin, and Alex looked up. "It was only once we got out of the factory that we realized you hadn't made it out with us," the tribe leader said. "You understand why we couldn't come back for you."

Alex shuddered with the memory. "The hunters . . .

"We had no reason to think you had survived," Daniel said softly. "Those beasts were everywhere, destroyed everything. I had the whole tribe to think of. You understand. Tell me you understand."

"I—I do," Alex said. The words sounded tentative to his own ears. He said, louder, "I do understand."

Daniel smiled warmly and nudged his half-full glass across the table. "Now tell me where you've been."

Alex took the glass and drained its contents in a single gulp. Daniel motioned to the bar with a wave of his hand. Moments later, a young woman appeared with two more glasses. Alex downed another, then told Daniel everything that had happened. He told him about the crazy old man and being presumed Icarus. He talked about the scent of gardenias and nearly going mad with silence, and finding the old photographs. He talked of the loneliness he'd felt, but even as the words left his lips he thought of the old man. He, too, would feel that loneliness. Alex fell silent.

"You'll come home to us," Daniel said. "Tomorrow morning, we'll all be together again."

Alex kept his gaze focused on the empty glass in his hands. "Of course."

"But first you have to take care of the old man."

He looked up. "Kill him?"

"You know the rules," Daniel said gently, and reached out to hold his hand again. "No mortal can know of us and be allowed to live. You understand the danger. If given the chance, any mortal would turn hunter and kill us."

Alex shrugged. "There's no need to eliminate him, really," he said. "The old man, well, he's crazy. He thinks I'm Icarus. He doesn't know what I am."

"That's only what he wants you to believe."

"Why would he nurse my wounds?" Alex asked. "Or—or sit by my bed, or tell me those inane stories of his?"

Daniel shook his head. "My poor Alex," he murmured. "Your injuries have been far more severe than I thought. You're not thinking straight. You know the legendary duplicity of mortals. I've told you before—the mortal hand that caresses also slaps. Have I ever been wrong before?"

"I suppose not," Alex said. Daniel's eyes narrowed, and his grip tightened almost imperceptibly. Alex lowered his eyes. "I mean, I know you haven't. Of course you're right."

The hold on his hand softened. "You'll do it, then."

Alex nodded once. "I'll kill the old man."

He took his time in making his way back to the old factory. Perhaps the old man would come to his senses, realize what kind of creature had really fallen into his garden, and flee before said creature could return. Alex walked as slowly as he could, but the sun would be up soon. He comforted himself with thoughts of being back among his tribe. After all, he'd already spent enough time alone.

Except he hadn't been alone. The old man had taken care of him, nursed him back to health. Daniel said that had all been a ruse, and Daniel knew best. Better to kill the old man as Daniel had instructed and get on with the uncomplicated life he'd known with the tribe.

An animal howled nearby.

Alex stopped and lifted his head. The factory was less than a block away; he could see the entrance defined by the angle of light on the sidewalk. The howl came again, but this time he realized a human being had made the sound.

The howl cascaded into laughter, and the laughter into shouts. Glass shattered. Piano keys were struck hard and tunelessly. More laughter.

He slipped into a pool of shadows just in time to see the factory door disgorge half a dozen black-clad mortals.

Hunters.

He recognized the yellow-haired girl who had poured the wax onto his skin. She headed off into the distance at a trot, and the others followed her like a pack of animals. Alex waited until he could no longer hear or see them before venturing out of the shadows.

The hunters must have been looking for him. When he entered the factory, he saw the piano had been set afire; it still smoldered like a burnt offering to an arbitrary god. Broken glass crunched beneath his feet, and books and paper littered the floor.

Alex bent to pick up the nearest book. *Bulfinch's Mythology*. The pages had been touched and perused so often as to feel almost like cloth. When he opened the book, a long white feather fell from its pages. It had marked a passage about Icarus and Daedalus.

Someone moaned.

Alex got up and followed the sound across the factory floor to the windows. He peered through the glass to a scene of devastation in the garden beyond. Spilled soil surrounded overturned pots like black blood. Topiaries lay like slaughtered animals. He searched the wall and found a door that, when he opened it, led into the garden.

He picked his way through broken pots and toppled shrubs to find the old man lying on his side amid his ruined gardenias.

Alex reached down and nudged the old man's shoulder. The mortal rolled onto his back with a cough that rattled his whole body. His robes hung like rags on his frame. Bruises darkened the pale face.

The old man's eyes opened. "Icarus." Something sounded wet and broken in his chest when he breathed. "My Icarus, my darling son. Thank the gods you've returned."

Alex got on his knees beside the old man and bent down to the delicate white throat. He shut his eyes and tried not to think of what he was about to do.

He felt the old man's hand in his hair. "When I came home you were gone," the old man said. "I called out to you, but you didn't answer."

The familiarity of those words stopped Alex before his teeth could find their mark. *I called out to you—Why didn't you answer me?* He shuddered.

He pulled back. "Tell me something," he said. "Why did you continue to look for your son—to look for me—for so long?"

Alex felt the old man's hand move from his hair to the side of his face. "Because you are my son," the mortal said. "You are my family."

"Did you have any reason to think I was alive?" Alex asked. The words sounded like a plea. Desperation strained his voice. For a moment, the old man became Daniel. Alex asked the questions the answers to which he'd been too afraid to hear from his tribe leader. "Did you have any proof I was alive?"

The old man managed a weak smile. "I had no proof you were dead," he whispered. "I would have searched the millennia for you."

Alex sobbed. It came as unexpectedly as a blow to the chest. He slumped into himself and clasped his head in his hands. "Why couldn't you be Daniel?" he asked no one in particular. "Why couldn't he say these things to me? Why?"

Silence answered him.

He looked down at the old man. A ribbon of blood fell from the corner of the slack mouth. Alex thought the old mortal was dead. He crawled toward him and took hold of the frail shoulders. Then, like a clock winding down, he heard the faintest heartbeat.

Tears shone in the pale eyes. "When I lost you, it broke my heart," the old man whispered. "To watch you fall into the sea . . . There could be no greater pain."

"I—I could take you to a hospital," Alex said. "Isn't that where mortals go when they're broken?"

The old man didn't seem to have heard him. "Do you forgive me for making wings that couldn't carry you?" he asked. His voice was barely audible, even to Alex's keen ears. "Do you?"

"I can't." Alex felt warmth at his eyes. "I'm not your son."

Tears shone on the old man's cheeks. *"Do you forgive me?"*

In that moment, Alex realized something. The old man needed forgiveness. He needed it as much as Alex had needed to know his tribe had searched for him. But it hadn't. Daniel hadn't. But where Alex had no proxy to give him what he needed, the old man did.

He clasped the old man's hand. "I forgive you."

The mortal smiled and his eyes closed. "Thank you," he said, and nothing else.

After a moment, Alex could no longer hear the heart beating.

He returned to the club just before dawn and found the place nearly deserted. Alex found Daniel still at the table in the back, holding a glass in his hands, staring at nothing. He looked utterly alone. Small.

Daniel looked up at his approach. "Is the old man dead?"

Alex nodded. "He is."

"Good." Daniel smiled. "Now the tribe is whole again."

The tribe leader got up and headed for the door, but Alex didn't follow. He called out, "Why didn't you look for me?"

Daniel turned around, blinking. "What?"

"Why didn't you look for me?"

Daniel moved toward him and laid an open hand on his shoulder. "Alex, try to understand. We thought you were dead."

"You had no proof I'd survived?" Alex offered. "And therefore, no reason to look?"

"Exactly!" Daniel reached up and touched Alex's face, but

the touch no longer brought him the comfort it once had. "I'm so glad you understand. You do understand, don't you?"

Alex tasted something bitter in the back of his mouth. "Oh, I understand," he said. "That old man who saved me, he said he would have looked for a thousand years. He said he didn't need proof or reason. I understand, Daniel, that I would have done anything to hear you say those things to me. *Do you?*"

He turned and started toward the door. Daniel grabbed his elbow, but Alex jerked away and kept going.

"Where are you going? Alex! Come back here!"

He left the club and kept walking. He was not surprised to hear footsteps gaining on him. A moment later, Daniel fell in step beside him.

"I looked into the old man's story," Daniel said. He laughed, but the sound was joyless. "To see what I was up against, I guess."

"It doesn't matter anymore."

"His name was Edward Brand." Alex walked faster, but Daniel matched his pace. "His son Jacob died over forty years ago. His plane went down without a trace during the war the mortals fought in Korea."

Alex pressed on, but Daniel grabbed his arm. Desperation shone in his eyes. "Alex, Brand owned the factory that made the parts on his son's plane. That's why the old man thought you were Icarus. He was crazy from the guilt, Alex. Don't you see?"

Alex pulled back from his once-leader. "He was Daedalus. He had a son named Icarus, who fell, burning, from the sky."

Daniel shook his head. "Oh, Alex, don't tell me you've gone mad, as well."

Alex glanced over his shoulder. The sun was rising. He smiled and shook his head, knowing that Daniel would not understand that Icarus had not died the day he fell from the sky. His father had saved him, and in more than one way.

Alex turned and walked away, still smiling, in search of shelter from the sun that would melt his wings.

After the Fire

ROBIN SIMONDS FITCH

Kat stepped out of the shadows as the bus approached, her eyes narrowed against the glare of the streetlamp. The bus stopped and she boarded silently. Unable to find another seat, she squeezed herself in next to a large woman wearing a wooden cross around her neck. She shifted as a spring in the cushion probed her obscenely, and watched through the dusty window as darkness crept over the city. She felt as old and worn down as the abandoned, burnt-out buildings they passed. She hated Harlem, wanted to be out of it before the hungry woke and rose from the gutters and the ruins to feed. At least in Midtown they were willing to pay.

The woman leaned into Kat, staring out the same window as they passed a small group of men standing on a corner in front of a burnt-out bodega. One of the men carried a flamethrower, a bright tongue of blue flame curling up from the nozzle, panting for a target. Kat fought back a wave of nausea and ducked her head, wondering if they were the ones responsible for the drive-by flamings, or the firebombing at CrossRoads that put her in the hospital. Like it was her fault, or Alek's or Delilah's or any of theirs, that the dealers couldn't synthesize Venom.

The woman beside her held her key chain a little tighter, fingering the small lighter that hung beside a cylinder of pepper spray. Kat shook her head mentally, hiding her disdain behind an impassive mask. Aiming that thing at a vampire was like poking a rottweiler with a stick. It would only make him mad, and they were so much more dangerous when they were mad.

"Drug dealers and dracs," the woman spat, her face contorting as if tasting her own disgust like bile. "I hope they destroy each other. The city's better off without either of them."

"Have you ever met a vampire?" Kat asked, taking the middle road. She wouldn't call a black man a nigger or a homosexual a fag, so she damned sure wouldn't call a vampire a drac. And as for the PC term, "hemobiont," she found it too sterile. Nobody but doctors and biologists knew what it really meant anyway.

The woman touched her cross and moved back into her own space. "No. And I hope I never do. Only an idiot would want anything to do with one of those demons."

Kat knew all too well what someone would want to do with a vampire, why people sold body and soul for the brightness of Venom in their veins, but she kept her reasons to herself, the same way she kept her neck and arms covered by her oversize black turtleneck. This woman would not be sympathetic. This woman would condemn her as quickly and thoughtlessly as she condemned the five million people in the world who needed to ingest blood to live. In this woman's world, the words "vampire" and "love" could not exist in the same sentence, the same thought, the same breath. It must be a sad existence.

"Idiots and Venomheads, they all are," the woman continued, rocking in her seat until it creaked, clutching her keys and stroking the cross. Kat considered telling her the cross was useless. The "normal" hookers in Times Square had started wearing large fluorescent crosses in the seventies to distinguish themselves from the Venom whores, but people got confused and thought they were for protection, not identification. She didn't think the woman would appreciate a history lesson, so she said nothing, and the woman let the subject drop. "You were in the hospital," she stated almost coyly, as if hoping for a handout of gossip without having to beg.

"Yes."

The woman seemed to realize she wouldn't learn more without digging and sat back in her seat to sulk. They fell into silence as the bus moved on past the void of light that during the day was Central Park. At night it was a black hole, sucking light and energy from the world around it until even the stars above seemed more pale. No one went into the park at night, unless they were looking for something most people didn't want to find. The vampires in the rest of the city were more or less civilized, but in the park, that chunk of wilderness in the middle of a concrete island, they were nothing more than predators, without honor, without humanity. Man-eaters.

The bus chugged along the nearly deserted boulevard, past clubs like Love in Vein and Blood Lust, patronized by hemophiles—vampire "groupies"—and awestruck tourists who liked sanitized, amusement park terror. CrossRoads, where Kat plied her trade—*had* plied her trade—catered to Venomheads and Venom whores, those who slipped over the line between fantasy and reality and found themselves unable, or unwilling, to get back.

The bus moved around Columbus Circle and onto Central Park South. Kat stood, preparing to leave this ignorant woman with her cross to bear. The woman grabbed her arm, obviously preparing to give her some dire warning about innocent little girls out in the big bad world. Before she could, the pressure of her hand caused Kat's sleeve to ride up, exposing several pairs of small puncture wounds, like tracks on a junkie's arm. The woman pulled her hand back as if scalded, and stared at Kat, her expressive face registering horror and disgust.

Rage uncoiled within Kat, overshadowing her mild contempt. This woman was her enemy now. That prejudice, once broad and laughable, was now aimed directly at Kat's soul. As if she could know Kat, could understand the decisions she'd made. As if she were somehow better because the only Venom she knew was her own.

Kat leaned down in her face, sneering. "What's the matter, ma'am? Never seen a Venom whore before?"

The woman sputtered, finally dumbstruck. The bus lurched to a halt and Kat turned, holding her anger in her fist and walking stiffly out into the city. The wind beat against her like the wings of a bird trying desperately to escape the beast that has it pinned. The dark sky seemed far away, a cloak lain across the tops of sharp, angry buildings that closed in on her from above. She shrugged her shoulders, adjusting to the burden, and as the bus pulled away she turned into the darkness.

The old stone building that had housed CrossRoads for almost a century was still there, a ghost lit by the lights in the parking lot next door. She stared at it for a long, aching moment, slowly summoning the courage to approach. One of the front doors hung drunkenly askew, and she slipped past them silently. Inside, the odor of smoke still hung in the air, the dampness from the fire hoses sunk deep into what was left of the furnishings. Where light shone through the broken windows she could see black fingers reaching up the wall, their destructive touch caressing the ceiling, teasing, promising.

She hadn't seen the fire, didn't know who, if anyone, had survived. All she knew was that the bomb that had killed so many of the people milling around outside hadn't killed her. If she had survived, maybe someone else had, too. She could hope.

Hope. The concept seemed so foreign, a foul taste on lips that knew the pleasures of the present, not thoughts of the future. Hope reeked of a belief that there was something beyond this night, these precious hours. She had given that belief up long ago. Or perhaps not so long. It seemed an eternity, but nothing was forever. If vampires could die, then she could remember.

She walked through the front parlor to the great room, full of echoes and ghosts still dancing to music she could hear in her mind, a haunting harmony of strange and different songs from across the decades. Long before her time people had done the jitterbug and the Charleston and even a waltz or two in this room. This room had been a ballroom and a disco and a different world. She had never danced here but she spent many nights on the balcony above, watching people drunk on life and lust and Venom. This had been the heart of CrossRoads.

She picked her way across the ruined hardwood floor to the massive marble fireplace beside the bar. Not even embers—of course not. She'd been gone so long, nothing would be left of that night, and no one would still be here to light a new fire. She curled herself into a ball against the marble and closed her eyes. It was true. Max was gone. He'd never been a gentleman. If he wasn't here, he was either dead or five states away, with no intention of returning for her. She almost wished him dead, so she could know he'd loved her, but she knew she wanted him safe. She would've died to save him, and everyone would've been better off. What was left for her now? She leaned her head back, finally releasing the tears she'd held for so long.

Beneath the muffled sounds of traffic outside she heard footsteps and she raised her head, heart pounding with anticipation. She knew no fear here—this was her home, the closest thing she had now. No one would come here to harm her. *Please let it be Max,* she prayed, knowing better but unable to stop herself. She stood and took a few uncertain steps towards the door.

Two men appeared in the doorway, and she knew neither was Max. The taller, a lean, handsome man with dark hair and darker eyes, stepped forward when he saw her. Alek. "Kat," he breathed, moving towards her. She tried to hide her disappointment, but she knew he could tell. He reached out to her and she let him fold her against his chest. He was so cold, colder even than she remembered. "Are you well?"

She nodded against the softness of his shirt, then pulled away, trying to catch his eyes in the light. "But the others—?"

He looked away. "I'm sorry, Kat. Only you, Delilah, and

I have survived, and Delilah is not strong." He touched her face. "Max died to protect you. Perhaps he was more noble than any of us believed. He loved you very much."

Kat began to tremble and shook her head, pulling away from him and trying to swallow her sobs. She'd spent a lifetime in that hospital dreaming about Max, seeing him die, *knowing* he had died his second death but refusing to believe it. How could he leave her? What would she do without him?

"Is this her?" the other man, a young, unkempt thing trying to hide his fear behind a paper-thin cockiness, asked. "I guess I could let her suck me."

"No." Alek said tautly as Kat glared at him through her tears. If she were a vampire, she would tear him to pieces right now just to listen to him scream, insensitive little prick. "Come with me." Alek looked at Kat and his features softened. "Please."

Kat and the feeder fish followed Alek through the public areas of the house to the kitchen. The fire hadn't reached back here, and though nothing had been moved or ruined, it was different from how Kat remembered it, no longer lively and inviting but instead strangely static, old, unused. Like a ghost town. She shivered, following Alek down the stairs to the catacombs because Delilah was down there, and that meant she and Alek were not alone.

Down in the catacombs the lights still shone dimly—the electricity here, like everything else, was stolen from the city to prevent any cutoff in an emergency. Like now. This was their safe house, a place where vampires could hide whenever the world above became too adversarial. But it hadn't saved them this time, not if Alek and Delilah were the only ones left.

Alek led them down several twisting corridors before reaching a small, Spartan room that was probably just under the kitchen. A bundle of blankets that must be Delilah lay on a simple cot. Alek pointed to a folding chair in the corner and motioned for Kat to sit. When she was settled out of the way he brought the young man forward.

Delilah didn't stir, and Alek slowly began to unwrap her face.

She was alive, or still undead, but barely. Kat couldn't believe a human would be able to survive burns like that, let alone a vampire. Most of her hair had burned away, and her face, what was left of it, was almost too much to bear. Kat turned away.

The feeder fish was more vocal. "No fucking way, man. Ain't no fucking Phantom of the Opera gonna suck me, asshole." He backed up into Kat, almost knocking her and the chair over, then broke and ran for the door. Alek let him go, although Kat doubted the kid would ever find his way out.

She watched the muscles in his shoulders tense and she touched him, wishing he didn't have to feel this pain, that somehow she could make him feel better. "It'll be okay, Alek. We'll find someone else. Or she can use me." A feeling of liquid warmth ran down her spine, pooling in her groin. It had been so long since she'd felt that ambrosia in her veins. If she could save Delilah and feel that way again, how could she refuse?

He turned to face her, the anguish on his face plain. "You don't understand, Kat. If she is to heal she must . . . she must drain whoever I bring to her. If you offer yourself to her, then you will die."

"You love her, don't you?" she asked, coming to sit on the edge of the bed.

"With every fiber of my being." He raised his hand towards Delilah's face but stopped as if fearing he would hurt her. "She made me remember what it was to be human. She saw the good in me. When Max stole her . . . you know how I was. I felt like an animal. To lose her so soon after getting her back—I don't think I could stand it."

Kat kneeled beside the bed and removed the turtleneck to reveal the strapless bustier she wore beneath. Scar tissue from her own burns twisted and undulated across her back like waves on the ocean, and bite marks ran up and down her arms, around her neck like a choker. She felt tears and closed her eyes, trying to stop them before she lost control. But she couldn't. Something tore open deep within her, pouring out a pain she couldn't bear. Sobs tore from her throat and she leaned forward, resting her forehead on the cold floor. Alek came over to wrap his arms around her, pulling her back up and cradling her.

"Sometimes it is worse to be left behind than it is to face the light," he said, stroking her hair. He rocked her back and forth, his cool hand running lightly over the ridges on her back.

"Let me do it," she said suddenly, pulling away from him and wiping her eyes. "Let me save her, Alek."

"I can't. I need you to help me find someone, and quickly, but I can't let you make that decision. You're still torn up over Max."

She shook her head. "I had to live without Max, you know, same as you had to live without Delilah. I don't want to do that again, *ever.* And even if I did, there's nothing for me here, now." *Should I go back to whoring, when I only did it for Max in the first place?* she asked herself, unable to put the thoughts into speech. *Should I go back to school, get some meaningless degree, live my whole life trying to forget what he made me feel, what no mortal man could ever make me feel?* She took a deep breath and found her voice again. "Don't leave me to slit my wrists in some filthy bathroom, Alek. Let my death mean something."

He raised her chin until she was staring into those deep, chocolate eyes of his. "I can Convert you," he said. "You don't have to die. You can travel with Delilah and me, and you will understand why eternity is such a gift."

She laughed harshly. "If I can't stand the thought of a mortal lifetime, how could I possibly want what you offer? No. I want death. If there is a God, maybe he will be merciful and allow me and Max to be together in Hell."

"There are no angels in Hell," he told her, taking her hand. He stared deep into her eyes and she could feel him giving in. He had no choice; they both knew it. She saw sadness in his eyes as he turned her wrist, tracing her veins with a feathery touch as he raised it to his mouth. "He is waiting for you," he whispered against the tender flesh of her wrist.

"Then let me go to him," she replied, lowering herself to the floor and closing her eyes. She felt the sharp prick as his Venom flowed into her veins, numbing the pain so quickly she almost didn't feel it, and her breathing grew ragged. She heard him moving, felt him raising her until she lay cradled in his lap as he sat on the chair. And then he placed her wrist against Delilah's mouth and none of it mattered anymore. When he bit her other wrist she cried out, the need and desire building so painfully within her that the experiences of her past faded and curled in on themselves like paper in the blaze she felt now, burning her alive from the inside out. The blood was draining faster now, and as she felt a mouth on her throat she reached up and let her hand tangle in long, silken hair.

"Let me see you," she whispered, opening her eyes. Delilah pulled away and stared at her with eyes as dark a blue as Kat imagined midnight on the bayou must be. She was beautiful again, smooth and soft and achingly beautiful.

"Thank you for my life," Delilah whispered. She pressed her lips to Kat's, let her taste her own blood. *I did that,* Kat thought with a serenity that her body did not feel, and when Delilah slid her mouth back down to Kat's throat, Kat pulled her closer, wanting more, ever more fire in her veins. Delilah gave it to her and Kat gasped her final breath, back arching like a bow as she reached a frenzied climax, her heart exploding in a storm of pleasure.

Max stood with Death beyond the shadows and beckoned. Kat went to him willingly.

His Essential Nature

Laura Anne Gilman

*Rumor and Hollywood have it that vampires are born
from a bite, drink blood to survive, and live hundreds of
years until someone puts a stake through their heart. Or
exposes them to sunlight.*

*Truth is, your average vampire is born to a mommy
and a daddy, requires one square, if small, meal a day to
supplement the hemoglobin, and generally lives to about
110, assuming that we don't get hit by a truck or taken
out in a drive-by shooting. As for the stake through the
heart—hell yes that'll kill a vampire. Kill most anything,
you do it right.*

*You see, when we're kids we can bear the daylight,
make friends, play by the daylight rules. Be "normal."
It's only when we hit puberty that things begin to change.
And by then, most of us have made our peace with the
way things are.*

Westin looked at the words glowing on the screen and
rubbed one eye wearily. He'd made his peace, but it hadn't
been easy. And now he was going to put someone else
through that. Maybe.

Looking across the home office to where Dani sat at the
old-fashioned rolltop desk, test papers and grade book laid
out with frightening precision, he felt a rush of adrenaline
run through his veins that had nothing to do with the blood

he had consumed not half an hour before. His wife. And, god help him, his child. Because they were really going to do this. They were going to have a kid. In about six months, give or take miscalculations.

Looking back at the words he had typed, his contribution to his child's education, Westin saved the file and stood abruptly, gliding out of the room without a word of excuse or explanation. He knew, without looking back, that Dani watched him go. He could see that smile on her face, the amused glint in her eyes. She knew him entirely too well, dammit. Couldn't a man keep some privacy?

Grabbing his camera from the hook where it always hung ready, Westin dragged his "working" jacket over his arms, let himself out the back door, and stood a moment on the yellow-lit porch, breathing in the cold night air. It was time to work. He'd been home for almost two weeks, trying to choose the negatives for the book project his agent wanted to put together, when Dani had dropped the baby bombshell on him. That, he admitted wryly, had stopped him cold for a few days. But worrying wasn't going to get the bills paid, and while it was satisfying to compose the things he was going to have to tell his unborn child, words weren't the same as images. They didn't have the same power, the same corporeal dimensionality.

He snorted, shaking his head in disgust. Fatherhood was making his brain soften already. Corporeal dimensionality. Jesus.

Stepping off the porch, he strode into the darkness, sensitive eyes adjusting automatically to the play of shadows and starlight. The adaptations of a night creature. Following the needle-sharp tracks of deer, he moved into the spaces between trees, letting his breath float like mist. There, over to his left. Stopping, he raised the camera slowly, forcing himself to take the time needed. A buck lifted his head, slowly chewing, a strip of tree bark hanging from his mouth. His sides were scarred, and his shoulders strong. A survivor. But the buck was thinner than he should be for what had so far been a mild winter. He might not last the season, leaving a space for a younger buck to get himself into the gene pool.

Two vampires made for a vampire. But a vampire and a human . . .

Westin tried to shut the thought out, snapping a quick succession of frames before the buck reacted to the clicking and bolted for deeper shelter. The last shot, of the old buck risking one glimpse over his shoulder, hooves kicking up dried leaves and white tail flicking, gave Westin a deep satisfaction. He was good at this. His photos of street life were in great demand, and critics referred to his "uncanny ability to ferret out the still beauty of despair, and the clarity of peace within misery." But it was this, his nature photography, that gave him the most pleasure. Animals were what they were, and his lens revealed only that. He exposed no one's secrets in these photos, laid no one's soul bare for the world to gape at.

He had met Dani during one of his nocturnal rambles through the city, camera at the ready. It was early in his career, when he was taking heat for not doing the "commercial" thing. Just in his mid-twenties, he already knew what he didn't want to spend the rest of his life doing. The fact that he couldn't work under sunlight had, thankfully, limited his options, and his talent turned his reputation into eccentric rather than obstinate, temperamental rather than brat. A few carefully chosen projects bombed, allowing the world that had heralded his early work to promptly forget his very existence, leaving him to his darkened streets and crowded tenements. Over the years he had learned the secret tricks of nighttime photography and invented a few of his own. It helped that he could see the shadows, sense the light. His eyes were a better meter than any mechanical contraption, and his judgement hadn't failed him in years.

Dani had been walking up Eighth Avenue, the light from a streetlamp catching her face as she stopped to look at her map. An obvious newcomer to the city that Westin called his own. The clarity of her face in that instant was too much to resist. He'd taken her photo. Had fallen into step beside her, offered his help getting her to where she was going. Made advances. Felt her pulse stir a hunger not expected.

Later, over coffee, he had scolded her for accepting a stranger's invitation. She had merely smiled at him and said that she knew he would never hurt her. Fool, he had thought then, not unkindly.

Two weeks later he had fed from the delicate veins in her wrist, bringing this undauntable woman into the small circle of human friends who willingly supplied him with the sustenance he needed to survive. Three months after that, he tasted the heart-blood running in her neck, and that summer they had been married. His father had been the only member of his family to attend the dusk ceremony, sadly outnumbered by Dani's innumerable, exuberant family.

Leaning against the cold fencepost that marked the end of his land and the beginning of their neighbor's, Westin scanned the field in front of him, hunting for owl sign. He'd gotten a decent shot of one of those horned hunters taking a mouse, but the angle hadn't pleased him. Hunching slightly to allow his jacket to bunch around him for warmth, Westin allowed himself to blend into the surroundings, his grey down jacket and heavy cords becoming just so many more shadows.

Born to the ever-neon, ever-bustling city of Las Vegas, Westin still savored moments like this, knowing that except for Dani back at the house, and the Fillinghams in the old farmhouse across the field, he was alone for miles. There was no blood-sense to distract him, nothing beyond the faint pulsing of animal blood too gamey to appeal. He loved Manhattan, but the coolness of Nature, her insistence upon ignoring him, was too much a challenge to resist.

Hearing the smallest rustling behind and above him, he forced his body not to tense. A few minutes later he was rewarded by the heavy flap and swoop of soft-feathered wings and the inaudible scream of a field mouse.

* * *

The CD player clicked and whirled, and the soft voice of Mary Chapin Carpenter filled the oversize darkroom. Echoing off recycled plastic walls, the upbeat music made the eerie black-lit darkness seem even more surreal. Reaching up, Westin adjusted the magnification and hit the light timer. While the seconds slowly ticked off, he checked his watch. Julianne was supposed to stop by tonight, and his sister wouldn't hesitate to storm into the darkroom if he weren't there to greet her.

Opening the black metal cabinet against the far wall, Westin carefully aligned the sheets of photosensitive paper and closed the lid of the box so that no light could reach it. He reached up to recount the large plastic jugs of fixative on the top shelf, his fingers sliding over the base of the jugs with the familiarity of a blind man reading Braille. Everything was as it should be, and he was simply filling time. Worried about telling his sister his news. Their news. Jules' children were her delight, even if the man she'd married had turned out to be one of the lowest bloodsuckers, in every sense of the word, he'd even encountered. There was no way that she would understand the apprehension ripping through him. Or worse yet, if she did, it would be with a painful I-told-you-so kind of sympathy. While fond of her human donors, and cheerfully willing to agree that Dani was five times the spouse her ex could ever claim to be, Jules had never understood his desire to marry outside. His need to make a life with this quiet, loving human woman.

The timer *pinged* and he swung around, slow strides taking him back to the machine. Unclipping the paper, he moved with that same careful grace to the row of plastic tubs. Dropping the sheet carefully into the first bath, he reached over to the small shelf by the door and lifted a neon-green squeeze bottle to his mouth.

His old instructor would have screamed to see him eating or drinking in the darkroom—there were so many chemicals, all toxic, that could get into the mouth without adding any risks. Westin's lips pursed in a sour smile. He was going to have to put a lock on his studio once the child began walking. Inquisitive little fingers were dangerous. And, if his nephews were any indication, a child that didn't mind darkness would home in on this room, with its kid-friendly revolving door and black lights.

Of course, the child could be afraid of the dark. . . .

A chime rang out, startling him from his ruminations. For an instant he was confused, looking to see what piece of machinery had made the noise. The chime rang out again, two quick bursts, and he recognized the sound this time as the bell outside the darkroom.

"Damn," he muttered, looking at the proof sheet still developing. It was unusual for Jules to be early—she was the original night owl.

"Mind the door!" he shouted.

The lightweight door began to revolve slowly, his visitor heeding his warning that there was work in process. But the body that appeared wasn't that of his reed-slim baby sister.

"Keeter?"

Six-four of Nordic god filled his doorway, making the darkroom suddenly shrink in on itself.

Westin put the bottle down slowly, not moving. His eyes measured the distance between them, taking in the other man's posture, noting the muscled arms held loosely to the side, shoulders relaxed, knees straight, not flexed for action.

Augie "Mosquito" Bick. Old childhood buddy. Sculptor. Art gallery owner. Part-time vampire hunter.

Not that Westin hadn't hunted a vampire or two on his own. Not every member of his rather extended family felt as he did about humans, and there had been a few times when Westin had been forced to explain his philosophy of coexistence at fangpoint. But Keeter did it for pleasure. And revenge.

Now his friend loomed like a minor god, one hand slapping a flat manila envelope against his left thigh. "We've got problems."

Keeter's voice still flowed like warm honey, seducing everything in sight. But the eyes were cold. And angry.

Westin turned his back, stirring the chemicals thought-fully. Keeter always brought problems. Usually fanged ones. Almost always messy ones. And despite the fact that it had been three years since their last joint venture, the memories of the blood spilled hadn't left him yet. Picking up a set of plastic-tipped tongs, he removed the proof sheet from the first bath, shook it gently, and dropped it into the second shallow tub. Images were forming there, rows of small boxes, holding a world of secrets to be unearthed, picked over, chosen. Shown to the world in a triumphant declaration: Here is how I see your world. Deal with it.

The CD clicked off, and nothing replaced the silence except Keeter's patient breathing. The human could sit for hours, waiting. Westin knew that, had taught him that. Had taught him how to make the first stroke count, and finish the job without hesitating. Vampires died badly. But so did humans. This is our world, too. Deal with it. What had Keeter brought him to deal with?

He could tell the human to leave, to take his trouble and walk out the door. Keeter would do it, he knew. Walk, without question. Never bring it up again.

The silence in the darkroom was unthreatening. They each knew what the other was about, the demons each danced with. Keeter found a space on the worktable that was clear to sit on and let his long legs dangle above the concrete floor while he waited for the photographer to finish his work. In the black light of the darkroom, his hair and skin seemed to glow with health, vitality—blood. Westin had often wondered what Keeter's blood tasted like. But the human had never offered, and he had never asked.

The tongs raised, lowered, and the proof sheet moved into the next bath, and on through to the waterfall of cold water that finished it. Westin found a feeling of satisfaction in the accomplishment. The taking of photographs was his love, his passion. But this was his religion, complete with ritual, offering, and resulting miracles. Dipping his hands directly into the water to remove the sheet, he lay it on a towel draped over the far end of the worktable, blotting it gently until damp.

Taking it and three other finished sheets carefully in hand, he moved into the revolving doorway, pushing out with a forearm. He didn't look behind to ensure that Keeter followed.

Hanging the results of a week's work on the drying line strung across the far length of the basement that housed his darkroom, Westin could feel the cotton of his shirt rubbing against his skin, the weight of his cords against his thigh. The flesh was tight, dry—active. Anticipating a Hunt. Damn Keeter anyway.

Someone—Westin couldn't remember the name, only that he had been a short, overweight little man with a wicked gleam of humor that made you trust him at the same time you watched his hands—had once approached him to work for the local police department. Night shift, where all the action occurred. He had declined, not graciously. He hadn't found any art in that work—too much anger in that profession, and damn little joy. But, looking at the black-and-white positioned on his light board, Westin was ready to reconsider. These shots were Art. Unfortunately, they were also of dead people. Dead humans. Their throats sucked dry with a considerable lack of finesse and a very definite message. Vampire. To Keeter, it might as well have been a neon sign. Come and find me. Catch me. Stop me.

And Westin knew that Keeter could no more refuse that invitation than he could stop breathing.

Catching a glimpse of himself in the small mirror by the door, Westin catalogued his features: Eyes, tired. Skin, papery. Mouth, tense. Well, hell.

"You couldn't call Nick Knight?"

Keeter actually laughed, rare for him. "He's been canceled. You're all I've got."

"Dammit, I'm going to be a father."

"Congratulations." He must have encountered Dani on the way downstairs; he showed no surprise. The blond indicated the photograph he had brought. "You want whatever did *that* to be her role model?" Frontal attack.

"Could be a boy." Sidestepping the issue.

"Nah. You were born to be whipped." Unspoken: Don't dodge my question.

There was silence, less comfortable this time. Westin placed a magnifying glass over one victim's neck, inspecting the wounds more closely. Keeter looked as though he were contemplating quantum time. He might, however, just have been counting the holes in the boards of the ceiling. With Keeter, Westin thought sourly, you could never tell.

The sound of a door closing upstairs made the human tilt his head in anticipation. Dani, apparently giving up on her work for the night, came down the stairs, her steps light, almost skipping. The two men sat up, shoulders broadening. Fourteen years married, Dani still had that effect on the male of either species. Not for her beauty, which had never been breathtaking, or any overwhelming sensuality, but the sheer light that she emitted.

"I left a message with Julianne's service that you were busy this morning," she said, wrapping her arms around her husband's neck and nuzzling into his throat, unabashed by Keeter's presence. "If she comes by anyway, should I divert her?"

"That might be best," Westin said, looking up at Keeter, who nodded slightly. Julianne, despite her aggressive manner, was not the vampire to include in a Hunt. She even had trouble taking blood from her human donors, preferring to let them siphon it off and store it, something most vampires did only for emergencies. Her small fridge was filled with bottles dated and labeled like some bizarre wine cellar, and it always gave her big brother the creeps.

Dani nipped at Westin's neck, causing him to yelp and then engulf her in a strong hug that cracked several ribs satisfactorily. Belatedly he remembered the baby and gentled his hold considerably.

"Late Movie's *Smokey and the Bandit*," she told him, extracting herself and straightening her nightshirt primly. "You boys get bored, I've made extra popcorn."

"Doesn't anyone around here keep human hours?" Westin wondered to the ceiling. "Thanks anyway, love, but we've got guy stuff to discuss."

Dani rolled her eyes at the obvious dismissal and left the room with a sad pout, well aware that two pair of eyes were fastened to the roll of her hips.

"Hey. *My* wife, remember?"

"Only 'cause she has a thing for hickeys," Keeter said dryly, returning his attention to the photographs. "So, what do you think?"

"It could be some bloodsport wannabe," Westin said, running his fingers through the air a few inches over the images. He didn't want to know through what arcane network of barter Keeter had acquired these.

"Could be." Keeter wasn't agreeing.

"Or it could be something completely unrelated—your normal garden variety murder spree."

"Could be."

Westin stood and paced from one end of the basement to the other, stopping in front of the small blacked-out window as though he could see the night-shrouded landscape outside. A lethal feeder. Just what this city needed. "These three the only ones?"

"The only ones the cops know about. The fems are sisters; they lived in the apartment. The guy is a friend of the younger girl, were going to art school together." Keeter stopped, knowing he'd just delivered the final blow.

"Art school, huh? They any good?"

"Oh, yeah."

Westin reached up and splayed one hand on the painted window, feeling the cold through his skin, down into his veins. Damn. Artists. Painters, he would lay even odds. Some of them were hacks, technicians—draftsmen and Xeroxers. But those with talent carried something special in their blood, something sweet, something appealing. Something that would call to a vampire from across town, and make him hunger for just a taste of that deep garnet wine. Look back closely enough, and most of the great creators in human history had a patron who shunned notoriety, content merely to ensure the artist's survival. Aesthetic appreciation was only half the equation.

But, by that same reasoning, no vampire would destroy the source of such intoxicating blood. Not if there was true talent. Not unless he—the vampire—were mad. And a mad vampire, unlike a lethal feeder, could not be reasoned with, or restrained. Like a rabid dog, there was only one solution.

He looked down at his solution-stained hands, his mind reshuffling priorities. He didn't have time for this, not with a show so close. But there was no other option. A dayrunner—a vampire who coexisted with humans—had that responsibility to those unaware of their danger.

"You should stay out of this," he said, not looking over where he knew Keeter still sat, swinging his legs as though he hadn't a care in the world. "This isn't your fight."

"They're all my fight." Cold, unemotional. But Westin heard the pain underlying the words, and flinched from them. He still owed Keeter a life, and the human's refusal to remind him only deepened that awareness. And so they moved on, each pretending to forget, to believe that the other had forgotten.

Shoving those memories away, Westin rubbed his hands roughly against his thighs as though trying to stimulate thought. There wasn't much time, not if the killer had targeted the artistic community. Despite the high number of people in Manhattan who claimed "artist" on their tax forms, the percentage of true talents was likely to be low. Mostly they moved out of the city, finding cheaper places to live on their limited incomes. But they came here first to study, to attend the schools and scope the museums, and talk in the cafés until they found the city's bustle more distracting than inspiring. That would be the place to focus, then. The students. The killer had found his first victims there, and the odds were good that he would return to that source. They just had to find him before more unwilling blood was taken.

Westin knew that there would be no outcry from his kin on this—a maddened vampire was something even isolationists would not allow to exist. But they would receive no help, either. And certainly no thanks if—when—they succeeded.

"Sometimes I wish you'd grown up to be a cop instead of a prissy shopkeeper," Westin said in mock complaint, turning to face his companion. "You'd be a lot more use if you had some official standing."

"Deal with it, fang-boy." Keeter sneered, ignoring the crack about his gallery. "If I were a cop, I wouldn't let you play in this game at all."

He could feel her watching, but every time he turned his head, she was engrossed in the book she was reading. She even turned pages at a reasonable rate. He turned back to the screen, one hand reaching for a handful of popcorn from the oversize ceramic bowl at his feet. A few unpopped kernels fell on the carpet and were crushed underneath the wheels of his chair. Westin winced guiltily, but Dani didn't look up at the noise. She was definitely ignoring him. She still had a mad on from being excluded from the conversation the morning before with Keeter. Westin gave an inward shrug. It couldn't be helped. Even if there were something she could do to help, he wouldn't endanger her now. Not with the baby to consider.

He stared at what he had typed, hearing his father's voice speak the words.

Three days, maximum. If the blood sits longer than that, it will taste so awful you won't be able to choke it down, even if it is all that stands between you and starvation. That's why it's so important to have a network you can rely upon. At any time, you must be able to call upon a donor, if not for immediate need, then for that three-day window.

Thinking of his own small circle, he added,

A good donor is one who is healthy, with no addictions which would taint their blood. Obviously, drug addicts and alcoholics are out of the question. Not only is the nutritional value of their blood almost nonexistent, but you also run a good chance of acquiring their addiction. On the other hand, health nuts are not a good choice either. Your mother claims that I'm too picky, but I believe that tofu thins the blood.

"This is starting to look more like a manifesto that a friendly letter of advice."

Dani's voice didn't startle him, but her breath, warm on the back of his neck, made more than his hair rise. It felt like he was forgiven. Swinging around in his chair, he swept her onto his lap. "I want to make sure that I don't leave anything out," he said seriously, hitting the save button with his free hand. The machine hummed for a second, then went silent.

"Michael. You're going to be here for Junior," she said, leaning back into his embrace, accepting his silent apology and offering one of her own. "He won't need it."

"Keeter says it's going to be a girl," he said absently, his hands busy.

Her hands covered his, guiding them. "Keeter doesn't know everything." Her head fell back against his shoulder, baring the dusky skin of her neck. He bent forward to breathe softly on the sensitive flesh, feeling the warmth and blood-scent that rose off her when she was aroused. He was bred to crave that smell, to cultivate it, but the flush of affection was purely between them, something he treasured above all the other gifts in his life. Grazing teeth slowly, he drew a gentle shudder from her; then her hands were stilling his, her body withdrawing ever so slightly.

"We need to talk about this."

He sighed, folding his hands around her waist in surrender. "Okay," he said, not knowing if she were referring to the Hunt or the baby.

"Nobody's ever presented the kin with a human half-breed before, huh?" Baby, then. Good. She knew the answer already, was just making an opening gambit. But he responded anyway.

"Not that I've heard of, no. There aren't many dayrunners to begin with, and damn few marry out."

"So we don't know that Junior—whatever his or her sex—will take after one side or the other." She was the voice of reasonableness, and he resented it. And resented resenting it.

"And you say that for the first ten or twelve years, our child will appear to be human, no matter the eventual outcome."

He nodded, knowing what she wanted him to say. "Dani, I can't put off worrying until then. There's too much that could go wrong. What if our genes don't mix? I know the doctor said everything's perfect, but what if there's—?"

She slapped at his hand. "What if I get hit by a truck tomorrow? What if you pull another damn-fool stunt like last year and get caught in the sunlight?"

He winced from that. It *had* been stupid.

"So we shouldn't borrow trouble, is what you're telling me."

"There'll be enough of that soon enough."

They swung towards the door to see Keeter leaning against the frame, a beer in one hand. Westin scowled at their houseguest, who ignored him with the ease of long practice. "Sorry. Didn't know that this was a private conversation."

"The hell you didn't," Dani muttered, and then laughed. "Oh, come in. Join the party."

The tall human sauntered across the room to the leather chair Dani had vacated and dropped himself down onto it, moving her book to the floor and carefully balancing his beer on his stomach.

"Why worry about the kid being norm or vamp? I mean,

by the time she's five or six, you'll have had to explain why daddy doesn't take her to the playground, or drive her to school, or any of the million stupid parent tricks daddies do during the daylight." He stopped, amused at the alliteration. "And then you'll have to explain about her Aunt Jules, and all those nifty cousins who don't want to go outside and play. . . ."

"All right, all right," Westin said, making a gesture of submission. "I get the picture. Thank you. You're always such a comfort."

"I try. I do try."

Dani drew the covers back over him and left the bedroom silently. He could hear her moving downstairs, the sound of dishes being moved, the rumble of Keeter's voice and the *swish-chunk* of the dishwasher starting up. Outside, he knew, the sun would be overhead. The sky would be endlessly blue, the air thin and piercing, the wind dragging smells for miles. Not for the first time he cursed his visual sense, that could carry memories from thirty years ago with such clarity. It would be kinder to forget, or to dull the senses with time and darkness.

Pulling the covers over his head, he rolled onto his stomach and tried to go back to sleep. Eventually the sounds from the kitchen faded, and he fell into a dream of being twelve, and playing baseball under the deadly rays of a June sun.

The sound of something ringing dragged him from the depths. His hand shot out and slapped the top of the alarm clock. The ringing continued, so he slapped it again. When that failed to stop the noise, he pulled the covers off his face and squinted in the darkened room. Phone. The phone was ringing.

"Yalo," he managed to mutter into the right portion of the receiver.

There was a long silence; then he dropped the receiver back into its cradle with a snort of disgust. He had better things to do than listen to some mechanical voice offer him low-interest loans. Sleep. Sleep was definitely a better thing. He, Dani, and Keeter had been up until past dawn talking over their plans, and while he could go for a long time without sleep, if need be, Westin had never seen the appeal. REM sleep was more than a necessity to him; it was a hobby. One to be indulged at every available opportunity.

A soft creak of the door opening warned him that the opportunity was slipping away.

"Good, you're awake."

"No, I'm not," he said testily. "Go away."

"I've got a lead on the victims."

That made Westin open one eye, if slowly. Peering past the sleep gunking his vision, he stared at the mirror that hung on the far wall in place of a window. His hair slicked back and his eyes heavy-lidded, the flip-sided reflection of Keeter looked like something the cat wouldn't bother dragging in. Westin felt a smug flash of gratification at that. Apparently someone had gotten even less sleep. Good. "Go make me coffee," he ordered, letting his head fall back onto the pillow. "And pour some for yourself. You look like shit."

"I hear and obey, Lord and Master." The human salaamed out the door. Westin rolled over to stare at the ceiling, frowning. Keeter was in a good mood. That meant he had found ass to kick. Terrific. Throwing back the covers, he hitched up his shorts and staggered into the bathroom to throw himself under the shower. That coffee had better be *strong*.

By the time he toweled off, Keeter was back with two mugs of finest kind Colombian roast. Standing nude in the doorway of the bathroom, Westin drained half the mug in one long pull, then put the mug down on the low dresser, and opened a drawer, rummaging for clean underwear. Keeter paced the room, taking small sips of his coffee simply because it was in his hand.

"The husks," and Westin flinched to hear the crude term coming from a human, "were known to hang out in the Village. One place in particular. A bar called The Basket."

"As in 'going to hell in a'?" Westin asked, sitting on the edge of the bed and snagging a pair of socks up over his ankles.

Keeter shrugged. "Whatever. The owner's a former teacher at the Ashkeleon School, so it could be basket weaving, all we know."

Westin hid a grin at that. Keeter was such a snob when it came to art schools.

"So we've got three bodies, two of whom were studying—" Keeter paused midstride, looking into the air to his left as he mentally checked his facts"—studying *watercolors*." The word came out on a sneer. "They met the girl's sister at ten-thirty last Wednesday night, and consumed two pitchers of Red Stripe." Keeter's voice was more approving now. "Then they trundled for, one assumes, the nearest subway station, since no cabbie will recall having fares to match their descriptions."

Westin stopped toweling his hair long enough to question the wording. "You think they took a cab and nobody's willing to say? Why?"

"I'm just naturally suspicious. But we haven't anything to go on, so let's say subway. The time of death is somewhere around daybreak, which figures. He's waiting until the last minute, drawing out the danger. So somewhere between ten-thirty and five a.m. we've got three young'uns meeting up with our rabid batboy and getting all comfy on their apartment floor."

"They were killed there."

"Yeah." Keeter finished his coffee, then looked down into the mug as though only then noticing it. "The local gendarmes are claiming not, 'cause the splatter doesn't match the wounds. But we know the reason for that."

The vampire got up and went to the dresser, pulling a pair of cords out of the lower drawer. He stopped, one leg inserted, and half turned.

"If he took all three on, they must have been off-guard. Drunk."

"Probable."

"He follows them home from the bar," Westin plotted out loud, pulling the slacks up and buttoning them as he spoke. "Maybe approaches them outside their apartment, claims to—what? How does he get inside without alerting them?"

"Hell, how did your kind ever do it?"

Westin stopped, taken aback. "Oh, come on, Keeter. That's a myth. Trust me, we'd have a lot larger population if taking blood were that easy. And even if you did have someone who could pull off that kind of mesmerizing, there's no way the other two would stand still while he took the first one out. There's not a vampire alive that has that kind of strength."

"You sure about that?"

Westin went to the walk-in closet and disappeared into the row of shirts. His voice, when it came, was muffled. "No."

The night was colder than he'd expected. Three layers of clothing kept the wind out, but did nothing for the claws of ice digging into his marrow. The street was deserted, most of the streetlights either dimmed or gone out completely. This wasn't a neighborhood that read its Neighborhood Watch booklets. Two windows were still lit, but he wasn't concerned with them. Raising the brim of his hat barely an inch, he shrugged so that the coat collar protected more of his ears. Vampire blood didn't run thin. Something more than weather made him shift from side to side, shuffling his feet soundlessly.

A noise made him swing carefully to his left, one hand automatically reaching for the camera not at his side. A pigeon cocked and bobbed disdainfully, indifferent to his presence. Reaching into one pocket, he tossed the filthy bird the rind of his sandwich.

Four figures came around the far corner, laughing and gesturing, coats open despite the weather. More than hemoglobin was warming them tonight. One figure peeled off, staggering to a wall and facing it, stood there for a moment.

The acrid smell of urine shot through the still, cold air, assaulting Westin's nose. Lovely. He couldn't have waited?

The group staggered on, unaware that they had lost one of their members. Coming to a doorway that still maintained a fading grasp on respectability, one figure struggled with a key, then swung open the door with a flourish, waving the rest of the party inside with a wide-armed gesture.

Westin tensed, feeling his tendons ache with the need to leap. He'd fed the night before, but the availability of so much ready prey was a fang-tease if ever he'd seen it.

That, of course, was the whole idea.

Three times, Keeter had swept down upon unsuspecting groups of struggling artists, buying them drinks and praising their works. His cachet as a gallery owner was enough to make them all but bare their throats in submission, making them perfect goats, ready to be staked out as bait.

In his defense, Keeter had drawn up plans for two of them to have student exhibits—they truly were talented; otherwise they wouldn't have been targeted. And the others had come out of the setup with nothing worse than a splitting headache from booze Keeter had paid for and a vague sense of disgruntlement that they hadn't been singled out for fame and fortune. But despite dangling the perfect feeders, their rogue vampire hadn't so much as nipped. And he—or she—would need to feed again soon. Even a relatively somnolent vampire needed to replenish every three or four nights, and it had been over two weeks since the bodies had been found. Where was he hiding?

Their quarry might have moved out of the area, but Westin doubted it. Once a vampire began lethal feeding, it rarely stopped of its own accord. Even if there were vampires casual enough about their existence to allow such a headline-grabbing killer to run through their community, the news wires would have picked up the story. The grisly triple murder earlier that month had gotten enough airplay in the New York markets to ensure that.

The door slammed shut behind them, and Westin sagged against the cold brick wall, letting the tension flow out of his body. Another night wasted, and he didn't have any suggestions to make that might bring better results.

Feeling the pinch of his fangs against the sensitive skin on the inside of his mouth, he opened his mouth wide, flexing his jaw. Canker sores were a side effect of fangs that no one ever seemed to consider in vampire fiction. Pushing himself off the supporting wall, he was about to head for his car, calling it a bad Hunt, when something wafted on the air, into his still-open mouth.

Westin froze, tilting his head in a pose of alert listening. Spinning, he was too late to avoid the arm crashing into his face, knocking him backwards and opening a flow of blood from his nose. A flash of bone-colored skin passed in front of him, a wave of inhuman speed. Snarling, Westin got to his feet, fangs in full view now.

His opponent stood still long enough to taunt him. "You. *You* thought you could stop me? You thin your blood with wine before you take it!"

With that insult, the speaker dodged away from Westin's lunge, chuckling on a wheezy exhale. "You've weakened yourself, fouled yourself, feeding from your tame humans. But I'll put an end to that. I'll teach you to turn your back on what you are." The eyes were all pupil, hard and cold. There was nothing that might pass for human in those eyes.

A setup. Westin blinked, trying to keep track of the dervish taunting him. Not a maddened vampire—a setup. If he died here, Keeter would never forgive himself. And if he survived, he was going to *kill* that damn obsessed human for letting them both be manipulated so easily!

Drawing his emotions under control, he slipped into a crouch, moving in time to the figure play-stalking him. The isolationist was in the mood to scuffle, it seemed. Tough. It had been a long night, he was hungry, and Dani would be waiting for him at home. Westin wasn't in the mood to play. Not when there was human blood to settle between them.

Fangs bared, he thrust his upper body towards his opponent, arms reaching as though to grab him by the throat.

The other vampire dodged easily, stepping in closer to the dayrunner and curling long cold fingers around his shoulders. Even through his heavy wool coat and army-issue sweater, Westin could feel the newly fed strength in those muscles. His head turned, and he sank fangs into the other man's hand, letting his canines come down in a secondary crunch. The taste was bitter, too much salt present in the skin, and his gorge rose, urging him to gag.

His attacker hissed, a long, silibant sound, and wrenched his hand free, spinning Westin and sending him to his knees on the sidewalk.

Not bothering to rise, Westin wrapped his arms around the other's legs, raising his hatted head into the groin area above him. His opponent buckled, and Westin let himself grin, a serpent's grin of white teeth and tongue. And so all men were created equal, he thought, taking advantage of the moment to push the vampire backwards onto the pavement and get a good look at his assailant's face. He saw an unfamiliar face, now covered in shock. Obviously, this stranger-kin had believed his own words, that willing blood weakened the taker.

"Idiot."

With that one word, Westin reached down and tore his opponent's throat out.

> There are those who would say that might is right, that those who can, should. And there will be moments, deep in the uncomfortable areas of your soul, when you will agree with them. We were created to be predators, to feed off others, and humans are our preferred targets. Come to terms with this. Accept it. Deal with it. Anything else, any denial of your essential nature, and you will end up maddened.

His fingers curled into his palms, hands falling onto the powder-blue foam wrist rest. The words mocked him, stirring eddies of emotional dust that clouded his thought process, clogged his mental gears. Did one ever really come to terms with it? Or was it all an illusion, a hypocrisy of good deeds to whitewash his essential nature?

Swearing, he pushed himself away from the keyboard, rolling the chair across the room with the force of his movements. The wheels squeaked softly on the hardwood floor, and Westin was suddenly struck by a burst of energy, as though he could run up the side of a mountain. A creative flash, and he knew that staying inside was beyond impossible. With a guilty glance at the clock, to ensure that Dani would be in class for several hours yet, he went to the door and looked down the long hallway to the window at the far end. The light coming in was grey and muted, the after-weather of the snows that had begun two days before.

"Live dangerously," he told himself with a grim, determined smile, his feet finding the path to the stairs and out the door as though by their own accord.

The snow clustered in his hair, thickening the strands into wet clumps. Westin moved along the unplowed road, snowshoes making soft noises in the overcast afternoon gloom. A series of clicks captured the vista of frozen pond melting into snowbank. The cacophony of greys was disquieting, too much, an overload of calm after his recent frenzy. It gave him the beginning of a headache. Letting his arms relax back to his side, he looked up to observe a vee of late geese swing overhead, heading east. It was a rare occasion, the heavy layer of clouds making daytime safe for a little while, and he wanted to soak every moment allowed him.

Leaning forward, he continued down the road, letting the unaccustomed afternoon air hit his face. He couldn't have said the differences between day and night breath. Something about the quality of stillness, perhaps. Or maybe it was all in his mind. He'd have to remember to ask Dani. Now that Keeter had gone home, she was actually talking to him again. In between bouts of throwing up.

Moving to the far side of the pond, he raised his lens to scope the tree line, scanning for something to trigger his instinct. Life slowed to an easy drawl, his breathing in tune with the pulse in his forehead, all concentration centered into that sphere of vision. Nothing. A heavy sigh—then he chuckled. A chance to take daylight photos, and he couldn't find a thing worth shooting. Pitiful.

A faint scuffling made him swing around, camera rising to eye level in an instinct he swore he'd been born with. The viewfinder settled on the ground where the road would have been. A crow sat, hock-deep in snow, and picked at the carcass of something that might have been a rabbit.

The bird raised its beak and stared directly into Westin's eyes. A shiver crawled down the photographer's back. *Dead eyes, staring at him. Dead eyes in a corpse. Dead eyes still open as he and Keeter slid it into the snow-lit waters of the East River. The dead eyes of an animal.* Then the moment was gone, and he snapped the picture.

Drink the Darkness

SIOBHAN BURKE

"Oh, there you are, Polly. Did you have an enjoyable walk?" Malice dripped from Lord Byron's voice as he turned from my faltering companion to me. "What have you done to him? Is he drunk?"

The terrace of the Hotel d'Angleterre was almost deserted, the night having become chill. I helped Polidori to sit before replying. "No," I said, pointedly ignoring his previous question. "He is merely tired."

"Oh, I believe that there is considerably more to it than that, Marlowe, considerably more," Byron said. Our paths had crossed often in the past few months, and although I had become quite friendly with his physician and traveling companion, John Polidori, the poet himself did not hesitate to avail himself of the least opportunity to display the violent antipathy I inspired in him.

During our brief absence Byron had graduated from wine to spirits, though he did not appear drunk, only somewhat agitated. He leaned toward me, his voice breathless and urgent as he continued. "While traveling in Albania I uncovered a most curious legend. Have you heard of . . . vampires?" I could see the glittering as Byron kept his feverish eyes fixed upon me, watching for any hint of a reaction to the word. He was disappointed.

"Vampires?" I allowed a note of puzzlement to creep into my voice. "Some sort of blood-drinking ghost, aren't they?"

"Not exactly. They do drink blood, but they are the undead, those that return from their deaths in their physical bodies to prey upon the living." He paused for effect. "I believe that you are one." Polidori's head snapped up at the extraordinary accusation.

"Are you mad, George?" he spat. "Or have you been at the pipe again?"

"No, I am not, and I have not. Be still, Polly. Have you nothing to say, Marlowe?"

"I admit that I am rather taken aback at the thought. What, if I may ask, has led you to this remarkable conclusion?"

"Little things. That you are never about by day, for instance. That you never eat. And, of course, that every time poor Polly has gone walking with you, he has come back pale and 'tired.'"

"Rather flimsy evidence upon which to risk a man's life," I said, disturbed to think that I had become so careless as to let my nature be detected. I nodded toward the waiters, who had stopped all pretense of work to listen and to mutter among themselves. "How am I to refute such an absurd flight of fancy?"

"Dine with me tomorrow at Diodati. Come early, at about three—I have something special planned for the evening."

"George!"

"Stow it, Polly!"

I looked thoughtfully at the pair, troubled by an echo from my past. *"Dine with me tomorrow at Deptford,"* Tommy had said fully two hundred years ago, and I had dined and died there. I would certainly dine tomorrow at Diodati, and if death should come, it would not come for me.

"I would be honored. Until tomorrow then, my lord. John," I added, and put out my hand to Polidori, who recoiled from my touch. Ah. I walked away without looking back.

*   *   *

The next afternoon was sullen, with a lowering iron-colored overcast that would occasionally part to show towers of brilliantly lit clouds above, almost too bright to look upon.

As I approached Diodati, a large and extremely ugly bulldog rushed out at me, seemingly intent upon tearing out my throat. I stood my ground, and the brute slowed his pace, until, when he reached me, he was moving doubtfully, unsure. I held out my hand, and he started to wriggle ingratiatingly, like a puppy. I knelt to pat him for a moment, and when I rose Lord Byron was watching, as I had thought he might be. "You have a way with animals," he said, and I nodded. "Moretto is, as a rule, not . . . gentle with strangers."

"And yet you let him roam free?"

"He broke his chain." He said nothing more, and I accompanied him, also silent, to the house. He preceded me through the door, then turned to watch me enter. As I stepped across the threshold, I heard Polidori laugh spitefully.

"The third test!" he cried. "Abroad in the daylight, entering without being invited, and—" He pointed to the large mirror hanging across the hall, where the three of us were perfectly reflected: Polidori the shortest, but well-favored with his Italian looks; Byron, elegant and romantic-looking, with his tumbled hair and careless cravat; and myself, the tallest and least handsome of the three—lean as a predator is lean, almost thirty, but my otherwise pleasing countenance severely marred by my eyes. My left eye is dark, but my right is a pale steely blue, and the eyelid droops slightly, webbed with the silvery tracings of old scars. Byron looked at the reflections, and then at the door, appearing somewhat vexed. I could not help but smile.

"In point of fact, you did invite me, yesterday," I said, and he brightened, even managing a smile of his own. He was a most attractive man when he wasn't being corrosive.

"I missed milord's grand arrival yesterday afternoon. I

trust it was suitably impressive?" I asked Polidori at one point as we wandered about the villa.

"Oh, very," Polidori grinned. "All the scandalized tourists hanging over the balustrades like laundry à la mode, all trying to catch a glimpse of the devil incarnate." His grin faded. "And Shelley with his harem in the forefront, of course. George had scarcely stepped from his carriage before that Clairmont harpy was clinging to him like some monstrous leech."

"Oh, unfair, Polly!" Byron laughed maliciously as he rejoined us. "After all, you are the only qualified leech here!" We laughed politely at his barbed pun, but I did not think that Polidori found it particularly funny.

The rest of the afternoon passed pleasantly enough, and at seven we went in to dine, where I disappointed milord once more by partaking of each of the five courses. The poet Shelley, Mary, his wife, and her cousin Clare joined us for coffee afterwards, at about nine o'clock.

By ten I was beginning to feel truly discomforted by the oppressive weight of the meal resting in my stomach, and more than a little weary of Shelley's efforts to scandalize the company. I interrupted him to mention that it was my habit to walk after a meal and that I would like to stroll the grounds for a time. I was graciously excused, and quite pleased that no one cared to come along. As I wandered, looking for a secluded spot, the dog joined me. I soon found a likely place and rid myself of the noxious meal, which Moretto was obliging enough to lap up, relieving me of the necessity of burying the evidence.

It was after eleven when I returned, heralded by the crack of thunder. Huge drops began to fall, mixed with hail, hitting the windows like gunshots as I paused before entering, an apparition lit by lightning. The blonde, Clare, pretended to faint, but when the only one eager to revive her was Polidori she recovered quickly enough. Shelley laughed outright at this byplay, Byron looked amused, and Mary bored. Her expression changed at Byron's next words, which were directed at me.

"We have a small—entertainment planned for this evening. Would you care to join us?" A ripple of emotion washed over them all as they awaited my answer.

"Why not?" I said.

"Shelley," Mary began apprehensively, but he soothed her.

"Have we not pledged this as our summer of sensation?" he murmured against her throat, so softly that I doubted the others heard. She shivered against him for a second, then nodded. Byron smiled and crossed to a table to pick up a large volume.

"This is an ancient book of rites and celebrations such as our ancestors held before the coming of Christ, and that some have continued even since," he said. "I have marked one for our revels tonight. If you will all follow me," he requested, tucking the book under his arm and taking up a candle. I found myself growing excited: I had never lost my fascination for the arcane.

In single file we trailed him through the hall, and through a passage that led to a chamber at the back of the house, possibly an old chapel, as it was vaulted. It had been quite recently scoured clean, and the walls were draped in heavy velvets and tapestries, the floor overlaid with lush oriental carpets and softened with cushions. At the end of the room stood an altar, swathed in velvet and satin in shades of purple and dark red. Upon it were placed six heavy gold candlesticks, each holding a stout candle of purple wax. At one end a large glass jug rested, filled with a dark liquid, and surrounded by six generous, stemmed cups. At the other end stood a heavy vase filled with roses of so rich a red that they appeared black in the candlelight. A crystal flask stood at one side of the vase, and a small vial to the other. About these objects, and trailing to the floor, all manner of vines were twisted, ivy, grape, clematis, woodbine, and moonflower among them.

"The time approaches," Byron said, "but first we must change our attire. Ladies, your robes await you behind the screen." He motioned them to a corner near the door. "We will change here." As Clare and Mary retired to change, Shelley began to strip unashamedly, reaching for the robe Lord Byron held out to him. Polidori claimed one for himself, and another which he handed to me. Byron undressed behind the altar and came forth just as I finished donning the garment I had been given, a chlamys of a deep purple silk shot through with dark red and trimmed in glimmering gold. I was aware of the eyes upon me, and glanced at the others in my turn, as we placed our discarded clothing in neat piles near the door. Shelley stripped well, looking quite at home in the diaphanous silk and losing the coltish, ungainly appearance that modern clothing imposed upon him. Polidori, on the other hand, fared rather ill, being somewhat soft from want of exercise. The ladies stepped from behind the screen also dressed in chlamyses, though their simple gowns fastened upon both shoulders while ours were pinned only upon the left. We wore nothing beneath.

Shelley, eyeing Mary and breathing fast, asked why we were clothed at all. "That we might have something to remove," Byron answered him in a voice more gentle than I had ever heard him use. Shelley grinned and nodded, the candlelight dancing red gold in his brown hair. Polidori came to stand beside me as Lord Byron walked around the altar. The rest of us were barefoot, but he wore soft buskins of purple suede, with soles and heels cleverly built to mask his deformity. He also wore a pendant in the form of a looped cross on a heavy gold chain. He lit the purple candles from the one he had brought, then pinched it out and had Polidori put it outside the door. Byron brought out garlands from beneath the altar, chaplets of flowers for us to wear. For Shelley there was passionflower, for Mary, moonflower. Clare had red roses, Polidori yellow. My garland was formed of nightshade, the grey-white flowers gold in the candlelight, and Byron, like Bacchus, wore wild grape and ivy. "Let us begin," he said quietly. He gazed for a moment at the candle flame, then straightened, raised his hands and spoke:

"We who have attained all life now ask still further joy:

*For what is sovereignty that turns aside from pleasure,
what is power that it may stand still and rest content? Having flown from flesh to spirit, having laughed at Death,
should we not rejoice even in the realm where flesh and
Death prevail?*

*"Turned invincible, we may descend upon our conquered
lands and claim our spoil. Where we have lived before,
fixed to Earth, we now may live again: thus, with new
strength, as the long vine that hangs upon the tree of life,
we wind our wisdom home again and seize what we have
won. Night shall be our drinking hall, no longer held by
Death and his dull minions: crowd them out, those joyless
hordes who will not laugh, and pour the wine of victory! As
we have conquered blood, now blood we shall enjoy."*

He poured the six cups full of the dark liquid, which indeed looked like blood, and added to each a pinch of powder. He beckoned to Polidori, who went and took a cup,
which he brought to me. He repeated this until all the cups
were distributed, the last being his own, and Lord Byron's
still resting upon the altar. Byron bade us drink, and drink
again. I tasted the cup. It held a dark red wine mixed with a
fruit brandy—blackberry, I thought, and the powder was
cumin seed. I sipped again and caught an aftertaste that I
had missed before: a tincture of hashish, one of the few
drugs that will affect my kind. I felt Lord Byron's eyes
upon me and drained the cup.

Polidori was at my side immediately, taking the cup to be
refilled. Without seeming to, I watched closely and this
time I saw Byron add the tincture to my cup alone, from a
bottle secreted among the vines. Three times my cup was
filled, and each time the admixture was stronger than the
last. Faces grew flushed, and eyes glittered in the candlelight, even mine, I suspected, not from the alcohol, but
from the hashish. Our cups were filled for the fourth time,
and Lord Byron bade us drain them. As we did so he began
to speak again:

*"Upon the hills and in the forests now the trees and vines
are warm and full of leaves: And Lo! The tree of Life, the*

*tree of Sun, is crowned with golden vines in the wood where
we have hidden it: hidden in the darkness of the grove . . ."*

I was drifting, now hearing, now losing the sense of his
words, when I realized that he had stopped speaking and
was taking the crystal flask from beside the vase. He beckoned to Clare, motioning her to hold out her hands. He
poured fine oil over them, and the heavy scent of roses,
patchouli, and lavender filled the chamber. He continued
around the circle until all had been anointed, then set the
flask upon the altar and tipped it onto its side to pour the
last of the oil over his own hands. Byron began to stroke
the oil down Clare's body, molding the silk to her skin; she
shivered and began to stroke him in return. John came
shyly toward me and ran his hand down my arm. I returned
the favor, feeling my hunger begin to rise, even though I
had fed from him but the night before. Byron spoke again:

*"Let us glorify our flesh, let us celebrate our bounty and
the sweetness of our flowering. For we are yet the flowering of all the universe, yea, even so we are its flesh and
blood and fruit. Who shall stay our hands when they would
act, and who shall starve our mouths when we would feast?
Gods we live and none may call us mortal: save for the dry
and lipless mouth of Death, but where is Death? We see
him not; we recognize him not. Even if he should gnaw the
root beneath the Earth, even while he gnaws the hidden
root that binds the tree of Sun to Earth, the tree of Sun
wherein we climb and feast on life, even while he gnaws the
root and starves the vein, the fruit is ours: And Lo! We see
him not, neither are we blind. . . ."*

I began to drift again, and I lost the thread of words for a
time, but was pulled from my reverie when Byron asked
sharply,

*"Whose blood may then be drained? Death's blood
alone, and not the tree's wherein we climb rejoicing. Sweet,
sweet, our own dark blood, as we are filled with life. Let us
drink up sweetest life with our dark lips, let us cleave unto
the heart of life and suck its juice, let us kiss the heart, the*

*vein, the hand of life whence all our highest sweetness
springs."*

We were all swaying then, bodies glistening with the oil,
the distant thunder drumming in the background. Byron
took Clare's left hand and kissed the palm, then took the
small vial from the altar, poured a drop from it into her
hand and closed her fingers over it. He then opened her
hand and raised it to show us the purple stain left there. The
action was repeated until we all were marked by the gentian
violet dye, and Byron began to speak again.

*"Now we are marked with the wine and the blood, now
we are marked with the fruit and the flower, now we are
marked with our lust and our power. So let this mark be a
sign to Death: that laughter is stronger than mourning, that
blindness is more radiant than sight, that excess is nobler
than abstinence, that pride is stronger than meekness. We
shall not lie with Death in the sober grave while there is
life with whom to lie, and to drink, and to celebrate: better
to lie upon the Earth, drunk to excess with the glories of
flesh and blood, better to kiss and be marked by kisses of
flowering blood, even if they should wound us, even if they
should drain our veins to death-white ropes, even if they
betray us and deliver us into the knotted bone-white bonds
of Death."*

He motioned for us to each stand beside one of the tall
candles before continuing:

*"We shall dare even to put out the candles now, and
drink the darkness."* Polidori reached up and pinched the
flame of the candle before him.

*"O put out the candles, then, and kiss the darkness of
blood: but call it never the darkness of death, for we have
refused all death. Call it the darkness of life, for we go
blind, and admit no darkness but living darkness."* And
Mary put her candle out.

*"Put out the candles now, even while we grow blind, and
we do not see, and we insist that we will not see."* Shelley
reached an unsteady hand and snuffed the flame.

"Put out the candles, and we shall embrace the dark-

ness, we shall insist upon darkness, kissing in darkness, living forever in darkness, our flesh and our blood and our wine as dark as all darkness itself." Clare, scarcely able to stand upright, pinched the candle flame and licked her wine-red lips, gazing hungrily at Byron.

"Put out the candles, give us even the darkness of Death, that we may make love to Death, and warm him with blood and wine, and cover his bones with kisses, and turn him to flesh and blood in the tyranny of our sweetest darkness of flesh and blood." Byron nodded and I snuffed the candle before me.

"Put out the candles!" he cried, and extinguished the last one. *"Thus in darkness shall this ritual be consummated,"* he said, and I heard the bodies moving around me. Hands found me, pulling me down before the altar. I had expected Polidori, but this was a stranger's hungry mouth claiming mine, a stranger's tongue thrust hotly against my own. The long windows were muffled by the tapestries but enough light penetrated to reveal Lord Byron to my vampire's sight. I wondered for a moment if this whole evening had been but a stratagem to bring me to his jaded bed, his apparent antipathy nothing but an attempt to cover an attraction he was loath to admit; his fervid hands commanded my attention, and I abandoned thought for desire.

I could hear the sounds the others made as they found their release, and I caught his flowing hair, pulling his head back, baring his throat. My hunger coiled, and I was aroused as I had seldom been before: I would master this volatile, passionate man, and in return for his submission I would reward him with such pleasures as he had never known. He shuddered, more in anticipation than fear, I thought, as my teeth found the pulsing vein below his jaw. I held him so for a little time, savoring the moment to come when my teeth would free his dark, salt-sweet blood, when this wild poet who bowed to no man's will would be ruled by me. I felt a tear drop from his cheek onto mine, and I let my teeth sink into his flesh.

I jerked back, gagging and spitting his blood from my

mouth. He had made the exchange! Somewhere, sometime he had met another vampire, had fed him, and drank his blood. Byron pulled away at my recoil, and I heard him making his way to the door, his breath coming in ragged sobs as he stumbled into the passage. I rose to follow him, but I was sluggish from the drug, and he was gone before I reached my feet. The sudden glare from the open door lit the chamber like a stage, revealing Shelley as he lay with Mary's head upon his shoulder, his hand idly cupping her breast. He watched with no apparent curiosity as I stepped over Polidori and Clare to follow Byron. They were sprawled together like corpses in a plague-cart, and about as lively.

Byron had fled out of doors by the time I reached the end of the passage. I wished I had thought to snatch up my boots as I followed him outside, past the apathetic gaze of the servants; the English were all mad, their eyes said. Raindrops the size of shillings were battering the terrace, plastering the thin silk I wore to my body. I could see no sign of my host. Another flash of lightning splintered the sky, and as the thunder cracked I heard a sharp cry come from the wood. I raced toward the sound, cursing the stones and sticks I trod upon, and almost ran my quarry over before I saw him huddled at the foot of a burning tree. I feared that he was dead, struck by lightning, but he drew himself up at my approach, preparing to flee again. I caught him and held him, his strength no match for mine. He was staring, the firelight reflecting in his wide, fearful eyes. I slapped him, and he focused on me. A blush suffused his face, and he looked away, still struggling against me.

"Leave off, my lord," I said, and shook him lightly. "I will take you back to the house, and we will talk. I believe that we have much to discuss."

When we reached the house, his man, Fletcher, met us at the French windows of the study, with towels, robes, and a perfectly impassive expression. Behind us the rain stopped, and we had hardly dried and donned the robes before the moon broke from the clouds, drenching the world in liquid silver. We stood at the window side by side, hardly breathing, until Byron suddenly sneezed. "So intrudes the vulgar upon the sublime," he said mournfully, and led the way to the armchairs near the blazing fire. Fletcher brought wine and our clothing, and told his master that he had taken the liberty of covering the sleepers in the chapel with blankets. He then excused himself, leaving us alone.

"So," Byron said softly, his fingers exploring his throat, searching for the place where my teeth had pierced his flesh. "So, you *are* a—a vampire." The final word was no more than a whisper. Denial was useless at this point. I nodded, wondering how I was going to control the situation. Normally, it would be by ingesting enough of his blood to enable me to bend him to my will, but that was impossible under the circumstances.

"How is it, then, that you walk by day, and eat, and reflect in mirrors?"

"A noonday summer's sun would be painful for me, but soft, cloudy days are not," I answered. "I purged myself of the dinner during my walk, though I can consume fluids with no discomfort. And I fancy that the idea that we cast no reflections came about when men believed that what was reflected is the soul: we are supposed to have none, you see. Be that as it may, as we have physical bodies, Newton's laws of optics do apply," I said, smiling slightly. "But tell me about your travels in Albania, my lord."

He looked at first startled by the apparent non sequitur, then comprehending. His journey had not been at all unusual, until he was stricken with a mysterious fever and befriended by a caliph. It was then that the dreams had come, nightmares of a relentless being who drank his blood and forced him to reciprocate. He shuddered at the memories, but kept his voice steady.

"They were not dreams, were they?" he asked, his hand drawn once again to his throat.

"No," I said, "they were not dreams. You have made the blood exchange that passes the condition of vampirism on, one to another." That was how he had detected my nature, I thought, with no little relief, not by any carelessness of mine, but by his own heightened awareness.

"Then, when I die, I shall be as you?"

"Not exactly as I: he was not the vampire that made me. And you may not rise at all. Not all do." I told him plainly what he might expect upon his death and how to prepare for his possible renascence. I pitied him, and there was no one else to whom he could turn. He considered my words for a time.

"Then, when I am—undead, I shall seek out this monster that created me, and kill him, for what right had he to so force such a life upon me!" he said fiercely. There was an answering cry from the doorway.

"Cursed, cursed creator! Why did I live? Why, in that instant, did I not extinguish the spark of existence which you had so wantonly bestowed?" Lord Byron and I both leapt from our chairs at this low, throbbing voice, but I sat down again, startled by the vehemence of Byron's whispered order not to touch her.

Mary stood in the doorway, her eyes unseeing, shrouded only in her dark, abundant hair. She was asleep. Speaking softly, Byron crossed to her, taking her unresisting hand in his. He had succeeded in turning her toward the stairs that led to the upper floor when a bolt of lightning struck a tree at the end of the terrace, and the thunder cracked overhead like a large-bore rifle. Mary shrieked and collapsed into a heap at his feet. He gazed at me darkly for a moment, then, cursing softly, bent to pick her up. He easily lifted the unconscious woman and carried her up the stairs. As he did so I heard her mumble a strange, German-sounding word. He was gone some minutes, and when he returned to our interrupted talk, I asked him about the German word Mary had muttered.

"It's from the story that she is working on," he told me, "as were the words she spoke from the doorway. Our conversation touched upon it—life, a sort of life, rising bitter and reluctant from death." He stared moodily at the fire for a time, then turned to face me again. "If it—happens, if I become undead, I shall be friendless, utterly alone." I could plainly see the effort it cost him to admit that.

"No, my lord, I think not," I said gently, and fumbled through my piled clothing, looking for my card case. When I found it I extracted several cards, which I handed to him. "In seeking to entrap me, you have saved yourself that, at least. Here, these are my cards, and these the cards of persons who will help you for my sake," I told him. "Just try not to die in a too inconvenient or out of the way place. This last card is that of my solicitor, Mr. Tulkinghorn, of Lincoln's Inn Fields. He will see to it that any correspondence is passed along to me."

He nodded absently, then turned his stormy eyes to meet mine. "Were you Marlowe? *The* Marlowe?" I admitted that I was. He nodded again, then grinned most provocatively, and I could feel the allure, the charm that had attracted so many to him.

"We, you and I, did not . . . consummate the ritual, Mr. Marlowe," he said.

"No, we did not, but my hopes aside, I do not truly think you desire me." I had seen his face as he had gathered up the senseless Mary, noted the caressing way his hands held her. No, I was not so foolish as to think any longer that I was an object of lust for him; I was merely a straw at which he had grasped, a possible means to the knowledge he so desperately needed. He raised an eyebrow and I shrugged. "In truth, would you desire me, were I not—what I am? Do you share your bed with men, as well as women?" I asked him bluntly.

"Has our Polly been so discreet that you do not know the answer to that? I did not think him so virtuous," he replied maliciously.

"You evade my question, my lord, but let it pass." I did not care to wound his feelings by telling him that his tainted blood made the thought of such an intimate embrace utterly repugnant. "Perhaps in the heat of the moment, during the ritual, it would have been different. In other circumstances I could have—would have—taken you, and you would have most thoroughly enjoyed my attentions. But now? No, not, I think, in cold blood." He nodded and flashed another grin when I added, "And my friends do call me Kit."

The storm had blown out, and I could hear the soft sounds that meant the dawn was approaching. I began to dress, wincing as I stood upon my abused feet. Byron looked embarrassed at my discomfort, as he knew himself to be the cause, but said nothing as I pulled on my boots. I would be able to make it back to Villa Rózsa before sunrise, but walking would be painful.

"Would you care to borrow a horse, K-kit?" he inquired suddenly, stumbling a little on the fond name.

"I would," I said with gratitude. He rang and gave orders for a mount to be saddled, and as we waited, I took the opportunity to mention something on my mind.

"Do you know that John is addicted to laudanum?" I asked, and Byron shook his head.

"We all use it from time to time," he told me.

"It is considerably more often than that for him."

"How do you know?"

"I know," I said, and smiled, showing my sharp canine teeth. He started as he realized that I meant I had tasted the drug upon the man's blood. "I believe it contributes mightily to the uncertainty of his temper," I continued. "Be wary of him, my lord, that he does not turn his hand against you—or against himself."

"What is he to you, besides sustenance?" He was not being spiteful, merely curious.

"He is not a happy man, my lord, and feels himself inferior—"

"He is!"

"That may well be, but no man enjoys having to admit that about himself. He fed me, and I made him feel . . . desired. Important. At least for a time."

"You speak in the past tense," Byron pointed out.

"I do. Now that he is aware of your suspicions about me, I think it best not to see him again. I will leave for London tomorrow night. It is quite all right," I added, "I would have left soon in any case."

Fletcher brought word that the horse was waiting. I stood then, and offered Byron my hand. His grip was warm and firm against my cool flesh, and he followed me to the door. "Au revoir, Kit," was all he said as I mounted my borrowed mare. As I reached the lane I looked back. My last sight of George Gordon, Lord Byron, was his silhouette in the lighted doorway. He raised his hand in what might have been a farewell, but perhaps he only brushed his tumbled hair from his brow.

It was several years later when word reached me of Byron's death. I was in Scotland at the time, and in the long twilight I went to look out over the grey North Sea, to think upon the man I had met, a man so wild and wicked, and yet so vulnerable. I had heard he died of a fever in Greece: a very inconvenient and most out of the way place. I thought of the ritual he had chosen to perform that extraordinary night on Lake Geneva, with its overtones of vampirism, its lust for life and its infatuation with death, and I wondered. . . .

Colour Vision

STEVE PATTEN

Through the grime-covered window of my studio apartment I watch the moon come up over the Boston skyline. The small gray cat I call Ghost, because I have not yet decided if he is alive or a spirit, is curled next to the radiator, watching me with one eye open.

No clients have come for a while and the warmth is fading from my coffee like the warmth of life fades from a dead body. I raise the cup to my lips and wonder why my coffee is blue. A drop falls into the cup, dark red—blood, I'd know that smell anywhere. It swirls and mixes with the blue of the coffee, another red drop, then a third. I stare at the mixture, red swirling with blue. Next to the white rim of my coffee cup, it reminds me of an American flag. I smile at myself and the spell is broken, my coffee is coffee again. I drink the brew and do not worry too much about the vision in my coffee cup. Such things invariably make their meanings clear whether I ponder them of not. It strikes me that it may not have been a vision at all. I might have a bloody nose. It would not do to greet the night with blood in my mustache; that would not do at all. A quick dab with a tissue confirms that my nose is not bloody, and that the blood in my coffee was indeed of a visionary, not a corporeal, nature.

All around me I can hear them stirring: the pimps, crack dealers, exotic dancers, artists and prostitutes that live and work in Boston's Chinatown. It has been only two days since I last drank from the river of life, so I am painfully aware of everything. I can hear the mouse chewing on an old cracker behind the walls, can smell the duck cooking in the restaurant a block away, mixed with the odor of stale beer and piss from the bar across the street.

The voices are the worst of all, almost deafening in their intensity now, the ceaseless, incoherent roar of a waterfall when what I want is the calm babbling of a brook. They never cease, those voices, the minds of those around me, never cease chattering away. If I didn't need to drink, for my readings, I'd never do it. A person could go mad, being so aware of everything all the time.

Luckily, like all drugs, the effects fade. Day by day the sounds get softer, the voices in the darkness quieter and the visions less frequent. I use those days and nights to sleep, sleep without the hyperawareness of the dreams of those nearby me. There is nothing so disorienting as being caught in another person's dream. Sometimes I can go for a month before drinking again, almost.

I light some incense. The customers expect to smell incense when they enter a fortune-teller's shop; in my present state, however, too much of it makes me ill. After the incense, more candles. I decide on five. Six disks of appropriately space-syrup music go into the CD player, I hit random play and I am set. I open the doors, admitting to my home a few stray breezes, along with anyone from the neon-shattered night who may choose to enter.

I stand in my doorway, inhaling the decay-laden air. Tsi Yu appears from around the corner and strolls toward my shop. Suddenly the meaning of the blue coffee becomes clear; my first visit tonight will be from the police. Even though he dresses in a conservative business suit and has been a detective for three years, Tsi still has not lost the casually purposeful stride of a beat cop.

He is not smiling. His lips are pursed, as if he is humming a tune under his breath. His short black hair is tousled, not good on a windless night.

"Good evening Sothe, how's business?"

"Wouldn't know, I haven't had any yet."

Tsi opens his mouth to speak. I hold up my hand, silencing him. His eyes narrow and his pulse quickens ever so slightly. He doesn't like it when other people take charge, but he plays a good game of chess and reads Edward Abbey, so he can't be all bad. "Please Tsi, let me have my theatrics—it's part of my trade. You have come to talk to me about three dead people. Am I right?"

His chuckle lets me know I have not overstepped my bounds. "Every time I think I'm through being surprised by you Sothe, I end up wrong." I motion him into my shop and after a quick glance down the street to see who is watching, close the door. "It's only two stiffs, though."

I pour him a cup of coffee and put mine in the microwave to warm again. I use the time to rethink. I was sure I'd had those three drops of blood pegged. I hand him his coffee and he nods his thanks. "So, what's so special about these two," I say as I sit my usual chair.

"They died from the bite of a cobra."

"Well, that is different."

"Yeah, real different. The only thing we have to go on so far, except same cause of death, is the fact that they had both been through this area to pick up a hooker less than an hour before their deaths."

I whistle slowly. "You figure it might be Yueng?"

"Well, he was known to put cobras in his coke stash. Most other crack pushers use dogs or old hand-grenades to trap their goods. Yueng was the only one who used snakes, so far as we know." I nod slowly. "Listen, Sothe, could I ask you to do a little sniffing for me? I got put on this case 'cause the department thinks the locals will talk to me just because I'm Chinese. But Yueng and his people know I'm a cop—he may have skipped town; he may not have. I'd rather not take that chance. All it would take would be one of his hookers recognizing me, and I'd end up floating in the harbor.

I consider for a minute, sip my coffee, and consider some more. "I don't know who belongs to who in this neighborhood, Tsi. I don't have time to get out and look around much. Plus, about the only people that come to me for readings are people wondering if their spouse is cheating on them, or drunk college kids." After another sip of my coffee I say, "I do know an herbalist or two that sells snake-bile tonic, and at least one place where you can get fried python. I'll check into them if you'd like."

"Thanks, Sothe. I appreciate it."

"So," I say, having weighed the risks and found the information I might gain to be worth it. "How are things going with Yueng's case, anyway?"

There is a long pause, during which Tsi looks around my room. He looks at the cheap oriental carpet on the floor, the bookshelves, anywhere but at me. He's wondering how much, if anything, he should tell me. Perhaps he's beginning to put two and two together. I will have to be much more circumspect with him in the future. He's been a good source, chess partner and friend for six years now. I'd hate to lose him. Eventually he decides. "It's still an ongoing, so I can't tell you much. But Yueng is one cagey bastard. We'll get him sooner or later. It's just getting him and the goods in the same place that is the problem. We want him cold, red-handed. His lawyers are good enough that circumstantial evidence won't cut it. We thought he'd left town; he used his credit card to buy a Greyhound ticket to Phoenix. But it looks like he's back. Perhaps the ticket was just to throw us off the scent so he could pull together what he's up to now."

"But what would he gain from killing johns? They're one of his best sources of income. I've seen his hookers pushing crack to the johns; it's a nice system he has going. Killing your customers is bad for business. You figure it might be a turf war or something?"

Sensing that even though he hasn't told me much, he has

told me too much, Tsi stands to leave. "I should be going. Thanks for the coffee. I'll be by in a day or two."

I nod. "Should I bring you an order of snake and chips?"

"Nah, it tastes like chicken. I do have one question, though."

"Shoot."

"How can you stand this music? It would drive me nuts in an hour."

"I am very good at hearing things I need to hear. Along with that goes being very good at not hearing things I don't want to hear. I just ignore the music. My customers expect to hear music like this in a card reader's shop."

"Well, better you than me." With a wave he is out the door and into the night. I take the twenty-dollar bill he left on the counter, put his empty cup in the sink and think on who killed those two johns. It can't be Yueng, that much I know for sure. Whoever it is, I can't allow it to continue. Not only will it draw an uncomfortable amount of police attention, but we predators are notoriously territorial.

The wind chimes I keep above my door ring. Turning to see what the night-winds have brought to my shore, I see a young girl. She is Japanese and looks to be no more than twenty. Long straight hair sets off her two large gold-and-jade hoop earrings. She is dressed too much like a hooker to actually be one. Her eyes are wide, darting around the room, searching the dark corners first. Her pulse is rapid; the heavy perfume she is wearing masks any other odors. She is more nervous than most of my customers, even the first-time ones.

"Can I help you, miss?"

"You are South, a reader of cards?"

"Sothe, it sounds like *moth* only with an *s*. And yes, I read cards."

"Oh. They say you are very good. I can come back later, though, if now is not good. I saw the policeman. . . ."

"No, now is a very good time, actually. Would you like some tea or coffee?"

"Yes, thank you, tea would be nice. You must be very good if you work for the police."

"I'm better than most, not as good as some others. And I rarely work for the police. Tarot cards and I Ching are not admissible in court. Which kind of reading would you prefer?"

"What is the charge?"

"Well—" I take in her wide eyes, not wandering now but looking directly at me, her thin sweater and worn, scuffed shoes. "Normally I charge fifty dollars, but since you're my first real customer tonight I'll make it twenty-five. For whichever kind you like."

"You are better at cards?" I nod. "Then I would like cards." I motion her to sit.

"Have you ever had a card reading before?"

She shakes her head, causing her earrings to jangle.

"It's very easy." I take my seat across from her, unwrapping my cards from their silk winding. I hand them to her facedown. "You just shuffle the cards, while thinking of what it is that concerns you. It need not be a specific question you want answered, just something that is troubling you, perhaps. When you feel ready, hand the deck back to me." I watch her as she shuffles, awkward at first, but after a few tries she gets comfortable with the deck. Her face is serene as she shuffles.

I don't take much stock in the ability of the cards to predict the future, actually. What I do is watch people react to the pictures on the cards. The images are powerful, and you can learn an amazing amount just by watching someone closely. You can learn what they love, what they hate and care about. You can learn how they think. In short, if you are good, you learn more about a person than they themselves know. That is what my job as a reader is: to know a person better than she know herself and then impart that information to her in such a way that she does not suspect how much I know about her . . . or him. I do not so much tell the future as I do prepare people to better deal with what it will bring.

She finishes and hands the cards over to me. I cut them and begin to slowly and methodically turn them over, laying them out in the ancient pattern. As I turn the cards I watch her face, noting the tiny muscle movements, a slight shifting or narrowing of the eyes, dilation of the pupils. The first card gets nothing but mild curiosity from her. I glance down at it; the six of swords, it shows a man in a boat with six swords arranged around him. The next several cards get the same reaction, mild curiosity and nothing more.

As I flip over the eighth card, her gasp is audible; her muscles tense, her eyes narrow and her pulse races. I look down and see I have turned over the Lovers. The card shows a man and a woman intimately intertwined and in one hand the woman hold a chalice of wine with a serpent wound around it. I continue turning cards. The only other cards to get any reaction from her are the Emperor, with its picture of a very stern-looking man seated on a throne, and the Tower, which depicts a tower being struck by lightning. As I watch her eyes however, they keep straying to the Lovers, and the smile on her delicate lips is not one of pleasure, but of grim determination.

I surmise that she is in a relationship with which she is unhappy—most people are, after all, and if they are happy, they rarely come seeking advice from me. This relationship, however, may be abusive or even life threatening.

As I talk to her, telling her in the most general terms what seems to me to be obvious common sense about relationships, trust and the misuse of trust and abuse of power, and about keeping ones options open, I see that I am wrong. She is hardly listening to me. She has already seen what she wanted to see in the cards. I know that look, when it appears it is fruitless for me to continue talking. When people have seen what they wanted to see, it is almost impossible to convince them they did not see it. So, I try to gently and gracefully end the session by saying, "I can tell that perhaps I may not have been as much help to you as you thought I might be."

"Oh, no. You have been a great help, a great help indeed." She fishes twenty-five dollars out of her sequined purse and lays it on the table. "Thank you. What they say about you is right. You are a very good card reader." She says this last as she hurries toward the door. I wish her well and begin cleaning up the teacups. I think about which shops I'll visit on my errands for Tsi, and what time they close and what kinds of things I might need to buy there. I'll need tea for sure; in this business you go through a lot of tea.

The chimes above my door ring again and I curse under my breath. I cannot really afford to turn a customer away. I will just have to hope this reading is a brief one, as I have less than an hour before the stores in the area begin to close.

I turn to greet my visitor, and standing in my doorway is a corpse. I can tell, just barely, that it used to be female. Flaccid sheets of flesh are peeling, and they hang off the body while entrails spill out of its abdomen to lie in a greasy pile on my floor. The smell of the sea and putrefaction fills my shop. The teapot I was holding shatters on the floor.

"Jesus Sothe, I didn't mean to scare ya. You OK?"

The voice emanating from the decaying horror is familiar; it's Iesha's. I shut my eyes, willing the vision—at least that's what I hope it is—to go away. When I open them again, Iesha, with her skin as black as obsidian, and not her decaying remains, is standing in my doorway. The rows of wooden beads in her hair click in counterpoint to her heels as she walks across the room and sits down at my desk. I should have remembered this was her night to visit. If I look just to the side of her, I can see the apparition from my doorway, and the smell of the sea is faint, but unmistakable. I hate it when this happens.

I regain my composure as I clean up shards of the teapot. Replacing it will cost all the money Tsi gave me. But what am I to tell Iesha? That this will be the last time she will come for her monthly reading, because within twenty-four hours she will be dead, her body food for fishes? No. What

I have seen is how she will be in the near future. I have seen it, so it cannot be changed. There is no use distressing her over it.

"What'd Mimi want? You to toss those funny Chinese coins for her?" Iesha's statement is as much a question as it is a way just to break the silence.

"Mimi? And do you mean the I Ching?"

"Yeah, Mimi, that girl who just dashed outta here like her tampon was on fire. She's new over at the Slip. One hot number, let me tell you. She don't take no johns, though, just dances."

"Oh. I didn't know her name. I just read the cards for her, not the I Ching. So, how have you been?" I feel like an idiot for asking this last; it seems monstrously wrong somehow to begin our familiar ritual knowing that I will probably never see her again.

"Not so hot," she says as she picks up and shuffles the cards. She knows the routine well by now. Her voice is rich, deep and resonant with laughter. It's hard to believe I'm talking to a dead woman. I'll miss her. "My sister totaled her car again, her third DWI, so she call me up to see if I can give her a lift. So, there we are driving down the expressway, and do you know what that bitch does? . . ."

Her words trail off as my mind tunes her out, the rest of what she says will be idle chatter. She has gotten what she came for, someone to ask how she is, to care for her, or at least pretend to care, even a little bit. I wonder who will kill Iesha, or whether she will die in an accident. However it happens, I hope she does not suffer. She's done enough of that.

Eventually she stops shuffling the cards and talking. Then she hands the cards to me and gets out a cigarette. She is trying to quit, has been for years. Her hands always have to be doing something, shuffling cards or just holding an unlit cigarette, something. I make a show of concentrating, cut the cards and lay them out. I am glad the death card does not show up—I hate explaining that one. I watch her eyes. She knows the cards pretty well after five years of monthly readings, the ones her eyes linger on tell me what she is worried about, what she's been worried about for every month for the past five years. Money.

I giver her a pronouncement about money coming her way, hard times that will be endured and all that. I also add a caution about an unforeseen journey, and how it is very important to make sure all her affairs are in order, debts paid, papers signed and so on and so forth. I also tell her that it is very, very important to tell her children that she loves them, and to make sure they know it. She listens to what I say about as carefully as I listened to her. Over the years our monthly ritual has become familiar and comfortable, like an old sweater you just can't bring yourself to throw away. I will miss her. Too soon it is over, and with a clatter of beads and a jangling of the chime, she is gone; one of the true children of the night, under the care of a harsh and unforgiving mother.

I am torn. Should I follow and perhaps see her killer? Or should I see Yueng and perhaps learn something that way? And then there are the errands I have to do for Tsi. I cannot help Iesha; all I can do is hope she does not suffer much. I decide to pay a visit to Yueng.

I turn my window sign from OPEN to CLOSED, a needless gesture in this case, because no one can see the sign behind the heavy steel security gate I pull down over the windows and doors of my shop. Ghost is nowhere to be seen—he must have slipped out the door after Iesha. Safe behind my screen of steel I shove my desk to the side and roll up the carpet beneath it. The trap door in the floor lifts easily enough and shuts after me with a bang as I descend the old iron rung ladder into the maze of storerooms and interconnecting tunnels that exist beneath Chinatown. Through storerooms full of dry goods, down narrow brick tunnels that turn for no apparent reason, down another ancient iron ladder I go. The floor of the tunnels turns from cracked and mildewed concrete to cobblestone, and then to brick—the remains of sewers long forgotten by the engineers above. The air is chill, and sharp with the odor of rats and decay.

Eventually I come to a steel fire-door locked with a new combination lock. In a small niche next to the door sits my goblet, its sides etched with the sign of the cross, its interior plated with gold. Why I use this chalice, I really can't explain. Put it down to one of those eccentricities that a person accumulates during his lifetime that he is at a loss to explain. I am sure that deep down in my subconscious, my use of this once holy chalice is symbolic of something, but what it is I am not sure; it's not worth bothering about. All that really matters is the lining of gold.

I turn the lock's tumbler quickly, having done this many times before. Ghost comes scampering down the tunnel, and upon reaching me stops and looks up, expectation in his eyes. I push open the heavy door and enter the small room beyond. At one time this room may have been a secret bank vault, or wine cellar perhaps. Now it serves a very different purpose. Ghost pads silently in after me, curls up in a corner and begins to purr.

Yueng looks up at me from the cot; the chain connecting his neck to the wall rattles as he moves. The look he gives me contains a hatred so intense it would be unbearable if I had not seen that look a thousand times before, and behind the hatred in his dark eyes there is something else: fear. His short black hair is matted, and he has not eaten any of the food I gave him yesterday and taken only a few sips from the plastic two-liter bottle of water. Men with Yueng's temperament rarely do well in captivity, no matter how nice the cage.

The police and the people of Boston would be outraged if they ever learned of this cell. They have no reason to be—there are government sanctioned cells all over the U.S. where men wait to die. This cell is much nicer than most of those, with its soft bed and television set—securely bolted down, of course, so it cannot be used as a weapon. There is also a wide selection of paperback books. The people should actually thank me, for when one is addicted to human blood, then killing those people who kill humans is only common sense. By killing Yueng, I save the lives of perhaps thirty or forty people who would have lost their lives to his drugs, or innocent bystanders shot down in turf wars. And if I later take one of those people for my own needs, the human race is still at a plus. For me, murder is not murder, but merely resource management.

Down here, sheltered by the earth, the voices in my head are quieter, less intrusive. Having the ability to hear people's thoughts is more a curse than anything. It's like being on stage in a huge concert hall. There you stand, all alone; you know the audience is out there; you can hear them whispering. In all that whispering, you cannot make out any distinct words, cannot separate even one voice from the vast susurration that hangs just outside the edge of your perception. They are always there, that audience, that crowd of chattering monkeys, always watching you and whispering in the darkness—until one of them dies.

The human mind can accept many things, but rarely can it accept its own death, the cessation of its existence. When confronted with the end of itself, the human mind does what most humans do in such a situation: it screams. A scream can be heard over the whisperings.

Yueng is still weak from the last time I bled him. He slowly sits himself upright on the bed, fixing that hateful glare on me. Throughout his time here he has never said a word, just glared, and tried to break the chains holding him when he thought I could not hear. This is good; it makes the process so much harder when they beg and cry and plead for mercy.

With careful rationing, Yueng's blood could have given me "the sight" for several more months. Now I have to kill him. What's more, within a month or so I will have to find someone to take his place. That will not be easy. I will have to travel. Too many disappearances in one area in a short time will always be noticed.

Ghost will drink well tonight, for I cannot drink so soon again after the last time. One common complaint of the insane is that they see too much. Perhaps they do; who knows. I prefer not to risk seeing that much.

I set the goblet in Ghost's saucer, which lies on the floor next to me. Where did it come from? I don't remember bringing it with me. Nonetheless, it is here. Yueng resists as I stretch out his arm and hold it firmly over the goblet. His strength is not what it used to be and I have no trouble making the incision in his wrist. The red river that was Yueng's life flows into the goblet.

When the goblet is full, and the thick red wine is running over into Ghost's dish, I let Yueng's arm drop. His eyes are dull and fluttering. This second bloodletting in under three days has him floating on the edge of consciousness. He watches with a detached expression as Ghost begins to lap at the blood flowing down the sides of the chalice. Ghost, like me, has use only for blood that has been touched by gold, the metal of the sun, and has overflowed from a cup. The blood is the life, and to see more than most people, you must have more life than most people. You must drink from a cup of life that is overflowing, so then your life shall likewise overflow.

"Listen to me, Yueng. You are going to die tonight." That gets his attention. He looks up at me and tries to focus his eyes. "There is someone using your snakes, Yueng. Who would use your snakes to kill, not to guard but to kill. Who else knows where you keep your snakes, Yueng?"

The mind will usually scream about what it was last thinking. People think the oddest things when they die: a favorite toy they had as a child, or their first pet and the day it died. I am trying to make sure Yueng is thinking about something useful. Standing, I put my hands on either side of his once strong and arrogant face. "Your snakes, Yueng? Who would be using your snakes?" With a sharp twist and a sound like the cracking of knuckles, I snap his neck.

As I sit there and listen to the whispering darkness, I watch the life fade from Yueng's eyes. The body may cease functioning quickly, but it takes the mind a while longer to die. When Yueng's mind begins to die, the whispering is broken by a faint buzzing, the sound of a panicked mind trapped within a cooling body, knowing that it has no option but to be sucked into the black unknowingness that is death. The buzzing erupts in a picture: a woman kneeling before a blank wall with a large white snake coiled around her. She is naked except for the gold-and-jade hoop earrings that sparkle in the dim light of a single candle.

When I come to, my head feels like it has been split open. I rarely listen to people as they die, but every now and again I am forced to remind myself why; it hurts, a lot. Looking at my watch I see it is 3 A.M. I have lain unconscious for three hours. Damn.

It takes me another hour to drag Yueng's body to the place I call the Hole. I am not sure what it is or where it goes. It is a black and yawning pit in the oldest and by far most distant part of the tunnels I have yet explored. I have tossed over two dozen bodies down it and never heard one of them hit bottom. Judging by the smell, which is what led me to the Hole in the first place, it must lead to some long forgotten cistern or industrial cesspool. It smells bad enough that the stench of a few rotting bodies will not be noticed. I heave Yueng's remains over the edge. As fast as my legs will carry me through the warren I return to my shop and take a long, hot shower, scrubbing till my skin is raw to remove every trace of that abominable odor. I read for a while and then retire to my room to sleep the day away.

I do not open my shop this evening. I hope Tsi does not stop by. This evening I am hunting, and my first stop is the Vingh Kong Trading Company. When I open the doors, the smell of dried herbs and desiccated animal parts, along with the thick smoke of the incense that is kept continually burning in a small shrine in the back, combine to make me dizzy. I lean against a stack of ten-pound bags of dried mushrooms and recover myself.

After a minute I walk over to the herb counter, glancing at the shelves as I go. This day the shelves are stocked with cans of grass jelly, black bean paste and more varieties of tea than I shall ever have time to try.

Once at the counter I stand and watch Chau the chemist grind up herbs in his mortar. When he is finished he meticulously cleans and puts away the mortar and pestle; only then does he turn to me.

"Good evening, Mr. Sothe. How may I help you this fine evening?"

"Good evening to you, Dr. Chau. I could use some bai shao, some ginseng extract—the Hunan variety, please—and a large tin of Special Dragon tea, and that small brown teapot, the one with the leaves on the lid. I was also wondering if I might ask you a few questions concerning snakes.

Without so much as a raised eyebrow Chau goes about preparing my order. "What kind of snakes?"

"Cobras. I was wondering, if I was interested in tonic of cobra, where could I get such a thing?"

"Ah. Very difficult. You have to have license to import cobra. I have no such license. I can get you python, corn snake or king snake, but no cobra. What you want it for, anyway? Usually python bile much better than cobra—cheaper, too. You want me to add some to this?"

"No, thank you. What about cobras raised here, not imported?"

"Hmmmm. I don't know of any place to get such a cobra. Tonic must be fresh to work and keeping cobras is expensive, not worth the trouble." Chau finishes assembling my order, wraps it neatly and sets it on the counter. "Anything else?"

"Yes, just one more question. I always thought cobras were black. Can they come in any other color, like, say, white?"

Chau nods. "Many cobras are black, but some are also green or brown. A white cobra, that would be albino. Very rare, albino cobra, and very valuable. White snakes are sacred to Benzaiten, a Japanese goddess of fertility. It's very bad luck to kill one, but very good luck to have one in your temple. Many people would pay much for such a cobra, for the temple, not tonic."

"I see. Thank you very much."

After I have taken my purchases back home and put them away, it is time for my second foray of the evening.

I walk the few blocks to the Glass Slipper, or the Slip as it in known to the residents of the area. There is a light rain and the oil on the damp streets fractures the neon and halogen lighting into rainbow rivers and pools of swirling color.

The doorman at the Slip knows me. He's been working here for almost a year now, and even came into my shop for a reading once. "Evening, Dave. How's things work out with that investment deal?"

"Heh, you hit that one on the head, Sothe. I took your advice and didn't give them one dollar. Damn good thing, too. Turns out it was some kind of pyramid scam, and all the original investors are up on charges of mail fraud."

"Good. I am glad to hear it."

Dave nods and holds the door open for me.

"What'll you have?" The bartender is a young man with short black hair. He wears too much Brut aftershave.

"Wine, a Burgundy if you have it."

"I'll have to charge you extra—full alcohol drink, you understand."

I don't understand, but don't want to make a fuss. I lay a twenty on the counter. He gives me a small glass of wine and a ten in change. I sit for a while and watch a woman with long blond hair, which is returning to its natural brown at the roots, go through a desultory series of dance steps and contortions in time to some piece of music that has a beat and not much else. The air is thick with smoke and the smell of human sweat; my nose itches and my throat burns from the combination. Even the wine can not wash away the gritty feeling on the back of my throat. The music is very loud, even by normal standards, and its assault on my ears is almost too much to endure—the joy of the hunt, indeed.

After the blonde, several women unremarkable in any

way except for the amount of makeup they wear, come on stage, do their routine and leave. I am struck by the similarities between these women and trained monkeys I once saw at a circus, or the machines you used to find at carnivals where you would put a quarter in a slot and a chicken in a cage would dance to a simple tune.

My thoughts are interrupted as the lighting changes from red to blue, and Mimi emerges from behind the red velvet curtain. The moment she starts to dance the hum of conversation in the bar stops as people stare, entranced. Her movements are fluid and graceful. The music she has chosen is modern, but with Arabic time signatures and no lyrics to distract the audience from her dance. The music flows and Mimi flows with it. Her hair flies about her head like a net, snaring the lusts and imaginations of the entire bar, men and women alike. The smile on her face as she dances is ecstatic; looking at that smile lightens a person's heart and spirit.

All too soon the music fades and she is done. She stands on the stage covered in sweat and breathing heavily while the applause, and more than a few wolf whistles and lewd suggestions flow around her. After a few seconds she executes a bow and leaves. Very rarely have I felt privileged to be a witness to anything. I feel that way now, though.

It takes several minutes for the shouts of "encore" to die down. The lighting changes back to red and a tall heavy-breasted woman begins to dance. I don't envy her, having to follow an act like Mimi's.

I sit for a while, sipping my wine occasionally, and look over the room. There is a security camera over the door that has a view of the bar and the customers seated at it. If I lean over slightly I can see the trapdoor that leads, presumably, to their liquor cellar. It is locked, but only with a sliding bolt on this side of the door, set into a recess so that the bartenders will not trip over it as they work. I can see no motion detectors or sound sensors, and this room is so smoky that any infrared beam would surely be visible, but I see none. Good.

After twenty minutes or so, Mimi emerges from behind another curtain, a blue velvet one that leads, presumably, to the dancers' dressing rooms, and perhaps the upstairs apartments where most of them live, as well. After a quick scan of the bar, she comes over and sits next to me. She is wearing form-fitting blue jeans and a Harley Davidson T-shirt.

"Hello, Sothe. Buy me a drink? The bar likes it when the dancers try to sell drinks. I've never seen you in here before, didn't think it was your kind of place." She is wearing the same heavy perfume she did when she came into my shop, something with a lot of orange in it—badly mixed patchouli, perhaps. It does, however, overpower the smell of sweat and lust that permeates this place, and for that I am thankful. I nod, she waves her hand at Brut boy and he brings over a pinkish drink in a tiny champagne glass, takes the ten that I had left on the counter and brings me a five in change.

"So, you like my dancing?"

"Yes, it was wonderful. You should be on Broadway and not in this place." She smiles and sips her drink. A slight blush colors her cheeks. I sip my drink while Mimi sips hers. Mimi watches the dancer and the crowd; I watch Mimi. She is about five feet three inches, 115 pounds, perhaps, a very nice size. It's time to see if my theory is correct. I hope it isn't—I am actually starting to like Mimi a bit.

"Have you seen Iesha this evening? I came in here looking for her."

"No, she was supposed to work, but never showed up. If you see her, tell her Charlie is very angry." She's lying, her pupils dilated, her pulse shot way up and her back muscles stiffened—not the reaction of a coworker angry at another, but fear. So, she either killed Iesha or knows who did and is protecting them. That's a damn shame.

Now, what to do? I have my target, but which arrow to shoot? After another sip of my wine I select the barb that I hope will snare the quarry. "Well, if Iesha is not around, perhaps Benzaiten will do." Her response is dramatic and unmistakable, her pulse rockets even higher and for a second she even stops breathing.

"How do you know about Benzaiten?" Her voice is no longer light and airy, but a forceful whisper, full of menace and venom.

"You forget, Mimi, I read cards and coins. It is my business to know things that are hidden."

"You had better leave now, mister, or I'll have you thrown out." As she stands Mimi flings what little is left of her drink in my face. She turns and stalks back down the bar. Brut boy and the rest of the bar are giving me definitely unfriendly stares. Time to leave. I set my half-drunk wine down and exit out into the street. After wandering the streets of Chinatown for a while I head home, doubling back and using a few alleys of decidedly unwholesome appearance to make sure I am not followed.

There are still a few hours left before I can begin my errand, so I open the shop. Three young women from Wellesley are my only clients. They concentrate mainly on looking around my shop and pointing at some of the many objects I have collected over the years, each one eliciting a furious bout of whispering and giggling. Eventually I finish readings for all three of them; their questions were uniformly about their boyfriends, and what they could do to keep them or get them if they did not already have them. They did not seem pleased with my answers, but at least they paid their fee.

Eventually 1 A.M. rolls around and I close up shop. I put the security screen down again, not only to hide my activities from prying eyes, but also because if I didn't, my doorway would soon be filled with drunk and frustrated vagrants looking for a place to sleep.

Now is the best time of the evening. At this time of night most people are asleep, or close to it, the faint whisperings of their minds in the darkness fade below my perception. There are still those who inhabit the bars and brothels, leaving to go home only when they are kicked out, but they are few in number, and their minds are so numbed by alcohol or drugs that I can scarce perceive them at all.

I almost feel as if I am alone. I pour myself a glass of wine, real wine, not the acidic Kool-Aid they serve at the Slip and other places like it, and revel in my aloneness. Solitude, darkness and fine wine—what else could a person want?

The clock in the corner strikes 3 A.M., time to get to work. I gather together my tools for the night's errand: an old army duffel bag, an assortment of thin files with felt along the edges, small pliers, lock-picks, a slim-jim, a gag and various other restraints purchased from the "marital aids" section of the corner video store and last but definitely not least, my stun gun. These little devices are one of the true advances of this age as far as I am concerned—much more humane than a blow to the back of the head, which is as likely as not to kill a person outright. And gloves; mustn't forget to wear surgical gloves; they allow for a light touch while not leaving inconvenient fingerprints all over everything.

With my bag and my bundle, I descend again into the tunnels. As usual, Ghost is there, silently watching me; he follows me as I head off down the cramped brick conduit. I take a different and much shorter route than before, and arrive at the door to the storeroom of the Glass Slipper. It is a large metal affair, barred from the inside.

I slide the slim-jim between the door and the frame. A few minutes' work and the bar is lifted. I crack the door open and spend a few minutes peering into the musty gloom; just because there were no beams or motion detectors upstairs does not mean that there are none here. The room is full of cases of wine and cheap champagne, kegs of beer and boxes of soda syrup with their lines running up to the bar. After satisfying myself that there are no security devices present, I slip inside and close the door. I didn't see Ghost follow me, but he is here, as well. The ladder up to the trapdoor is at the far end of the room. As I climb the old ladder, every squeak of the rungs as they adjust to my weight seems louder than a scream. Once at the top, I wait several minutes, sure that someone must have heard me.

When no one comes, I slide a pair of the thin files between the door and floor on either side of the bolt. Gently I give the bolt a quarter turn. Once the bolt is rotated, it becomes only a matter of patience and repetition, working the bolt back a millimeter at a time, until it is free of the latch. Slowly I push the trap door open and raise myself into the bar. Keeping low, and next to the bar so as to avoid the camera, I make my way to, and then through, the blue velvet curtain. There is nothing behind the curtain except a flight of rickety wooden stairs leading up into the darkness of the building. I climb the stairs, keeping near the edges to reduce the creaking and groaning of the ancient and long-unpainted wood. I emerge into a corridor, with another flight of steps continuing up. A single electric bulb lights the hallway, showing every bare spot and stain in the thin gray carpet that runs the hall's length; there are eight doors.

Keeping my footfalls as light as possible, I reach the first door, bend down and cautiously sniff under the wooden portal. The scent of sex, cheap wine and Blue Rose incense assails my nose. I move on. Door after door I check in this way.

Eventually, I find what I am looking for. At the far end, the sixth door I try, the odor of heavy orange mixed with something else; the combination is reminiscent of burnt plastic. Again the lock is a simple bolt, and again I use my files, hoping that none of the women on this floor emerge to use the bathroom at the end of the hall while I am out here—none do. Once the bolt is open, I slide into the room, close and bolt the door behind me.

The room is decorated in cheap oriental. There are several small lamps with red paper shades that hang from the ceiling. A large tapestry showing a woman riding a sea serpent through breaking waves is hung over a bookcase against the far wall. A small table draped with a deep blue cloth holds an incense burner and the statue of a slender woman. A stuffed panda sits in the corner, next to a crum-

pled and tossed pair of jeans and T-shirt. Next to the bear
and cloths, a window even dirtier than mine at home looks
out onto a fire escape. Several trunks, covered with cheap
Indian batik prints, hold a variety of stacked books, candles, a pack of cigarettes, a stereo and a haphazard stack of
CDs. In the other corner is a futon spread on the floor, and
Mimi sleeping soundly beneath a thick down comforter.

I look at her sleeping form and ponder what I am about
to do. Once I move again, there is no turning back. I think
back to the vision I ripped from Yueng's mind as it died.
The woman with jade earrings and a white snake . . . She
was as thin as Mimi, and had hair exactly Mimi's color and
length . . . and Mimi did react with fear when I mentioned
Benzaiten. How many people would even know who Benzaiten is? And she did lie when I asked her about Iesha. I
wonder if Iesha is still alive, or floating in the harbor, food
for the lobsters, which will then be food for the diners at
fine restaurants all over Boston. Thoughts of Iesha bring to
mind the vision I saw of her, right after Mimi exited my
shop. Mimi, who when she entered my shop had said "You
must be very good if you work for the police." The police,
meaning Tsi. I would have preferred to travel to take my
next source, but I think things can be arranged to draw sus-
picion away from this area. But Mimi will have to be the
last, for a long time.

Without further hesitation I bring out the leather goods.
When I am ready I walk quickly over to her sleeping form,
grab her delicate face in my hands and shove the gag in her
mouth. In the instant it takes her to wake up I have flipped
her over and cinched the strap tight. Her reaction is instan-
taneous and unthinking; she tries to scream. She's quick to
recover, and lashes out with her leg, landing a solid heel to
my solar plexus. I double over, and before I can recover she
is on her knees, getting ready to stand and run. She almost
manages it before I regain my control; grabbing her retreating ankle, I bring her down again. This time I apply the
stun gun to her bare flesh. One quick, violent spasm and

she is still. Her eyes flutter and she breathes in heavy gasps, barely getting enough air around the gag.

The shock of the stunner lasts only a short time, so I quickly handcuff her wrists and tie her feet together. When I am done she is wrapped up: a nice, neat, very angry and afraid package.

She glares at me as I search her room. Under her futon I find a small book, presumably a diary, which I tuck into my back pocket. The curtained bookcase yields nothing, only a few rolled scrolls of paper filled with Chinese characters. I leave these in their place. Just then, I hear something moving—not Mimi, she is lying on the futon, still glaring my death at me. The sound came from the chest with the CDs on it.

Carefully I remove the CDs, lighter and ashtray from the cloth, then the cloth itself. The first thing I notice about the chest is that it's locked; then I notice the holes. The chest has a row of small holes around the top—air holes, presumably.

After a bit more searching I find a set of keys in the pockets on the jeans lying in the corner with the panda. After several tries I find the correct key. I open the chest slowly, lest whatever is making the sound leap out and attack me. Within the chest is a large glass aquarium with a screen top on it. Something slams against the screen top, hissing and showing inch-long fangs, its black hood spread wide in threat, a cobra.

Taking the batiks off the other chests and opening them reveals more cobras, one of them particularly large and all white with pink eyes. One of the trunks also contains about a dozen baby cobras, white with pink eyes, all glaring at me and spreading their hoods. Charming.

This is too good an opportunity to pass up. Glancing over at Mimi every few seconds to make sure she is behaving, I gingerly take the tank containing the baby albino cobras and secure the lid shut with several of the leather straps I brought along. As I am cinching the last buckle something solid slams into my legs from behind, knocking me down. Luckily, the cage containing the baby cobras does not break. Then I turn my head to see what hit me, and freeze.

Mimi had swung her legs around, knocking over the cage with the large white cobra in it. The huge serpent now sits in the middle of the floor, even angrier than before, spreading its hood, hissing loudly and looking for the cause of its disturbance. Neither Mimi nor I move.

After a minute of the tableau with the white serpent swaying slightly, regarding first Mimi, then myself with its baleful pink eyes, there is a soft knock on the door and a quiet voice. "Mimi, are you OK? I heard a noise. Did you drop something? Are you OK in there?" Mimi begins to scream. Even through the gag the sound is loud in the still morning of the building. The knocking comes again, more insistent now. "Mimi, is that you? Open up now, Mimi, please, or I'll have to call the police! Mimi!"

Mimi screams louder. The sound of footsteps running down the hall, away from the room comes to my ear. I must do something; in Chinatown the police usually respond quickly. Within ten minutes there will be police, perhaps even Tsi himself swarming through this building. If I move, the cobra will strike, but I can't stay here to face the police. I make a grab for the stuffed panda. The serpent swings its head my way, rearing up even higher. I hurl the stuffed bear at the advancing reptile. The toy strikes the snake squarely in the head. There is a loud hiss and the cobra strikes, impaling the stuffed bear with its fangs. As the snake disengages its teeth from the toy's fluff, I stand up and in two quick strides am standing over Mimi. Having dealt with the panda, the snake once again swings its gaze toward the only movement in the room: me. As the serpent advances, I roll Mimi off her futon and fling the thin cotton pad at the snake. The futon flops down over the serpent, covering it.

Who knows how long it will take the snake to extricate itself? I open my duffel bag on the floor, mouth up. Picking Mimi up unceremoniously by the waist I set her in. Her screams are becoming quieter—perhaps she's getting hoarse. I raise the sack and draw the top closed, fastening it securely with the metal clips the army so thoughtfully provides. They make good equipment, the U.S. Army. I heft the bag over my shoulder—heavy, but not unmanageably so. I then pick up the tank of young serpents by the leather straps. In the distance I can hear the wailing of sirens.

The large cobra seems content to stay under the futon, a nasty surprise for whoever turns it over. With a last look around the room to make sure I have not left anything, I open the window and step out onto the fire escape. I make sure to close the window again, nothing points to where you have gone like an open window in a locked room. From the fire escape, it's up to the roof and across to the other side of the building.

Two police cruisers have arrived. I wait, peering over the edge of the crumbling brick edifice until the police rush inside. I descend an old rusty ladder built right into the side of the building. It was originally meant to help service a huge electrical sign that hung off the side of the building. The sign is long gone, but luckily the ladder remains. Halfway down the ladder, I swing out and open a window into the warehouse of the Hoy-Toy noodle company, which shares the building with the Slip.

Mimi is struggling violently, unbalancing me every so often. I am glad I am done with the aerial part of this escape. Closing the window, I cross the room full of sacks of rice flour. Down the service stairs and into the basement, then through an old electrical service crawlway, until I am once again safe in my shadow world of decay-ridden tunnels and forgotten rooms. Ghost is waiting for me, and accompanies me as I haul my night's harvest back to my waiting room.

In the still dampness of the small chamber, I remove Mimi from the bag. She tries to struggle, but her bonds hold. She watches as I fix the collar around her neck and the shackles around her wrists to the iron chain embedded in the wall. Only then, once she is secure, do I remove her gag. She is silent, hatred pouring out of her so thick it is almost tangible.

"Kicking me, and that snake over up there was stupid—it could have bitten you just as easily as me. Are you so anxious to die?"

"Death by the fangs of Benzaiten's servant is better than death at the hands of some mass-murder-child-molesting-rapist like you."

"Ah, so you are a servant of Benzaiten. You know, until last night, I'd never even heard of her. Tell me about her."

"Hah—she is a goddess of love, beauty and fertility, youth and springtime. Her virtues are so far from you, I'll not waste my breath. If you're going to rape and kill me, then just get it over with, asshole."

"Don't be in such a hurry to die, and as to raping you— my appetites don't run along those lines. Now, are you going to tell me why you are killing johns? Does it have something to do with Yueng?" I can see that at least one of my theories is right. The mention of Yueng's name causes her eyes to narrow.

"How do you know Yueng—what have you done with him, you asshole?" The concern in her voice and change in tone from a moment ago tell me just how well she knew Yueng, which is very well, indeed.

"It was easy to piece together. My friend Tsi tells me that people have been dying from cobra bites, and Yueng was known to keep cobras. But I know Yueng isn't around, so it couldn't be him. Then Tsi tells me Yueng and his people know he's a cop, so could I ask a few questions around for him. The minute he leaves, bang, you show up and say that you saw the policeman and if it's convenient you could come back another time. It doesn't take a genius to figure it out. The only thing I can't figure out is why."

"It's simple, you asshole. Love. I love Yueng and he loves me. But love is something you will never understand."

"Perhaps. But let me get this straight. You love Yueng, so you kill johns and hookers. I still don't get it."

"I kill those who would take him from me. Yueng has love—that is the most important. But the men who pay for women, and those who buy the drugs, they pay so much money. Like all men, Yueng is weak when it comes to material things. The money was too strong. He did wicked things to get it. He was selling his soul to buy things. I couldn't sit by and watch that happen."

"So, you decided to remove the temptation. What did you think, that you could kill all the prostitutes, crack dealers and johns in the whole world?"

"No, just enough to make the others afraid, make them take their business elsewhere, to leave us alone." After several minutes of silence, I get up to leave. "Hey, where are you going? You take me to Yueng—tell me what you've done with him!"

It has always been my experience that not knowing is worse than knowing; ignorance is not bliss—it's torture. "I killed him. It was a quick and painless death, just as yours will be. To kill an innocent is wrong. Yueng killed innocent people with his drugs, and you killed them with his snakes. True, not all the people you killed were innocent, but some of them were—Iesha was."

"She was not! She sold herself to men, she made a lot of money—" Her next words are silenced as I shut the steel fire door and secure the lock.

Back in my apartment, after a good long shower, my last action for the evening is to visit the Greyhound Web site and book a one-way ticket for Phoenix, Arizona, using Yueng's credit card. With luck, that will throw the police off the trail. Then it's off to bed for a well-earned day's rest.

The cab closes its door and roars away from the curb in front of my shop. Inside the cab is a young girl with dark hair, a runaway most likely. I paid her cab fare to the bus station last night, and paid her forty dollars to pick up Mimi's never-to-be-used ticket and bring it back to me; and just now paid the cab to take her wherever she wanted to go, which was some mall I'd never heard of. Already it has been an expensive evening. I don't mind, though. With what Chau paid me for the tank of baby cobras, I'll be able to live comfortably for a year or more, even without doing another reading; that thought does hold a certain appeal.

As I open the door to my shop, Tsi appears from around the corner. "Hey, Sothe. You busy?"

"No, just doing my usual haunting of a few used bookstores. Nothing interesting this time, though." I open the door and motion for Tsi to enter. As he does so he glances quickly at the brown wooden box that my chess set rests in.

"Ah well, better luck next time. I was wondering if you'd been able to come up with anything." Tsi sits down in the chair my clients usually use.

"Care for a game of chess?" I ask. It is a familiar ritual between us. His eye movements are unconscious. He is unaware of them, so is continually on the verge of believing I can indeed read minds, but, being the detective he is, believes that there is a logical, rational explanation somewhere, if only he can find it. I doubt I'll ever explain that it's not so much reading minds as feeling them—he wouldn't understand.

A heavy sigh escapes him, "Well, it has been a while—sure."

I move to get the set and begin laying out the board and pieces. "And about the information. I found out that Yueng seems to have left town. Some people say he left with a woman, some don't. No one knows anything about cobras, except that rat snake tonic is better, and they were fresh out of fried python. Will takeout Chinese do?"

Tsi smiles and nods. "That fits with what we have. Yueng seems to have skipped town. Took his girlfriend with him, too. She was a dancer over at the Slip, maybe you even knew her?" Tsi flips out a black leather photo holder and shows me a picture of Mimi, wearing her hair and nothing else.

"I've seen her dance over there, and gave her a reading once, but I wouldn't say I know her." I gesture to Tsi, indicating it's his move. White always moves first, and I invariably chose the dark pieces.

"Hey, just thought I'd ask. Yueng must have sent for her last night from wherever he's hiding out. He purchased two bus tickets to Phoenix, one a few weeks ago, the other one last night, over the Internet. A woman fitting Mimi's description picked up the ticket last night, only a few hours before we got there. She left a surprise in her room, too—the biggest damn snake I've ever seen, a cobra. Nearly killed the officer that entered the room. We couldn't get in there for an hour until Animal Control came and took care of the damn thing.

"Yueng really must have liked her—that's a big risk to take, using his credit card. He's usually more careful."

"Yeah, he must have." I weigh my next words carefully, and decide it's worth the risk. "So, you think you'll get him?"

Tsi considers awhile before answering. "Don't know. Now that he's crossed state lines, it's a matter for the feds. We've already sent them the files. I think I'm gonna use this break to take a vacation."

"Oh?"

"Yeah, maybe Florida. Word on the street is that Yueng's territory is up for grabs. Several small-timers are doing the grabbing, but not very hard. What with the porn theaters being torn down and the strip clubs on their way out, all the sleaze in the area is nervous, looking to move out to the suburbs. Besides, this area seems to be getting a rep as 'unlucky' since anyone who sets up shop in it seems to take an unannounced permanent-like vacation within a year or two. I don't think there'll be much going on here for a while."

"That's good to hear."

After a few moves in silence Tsi wins. With a nod of his head and, "Be seeing you around, Sothe—take care," he is out the door and into the drizzly Boston night.

"Be seeing you, Tsi," I say as I watch him walk down the narrow street, slick now with the damp. Before he rounds

the corner, he turns to look at me, and winks. A wink—
now, what could that mean?

I start coffee brewing and carefully tear up the bus ticket,
dropping the pieces into the wastebasket. When the coffee
is ready I pour myself a cup. I stare at the swirling black
liquid, waiting for it to turn color. Perhaps red, indicating
that blood will be spilled—around me, that would be a useless prediction. Blood is always spilled. Or perhaps green,
indicating that I am going to be meeting someone wearing
emeralds. My beverage remains resolutely black. I take a
sip and decide that it is going to be a good evening.

The Blood Like Wine

SARAH A. HOYT

He stood by my hotel bed yesterday.

In the cool artificiality of a twenty-first-century hotel suite, with the curtains shut tight against the harsh light of day, beside the massive, white wardrobe, François stood.

He wore his best suit of blue silk—long jacket edged with lace, and tight knee-length breeches that molded his tall, muscular body. His golden curls fell to his shoulders, and his dark violet eyes were oh so infinitely sad.

He walked to the bed and opened his lace collar with a gloved finger, revealing the red line where the guillotine had separated his head from his body.

And he said nothing. Nothing. And yet, I knew all too well what he meant.

He vanished when I sat up. He always vanished. Like cherished smoke, like unreachable paradise, like longed-for death.

I sat beside the small desk and smoked my mint-laced cigarettes till sunset turned the world outside as dark as my hotel room.

Then I'd showered, dressed in my fuck-me-red dress, which went with my fuck-me-red painted nails, and with my bloodred high heels, pulled back my straight, golden hair, got into my black sports car and hit the road.

I'd made contact. I had the address. I would do what François wanted.

I always did what François wanted.

It was all I had left.

We'd met when we were both seventeen. Which is not to say we were the same age. Born in Faubourg Saint-Antoine, where rats outnumbered people ten to one, where the streets were so narrow and the houses on either side so high that the sun never touched the shit-layered streets, I'd had no time for childhood.

But I was one of the lucky ones: I'd survived.

By twelve, I was an orphan. My mother died giving birth to me. My father, a poor cobbler, died of desperation and tiredness in 1786.

I didn't know the date then, but I know it now. I didn't know how to read then, but I know it now.

Look at the gifts death has heaped upon me.

They said that my father died of a fever. All were fevers, then, and it might have been anything at all: a cold, an un-healed sore, tuberculosis or cancer. All of it then was a fever—stinking sweat upon the dirty bedsheets, a strug-gling voice, breathing that sank slowly, slowly, into a harsh rasp at the throat. Then nothing.

The neighbor women had looked after my father in his last days, community being the only palliative for the harsh, grinding poverty of peasant France.

Just before the end, I was admitted to the small, dim room at the back of the house and allowed near the dank lit-tle pile of bedding, where my father lay.

His grey hair had grown all white through his illness, and his face had sunken, the skin drying and stretching, till it looked like parchment layered over the skull. His aquiline nose looked sharper, and his dark brown eyes smaller, opaque, lost amid the yellow skin, the white hair, the sharp nose.

He smiled and it was the smile of a skull, his irregular teeth gaping at me as I approached.

The hand that stretched out of the pile of covers and grasped my small, soft hand looked more like a claw, with long, yellowed nails. And there was the smell of death in the breath that flew past my face as my father spoke.

"Sylvie," he said. His eyes were soft, sadly sweet when he looked at me. "Sylvie, my daughter, you are too beautiful. Marry someone soon. Marry one of our neighbors. Don't let your beauty lure you outside your sphere. That beauty can be a curse."

Uncomprehending, I listened. Uncomprehending, I held his hand.

Though girls little older than I were often married, I had no thought for such a thing. As for leaving the neighborhood, I dreamt about it every day and every night and prayed upon it to any listening divinity as I told the beads of my rosary with the other women at my father's wake.

I knew I was beautiful and looked older than I was. I'd often seen the effect of that beauty in the lingering glance of passing coachmen, in the appreciative look of merchants in the weekly market.

I dreamt of leaving behind the small, dark streets, the smell of stale smoke and shit, the memory of my father's rasping breath sinking lower and lower into nothing.

He was thirty-two when he died. I had no intention of dying young.

Leaving the hotel parking lot, I drove away into darkness.

In the eastern United States, where I had lived for a time, as the sun went down other lights came up: neon lights of gas stations and drive-throughs, lights that shone on billboards, lights of hotels and motels and restaurants. All of them shone from the side of the road, turning the night into a continuous sunset and reminding me of what I could no longer experience.

But out west the sun went down and night came on, like a blanket obliterating all life, all reminders of life.

Driving at night, between Denver and the little town of Goldport nestled up against the Rockies, I saw no light.

No reminders of lost dawns moved me; no memories of

past noons disturbed me. No sharp, aching mementos of François's golden hair glimmering in the sunlight.

There was nothing in the world, nothing, except the shiny black highway unrolling in the headlights of my black sports car like a lazy snake, and the loud music drowning out my thoughts.

Here and there, clusters of distant, twinkling lights looked like stars fallen to Earth, like a Christmas tree in a cemetery.

I lit a cigarette from the end of the other, threw the spent butt out the window, my nails flourishing briefly in my field of vision, looking like claws dipped into fresh blood.

Smoke enough of these and they would kill you. That's what the surgeon general said. But his promises failed me.

What would he know? I'd died in November 1793, when terror reigned on the streets of Paris and blood flowed like wine over the stained boards of Madame la Guillotine.

My face in the mirror looked back at me, triangular, small, pink. Too pale. My grey eyes showed dark circles all around, the circles of those who hadn't slept for too long. The circles of the damned.

I looked twenty, as I had over two centuries ago. Twenty and still as pretty, still as slim, still as delectable as I'd been when the revolution had washed over Paris like a madness and drowned me in its waves.

Then, as now, my beauty bought luxuries: travel and fine clothes, a beautiful house, transportation.

But transportation now was a sleek new Viper, a horseless carriage that sped silently through the night, devouring the never-ending snaking road, and yet still incapable of taking me away from my guilt, from my fear, away from François's accusing violet eyes, his eyes that found me every time.

I caught François as one caught a fever. And fevers in those days came at a galloping speed, carried by the impetuous horses of madness.

At seventeen, I had left my miserable origins far behind.

I was beautiful, admired, the mistress of a member of the representative assembly, the hostess of a fashionable philosophical salon.

I'd clawed my way out of Faubourg Saint-Antoine, climbing over the backs of rejected lovers, over the proffered purses of eager new ones.

In my salon, with its satin-covered walls, its velvet-covered couches, gathered the fine flower of thinkers in France.

Not the fire-breathing revolutionaries, not the scabby sans culottes.

No. To my nightly assemblies came younger sons of nobility, well-dressed young lawyers, the heirs to bourgeois purses.

Their arguments spoke of Arcadia, of the natural man, the noble savage that never existed anywhere but in the dreams of well-brought-up men.

And I, little Sylvie, who still didn't know how to read and knew scant of anything else, listened to their arguments, never letting them guess my ignorance, never telling them that uneducated men were not near to angels and that nature was very far from nurture.

I sat and listened, and was bored, and dared not talk truthfully to any of them—not even my patron, who paid the bills for my fashionable town house, my fashionable wardrobe, my carriage and my maid. None of them knew about the dark, dank house of my upbringing, or of the sound of rats, rustling close to the walls, or of my father in his deathbed, with the smell of death and sweat, and his rasping breath, and his unheeded advice.

And then there had been François.

He'd appeared at the salon one night, brought by someone whose name I don't remember, as I no longer remember the names of my many patrons.

But him I'd never have forgotten, even had our destinies not entwined in blood and guilt.

François was tall and so pale that the light of candles shone on his skin with the subdued richness of fine silk. His features were finely chiseled, just one square chin, one sharp nose short of effeminate.

His fine golden curls spilled like molten metal to his waist and highlighted the squareness of his shoulders, the narrowness of his waist, the masculine beauty of his long, muscular legs.

He walked like angels must walk in paradise—with effortless grace, like a dancer who has forgotten steps and yet moves to the sound of unheard music.

François, someone told me his name was. François. He was the son of the marquis of something or other.

I never had a good ear for noble names. But I had a good eye for a well-cut manly figure. And I had learned the persuasive words, the easy laughter, the fan carelessly waved towards him so as to give him a scent of my perfume, the tilting forward that allowed him sight of the deep crevice between my round, silk-cradled breasts, the laying of a well-manicured, soft hand on his arm.

By the end of the night, sweet François was mine.

I drove out of the highway at the exit for Goldport, a small mining town that time had forgotten, nestled amid the Rockies.

Closed mines had given way to casinos and to motels and hotels of all descriptions.

The town itself looked like a splash of neon amid the dark mountains. I fished for my sunglasses from the passenger seat, and put them on, to mitigate the glare to my dark-loving eyes.

The Good Rest Motel consisted of several rectangular buildings, painted gingivitis-pink, nestling amid improbably tall pines at the entrance to the town.

I took a right by the lighted billboard that advertised king-size beds and a TV in every room, and parked next to the RVs and trucks beneath the trees.

Cabin number twelve was dark, but the sounds of the television came from it.

At my knock, invisible hands opened the door, with the

classical unoiled-hinge shriek of every B-grade horror movie.

And, from the darkness within, a voice spoke; a voice said, "Ah, Sylvie. Beautiful Sylvie. Still as pretty, I see."

I blinked. Pierre, with his dark eyes, his curly black hair still long enough to sweep his shoulders, stood in the shadows.

The shadows were bright as light to me.

And Pierre smiled at me, the smile of the damned. He wore a white suit, a strange choice for a vampire.

I closed the door behind me. The small room smelled of that dry dust of long-forgotten tombs. It smelled of Pierre.

But, behind that smell, I could sense another. The smell of blood, the smell of some living thing that Pierre had fed upon tonight.

That blood, coursing fast in Pierre's long-dead veins, made me lick my lips, made my heart quicken within my withered chest.

Pierre stepped back and smiled, his old, evasive smile. "You said you wished to see me, Sylvie? What did you want?"

"His name is Pierre D'Laubergine," François said.

François was twenty—had just turned twenty. The last three years hadn't been easy for us—for either of us.

I'd kept my home, but my patron and protection had vanished in the maelstrom of the revolution.

François had taken his place for a while, but then even he had lost the power to support me. His lands were confiscated, his money fast vanishing. He had secured us two small rooms in a middle-class town house. A far step down from my little town house where I'd held my salon for the luminaries of the more restrained forms of revolution. But well above Faubourg Saint-Antoine.

Lying naked and perfect in my bed, François looked unscathed by three years of living beneath his station, if above his means.

The suit folded over the foot of my bed was serviceable

muslin, in a greyish color. Not black, since black was assumed to mean one was an aristo, mourning for the king whom the revolution had guillotined two years ago.

But François's body was still pure white silk, stretched evenly over a muscular frame that would have suited a workman well enough. Only no workman had ever grown like this, tall and straight, not deformed. Workmen's bodies soon became twisted by work and bent out of their intended shape.

François was all that could be intended: soft skin and violet eyes; elegant, tall body and golden hair; a smell of mint; a lingering taste of fresh apples.

He turned in bed as he spoke and looked intently at me, his square-tipped finger drawing a circle around my dark nipple. "Pierre D'Laubergine is his name, as I said, and he's a guard of the city. He said he could get us passports out of the city, out of the country. We could get as far as Calais, and from there hire a boat to England. There are still boats. For a price."

"What . . . What would the price be?" I asked. I knew he didn't have much, though he'd never tell me exactly how much remained of his once-vast fortune. His father had been imprisoned, executed, and the family lands confiscated.

Yet, François paid for our lodging and for our food; but how long would he still have the money?

His broad, sensuous lips twisted in a wry smile. This wry smile was a gift of the revolution, something the pampered innocent of three years ago would have been incapable of. "Too much money, *ma petite*. Too much."

He pulled me to him. His taut neck tasted of fresh apples and smelled of pure mint. I buried my face in his hair. I savored the touch of his silky hands.

I loved François. But how could we afford to escape the revolution? And, already reduced to middle-class circumstances, how would we live when we got to England?

I didn't have the courage to ask.

I bent my head to his golden hair; I inhaled his scent of mint and freshly cut apples.

I wanted to know nothing more.

Pierre backed away from me, smiling still.

His dark eyes looked at me with sheer, blank incomprehension.

"What do you want, Sylvie?" he asked. "You said you had news . . . about the slayer?"

For just a moment, his eyes looked unfocused, his gaze tinged with fear.

The slayer. That was what we all called the mysterious figure who killed vampires. News traveled fast, nervously, through the vampire network. People who don't die easy, people who don't age all get to know each other over time. There weren't that many of us. Growing fewer by the day.

The slayer. Like someone out of medieval legend, a creature of right, slaying the evil ones, laying the undead to rest.

Only we weren't medieval vampires. We were Enlightenment vampires, born at the dawn of science, grown strong with it, harbored in its shade.

Science made people disbelieve things that went bump in the night. Science ensured that no one searched for us, much less slew us.

And now this creature traveled, as silently, as darkly as one of us, traveled swiftly around the world, slaying vampires.

I smiled at Pierre, "I do know about the slayer," I said. I smiled at him. I batted my eyelashes. Long, long ago I'd learned that what worked on mortal men worked on vampires, too. They might be dead men, but not where it mattered.

I walked forward, just little me, little Sylvie, tottering atop my high heels. I smiled my most innocent smile, and I stepped up, walked close. I leaned on Pierre, feeling his thick, muscular arm beneath my hand, and leaning in to kiss his black-stubbled chin. "It's been so long," I said. "Since I've been with one of my own kind. So long."

He looked down. He chuckled. Only the slightest bit of weariness remained in his dark eyes. "The slayer?" he prompted.

I reached for the black bow tie that provided the only contrasting note in his snow-white outfit.

My fingers brushed against the crisp, cool collar of his white shirt. His tie felt like satin. He smelled dusty and clean like the grave, but with the underlying spiciness of freshly drawn blood.

The recent feeding put color in his cheeks and a quick glimmer in his eye.

As if he were alive.

"Can we talk about it later?" I asked, pulling his bow tie free and unbuttoning the top button of his crisp shirt, and raining little, soft kisses at the base of his neck that, even two centuries later, remained golden tan. "It's been so long."

He sighed, then chuckled, a chuckle that was almost a giggle. His large hands engulfed my small waist. "Ah, Sylvie. Always the same. Dead or alive, Sylvie will be a fun girl."

Pierre was an officer in the city police—tanned dark, with black curls that brushed the shoulders of his white suit. Like most city police, he lacked a uniform and wore what he pleased. In Pierre's case, that was white satin, as cool and glimmering as new snow.

I remembered staring at his attire—the well-cut breeches, the loose, expensive shirt, and thinking that he couldn't possibly—he couldn't ever afford such clothes from his low-paying job. And I wondered again how much François was paying Pierre. And how much would be left for us. But I didn't dare ask until we were in the carriage.

Both of us wore dark, peasant clothes of prickly wool, clothes that reminded me of the shabby skirt and shirt I'd worn as a child. They were secondhand clothes and I could smell in them the mustiness of cramped corridors, of rancid smoke, of insufficient air.

Just putting the clothes on, I'd felt as though I were suffocating.

Now, in the narrow carriage, tossed shoulder to shoulder with François, with his arm around me, his hair tied back and hid beneath a liberty cap, I felt as though the last five years had been erased. I heard my father's voice telling me to marry a neighbor, consigning that neighbor and me to the same life of poverty that had killed my mother, that had killed him.

"You're very quiet, *ma petite*," François said. His arm over my shoulders brought almost stifling heat, and a feeling of confinement. He smelled of dirty wool and the acid sweat of fear.

I'd loved François for three years, and now he felt like a stranger in my arms.

"I was thinking," I said. "I was thinking." The carriage carrying us moved through the night, rocking on its unsteady, ancient wheels.

The curtains were drawn, all was dark. I could see François only because his skin was so white, his hair so golden.

He pulled at a strand of my own hair that peeked out from beneath my own liberty cap. "Thinking of what, Sylvie?"

"Of how we'll live in England. You have property there, yes?" I had a vague idea that almost all noblemen had property in both countries.

But François chuckled and shook his head. "No, my little one. No property at all. We'll live as God shall want. I know how to read and write, and have other small gifts. Something will offer."

The carriage trembled on and on, upon its unsteady wheels, along a rutted road. "No property at all?" I asked. "No family?"

François looked baffled, as though not understanding my question. He shrugged. "God will provide."

Oh, easy for him to think that. The son of a nobleman, raised in a palace. When had he known hunger—the sort of hunger that twisted your stomach at night, while you lay in the dark and listened to the rats run within the wall? When?

God didn't provide for most of us. For those without family, without connections, without property.

"We'll get married," François said. "I'll look after you."

There was only one thing I knew how to do, only one way of acquiring power, and that didn't involve—didn't allow for—my being a married woman. I looked at François, wondering if he would play along. But he wouldn't. I could never have François while living off other men.

François was too fine for that. Too idealistic. He believed God would provide.

He tightened his arm around me, in a thick smell of heated wool. "We'll be all right, Sylvie. We have each other."

Each other and nothing more. Together we could starve in the English equivalent of Faubourg Saint-Antoine.

I felt trapped, but I had nowhere to run.

Without François, I could remain in France and find someone else to support me—one of the new republican elite, perhaps, a rich bourgeois.

But I wouldn't have François.

And the thought of his body, his perfect, white, silken body in another's arms made my heart clench in jealous possessiveness.

"Of what are you thinking, little one?" François asked.

The carriage stopped, with a rocking halt, and our coachman, paid for by Pierre, yelled something.

It was much too early to have got to Calais.

François stood up, startled, as the door opened and a light shone in on us.

"Were you thinking of this, all along?" Pierre asked. "Did you have this in mind when you summoned me?"

I didn't answer. I covered his mouth with my eager one. "It's been too long," I said. "Too long since I've had you."

I tore off his clothes, frantically, and pushed him towards the low bed. The television still blared on, behind us, as I kissed his naked body.

The smell of fresh blood in his veins drove me on.

The light of a lantern blinded us, while voices yelled, "Aristo, aristo." Aristocrat. The death sentence. On such a word had people been hanged from lampposts, trampled by the crowd, bayoneted to death.

Trembling I rose, trembling I clung to François.

François blinked in surprise. He looked only slightly pale. "You are mistaken," he said, trying to infuse his well-bred voice with a popular patois that wouldn't have fooled a child. "You are mistaken. This is just me, François Ville, a farmer, and my wife, Sylvie."

But the crowd laid rough hands on us; the crowd pulled us out. Someone stood before us, someone wearing a patched-together uniform. He had the look of one in authority and he turned to the man all in white, beside him, and said, "Are these the ones, Pierre? Is this the little marquis and his fiancée?"

I realized then we had been betrayed. François's money, all that remained of his fortune, wouldn't even buy us slow death in an English slum. Only quick death in the guillotine.

This wasn't right. It wasn't proper. François was an aristo, born and bred, one of those for whom God provided.

But I had already paid my dues in sweat and blood, in tears and humiliation. I'd grown up in Faubourg Saint-Antoine. "I'm not his fiancée," I yelled, as years of cultivating my accent fell from my voice, leaving the gutter-snipe speech that had been my first expression. "I'm a prostitute. I was sent by this man, Pierre, to entrap the *si-devant* marquis."

The man in authority looked at Pierre as I detached myself from François to embrace Pierre.

For a moment it hung in the balance, as I frantically

kissed Pierre and thrust my tongue in his mouth. Then he laughed and said, "Yes, she's a prostitute."

I hardly dared turn, to see François as they pulled him away. He turned back to look at me, and his violet eyes showed a mix of dread and grief. They sparkled with tears like violets under the rain.

"Do you ever dream of him?" I asked Pierre.

"Of whom?" Pierre looked blankly at me. Funny how even vampires, after lovemaking, looked slack and stupid and slow. He lay on the rumpled bed. A ray of moonlight came through the window and shone on him, stripping him of his tan, making his skin look even whiter than normal vampire skin. Like the belly of a fish, dead and repulsive, pulled from the depths of a sea and left to rot on the beach.

Of whom. He didn't even remember. I'd lived with Pierre for a year, after François's death. But surely, he would remember how we'd got together. Wouldn't he?

"François," I said. "My little marquis."

I got my purse that I'd abandoned in the beaten-down armchair, and, by the light of the silver screen, got a cigarette and my lighter, and lit the cigarette.

Pierre looked blank for a moment; then a spark of intelligence shone in his eyes. "François? No. I had quite forgotten."

I'd gone to see François guillotined. I couldn't stay away.

I had to be there when the one man I loved coughed in the basket, in the droll language of the times for the sound a severed head made, in the basket with other heads, while dying.

Unlike so many prisoners, François hadn't aged, in his three months in jail. Instead he seemed to have matured. His beauty cloaked itself in a terrible dignity, the dignity of an emperor or of a god, of a supernatural being that no mere human could touch. He had procured, somehow, his best suit of blue satin, and it was what he wore to the guillotine.

Before putting his neck on the terrible rest from which no one rose alive, he tied back his hair, dignifiedly, slowly, ensuring that his neck was free for the blow.

The Place de la Concorde was full of men and women yelling and shrieking for the aristo's blood. Men and women who'd never known François and had no mercy on his tender, silklike skin, his soft sensuous lips, his violet eyes. They could not see his nobility, his terrible, brittle majesty. But I could.

And, at the last moment, before laying his head on the block, his gaze found me amid the crowd, and his lips formed the one word, *Sylvie*.

Then the blade fell, and his blood flowed like wine. So much blood, washing down the blade, the indifferent boards of the guillotine.

And François's head tumbled into the basket, amid the others. What was done could no longer be undone. My love had died hating me.

In the twentieth century, research found that a severed head could live as much as five minutes after beheading.

Had François lived that long? What had he thought?

And why did his vengeance still visit me?

That night, after his death, I dreamed of him. He came into my dream as he had been in life—whole and unharmed, save for a red line that showed where his head had been severed from the body.

He'd come, step by step, silently, to the bed I shared with Pierre, and stood by it, and smiled at me, a smile all the more ghastly for being gentle and soft.

His gloved finger had opened the lace of his collar to show his red wound. He touched it with his finger, and it bled, a trickle dripping down the front of his shirt.

"Drink," he told me. "Drink. You have become one of them. One who feeds on human need and suffering. You should have their rewards."

"François?" I'd asked. "François, but you're dead."

He grinned, a grin as gentle and as innocent as the one I'd first seen on him, but looking ghastly and wan on that pale face. "No, my dear. I'll live as long as injustice must be avenged. And so will you. Drink, my dear," he said, and pointed at his dripping wound. "You'll live forever."

To live forever. Not to die like my father, young and miserable.

I drank. It tasted like new wine, like newly stomped grapes, fermented and ripened and full of sugar and heady alcohol.

When I leaned back, satiated, François smiled at me. "Now you've become like them," he said. "Like everyone who commits great injustice, who feeds on the suffering of others. The worst of them do not die, you know? They become vampires, who hunt the night, feeding still on blood and suffering. And now you're one of them, my Sylvie, and you have what you want. You'll be forever young, forever beautiful."

Pierre slept, in the sliver of moonlight, looking grey and wan like a landed fish.

I crept close to him. I snuggled against his chest. He smiled, his teeth glimmering in the moonlight.

Fresh blood sang through his veins, pumped through his long-dead heart, put a flush on his cheeks.

Years later I figured out I'd died that night, when François first visited me. Perhaps it was the fright of seeing his ghost. Perhaps remorse. Perhaps thwarted love and realizing I'd never get to hold François in my arms again.

The symptoms had come on, little by little, over the next couple of years: the fear of light, the abhorrence of food, the need to suck fresh blood from human victims.

The latter hadn't been really difficult. I was still young, still beautiful. Any man would go with me into a dark alley, into a shady bar.

Five years later, I'd heard through the vampire circuit that Pierre D'Laubergine had been shot in battle as one of Napoleon's soldiers, and got up twelve hours later, and washed away the stink of the battleground, and become one of us.

*   *   *

When I was sure that Pierre was asleep, I nuzzled close to his neck. I found the pulsing vein of life.

I sank my fangs in so quietly, he never knew as I drained all the blood out of him, not leaving a drop that would sustain his life in death.

Vampires won't die from being drained, but it will make them unconscious for twelve hours—long enough for the sun to come in through the curtains I left wide open and reduce Pierre to what he smelled of: clean graveyard dust, with no life, no memory, finally washed of all guilt.

Last night François came to me, in my hotel room.

He looked as always, terribly near and impossibly far away, gratified but sad, terribly sad.

His violet eyes looked at me, as always, with a mixture of desire and revulsion.

I stared back with a clear vision.

François said I would have to do this while there were vampires left in the world, while there were those who lived from others' blood.

I was his vengeance, loosed on malefactors.

When I killed the last of them, I knew, I would finally be able to clutch his insubstantial body of smoke and fog in my trembling arms. I'd feel his silky skin once more, I'd savor his fresh apple taste, I'd smell his fresh mint smell.

I would step with him through the archways of life, into restful, serene death.

But then, François had said, I would live forever.

There would always be evil men to kill. And François would be forever out of reach.

I got out of bed, and lit a mint cigarette, and looked at the place where I'd glimpsed François, by the big white wardrobe.

To live forever had once seemed so sweet. How quickly it had grown weary. How quickly did I, like a child at the end of a long and fretful day, come to long for rest.

My task is impossible, and yet I must do it.

I have beauty and youth and life eternal. But death is the only gift within my giving.

Borrowed Light

EMILY GASKIN

You, the elusive one—
the first unexpected thing.

I thought I would stay the lost one,
brooding with all the suggestibility
of shadow, where a thought
is all one feels and clings to,
never envisioning myself the guide,

that I, a mirror like the moon,
should cast borrowed light
onto your burial mound seclusion,
seeking that place where you remain,
a solitude that dares only the endurance
of self-defined torments.

In those final moments before even I
can no longer pretend to light,
when I vanish from the sky
to shiver in a night that I created—
a darkness not so different from your own—

before I lapse uncertain,
too awkward as bringer of light,
I sense that you might almost look up,

if you would only will it,
and see what I do not understand
but try to reflect to you.
Perhaps you would then know light
and show me what it means.

Love Letters

BARBARA JOHNSON-HADDAD

I draw pictures with my own blood,
hoping that the pain of my open veins
will distract me from
the ache of my abandoned heart.
When I can no longer move my torn arms
or speak from my dripping throat,
I will stop sending you letters written in blood
apologizing for my failure to love you enough.

Understudy

S. L. ROBINSON

Red wine
fills the void
as best it can.
Graveyard dust
flakes from
patent leather shoes
Black crepe and lace
drape my body
and my mood.
Sunshine is something
I hear of
on late-night news.
A pathetic mortal vampire
since you revoked
your invitation.

Ravens

CARRIE PAVLIN

Dark sleek black shiny
Drawn to lights or pretty girls
Rapt over shiny objects
Here and nows
No futures, save the past
and the fear that always follows
Eat drink kill slay STEAL
Steal enough of mortal dreams
Take their prized possessions
Borrow their obsessions
We don't only take their blood
But that fear, that always follows
As they go about their lives
Makes them live each day much harder
Than the dark and violent creatures
Living in their shadows
Hard to think we once walked with them
We who cannot see tomorrow
When it reminds us what we gave away

Summertime

Antonia Mitchell

The days are so long now.

I stand at my window,
behind white lace,
and I watch people walk in the light.
Their features are blurred by the curtains, but I can see
the shine of their hair
and the copper their shoulders and arms have turned
from the sun.
They smell of coconut oil, and sweat.
I hear them as they walk underneath the maples, and I
    watch
from behind white lace curtains.

Five o'clock
(only three more hours until sunset)
grandfather chimes in the hall.
I wander from room to room, running my fingertips
over mirrors and rose petals,
and wait for sundown.
I can hear a lawn mower.
It can take forever, the night,
before it finally comes.

I press my cheek against the lace,
feel it scratching over my closed eyes.
A dog is barking somewhere, outside
in the last rays of light.
Children in scruffy overalls chant and jump rope.
I wonder if they smell like ice cream,
like trips to the beach, and rolling in the grass:
summertime.

The days are so long now.

Note Found on My Door, Friday

JEFF COPENHAGEN

You are an emotional vampire
feeding on me and other
vulnerable very post- or pre-
divorced self-esteem challenged
women. All of those late
night phone calls telling
us what we'd almost die
to hear
you are beautiful, you said
you are smart, you said
you can do anything, you said
you selfish bastard, I should drive
a wooden stake through your heart
why did you stop calling?

Lying in the Shade

Elizabeth Fuller

Color me sanguine
in your paint-by-number world
and I shall sing of the boldness
of color flushing out my veins,
racing-heart-engine crossing over
your lanes,
laughing out the light
from my bleached white refrains.

Color me sanguine
like the break of a drum when the
thumping rattles the breath of my sighs,
rumble-heart-thunder rolling over
your skies, bleeding silence in the wake
of stifled cries.

Color me sanguine
and I shall be, red as the life-blood
your love drained from me.

Murava

ANNE SHELDON

Slavic and Finno-Ugric peoples believe children born with
a tooth will become sorcerers or vampires. . . .
   Certain groups of Wends call them "murava."
      —*Standard Dictionary of Folklore, Mythology, and Legend*

I slipped out
in the blood of my mother
with one small tooth already budding.
Not even an incisor,
but it was known by all the village
within an hour
and they were ever after wary.
I wonder if I would have taken to the thirst
or at least so quickly
if there hadn't been that expectation?
And such a lack of friends
to show me how a girl behaves
and how her appetites
are best controlled.

I was otherwise a quiet woman
content to knead the supple dough
or rock and knit a nubbled stole
for my beloved's neck.

I liked my house in order,
the spices all by color
and the needles all by size.
I scrubbed the ironstone plates
and on my birthday
Janos always gave me
one more porcelain cup,
the roses on the shining white.

My husband came from Danzig
and set no store on rustic company.
He barely noticed that my neighbors held apart.
And what I wished from him
was just his heart, not what it pumps.

But sometimes while he slept
I needed just a little more
to make life perfect.
Mostly sleeping fowl or rabbits.
Rarely little misused children,
happy to be gently held
at any cost.

One night, however,
my darling woke up cold
and when he couldn't find me
took it in his head
I must be lying with another man.
He waited for me with the bread knife—
and hardly recognized the creature who crept in,
or I'd be dead. And happy so.

Without a word he crossed himself,
and, taking just his fowling piece
and all the gold we'd hid
beneath the hearthrock,
left our home for good.

No doubt he has another wife by now
and speaks of me as "dead."
He wouldn't want the world to know
what he had loved.
You say I have no right to feel betrayed?
being what I am?
I think I could just bear to give it up
if I thought that lighting candles at the altar
would bring him dreams of me
that made his blood rise in the night.

Azeman

ANNE SHELDON

In Surinam, a woman who changes her human form for
animal form at night and goes about drinking human blood.
—*Standard Dictionary of Folklore, Mythology, and Legend*

These dull-eyed pigherds
with their grimy rope and straightened locks—
ignorance fills their arteries.
Unworthy of the hunt.
Say we are slovenly tarts?
Only proper housewives could be driven
to such extremities by night—
and be caught as we are caught.

Just so, my love,
the blood of the righteous doth surpass
the juice of sinner:
so much desire and temper
simmers in the veins of virtue.
The priest, of course—
with his foot-water by the door
and all his pornographic crosses—
has always been too hazardous,
even for the slender orange cat
I was that night.

But you, my blacksmith,
had the troubled quiet of the sweet—
or so I dreamed—and dreamed for weeks
about the rosewood sinews of your neck,
and how I'd pick a path with easy paws
through the ironmongery
to a place beneath your blanket.
How could I imagine you'd be clever, too?—
leaving the ancient broom
across the bedroom threshold?

Thus magicked to my daylight shape,
I couldn't help but curl upon the hearth
and try to count its nimble straws.
Where you found me
clawless, easy to bind,
before you took advantage.
Perhaps I wouldn't find you
so tasty, after all.

And now in gaol I wait
and wonder—if you know so much,
do you know the way to kill
a thing like me?
And if you do, whom will you tell?

Gifts

Jude Lupinetti

Speak to me of love and roses.
Tell me all the lies my heart would hear.
Give me false hope and promises.
Show me jewels in the skies.

Show me jewels in the skies.
Lay me down on cold, hard stone.
Cut my heart with steeled incisors.
Suck my life's blood anew.

Give me false hope and promises.
Rub my wounds with salt, and
Wash me in the acid rain.
Cover me with kisses light.

Tell me all the lies my heart would hear.
Drown me in your rough embrace.
Take me to the door of night, and
Speak to me of love
    and roses.

Searchers in the Long Dark

WENDY RATHBONE

Why are you hidden
in my ancient thoughts
that even the void
has forgotten?

On black pathways
under star-gardens
strewn with your
graffiti,
in letters carved
on trees and stones,
in love poems

where glimpses
of you
trailing your evening capes
like some suffering
prince
form

Golden-eyed
your reflection in mine

Sometimes my mind calls it
madness

Night skies bloom
autumn planets

The wind brings
a fierce moon

I try to remember
in these unkind times
that all solid reference points
melt in eventual dreams

to longing
and only this
is what creates us searchers
in the long dark
for each other

Lifestyles of the Undead

ANGELA KESSLER

You're surprised by the way I live my unlife?

Of course I have a garden—
I love roses, despite the thorns.
Aren't the night-blooming flowers lovely?

Of course I sleep on silk sheets—
They give me sweet dreams.
Wouldn't you love such decadence?

Of course I keep a well-stocked kitchen—
I do have guests occasionally.
Isn't the garlic braid decorative?

Of course I sip human blood from crystal goblets—
I serve it hot, like sake.
When you want a steak, do you kill a cow?
Of course not. You have someone else do it for you.
Much more civilized.

Perhaps we're not so different after all.

Immortality

Lida Broadhurst

I live because I feared. Heights
Terrified, especially
The depth of six feet.

No longer allowed that
Which repelled delusions
Serenely I slipped free
From rotting dreams.

But my bones refused
Pine's reality,
Preferring a mattress
Of moss on stone.

Now I swallow my bliss
From those who reject fear,
Until the slope of my descent.

She Dreams in Color

ANN K. SCHWADER

Night bleeds all colors
from life but she dreams in them
anyhow:

retouches pale sketches of screams
with a burgundy
borrowed from death warrant seals
then shades in
silver kissed moon's razor shadow
descending
in finest Poe style against hyacinth satin
(remembered of course
from her own casket lining)

till gilding foils this timeless art
for Sun is the only
forbidden pigment.

Pomegranate Winter
(for Kore-Persephone)

ANN K. SCHWADER

Some come down
on their own to this land
of barren willow aisles
& cypress kisses.

They do not require
the cries of their mothers,
the breaking of summer
into frigid shards,
the retribution
of heart's harvest lost.

Theirs is the pomegranate
taste of awakening,
deep knowledge of the dark
reclaimed from the start.

Queens of the more than blessed dead,
they lift narcissus praise
to Sister Moon;
her slender fanged crescent
their only true chariot
carrying them home.

Supplication

Dawn R. Cotter

I am rage.
I am hate.
I am pain.
I am full of agony over this life.
Take me from this hellish normality
Into that sweet, cool, twisted darkness.
I will not regret the violence;
Anything would be better than this banality.

I ride the bus and see endless rows
Of blank eyes and blanker souls.
I go to work on a Monday
To deal with idiots and morons,
To cater to the whims of petty dictators
With no power,
Only the desire to inflict the same nonexistence
They have endured
Onto others.

My heart twists with every passing day
As the bitterness and anger become permanent features
    of my face
And the darkness within swells and threatens to burst
In a fit of insane screaming and violence.
I have not yet decided whether the target will be

Myself, or others. Perhaps both.
To release my frustration with brutal force
As I bloody my head and fists on a wall
Or my coworkers' bodies with bullets of hate.

I would rather stalk the star-filled night
Than trudge the sun-bleached streets of day
Silent witness to other people's tragedies,
Desperation, and defeat.
I would rather live in a world of nightmare
Than suffer a world with no dreams.
To end what torments me,
Rather than meekly shuffle toward my soul's true death.
I would surely be saner as a madman
Than as a corporate slave.

Let me walk in a world of mystery
Where I alone control my fate,
And that of others.
Give me eternal power
And I will wreak havoc in your name.
Let me be the hunter, not the prey;
The tormentor, not the victim.
Give me power
So that when I tell them to go to hell,
I can also send them on their way.

Give me strength, that I may destroy
Give me death, that I may live.

How to Write a Poem

LAWRENCE SCHIMEL

Open the windows at night
and invite him in.
Bare your throat
and let him drink his fill.
Dream until he stops,
then write about the dream.

To you the words will seem flat
but those who know will *know*,
remembering their own nights
of crimson dreaming.

Good News

Karen R. Porter

Death looks good on you—
pretty as a picture in your
bloodstained dress ripped
in all the right places and that
icy flesh peeking out to take
a gander at the creeping world.
No worms for you, my lovely,
just absinthe nights with a hint
of old-fashioned hospitality.
Never turn a stranger away
into the cold, the dangerous dark—
you'll get the hang of it soon enough.

Death looks goddamn good on you,
just take my word for it since the
mirrors won't talk, and water just
stares black as dried blood in the
corner of your mouth. Uncover those
crystal eyes blooming with atomic fire;
smash your glasses with impunity, toss
out the weight-loss books 'cause you'll
be drowning in a liquid diet from now on.
No more doctors, dentists, druggists,
Vietnamese hit men, dirtbag thieves
except when they're dinner on the hoof.

The Romantic Age

MIKE ALLEN

Polidori's nag lagged behind
the thundering stallion, spurned
as Byron spurred, a fallen god
become a demon of speed, flickering
in and out of twilit forest shadows.

The doctor watched his Lord fade,
an avatar of grace in flesh grown
ethereal, the void between them
expanding forever with distance,
the electric caress his soul craved
never to be given, that hand withdrawn
to somewhere far beneath the grave.

He thought of Padua, the ordeal ahead;
Himself a jealous shadow, his Lord
devouring the court with gestures,
enthralled women like leeches attaching
themselves to every hollow word
and casually apathetic glance.

Polidori watched his master
disappear into the dark, and thought:
How very much like a vampyre.

*The shadows
of two riders
fall across
a hidden face;
she watches
from the
undergrowth,
eyes widened
with a final
sight of
ancient
parchment-
yellow eyes;
her throat
opened by teeth
like hooks;
her unused
essence drained
into the soil.
No tales will
memorialize
her lonely
encounter
with immortality.*

Vampire Standards

Uncle River

Monstrous world—
It is not that people are evil;
Most are not,
Perhaps no more than ever.
But people,
Good and evil alike,
Maybe the good even more than the evil,
Believe evil normal.
How to explain?

When you've been fed every day
Of your childhood
On flesh of geese that
Would have laid golden eggs,
Of course you grow up accepting standards
Of people who kill them.
When the only stories you know of
Goddesses are of rape,
When the only story you know of
A God is of murder,
When slaves' and prisoners' guilty pleasures
Are the only good things you have
Or ever heard of,
When you believe that survival requires
Doing something both pointless and unpleasant

For benefit of someone despicable
And know this Hell by honorable name: work,
Knowing no other kind . . .

The world does not have to be monstrous.
Evil people are not that many,
Maybe no more than ever.
But when ninety-nine point ninety-nine percent
Of good people know
Only the monstrous as normal,
I despair. Better to die.
Leave this lovely planet to
Cockleburs and flies.
Let hummingbird moths enjoy the flowers.
Let beavers do the building.
. . . And that may happen.

Those who eat my soul,
Not because they are vampires,
But because the vampires taught them
That is the only food,
Will finish me off.
How many are left
Designated as food by reaching adulthood
Without a diploma . . . license to feed,
From the vampires' school?
When we are all gone, then what?
Surrounded by glorious Creation,
You will starve because,
Raised by vampire standards, innocently,
You do not know
There is any other way to live.

In Black

LAUREL ROBERTSON

Arranged in black
at a windless dusk, we gather
in a mourner's masquerade.
Our shades of sorrow, pale and deceitful,
why, we've even veiled our fury eyes
to mask our anticipation.

We weep for their memory of you,
but mostly out of joy
for what you will become.

Feigning grief as they lower you down
in an immaculate white coffin,
we slip away into the shadows
knowing you will find us,
remember our faces
when you come back . . .
in black.

To See You Again

LAUREL ROBERTSON

You came to me in a dream last night,
how long has it been
since we laughed together, held each other close?
Ecstatic, yet somehow uneasy, was our reunion,
you looked too weary
a shade of sadness had darkened your eyes.
The hollowness in your voice
the way you moved, so soundlessly,
I doubted it was even you . . .
still, we shared complete bliss.

Until you led me to a place,
a gathering of your dearest friends and family
though so familiar from before, all now looked dimly
    strange
and I felt lost as you mingled with the sallow faces,
so solemn you were when you called my name.

And turning around I saw the sky
changing from blue to black
storm shadows swelling, as did a fear inside of me
as you bent and kissed the warmth from my soul.

My dread remains . . . even though I am awake.

I got the news today
a voice that echoed from my dream spoke the words . . .
you died last week, buried only yesterday.

The chill of your kiss lingers on the curve of my neck
and I wonder when I will see you again.

Soliloquy

ALEXANDRA ELIZABETH HONIGSBERG

Another century dies with the coming dawn and its worn-out revelers. They say there is no millennium fever, but I see with older eyes and think maybe they're wrong, though this is my first. Ask me again in another thousand years and I might know better.

It is for this reason, foolish though it might be, that I've decided to keep some sort of chronicle of recollections, thoughts, a bit of rambling. After all, how many true confidants might my kind have? There are not many of us and we don't share with each other, especially scattered as we remain—we like our solitude and lands undisturbed. Our servants tend to lose their minds so are not likely to make for great conversation.

The newspapers are amusing, in their myriad fashions. And those who write for them seem to suffer from a hunger to know as much as I do for the blood. There is great potential there. Though many are little minds suffering from delusions of grandeur, still, there are those who see with sharper eyes and are very much aware that they can help build up or tear down dynasties—and do it with great relish. With those few, I feel a sort of kinship. We see. We hunger. We reach inside.

But I am no writer. I keep to my own ways and leave them to theirs. Yet, it is a comfort to know that I have some allies out there, unknowing though they may be.

This chaos, this London, still suits me. It has called me across the years yet again and who am I, even I, to ignore its potentials, its life? A hundred years is not an eternity, but it can feel that way when you're separated from your passion. Still, time has taught me nothing if not patience. Passion I always had.

'Twas the jewels—O the jewels!—and not the sickly blood of the Royals that flows too freely—that first drew me and calls me back. Their fire—life from the dark core of the Earth itself, from the sun I've long forgotten but which still tugs at some hidden strands within me. This speaks to me. Their spirit speaks to me even as the call of human blood does and does not. Yes, they had their cost in blood, as well, and carry within them sparks from their makers and keepers, though most who encounter them seem to be oblivious of their true nature. They are mostly unconscious, humans are, as I was. Years, six hundred of them, can bring fog or blinding vision. I have vacillated between both.

But these jewels, family chroniclers, dynastic artifacts, carry within them the seeds of conflict, inflammatory as their brilliance proclaims, in need of but that catalytic spark from outside. I could unleash the chaos again, though it seems well on its way. Little less than royalty I, in all but name. Once a warrior-king much like their legendary Arthur. Now there would be one worthy to walk as an Immortal! I believe that he sleeps. Whether he will rise again remains a mystery even to me. But I dream of my Wallachia, far away Carpathian homeland—it is not as I left it last nor as I would have it, with tourists and scholars all about. Yet freedom is a good thing for my people. I remember how that felt—to win it, then to lose it once more. Surely, to my people I remain a king and more, a legend. I upheld my father's house and am no stranger to riches.

Riches. I know them more intimately than most. After all, I have already had many lifetimes to accumulate wealth in all its forms, stash it away against a long sun and transform my persona in the eyes of the humans. The jewels warm my long-dead and unbeating heart, for I know that if sun or stake should find me, the living stones would live on. Every man wants to guard his immortality, even we so-called Immortals. Death could come like a thief with the dawn and still there are too many ways to die. But age and cunning are with me, besides the Dark Gifts. I have plans.

Let that fool of a doctor think me vanquished. Ah, Lucy the Pale, my Lucy of the Light, released. What a loss! None believed that I could truly love her, thinking my heart as ruined as my home. But I did—not as humans could ever understand it, yet with no small part an echo of the human I had been. It hasn't left me. I wonder if it ever will. They say the old ones lose it. What am I, if not old? But I know better.

Those meddling men dealt me a painful blow, but a temporary setback, only. They had been careless enough to leave behind my family medallion with its bloodstone there in the coffin with my shattered body. A few years, no more, and I was able to reach out once again, return to London with more care and a single purpose. The jewels.

They waited for me. Victoria had seen to that, having bequeathed half her treasure to the Crown in perpetuity. And I watched as her Danish daughter-in-law, the queen consort, Alexandra, too long in waiting for her husband to take the throne, built her own legacy upon Victoria's foundation. The photographers snapped endless pictures of her, proclaimed her a great beauty, bathed in the light of the stones, "dazzling, dizzying." I found her to be so, though severe and too short-lived. She gave them to her daughter-in-law Mary, who grew handsome and a great presence of a queen in her old age. And what merry madness the Romanovs and Bolsheviks made together, necessitating the Dowager Empress Marie's escape through her British in-laws to her native Denmark. The papers called her not quite so comely as her elder sister, who dazzled. They were right. She was rich in jewels, but little else, least of all sense. Still, she eventually added to the jewel collection that carries the life.

I was glad for the demise of Victoria, the perpetual widow. The other ladies had necks long and strong enough to make my day-long sleeps restless with dreams of taking them. And how they covered themselves in the living jewels, like none before them or since—that Bowes-Lyons woman and her brood more reserved, less striking, and sometimes with less sense than their ancient Danish aunt.

Carfuks, where the four roads cross, named by the Saxons—would that I had had their sheer numbers, their heart, their hot blood, in my campaign! My thoughts wander back there to the abbey. How I miss the place. I never got to finish its restoration and I so hate to leave things undone. But I dare not go back there. London is vast and teeming. I can get lost in its crowds easily enough.

I used to love to stroll its streets after the opera. One night I encountered the mourning Queen there. I caught her eye, penetrated the central stone in a brooch set over her heart—a bloodred Burmese beauty that called all souls to its depths—and left a piece of myself there within, with a suggestion. I had to smile when I read of how Victoria had carried out my plan, leaving the best pieces to the Crown. Crafty woman. Not even the Hanovers won all they sought from her. Strong, if a bit too stubborn and sentimental. I can forgive her that.

Oddly enough, it was the Prince Albert opals that disturbed the new Queen—her husband, at sixty, was already too tired to notice such details. She thought them bad luck. But that ruby and its ninety-five cohorts, a gift from the Indian government, were the culprits. Even she missed that. So Alexandra had them all placed within a necklace that Burmese believe guards against the ninety-six illnesses that assail the body. Ninety-six rubies to protect her, possibly grant immortality. Ninety-six rubies to urge her on. She was close. So close. But I controlled the keystone and could not bring her over. She was not the one. Elizabeth wears it now, and my essence survives within it. I did steal them away, once—that leather chest so stealthily carried on her coronation tour. En route to Wellington, New Zealand, it was— now there's a beautiful and rugged land! I mingled with their essence, strengthened the call, then returned them, as much as I wanted to set things in motion right then. It was not yet time. I waited, and still wait.

I have time to wander, amuse and educate myself. I love to go to the Tower, the Jewel House, on foggy nights and dissolve to mist to absorb the history, the life there. The Black Prince ruby—before my time—makes the Imperial State Crown too heavy with blood lust. Still, I like the feel of it. It echoes with histories of monarchs that I wish I had not missed, of a mortal with the hunger so strong within him that he might have been reborn a prince of blood. But his spirit failed him in the end, like so many others. And there was no vampire there to help him across. His echo remains in the stone to beckon monarchs to hunger and unleash more chaos, possibly birth another Immortal. Someday.

None seem to have the stomach for it, though Elizabeth—the so-called Virgin Queen—and her aptly named sister, the saintly Bloody Mary, also came very close. Fine companions they would've been. I find the Catholics and Anglicans understand about blood, sing to it more. They and the Byzantines certainly understand jewels the way the children of the Reformation do not. How foolishly the new churches threw all that away. They knew only parts of the story.

I go to Westminster Abbey, stand outside to watch as people visit the sisters' tombs. Stand there. I tell you, even at a distance, the hunger still sings in them. They sleep, ever watchful, awaiting a time when they might walk Immortal by some means. They love their country. They love their power more and have not let loose their Earthly bonds. Mark me. They wait. Desire knows no bounds.

Time has become one large reality, for me. It is hard to keep the lines in order, since I live within them and without. But I watch. The present monarchy, in disarray due to all its petty bedroom intrigues and the ravenous press— think they that Royals have never dallied, before?—leaves me sad. They could've been so much more. Frail Diana wore not Victoria's and Alexandra's rubies and was large-hearted and of the Light. That's as it should be. They need a tragic heroine, the people do. She was more like them than any royal before. Charles is a melancholy, almost Byronic, and has no ambition—not like his father before him or his beloved warrior-uncle, Mountbatten of Burma. I'm sure that old one knew the lore, but the stones were not for him. Yet he had the heart where others did not. But the Irish won that battle. The present Queen is tired and her mother too sweet, the other Royals too fun-loving. But in William I sense a spark, that longing for something more, that hunger, maybe even a bit of the dark—hard to tell in one still relatively young, though tragedy and responsibility have tempered him. Maybe he would rise to rule a country that would welcome the power of an Immortal. They forget their legends. He might give them what they write of, what they dream of, though never suspect is within their reach. Henry and his, Victoria and hers, they'd nearly found their way. Maybe this time.

The sun has long since set on the British Empire. Maybe now the bloodred moon can rise.

I, Count Vlad Dracula, am ready.

Deathlovers

ANGELIQUE DE TERRE

When I first saw Linda Meritt's file, I suspected that she was wasting our time.

Anton had that reaction, too. He had smiled, standing in front of my desk, picking up the folder with his elegant hands. The pose of nonchalance was perfect. It would have fooled me if I hadn't worked here long enough to know that he always just happened to appear within five minutes of a new application hitting the ADMIT basket. Now, as he read, he was frowning.

"You know better than this, Saundra," he said, his accent doing wonderful things to the first syllable. "She is twenty-three. How likely is it that she will stay with us to the end?"

I knew what he meant. Almost always, when young people come in and file death papers, it's a gesture. They're trying to throw a scare into somebody. During the three-day waiting period, the notice goes out to "interested parties and the general public" as required by law, and the applicant is hoping some particular person, usually a parent or a lover, will intervene, stop them from having themselves done in. If nobody does, they'll take themselves out of the process, either during cleansing or in the first few days of the feeding. Anton doesn't like to see young people come in here. He's been burned too often. If it were up to him, we wouldn't take applications from anybody under forty-five.

"It doesn't matter," I replied. "The law requires that we

refrain from discrimination on the basis of age, sex, race, or any other protected category." He looked at me with his lips set in a flat line. "Besides, I don't think she's all that bad a risk. Keep reading."

He lowered his head while keeping his eyes on mine, then abruptly shifted them down to the page. It's one of his little mannerisms, slightly unnerving, slightly fascinating. I don't know whether it's natural or deliberate.

"She is not a bankrupt," he observed as he read. "She is not an intellectual." That's the Kevorkian Classic: brain-proud individuals from a family prone to late-life loss of brain function, as the medical profession now terms what we used to call senility. They notice the first signs in them-selves and they want out while people will still remember them as sharp and in control. Linda Meritt was not that type; she did clerical work and had graduated from junior college in the lower half of her class. "She is not a depres-sive."

"She hasn't been diagnosed as a depressive," I corrected him. "But let me point out a feature or two from the bio. Her parents were legally married, but only briefly. Her mother's given her seven—count 'em—seven stepfathers since then, including the current one, with whom Mama's down in Florida running a seniors' resort. The notice didn't raise a peep out of any of them. Mama also has a history of admissions to alcohol detox programs that goes back before Linda's birth. This kind of background doesn't inevitably produce depressives, but it sure does up the odds. For her father's address, she put 'unknown.' She didn't know where he was. I would guess he's been out of the picture for a long time."

"So," he interrupted, "has he been located? Has he re-ceived his notice?"

"Come on, boss. You know Devi found him or the appli-cation would never have gotten this far." Devi is our re-search department. She's very thorough. "We notified him in his fishing cabin in Wisconsin. We notified her half brother in the air force, which takes care of the immediate relatives. None of them are local. This is not a tight-knit family. We notified her most recent ex-lover, whom she hasn't seen since school days. None of them have called even out of curiosity. No children, no pets, she didn't list any close friends. Under hobbies-and-avocations she put 'reading and watching videos.' She's in an entry-grade job at Hancock Health and Pension. One thing I know about entry-grade jobs at big insurance firms: If a person's any good they get promoted out of it in six months. She's been there two years."

"But she is not bad enough to fire," he finished. "You still have not persuaded me that she is not simply bored and seeking to create some excitement among people she fancies are neglecting her. If she were a depressive, why would she not have been diagnosed?"

"Because she can't afford treatment on her own and she's never performed badly enough, in school or at work, to trigger third-party intervention. Therapy isn't so easy to come by in the age of managed care as it used to be. It's not enough to be miserable. You have to mess up, inconvenience somebody with some power, and she hasn't." He still looked skeptical. I reached for the folder. "Look," I said as I slipped my hand in the back of it and came up with her picture.

That clinched it for him, same as it had for me. Not just the lumpy features. Plenty of people who don't have looks on their side still manage to enjoy life. Linda didn't appear to be doing that. The expression in the eyes was too old for twenty-three, and too tired. I saw his forehead relax as he looked at it, though his mouth remained in a frown. He didn't want to admit he'd been convinced this easily. He turned a page, read down it for another moment, then smiled.

"I owe a great deal to novelists," he said, closing the folder. "Very well. Admit her. She will be . . . an interesting change."

I knew what had got that reaction out of him. As her reason for applying, she'd entered a quotation from a Saint-

Germain novel: "I would like to know, just once, what it is like to be loved."

That's the lure, of course, the thing that makes Anton better than thirty Darvon and a fifth of vodka. When a vampire feeds repeatedly and exclusively from one person, the resultant emotional state for both parties is exactly (I've been told) like intense, obsessive, mutual romantic love. Let him finish you off and you will die happy. Guaranteed.

The rest of the file looked good, nothing to object to, so I initialed her into the cleansing program. She arrived the following Friday with an unusually small amount of luggage. We encourage people to bring every possession they might possibly want during their stay, since the idea is to keep them happy. Most of them take us at our word. I remember one man who had a four-poster bed brought in. But Ms. Meritt had only two suitcases and her purse. It was as if she'd packed for an ordinary trip.

I met her at the door, introduced myself, and got her settled. She was more or less what her file suggested: average size, working-class voice and manner, clothes too cheap to get respect and too drab to be any fun. She didn't mind if I called her Linda. She thought everything about her suite was fine. She had no objections to the schedule I showed her. Her attitude was more peaceful than her file had suggested, a phenomenon I had seen before. Once the decision is made, they seem to relax.

The first week of the cleansing is like time at a good health spa: green vegetables and mineral water, sweat baths, body work and breathing exercises. She didn't complain when the high-fiber diet gave her the runs, and she submitted to the body work in a tractable, complacent way, showing no discomfort even with procedures that most people find uncomfortable. I began to see why no one had noticed that anything was wrong with this woman. Outwardly, she was a complete stoic.

The second week is buildup. We gradually introduce more protein into the diet, more naturally oil-bearing foods, blood builders and toners. Toward the end of this period,

Anton begins looking in when the client is asleep, to check readiness. By that time, he's getting eager, bored with his occasionals, knowing what's coming. He judged Linda ready on the fifteenth night of her stay, and on the sixteenth he went in.

I didn't have to watch on the monitor to know how he was coming on to her. Old World charm, kissing her hand, the accent. He works on his accent. If he didn't, he would have lost it years ago. Most of all, he'd be using his obvious fascination with her. That is absolutely sincere every time, with every client. The scent of high-quality blood (and hers is very high quality by now) triggers emotional attachment in him. He really was falling in love with her, and there's nothing like love offered to stimulate love in return. He'd have his first feeding within half an hour of meeting her, and from then on nothing but daylight would separate them.

About eleven-thirty he buzzed me and ordered the midnight snack that I'd had waiting: eggs Florentine made with fresh spinach and English muffins baked that day. From now on it was gourmet luxuries at every meal. I doubted she'd ever had such food in her life. When I brought it in, he was ebullient, full of praise for my every move: the euphoria of the early stage. As for Linda, her face was transformed. I had a feeling it was the first time I'd seen her face, reflecting her genuine emotions, instead of the stoic mask she had presented up until then. It was going well. A couple of hours later, after he moved her into the bedroom, I came in quietly and cleared the dishes away.

The next afternoon, as soon as she was awake, I brought her a cafe latte in bed. The transformation was holding. Always before she'd had to put her robe on and brush her hair before she would let herself be seen. This time she said "Come in" as soon as I knocked, and didn't budge from bed, just let me arrange the pillows for her so she could slide up into a sitting position. She took a sip of her latte and leaned back into the pillows with that lazy well-fed-from smile familiar to me from other clients.

"It's true what they say," she remarked. "This is definitely the way to go." Not a controversial statement, it was still the first time since her arrival that she'd volunteered an opinion about anything. I looked at her face, lit by love and contented with good care, and it was as if I saw another person, one who could have been a friend of mine if things had been different. Maybe that's why I broke one of my own little rules. I sat down on the bed.

"Mind if I ask you a personal question?" I asked. She shook her head, so I went on. "Why?"

"Oh, come on. You have to know. I mean, don't you? Working here, being around him every day, you let him feed sometimes, right?"

It was my turn to shake my head. "Vampires don't like diabetics. Our blood's no good to them. That's why I can work here. But that's not what I meant, anyway. If you just wanted to experience a feeding, you could have come in here as an occasional, and gone home afterward. Why death? Why this program? It can't be my cooking." She laughed, a sweet, open, relaxed sound that I wouldn't have thought she had in her. Then she thought seriously for a moment before she answered.

"I guess it's so I don't have to take responsibility for it afterward. Does that make sense?" It did. An experience of joy would make her old life intolerable to her, and there was no new life beckoning. A less passive person could have made a new life, but Linda Meritt was not that person. She couldn't pay the price of joy, so by letting go of life she skipped out on the payment.

"You probably look to the world like a responsible person. You show up for work every day. You're always on time with the rent. Right? Little do they know . . ."

"Little do they know," she agreed, with more laughter in her voice. The idea of being a truant appealed to this obedient stoic. I told her to buzz when she was ready for breakfast and went out.

That was the last conversation I had with her. She went very rapidly into the next stage: total emeshment with him.

She was no longer really aware of me, or of Val when she came on for the early shift. He was only slightly more aware. He remembered that he could call in food or order a bath drawn or whatever, but he didn't look at us anymore, or thank us. Obsessive love is like that. I saw that even before she began to weaken much, he was bathing her and feeding her like a child. There's something basically infantile about the passive personality, and Anton is good at uncovering clients' unspoken wants.

She weakened eventually, though. Anton is not a heavy feeder, and there were all kinds of things in the food to keep her going as long as possible, but nobody can support a vampire for more than a couple of weeks. As they went into the final stage, where she couldn't walk without support, the atmosphere around them developed a melancholy flavor which did not, from what I could tell, reduce the pleasure for either of them. She was dying, and it made them sad, but it also made every moment sweeter and more precious. Actually it wasn't inevitable. At any moment she could have changed her mind, asked to be taken to a hospital, and probably been saved. But very few clients who get this far will choose to do that, and by now I was sure Linda wasn't going to be one of them.

The end came an hour before dawn on the twenty-sixth day of her stay. Anton can tell by the sound of the heartbeat when a client is too weak to survive another feeding. He buzzed Val, who woke me and then left me to get everything ready while she went to get the notary. The law requires three witnesses including a medical notary, plus an open video line to the public recorder. At that hour it takes no time at all to get an open line.

We all went in together. Linda was in bed, with a sheet pulled up just enough to make her decent. She had marks not only where you'd expect, but just about everywhere there was a blood vessel, and I knew there would be more under the sheet. Her expression was relaxed and happy but not unaware. Anton was beside her, on the bed but not in it, wearing tai chi pants. He backed off. Physical nearness may cast doubt upon how freely the choice was made, and we want to stay absolutely clean, legally. The notary handed her the papers she'd signed the first day and asked her to read one copy out loud. It was short, just a statement of her intention to die, to contract with us to bring about that death, and to free us from any liability in the event of something going wrong. The notary asked if this was still her intention. She said it was and countersigned the papers with date, time, and thumbprint. Then she set aside the clipboard, turned to Anton, and said "Now."

He kissed her on the lips one last time (that's Anton, an artist right up to the end) then reopened his previous holes in the left side of her throat. She said "Mmmm" as if it felt good. (Isn't that just about the ideal last word?) He fed rapidly to make it quick, tensing with the effort as she went limp with loss of consciousness and then, at last, even more perfectly still with the loss of life. Drawing away, he hovered over her a moment, looking troubled and weary. This is the hard part for him. His natural impulse at this point would have been, not to kill her, but to Turn her, to give her fangs of her own. The vampiric reproductive instinct is what drives this whole process. Staying with the contract required him to suppress that instinct by willpower. I've seen him kill probably fifty times by now, and it has not gotten easier for him. But he always does it.

Then he looked at us and said "It is done," and we went into action. The notary started attaching equipment to the body for the legal certification of death. Val got out clothes for it. Anton usually stays to help dress the corpse, which he always handles very tenderly, but this time it was too close to sunrise, so I did it, even though it wasn't my shift. By seven o'clock the physical remains of Linda Meritt were ready for the mortician's people. Val called in a message for them. I showed the notary out.

And then, while Val was still tying up loose ends, I went upstairs and let myself into Anton's rooms. As he lay there in a sleep so deep our ancestors couldn't tell it from death, I kissed him good night. Then I went out.

Anton doesn't miss much, so I think he knows that I do this. As often as he's been a deathlover, I think he likes having his own deathlover around. That's me, with my poisonous sugary blood and my unrequited longing. We've never talked about it, of course. The pretense of a business relationship, even in as strange a business as this, keeps things within bounds. But whenever I've thought about leaving he's gone to a lot of trouble to persuade me to stay. Maybe one reason he's so good with the clients is that he's a little bit like them; knows the attraction of death, the fascination of it.

And if he did decide he wanted it, wanted death after all the years of immortality, wanted me, I don't think I could refuse him, even though I wouldn't like to be walking around in a world that didn't contain him somewhere. Maybe I'd ask him to finish me, too, the way he finishes the clients. We could go together. Maybe I'm as much of a death freak as anybody who comes in here. Fixated on a vampire, what else would I be? I need a vacation. I've been at this too long.

Vermilia

Tanith Lee

He wrote, "She is a vampire. Now I know. I thought I was alone."

He felt the inevitable amalgam. Shock and excitement, jealous resentment, unease.

He would never have said, "The city is mine." How could it be? There must be several others, like himself. But he had never met one, here. Not here. And, otherwise, none for half a century.

They kept to themselves. Like certain of the big cats, they did not live easily together, the vampires. They drew together for sex, sometimes even for love. Then parted, eventually.

And if any were sensed, then generally, they would be avoided—by their own kind.

But now, now he wondered if he had wanted—? The one who said no man was an island was quite wrong. Every man is, every woman is, both prey and predator. Alone.

And she was an island lit by gorgeous lamps, smooth and lustrous in her approach, her hidden depths and heights alive with unknown temptations.

Of course. She was a vampire.

Flirtatiously he wrote, "What now?"

The first time he saw her was across a crowded bar. It was just after sunset, vampire dawn. She had that fresh look a vampire had, waking to the prospect of a pleasant "day." Obviously, there were others who had it, too—certain night workers who enjoyed their jobs. But vampires *loved* their employment. Most of them. The stories of guilt and angst were generally spurious—or poetic.

She moved about the bar, sometimes sitting, crossing and uncrossing her long pale legs in their sheaths of silk. She had black hair with a hint of red, and a bright red dress with a hint of blue, sleeveless and body-clinging, the sort that only a woman with a perfect figure could wear. And her figure was perfect.

The face was something else again—sly and secretive, with elusive eyes. The mouth crayoned the colour of the dress. For this vermilion colour, he coined a name for her almost at once: Vermilia.

She would be pleased, he later thought, once he had seen her at work. Vampires tended to obscure their true names, at least from each other. The invented name he would offer her, like a first gift.

Why she had initially caught his attention he was not so sure. Possibly vampiric telepathy, empathy . . . For there were other attractive women in the bar, even with perfect forms, and faces that were actually beautiful, if only in the synthetic contemporary manner.

Naturally, she did not look like that. She would have appeared as well in a sweeping Renaissance gown, or corseted crinoline.

From involuntary observation, he began to watch her. It was soon apparent she was there to secure company. But, she was selective. She would speak to men, engage their interest—even allowing a couple to buy her a drink—but then she would drift away. Not for a moment did he take her for a hooker. She was not—businesslike. You could see she liked what she was doing. For her, it was foreplay.

That night, himself, he had no rush. He had taken rich sustenance for three consecutive nights, draining his source with civilized slow thoroughness. She had died, happily, in the hour before sunrise. Tonight, then, was a leisurely reconnoitre, no more. He would not need blood again for seventy-two hours at least.

He felt nothing for his prey, or very little. He was seldom rough or cruel—there was seldom any need. To seduce, to entrance, was second nature to his kind. Was he thinking Vermilia might be a worthy successor to the last dish? Probably not. After someone so lovely as the last young woman who had died, he would have preferred a very different type, perhaps even ugly. You did not want always the same flavour.

Besides, he soon began to realize about Vermilia.

She was drinking red wine. It was a human myth that vampires could not eat, or imbibe any fluid save one. They did not need to, certainly, but they could. He himself disliked alcohol, and drank mineral water, but that was his personal taste. He understood also she did not favour red wine because it reminded her of blood. What else was ever like blood?

Finally, she was with a boy, standing right up to the bar now, across from him as he watched her. For a second even, her eyes slid over his face. Did she see him? Sense him, as he had begun to sense her? Maybe not. She was intent on her prey.

The boy—he *was* a boy, though probably forty years of age, arrested in some odd gauche slim adolescence of human immaturity—was fascinated at once. He bought her another wine. Then another.

"Yes," he wrote, "right then I did truly suspect. I was sure she was not a professional. Therefore, and in any case, why fasten on this oddball character, plainly not rich, not handsome, and not wise. A new flavour?"

They were there for about twenty minutes more. He even caught phrases from their conversation. "You do? Wow." And she, "Let me show you. Would you like that?" They were not talking about sex. It was a building, the building where she lived. Some old-style architecture, that had been used in a movie, she said. He did not catch the name of the director or actors in the movie. Conceivably she made it up. He was almost sure by then.

When they left the bar, he left also, sidling out into the hot night, to follow them unseen.

The city was black, jeweled but not lit up by its coruscating terraces of lights. Humanity idled by, skimpily clad, drinking beers and snorting drugs from cones of paper. Police cars shrilled through the canyons, rock music thumped.

They reached the famous building. It rose high above and did look extremely gothic, with some sort of gargoyles leaning out from the fortieth floor.

The foyer was open to anyone, at least to any vampire, dim and shadowed, with carven girls holding up pots of fern, and the doorman watching a TV. Either he waved to Vermilia, or thought he waved to some other woman he knew to reside there. To him, the doorman said, not turning, "Hot night, Mr. Engel."

"It is."

Vermilia did not turn either. She was showing her boy the statues and the cornice, and summoning an elevator.

He got in with them. Vermilia did not glance. The boy looked slightly embarrassed, then forgot, the way a vampire could always make a human forget.

They got off at the fifty-first floor. He rode up to fifty-two. When he came back down the stairs, they were still outside her apartment.

The corridor was dimmer even than the foyer. The doors were wide spaced and no one was there. He stood like an invisible shadow by the stair door, and looked.

"Oh—I forgot my key. Or I lost it."

"Maybe I can pry it open with this—" The credit card twiddled in boyish old fingers.

"Honey," said Vermilia.

It occurred to him she did not live here at all, liked the chancy stuff of doing it right now, in the corridor.

She had her arms round the boy's neck. The boy kissed her, sloppily, the way you would expect. Then she put her face into his neck.

He gave a little squeal.

"Ssh," she said softly. "It's sexy. You'll like it." Then a pause, and then, "Don't you like it?"

"Ye-aah, I guess. . . ."

It did not last long.

As she pulled away, a vermilion thread was on her chin. It might only have been smeared lipstick.

The boy breathed fast. He turned to try to open the door.

She said, "Oh, leave that. Let's go out. I'd rather go out."

"But I thought maybe—"

She was already by the elevator again.

The boy shambled after her, pressing a surprised handkerchief to his bleeding neck. "Hey—you drew blood—"

"Sorry, honey."

The elevator came.

He knew she would lose the boy somewhere in the crowds. He let her go.

He went back to his living space, and wrote about it in the book he kept. He wrote, "She did not relish his blood. She only took a little. Must then have gone looking for someone else."

And then, flirtatiously again, "What now?"

But he knew. He would go after her. As no one else could, he could find her. Hunt her down. Oh, Vermilia . . .

He had never thought of them much as victims, the ones he took. Some he even allowed to recover and forget him. The best, he drained over three, four, five nights, at the end eking it out. There was no other pleasure in the world like it. Sex, the closest, was anaemic beside it. He would never have tried to describe the delight, the power and the glory. There were no words in any language, or from any time.

The night after he saw Vermilia in the bar, he took a girl off the sidewalk near the park. Perhaps it was Vermilia's fault, in some incoherent way. He did not control himself, and drained the girl, among the trees. Her passage from slight surprise to thrill to ecstasy to delirium and oblivion was encompassed in two hours. Because he had been incautious, he had then to obscure her death, to cut her throat—almost bloodless—and roll her down the 3 A.M. slope into the kids' wading pool. One more puzzle for all those whirling car-bound cops.

The next night he began the hunt.

He was very perplexed not to find her at once, Vermilia.

But the reason he did not was very stupid. He had never thought she would return instantly to the bar, and do exactly the same there as before.

When she left with her new beau, a muscled moron, he let her have him. Did not even bother to go in the building with them—the same building.

Presently, about half an hour after, the moron came plunging out, looking both smug and unnerved.

He went up to him. "Say, are you OK, son?"

"Sure, sure—some weird babe."

"You gotta be careful."

"Yeah, old man, I guess you do."

He knew that the moron, who had a surgical dressing now on his thick neck, saw him as some cobwebby, bent old guy, leaning on a cane.

The moron swaggered off, proud of his youth. She must have let him have some sex, in payment. Perhaps the blood had been good, he looked strong. But it was not always that way; sometimes the puny ones had the nicest taste.

He went in, and the doorman, watching TV, called out, "Mind the floor, Mr. Korowitcz. Woman spilled the wash bucket, still damp."

The elevator took him up to fifty-one, and he walked along to her door. Presumably it was her door. Of course, she might have taken the stairs, as he had last time. But why would she? Unless she had seen him—there was always that.

He tried the door.

He was thinking, she might assume it was the moron back, angry maybe, or just wanting another helping.

Or she merely might not answer.

Then the door opened.

She looked right up at him in a cool still amazement that made him aware she had, somehow, not sensed him at all, not properly *seen* him, until that moment.

Later, he wrote, "Should I have been more careful? I? I was innocent after all, worse than the 'boy' in the bar. How could I guess?"

She said, "Who are you?"

"A . . . kindred spirit."

"Really?"

She looked glad enough to have him there. But that was usual. To the one he focused on, he was everything, a prince among men. With his own kind, it was not quite the same. Even so. He was all her conquests had not been, and more. What struck him was that she did not seem at all wary. No, she was inviting—if not exactly yielding.

"May I come in?"

She laughed. "I see. I have to ask you over the threshold."

"I think you know better than that."

"Do I?"

"We," he said, peremptorily, "decide. Asked or not."

"My." She pivoted. "Come on in, then."

As he passed her, she ran her hand lightly along his arm. Even through the summer jacket, he felt the life of her.

The apartment was in keeping with its grand façade and foyer, and just as dimly lit. What startled him was its total ambience of cliché. Velvet draperies hung, and tall white candles burned, dark perfumes wafted, Byzantine chant murmured, stained glass obscured the windows. There were no mirrors he could see. This room was exactly what *humans* expected a vampire's apartment to be. Yes, even to the skull on the real marble mantel, the ancient dusty books, and the chess-set in ivory and ebony standing ornately to one side.

He had never come across, on the rare occasions that he met them, any vampire who lived like this, and he himself certainly did not. His room was inexpensive and plain, without curios. Without, really, anything.

She had a piano, too.

Now she walked over to it, and ran her fingers over the keys, clashing with the chanting. He could tell from the way she did that, too, she could not play the thing at all. Show, then. Just for show.

"Like a drink?" she said. "Or am I being forward?" And she snapped her teeth.

He smiled. Grimly. Her vulgarity—he would have preferred to leave. But something—herself, obviously—held him there.

A drink . . . She was perverse, kinky, a freak. Vampires did sometimes like such games together. He, too, had done so, long, long ago. Acting prey–predator, drinking each other's blood. It could be amusing, as a novelty. But that was all it was. She, though, he could tell from some infinitesimal quivering in her, found the idea a turn-on.

Was it just possible she did not believe he was what he was—one of her own kind?

He walked over to the sofa and sat down, sinking miles deep. She moved about him, round the room, prowling like a cat, and now, to his disgust, lit some sort of incense. She must be very young. She looked about twenty-five—maybe less than a hundred, then. For vampires, though immortal, did age, in their own way. No sags or wrinkles, but something in the line of the bones, the way they *were*.

"But tell me about yourself," she coyly said.

And she came and sat down beside him, leaning back a little, displaying herself, her eyes gleaming now, yet still elusive—*reflective,* like the mirrors she did not have.

"Nothing to tell," he said. "You know that. Our lives are all very much the same."

"Why are you here?" she asked.

He looked at her. Why was he?

"You," he said.

"I've put my spell on you. I did that the other night, didn't I? Across the bar. I thought, my oh my."

"Did you?"

"Yes. I bet you spied on me with Puddie."

"With whom?"

"Puddie. That guy."

"Which one?"

She smiled, and her teeth glinted. He could see their sharpness. She was not being careful. Of course, with him, that would be a futile precaution.

"You know what I do. And I know what you do," she said. "Come on, let's do it."

"You want that with me?"

"You bet I do. Oh, yes. So much."

He did not want to drink from her. Later, he wrote, "I wanted nothing less than her blood. That was my fatal mistake. But she had—as she said so naively, fooling me further—cast a spell on me of some sort. And for me, Vermilia was the first of my kind for all that time."

He lay back, almost bored. "Ladies first."

"Oh, how sweet. Yes, then."

As she leaned over him, he had—he afterwards told himself—a premonition. But he was too indolent to heed it.

She smelled wonderful, too, new scents: fresh-baked bread and fresh-cut melon, and this perfume, and the incense smoke which had caught in her hair.

Her bite was clumsy. She hurt him and he swore.

Why put up with this? He was thinking, he would give her one minute.

He wrote, "Suddenly something happened to me. Unprepared—how could I be otherwise—I was flooded, overwhelmed. The—no other word is legitimate—*rapture*."

He did not, writing, compare it at all to sex. But again, probably, that was the nearest comparable thing. The tingling, surging, racing— And presently, the pleasure-gallop exploded as if it hit some crystal ceiling of the brain—a kind of orgasm. He blacked out.

When he came to, which, that first time, was only a few seconds later, she was sitting back, looking at him, licking her lips.

"Sorry I hurt you," she said. "I need them sharpened again. The teeth, I mean. But my little Chinese guy, who does it for me—he's off someplace. He's a great dentist, too."

He was thinking, *Is that what they feel, when I*—dizzy and wondering, when she put her hand up to her lips. She slipped the two eyeteeth out of her mouth. They were removable caps. Her own teeth—were blunt, ordinary.

"Did you like that, honey?" she asked, needlessly. "I'll make some coffee."

While she was gone, somehow he found the strength to get up and get out of the apartment.

In the elevator, he almost passed out a second time.

As he wandered across the foyer, the doorman said, "You don't look too good, Mr. O'Connor."

He thought doubtless he did not.

Having no intention of going back, the next night he hunted among the bars many blocks away from the Gothic building.

He took three women, and each time found he had killed them, which was a nuisance in the matter of disposal. The last one he did not bother to hide, leaving her among the trash cans in an alley. Despite the excess of blood, he felt enervated, and depressed.

The following night he overslept, waking two hours before midnight. This was not unheard of for a vampire. But it was rare.

Vermilia.

He found himself in some nightclub, sipping a mineral water that cost seven dollars, saying her name in his head—the name he had given her.

He kept thinking about what had happened to him, with her. He was pretty sure he had also dreamed of it. Again, vampires did dream. But not much.

He wrote, "I am like some little virgin bride after her first night. I infuriate myself."

He discovered that now, when he took the blood from his

prey, he did not enjoy it so much. At first, desperate for the blood, he had not noticed.

Did he, then, want the blood of Vermilia? Somehow, that thought revolted him. Almost made him, in fact, retch. Why was that? The blood of another vampire could not properly nourish. But, it was not repulsive, or poisonous—

He thought of her leaning to him, and piercing his throat with the peculiar caps she needed because somehow her teeth had grown deformed and useless. He thought of the rhythm beginning, and his head went round.

He bought a bottle of Jack Daniel's. Drank some. Threw up.

The next night, he threw up the blood he had taken from his prey. Twice.

He lay in the dark of his bare room, cursing her.

What was it? What had happened to him? A human might have feared some disease, but he, a vampire, was immune to such diseases. And she, a vampire, would not carry any disease.

The *next* night, he went to the Gothic building. And in the foyer the TV-doorman turned morosely and said, "Hey, bud, who the hell are you?"

He stood there, made stupid. Never before had he been seen like this, when he had not meant to be.

He mumbled, "Number fifty-one. The lady."

"Oh, who's that?"

Who indeed.

"She knows me."

"OK, bud. No funny stuff. Get outta here."

He walked out, and there was Vermilia, like in the best movie, dawdling towards him up the street. She wore black tonight, but her mouth was still the proper colour.

"Honey!" she cried. She ran and hugged him. "You look beat."

They walked by the doorman, who now seemed to see neither of them.

In the elevator she jabbered about some idiotic thing, he did not grasp what she said. Why was he here—with her?

In the apartment, she lit the candles, the incense. He stood coughing and trembling.

"Like a beer?"

"I'd like you to do what you did last time."

"Oh, sure. But let's get in the mood."

He fell down on the sofa. She caressed him. He writhed with need and dragged her mouth to his neck. "Do it. For God's sake—"

She did it.

It was the same as before. Ecstasy, racing, explosion. Out.

This time he was unconscious for an hour. She said so anyway, shaking him. "Come on. You always fall asleep. If you weren't so beautiful . . . I need my bed. I have to be at work in the mornings."

New stupefaction hit him only as he reeled towards the elevator. Mornings?

Three more times he went to her. Between, he was able to take a little blood, here and there. It was no longer easy to do this. Partly because he did not properly want it, and, besides, sometimes got sick when he had taken it. Also partly because his ability to seduce seemed strangely less. In the past, he had needed only to look, perhaps to touch or speak. That was enough. Even at the moment of impact, if there was a struggle, his great strength could subdue at once, but, more likely he could still them with a brushing of his lips, a whisper.

Now some of the prey got cold feet. Some fought with him.

And he did not have the energy to pursue these ones. And anyway, he knew, he was losing it. Losing it all.

He thought he had said to her, the third time, "What have you done to me, what *are* you?"

And she had said, "I'm a vampire, honey. Just like you. Only you just like to play it one way, don't you? But that's fine by me. I like it best this way. Sometimes."

More than the terrifying pleasure, it was something else that brought him back, and back. The spell. But what *was* the spell?

"How old are you?" he said.

"You're no gentleman," she said. Then she said, "Oh, hundreds of years, of course." She lied. He knew she lied.

It was worse than that. She was losing interest in him. She had by now told the doorman to let him up, but when he was with her, now, she said, "You might do something for *me*."

What was she talking about? Exhausted, he closed his eyes. Exhausted, he begged her to do what she did.

That time, when he came around, he knew she was killing him.

It had to stop.

But he was hooked.

"OK," she said. "Come tomorrow. I may have a friend here. You'll like her."

"Will you—?"

"Yes. Go on now. It's so late. You were asleep for *four* hours and I couldn't wake you."

"You have work in the morning," he drearily remarked.

"Sure do. My stinking job."

"But the sun," he said.

"Oh, get out of here," she said, laughing and impatient.

Outside—he leaned on her door and then he began to see. Swimming down in the nauseating elevator, he saw more.

The doorman glared. "Hey, you on drugs or something, mister?"

He got to his bare room and lay down.

Tomorrow night. He would go. He could not help himself. No one could help him. But he thought now he understood. And tomorrow, before he left, he would write it in his book. In case, in the future, to some other this same thing might happen, as well it might.

As well it might.

"This is Raven," she said.

Raven had long black hair and a face made up white as a

clown's. At the corner of her mouth she had painted a ruby drop, but her lipstick was black.

"My," said Raven, and she curtseyed to him, leering. But Raven was the same as Vermilia—the same kind and species.

Tonight it was to be different, Vermilia said. They would take off all their clothes. They took them off.

He stared at their bodies, Vermilia's perfect, Raven's not, both irrelevant.

In turn they ogled him.

Then they all lay down on the wide sofa. The girls drank wine, and tongued him, and all he could smell was hair and flesh and perfume and wine, and all he wanted was for them to have his blood, and he knew this time would be the last, and he cursed himself and them and the world and all his hundreds of years that had not saved him. Consumed with fear, he shook with desire.

"He likes to be the subserve," said Vermilia. He hated her accent. Hated her. "Go on, Rave, he'll like it."

Raven picked up his wrist. She sank in her teeth, also caps, he supposed. The pain was horrible. He wished he could kill her. Then, it began, even so, began—

And Vermilia's lips were on his neck, and then the bite, sharper, better—her dentist must be back in town.

Like an express train, a locomotive of fire, the surge rose up in him. He forgot he would die. Forgot he had been alive.

The fireworks erupted through gold to red and white, and to vermilion.

As his brain and heart burst, he screamed for joy.

Leaving him, Raven and Vermilia, whose true name was Sheila—but who called herself, on such nights, Flamea, which he had never bothered to learn—turned to each other.

When they were through, they got up. "He sleeps for hours."

"He's great-looking. But what a drag."

They left him, and went to get some chocolate cake.

While they were in the kitchen, since he had died and

was a vampire, he disintegrated quickly and completely to
the finest white dust, which presently blew off through the
air, coating the apartment lightly, and making Sheila-
Flamea sneeze for days.

Some human myths of vampires were true.

When the girls came back, they commented on his absence, and that he had rudely got up and gone.

"But look, he left his clothes."

They raised their brows and shrugged.

Earlier, he had written in his book:

> *I know now. She is no vampire. She is a human. A
> woman playing at being a vampire. This is how she has
> her fun. Pretending she is our kind. Acting it out.*
>
> *But why it should do this to me, I have no notion. Per-
> haps it is only me, but such a scenario may affect others
> of my kind in the same fashion, and to them I leave this
> warning.*
>
> *We have taken the blood of humans all these millen-
> nia. Now, unknowing, they are prepared to take ours—by
> accident, thinking we are the same as they—or not rec-
> ognizing us—or not thinking there is any difference be-
> tween us and them. And when they do take our
> blood—this may be the result. I have no answer as to
> why. I have no resistance to it. Perhaps it has evolved,
> this power, naturally. Like some virus or germ. Perhaps
> this is now their natural means of protecting themselves
> against us.*

His last lines were these:

"Her kind have always killed my kind. That used to be
with stakes and garlic, honed swords, sunlight and fire.
Now, is it this way? Her kind kills my kind with . . . kindness."

In the Market for Souls

MIKE WATT

I was right on time, but I didn't have to be: he'd have waited. Just as he had been waiting, hunkered down in the alley, in the dark. He'd've waited till the sun came up and blasted him into ashes, he didn't know any better. But I came and spared him, saved his life, if you could honestly call it that.

As soon as I had one foot in the alley, he was on me. Rushed up, shaking, his eyes wide and shining in the dark.

"You got it, man? Right?" he asked, desperation spilling from his mouth. "You got it?"

"Course I got it. Wouldn't be here if I didn't."

I opened my hand and showed him the two capped syringes. He made for them, but my fingers were faster and they closed around the tubes, hiding them from view. "What you got for me?"

His tongue lolled out. Wondered if I could be played. I could see it on his face. He was hungry enough, no doubt about it, but he hadn't been a 'breed that long, which is exactly why he needed me. The tongue licked at the new and sharp white canines. Then he pulled his lips over his teeth in a grimace, and his hand jammed into his pocket, coming out with a wad of crumpled bills, and thrust the wad at me.

It was enough, barely. I took the ball of cash and gave him what he needed. He wasted no time, ripping the cap off one and plunging the needle into his neck, a look of re-

lieved ecstasy washing over his white dead face. Yanking
the needle with one hand, the thumb fumbled to uncap the
other. The cap shot off, he hurled the empty tube into the
darkness and made to plunge number two.

"No business of mine," I said as I was leaving. "But I'd
save some. Price goes up next week."

He shot me a pained look like I'd just run over his dog,
full of anger and misery. "No way! You can't do that!"

"Got to." I spread my hands wide in a typical gesture of
"What can I do?" "Folks been noticing here and there. Heat
may be on. Ain't a public service, 'breed."

Panting, tongue licking out like a snake, he was going
into a panic. "How much?"

I shook my head. "Don't know yet. I'll get the word out
soon as I do."

"You prick," he said, getting shakily to his feet. He had
some blood in him now, felt stronger, healthier, like he was
human again. "I should just tear you up, get it over with."

I nodded. "Yeah, that would solve your problems." I
turned and stared him down. One syringe gave him the
strength to do me, yeah, but he didn't have it in him yet.
Which is why we had the perfect business relationship.
"You weren't so kill-shy in the first place, wouldn't be in
this mess. Learn some fuckin' survival instincts, junior, or
get used to the dark and get used to me."

He didn't like that. Didn't think he would. He growled
and faded back a bit, into the dark where I couldn't see him
well; then he lunged, his hands coming into the dim streetlight first. But I had my own hand up before he closed the
gap. Crosses and holy water and all that movie shit works
on these idiots only if you believe in it. Human faith. They
lost theirs at rebirth. I don't believe in any of that shit, personally, so I held up my own talisman, giving him a quick
burn on the forehead, making him yelp and jump back.
Holding his hand up to the smoking patch of flesh, his
growl was gone, but he was still glaring at me. I smiled—
didn't even singe the ten-spot I burned him with. Everyone
has their own gods.

I jammed my ten back into my pocket, shot him a look of disgust and pity for good measure and turned my back on him, just to show him what I really thought of him. "See you next week, 'breed. Do me a favor and pass the word around."

He didn't like that either, but what could he really do about it?

Vampires are a lot cooler in the movies. They're smoother, better looking, dress better, scarier. Even the punks in these new movies have more style than the 'breeds I deal with every night. These rotting, stinking morons who still think they're human, still think they feel human. Afraid to kill or even feed on live blood. Can't go out in the sun, think they should be afraid of garlic, for Christ's sake? What is that? It's like a human afraid of his own shadow 'cause someone told him it could hurt him. These 'breeds don't even know how to be what they are. Too scared to go sunbathing and get it over with.

Who knows how they got like that. Million different stories. Sloppiness by the 'bloods that made them, most like. Doesn't matter. As long as they can pay for the blood, I don't care if they evolve or die come morning. Once the money's in my hand, it ain't my worry.

I was telling the truth before, about the price jack-up. Buddy of mine's a paramedic, gets me what I need by siphoning some off his riders. Rest I can get through work, if I really need it. I get it from work, I can't charge as much. I'm a day morgue worker. My job to empty the corpses of their own fluid and pump them up with the embalming kind. 'Breeds like blood from lifers; dead blood's too stale for 'em, but generally, they'll take what they can get. Risks are different in this case. I don't worry about getting caught 'cause it's all refuse anyway. It's a haz-mat thing, but I'm reasonably sure anyone saw me'd look the other way. Even if they didn't, it's no big deal, really. Just you can't always know what's *in* the blood this way. 'Breeds who haven't killed yet are still susceptible to human diseases. Overly so, in some cases. No immunity yet. But then again, there ain't many who care, either. They know the risks. Hunt or get it from me. Only choices.

Dane and Cobalt caught up to me in the bar. I needed a few before I went home, and midway through my second, they came right up behind me. They looked as pissed off and self-righteous as usual. I think they figured out I'd been avoiding them and their little lectures.

Dane was a huge black guy—or 'blood, or whatever you want to call him when he ain't around. Mean-looking, but slow to bare the fangs. Cobalt used to be a hot club chick, and still was, in a lot of ways. Eternally sixteen, hair dyed "black number one," leather and chains and silver over cleavage. I liked looking at her, even when she was giving me shit, which was every time I saw her.

"Stivic—," Dane started, a deep growl of social conscience.

"I know, Dane," I said, not looking up from my beer. I could see them in the mirror. They weren't pulling their tricks tonight, not in a crowded lifer bar.

"You know, but you persist," he went on. I coulda mouthed it with him. First time I crossed with Dane, I thought he was trying to shake me down for a cut, like a pimp for 'breeds. But it was worse: a neighborhood watch, helping the 'breeds off the streets with tough love and all that feel-good lifer shit. Dane and Cobalt were new gen' 'bloods, wanted to teach the 'breeds to hunt for themselves. Teach them the gentle art of what they called "tapping"— getting lifer blood without making more 'breeds. Population control. Safe feeding. Social responsibility. And I'm the scum of the Earth.

"They don't buy from me, they buy from Willy, or Little Bob." There weren't many of us, obviously, but it was more than just me raping and pillaging out there.

"Willy's dead." That came from Cobalt. First time she spoke since they came in. I stopped, midswig, and turned around to look at her. She was easy on the eyes, but I wasn't sight-seeing just then.

"What happened to Willy?"

"Barlow and 'Sil," she said. "And Savin. And that whole group. They decided they didn't want him around anymore."

"Unanimous vote," Dane said. "They're cleaning up the nights."

I felt a little cold. Willy was a goofball, but he was all right. *Had been,* anyway. Barlow and that bunch were mean. Old school 'bloods. Top of the line hunters. Used to do it for fun before they got civilized.

"Doing this is serious, Stivic. Cobalt and I can't protect you anymore."

"I wasn't aware you two were my guardian angels."

"Only thing keeping you above ground is you haven't passed any bad blood lately."

"Hey, my stuff's clean. Quality, man. I even siphon off myself from time to time, rather than give tainted shit."

"Yeah, you're a prince," Cobalt said.

"You want to keep pushing, that's your business," Dane said. "You got no one to answer to now, Stivic. You are now without a net."

And then they were gone. 'Bloods are fast when they want to be. Faster than human sight. They wanted to remind me of that.

Shit. Dane and Cobalt were pains in the ass, but Barlow and that bunch weren't ones to piss off. I knew them by reputation only, never met a one of them. But a few years back, one of their private clubs got raided by some hopped up lifer group who found them somehow. Tore the place up with long bows. They got tore up even worse, though, when they stopped to reload. And since then, the unspoken truce 'bloods have with lifers has been a bit thin. If Barlow and Savin are cleaning up, then lifers like me gotta toe the line till the heat dies down. 'Bloods don't kill their own, but they'll rip me any day they think I'm trouble.

I don't think I'm trouble, just trying to make a buck is

all. Not that they'd see it that way. I finished my beer and got the hell out of there, just in case I was in high demand that night.

Message on my answering machine wasn't good. I had a big night coming up. Lotta regulars in need of a fix. Fridays are always good for a grand at least, but I was running low on stock. I pressed the flashing button and heard the voice of my buddy, Ron: my supplier and partner.

"Dude, this is Ronny. Listen, I mighta gotten busted tonight. Gotta new partner with high ideals. Might be nothing, just a blow up, but I better lay low, just to make sure. Hope you got enough to hold you a week or two. Later."

Of course. My luck had been going too good for too long. Something had to change. Can't ride a wave forever. But I was low, real low. Almost out of the good stuff. Which meant either I was tomorrow's cow, or I hope for a really good couple of stiffs. And the way things were going, I could see hoping was for suckers.

I don't like needles—I'm a real pussy when it comes to them. The line I gave Dane wasn't bullshit; I've tapped myself a couple of times in the past, when I was just starting out. It hurt, and it took a million tries to find the vein. I don't know how the fuck junkies do it. I almost pass out every time. Most times, I can't do it at all. So I wasn't too fond of the idea of tapping myself to get my big score. I'd have to play tomorrow by ear.

They fished two homeless guys out of the river the previous night. That's all I got. I didn't like the downward course my life was taking.

'Breeds don't scare me; they're weak and sick—they haven't the foggiest freaking idea what they're actually capable of. But without a fix, even the biggest pacifist on the street is bound to get irritable. I told myself they were depending on me, that I was keeping them alive till they learned. But what'd I say before? I ain't the Red Cross. I wanted the money. I've held out before on 'breeds who couldn't pay.

I wanted the money and I'm chickenshit of needles. So I siphoned off the two old bums.

The blood came out thin, watery, more river water and Mad Dog than hemoglobin. It had an odd odor to it I didn't like either. Had a weird color, even for dead blood.

It was shit. I knew it. Took it anyway.

My first 'breed that night took the syringes greedily and I took off before he used them. I'd mixed the dead blood in with the remaining good stuff, shuffled the syringes around so I wouldn't know. Maybe I could make it last a little, or at least, make it look like it wasn't done on purpose. Thin, yeah, I know. But I tried to tap myself. I mean, I *really* tried. Couldn't do it, man. Got sick at the sight. Couldn't get the syringe anywhere near the vein.

So I made haste after every sale, couldn't watch them stick themselves. Didn't know what the bad stuff would do and didn't want to find out. I had twenty-three customers buying two tubes each. I'm supposed to drain myself of all that? Come on.

Halfway through the night, my path doubled back and I stumbled over one of the evening's previous buyers.

He was sitting on the ground, propped up against the side of the building, and had both needles sticking out of his neck. I prayed to God that 'breeds can OD. Take it too fast or too much, whatever. But I knew they couldn't. His eyes were wide open, yellow, staring, still shining in the sliver of streetlight knifing through the dark. Thick black and bloody vomit caked around his mouth and chin, down the front of his shirt. His mouth was open, I could see the four sharp canines poking up beyond the other teeth.

My mind ran through its litany of denials. I didn't force him to take the stuff; he used too much at once. My favorite, my battle cry: He would have just bought from someone else. Whatever. Even if it wasn't the blood, it didn't look good for me. I sucked it up, though, tried putting it out of my mind as I headed for my last sale.

* * *

My last 'breed was a customer named Quick. Ex-lifer gang-banger you wouldn't think would have night-sweats about killing for food. I guess capping someone in a drive-by is easier than drinking a guy's blood.

Quick looked even jumpier than normal when I met him at our usual place. It could have been the flickery fluorescent lighting in the all-night McDonald's restroom, but he looked like complete shit.

"So, what, you're like the grim reaper now?" he demanded, keeping his back to the wall as I closed the door behind me. I played it cool, even as my stomach jumped and I felt my dinner backing up.

"What are you on? You got my money?"

"Fuck no! And stay away from me with that shit. You know you already killed six brothers? You on a killing spree or something?"

"Six!? What are you talking about?" Jesus H. Christ—*six*!

"Passing bad blood, motherfucker! It ain't like we can kick the habit, you son of a bitch! We need that to fucking live!"

I had to keep a grip, keep making like I had no idea what he was talking about. Leveled my gaze, got out the needles, said, "So, you don't want yours tonight?"

"Not that shit!"

I stuck the syringes back in my pocket. "Fine. See you round."

"Hey! Hey, man!"

I stopped, half turned, cool as hell. "Change your mind?" I was pissing myself. Six dead. I was toast. Had to get out of here. Leave for a while.

"I got wise to you, motherfucker. You heard of a bad-ass bitch named 'Sil?"

Dead. I was fucking dead.

"She coming for your ass, shitdick. She gonna get me off your ticket. Take me in. Take you out."

"Good," I said, hoping my voice wasn't shaking as badly as my hands were, jammed into my pockets till they were ripping through the lining. "Maybe she'll give you some brains. Or at least some balls. Make you a 'blood and stop being a pussy." Big words from a corpse.

He just smiled, showing me his teeth. "You goin' down, Stivic. Poisoning 'breeds, must have a death wish."

"It wasn't poison! They couldn't handle it!" I was losing it. He wasn't even listening, climbing up and out the window, shimmying up the slick, stained, broken-tile wall like a tarantula.

"Chew you up, Stivic," he said, almost giggling. "Spit you out."

"They'da bought from someone else," I said for like the fiftieth time that week. "I'm not the only one selling!" I backed against the wall, behind the door, as far as I could from his retreating back, from the open window, now empty of Quick.

"Have a nice night, chump." And he was gone.

I ran over to where he'd been. Jumping as I yelled, to get to the high-set window. "Tell them I never passed bad blood before! This was a bad batch! Quick! It was a mistake, you know me, man! I'll make it all up! Two weeks for free! Quick! Quick!"

Nothing. He'd vanished, and I'd completely lost it. I pressed my cheek against the cold hard tile, squeezed my eyes tight to make it all go away. I was so dead. So stupid. Pissed, scared, frustrated, greedy, stupid. A rage settled over me and before I knew what I was doing, I picked up the plastic trash can and began smashing it against the mirror over the sink, spilling garbage everywhere and yelling "Shit! Fuck!" and variations of the two.

Then some old rent-a-cop heard the noise and came in, hand on the butt of his gun, but I threw down the trash can and bolted past him. Once I got outside, I rounded the corner, got into the dark as fast as I could, forgetting that that was the worst place to hide from 'bloods. I don't even know if I cared just then. Panting, swearing, I ripped the last two syringes out of my pocket and hurled them down the alley as hard as I could, then took off before I heard them land, shatter in the darkness.

It suddenly dawned on me—I don't know why—but I had one last chance. Something Dane told me a long time ago, or maybe something I already knew from dealing with 'breeds and 'bloods these past two years. 'Bloods don't touch 'bloods. Or 'breeds. They don't kill their own, not like lifers. My one way out was to ditch being a lifer. To join up. Get a sponsor, a 'breed I was still down with, offer myself up. Get out of this mess, I was that fucking desperate.

Couldn't be a 'breed, though. Too new at it. Might take too big a bite, or suck too long, then I'd be done anyway. A 'blood, though. A 'blood would do it right. Make me. That'd be my shield. Save my ass. Then I could buy into Dane's crusade, or offer Barlow my services, even. Hell, I knew all the 'breeds, even the ones who hide down deep, hide from everyone. The 'bloods *needed* me to help their reform thing. Everyone knows: Stivic knows every 'breed.

So I took off, ran as hard as I could, checking every lifer club I'd ever seen Dane in. Every little nook where I'd ever run into Cobalt. Went to the places 'bloods liked. All the while, feeling the shadows closing in. Every alley had eyes looking out, watching me. Barlow's little coven, his inquisition.

My paranoia had me in a vise grip. I looked around me, behind me, stumbling over my own feet as I ran, not bothering to chitchat with any lifers who spotted me, oblivious of the fact that there were monsters all around them, every night. Not privy to the information I had. I knew though. Savin could be right above me, floating invisible over my head, keeping right up with my hysterical run. 'Sil, clinging ass-to-the-wall, past my line of sight, watching, waiting to reach out and tear open my throat, spill my blood into the gutter.

Barlow's group were serious 'bloods, doing the comic book parlor tricks. Some of them were centuries old, still knew how to become smoke or a wolf whenever they wanted. Could slide through the cracks of doors the width of a knife blade. They didn't fall for the garlic tricks. The faith thing didn't faze them much. Who cares about what lifers believe when you were around before they were out of the trees?

They were fast. Eye-blink fast. Hit a light switch and cross the room before it got dark. They could be on the ceiling, or in the wind. They were the monsters in the closet. They were all your fears in one box. Shadows with sharp teeth.

I needed Dane. I needed Cobalt. They weren't friends, but they wouldn't offer me up. I needed them to protect me from the monsters.

Finally, I found them. Rather, they found me. Before I knew what was happening—running down Furnace Avenue, heading for the Cellar Club—the wind whistled, cold all around me, and then I was dumped on my ass on a rooftop, looking out over the city and the river, the lights gleaming and twinkling far below me and into the distance. I could see only the two of them: Dane and Cobalt. But I knew they weren't alone. There were others in the darkness of the rooftop, watching us from the shadows, wanting no part of me.

Nobody spoke. Down on the street, life went on. Cars honked; people shouted. Music drifted up from the clubs. But it was still on the roof. I couldn't talk—too freaked out by the seemingly instant trip. They just stared down at me like I was some kind of new bug. Dane's eyes were blank, expressionless, but Cobalt's burned with fury. They both seemed very beautiful and alien to me just then. I realized I was actually looking at them for the first time. The facts became very clear to me, and I gasped out loud as the realization struck home, as if I had just now come out of some drug fog. They were a completely different race of creature, man-shaped. I'd seen the "true-faces" of 'bloods before, but the reality never hit me like this. They were *not* human. They were the most inhuman species you could think of. When I came across a 'breed for the very first time, I didn't think about were they human or not; my only thought was How do I cash in on this? How do I make a buck?

I was still panting, but I turned away from them, from their beautiful frightening faces, and looked down over the edge of the building, seeing the streets so far away, and the city all at once. And then my situation became that much more real. I was having a true moment of clarity here. And I didn't like what I was seeing. "Listen," I gasped, pleading, still on my knees, all ready to beg. "You gotta help me, Dane," I turned and looked up at them. What's the word? Beseechingly. "Cobalt, you know me. I don't pass bad blood. Please, they're coming for me."

"Can't help you, Stivic," Dane said simply and without emotion.

"It was an accident, Dane. I swear to Christ! You gotta believe me. I mean, it was like bad karma, you know? You say I don't pass bad blood, then what happens? I get a bad batch without knowing it, I mean, I didn't *know*, you know? I mean, how could I know?" I was talking fast. Not a grifter rap, but the panicked stream of words. Desperation pouring out.

"It was filth." Cobalt's voice, hard, cold. "You should have staked them out in the sun. It would have been kinder."

"It was bad luck," I insisted, not hearing her. "I didn't know. I didn't mean to hurt them!"

"Don't!" Cobalt spat, bringing her face dangerously close to mine. She seized my lapels and yanked me up on my knees. "Don't even think it! You didn't care about any of them! They were weak, and you wanted their money! You preyed on them! You could have helped them."

I was getting mad, now. I was running out of time and resented having to defend myself. "Hey, Cobalt. Don't lay that trip on me. You should have gotten to them the minute they turned 'breed. I was the only thing keeping them alive."

She started to answer back with a snarl and a closed fist, but Dane stepped in.

"We told you, Stivic, we're through with you. You coulda gone seven different ways with those 'breeds, including staying out of their lives altogether. But you played your sick dealer games and now you gotta pay for them."

He turned away, started to walk towards the shadows. Cobalt dropped me and went to follow. I was on my hands and knees, scrabbling after them. "Look, wait—" I grabbed Dane's hand, begging. "I'll make it right. I swear. Put the bite on me, I'll make up for everything. Everything. Just give me another chance, please. I know them. All the new ones. You'll never find them all. There's too many. They're sick, Dane. Dying. Please, I'm begging you, Dane, please. Make me! Don't let Barlow kill me, please."

He shook me off and kept walking, but I couldn't stop myself. "You don't even have to make me. Just take me in. Just till the heat's off. I'll take you to every 'breed, man. Every one. I'll never deal again. And I'll give back. They can tap me if they need to. Look, look, you can see it, can't you? I'll do anything you want, Dane, just don't leave me to them!"

They stopped and looked down at me like I was nothing. A worm. Then, all of a sudden, we were the *only* ones on that roof. The others, the ones who couldn't be bothered to show themselves to a worthless lifer, they were all gone. I couldn't feel them in the shadows, on the back of my neck. Just the three of us now. I looked up, willing to promise my soul to Dane. "Please," I whispered, too hoarse now to raise my voice.

Then they were gone, too.

I was too scared to cry, too tired to run. My knees gave out and I slumped over, dragged myself the few feet back to the wall, crammed myself into a dark corner of the ledge. Behind me and below me, Barlow and his friends were looking for me. And they'd find me, no matter where I hid, and whether Dane told them where I was or they looked for me themselves. I wasn't even good as food to them. This was a vengeance game. I was marked, a dog to be hunted down. I sat and stared into the shadows and waited.

I didn't have to wait long. I couldn't see them, any more than I could see Dane's companions when they were there. But I knew they were there, and I'd see them soon enough, though I did not want to. They were definitely there, in the shadows, watching me. They'd come for me slow, and hurt me slow.

They were going to have me for dinner and never touch a drop.

Irish Blood

Lyda Morehouse

Some French pasture is the last place I should be doing my dying. It irks me especially to be dying for a foreign king. . . . Ah, still, it seems unavoidable. The shrapnel from the mortar bomb sliced clean through something major in my chest. Blood is everywhere. I can feel its warm, stickiness on the hard ground beneath me. I wouldn't be so worried, except the pain disappeared an hour or more ago. Now, all that's left is a sort of gut-wrenching, floating feeling. Off in the distance, beyond the artillery fire, I can hear some birds singing. Between their twittering and that warm breeze bringing the smell of sweetgrass, a guy could get to feeling peaceful.

Not that I'm going anywhere without a fight. As another wave of nausea ripples through my body, I dig my fists into the frost-lined grass. Hell, I figure I'm holding on to this earthly plane one way or the other. There'll be none of this "may you be in heaven half an hour" crap for old Jack Mc-Cahey. If I'm going, the Devil himself is going to have to carry me away.

The way I've lived my life, I hardly can expect a choir of angels, now, can I? A more likely choice is the flying black horde of the bogie on their thistle brooms. Anyway, from the stories I've heard, the faerie are continually taunting the priests. Not a good track record for the wee folk, I'm afraid. It's the Devil for me, then.

Besides which, I've never been crystal clear what God's opinion is of Republicans. In my da's time, an IRA man could be pretty certain the Lord was on his side, all excepting the partition, of course. When I was a boy, the bad guys wore black and tan. The good guys were always in *green,* if you get my meaning.

Myself, I've been a good Catholic. Well, good enough to attend Mass every Sunday—not good enough to keep from spending my time in the church watching Fiona McCarthy bow her pretty head so fetchingly. That sight, my boys, was far more divine than anything coming out of the side of the mouth of Father O'Rourke. I can see how the wee folk get such pleasure out of teasing the likes of priests. Sure, and half what they say is nonsense. It's not proper Irish faith, at all.

Another wave racks through me, breaking my reverie. My fists grasp uselessly at the crumbling dirt and shriveled grass between my fingers. I moan lowly. I wish I had the strength to curse. It's time for going, but I'm not ready yet.

A shadow blots out the sun. I focus on a tall figure standing over me. Sure, and doesn't it look like the dark angel himself. His eyes strike me most of all. They're a piercing sort of black. I think they stand out so much due to his pale, almost Irish complexion. I smile. I always knew the Devil was Black Irish, like me.

"So, you've come for me, then?" I ask. My voice sounds strange to my ears, like it's coming from a long distance.

"I have." I'm disappointed not to hear a Donegal accent in his words.

He kneels beside me. Those dark, bewitching eyes flick over my wounds. I wonder for a moment if I haven't mistaken him. Perhaps he's a priest or a medic. Truth be told, he looks more like the Devil, with those eyes and that even blacker hair that seems to swallow the sunlight instead of reflecting it.

"I didn't know dying would be such a formal affair," I joke. I gesture at his clothes. He's wearing a tuxedo. It looks to me as though he was on his way to some grand ball, instead of kneeling in the gore of a spent battlefield. "If I'd have known, I'd worn my Sunday best."

"The uniform is more than acceptable." His tone is serious. "It's dress code in most black-tie places, after all."

I get a cold feeling in the pit of my stomach suddenly. "I'd rather not go wearing the British uniform," I find myself protesting. "Could you arrange to hold things off until I get a proper one? I'd rather be wearing the green of Óglaigh na hÉireann. My own sainted da would spit to see me in this."

His lips spread to a tight closed-mouth smile. "You should have thought of that before you got yourself in this pickle, my dear friend. But, it's not in my power to stop the inevitable, just ease your pain."

He opens his mouth, showing off pointed incisors, and draws nearer to me.

"Ah," I say, "I know you now. And, I wouldn't, if I were you."

He pauses to chuckle wickedly. He sneers. "Catholic blood isn't poison to me, fool."

In a swift movement, he plunges his fangs into my neck. The tearing pinprick of pain is brief, and nothing compared to the pounding in my chest. He drinks greedily from me. The wet smacking sounds he makes seem distant. I can see the dark curtain's frayed edges now, fluttering like crow's wings.

He coughs, then sputters. Strangled choking sounds bring me briefly back to awareness. He tries to retch, struggles to rid himself of the poison of my ancient Irish forebearer's blood.

"Not Catholic," I murmur, though I doubt he can hear me. "Fey. I'm half-faerie."

The Note beside the Body

LAWRENCE WATT-EVANS

If you let me in, I'll kill you.

You won't believe that, of course. No one ever does. I'm giving you fair warning, though—if you let me in, I really, truly will kill you. I will tear open your throat and drink your blood, and you will die of it. No, I can't stop myself before the blood loss is fatal; even when I've tried, even when I've struggled with myself so hard that I thought my bones would break and my head explode, even when I've left enough blood that I thought survival was possible, the end has always been death. Perhaps there's some toxin involved, some venom I produce; I don't know, and there's no one I can ask.

And no, you will not rise again, as I did. I don't know the technique of creating more of my kind, nor would I use it if I did. I remember my own rebirth, but I have neither the knowledge nor the desire to re-create it. The creature that made me what I am is gone, long ago; I don't know where or how.

If you let me in, I'll kill you, and you will be dead, dead, dead. Dust to dust, ashes to ashes—whatever lies beyond death, if anything does, you'll know it long before I do.

I imagine you standing there reading this, thinking, "The poor little thing has gone mad." You don't believe in vampires—or if you do, you don't believe that the pitiful waif you met at Ron's party could *be* one.

Believe it. I am a vampire. I am a bloodsucking creature of the night, and when I come to your door tonight, if you let me in, I will kill you.

Think about it—have you ever seen me by daylight? Have you ever looked closely at my teeth? And doesn't it feel unnatural to be so strongly drawn to someone you barely know? Especially a scrawny, pale slip of a girl who can't be older than nineteen, at the most?

But then, even if you accept that I might be what I claim to be, even if you begin to believe that I have existed for 124 years by drinking the blood of the living, you still can't imagine that I would harm *you,* can you? You're a head taller than I am and probably twice my weight, with broad shoulders and solid muscles. You don't fear me; you *can't.* You know the stories say that vampires are inhumanly strong—the strength of three men, or ten, depending which books you read—but I'm so small and frail that you can't see me as a threat.

That makes me all the more dangerous, of course. My victims never believe until it's too late. It's protective coloration, like a tiger's stripes. I can tell you this, and you still won't believe it.

If you let me in, I will kill you. In your last few minutes of life you will finally believe me, finally understand that every word of this letter it true—but it will be too late.

And of course, one reason you won't believe me is that I am writing this letter. If I were truly the heartless, murdering predator I say I am, why would I warn you?

I am a predator, a murderer, yes—but I'm not heartless, or at least I don't think I am. Sometimes, after so long, it's hard to be sure just what's honest emotion and what is merely memory or lingering habit.

I was human once. I loved, and hated, and was caught up in all the everyday concerns of life beneath the sun. I had a brother I adored, but when I had become what I am now I killed him. I was devoted to my father, and I murdered him, as well. I slaughtered my own mother. I loved them all, and yet I drank their blood, sucked the life from their veins, watched them weaken and die, and when the frenzy had passed I screamed with grief each time; I shuddered and wept and flung myself across their bodies.

I don't react quite so emotionally anymore. Anything can grow familiar with repetition, and the pain of knowing I've destroyed what I love has grown less acute.

But the pain is still there. I love you, Jim; I love life, and light, and laughter. I love *people,* love the flash of wit and the charming smile and the comforting arm. I'm alone in the world, and in the end I must always stay alone; what makes it tolerable is the brief encounters, the human contact, the genuine warmth that I find as I hunt.

To destroy a human life is a terrible thing, Jim, and yet I can't help myself. The craving is unbelievable in its intensity; the fiercest hunger you ever felt, the most unbearable yearning, is nothing to it. It builds slowly, very slowly—I feed no more than two or three times a year, and sometimes, when my will is strong, even less. Those tales of vampires striking night after night—nonsense! We're cold-blooded creatures, and a human body holds an amazing amount of blood; just as some snakes will go weeks between meals, we go months.

There's a cycle to it. When I have fed I'm bloated and torpid; I want nothing but to rest, to lie quiet somewhere in the comforting darkness. You'd hardly recognize me as the skinny little girl you know.

But then the torpor passes, and a certain edginess begins—an edge that manifests itself in that elfin smile you remarked upon when we first met. I long for human company—and at first, only for company.

So I find it. I seek it out. And sometimes I tell myself that this time, I will resist; this time, when the urge for companionship begins to turn to a lust for blood, I will force myself to withdraw, to go away, to leave my new friends behind—for, of course, I don't dare return to the same circle of friends after I've killed.

I never resist. I never withdraw. The transition is so subtle that I never notice it until too late. I will suddenly find myself looking upon the people I sought out for their warmth and intelligence not as companions, but as potential prey. Invariably, infallibly, the change occurs and the hunger begins to grow.

I think this is hell, Jim. When I come to realize that it's too late, that I must destroy everything I have been enjoying, that I will kill the one I love best and leave the others shocked and grieving—I think this *must* be hell.

I grow thin, and tense, and take on what one victim described as an erotic glow; I become almost irresistible to men and women alike.

And I choose my prey, Jim, as I chose you.

I fight it as long as I can, but in the end it's always the same—I come to my lover's door and knock, and when I am admitted . . .

Sometimes I lunge immediately. Sometimes I'm able to speak, to hold off, sometimes even to warn. At such times I must sound quite mad—I rave, I weep, I scream as I struggle against the hunger.

The struggle makes the inevitable so much sweeter, Jim. The pumping rush of blood on my lips is always a delight and a release, but when I have resisted it's heightened, infinitely more intense. This is the heaven that I survived hell to experience.

You know, I've never noticed that it matters whether my *prey* has resisted. Vampirism is selfish, to say the least.

Afterwards, when I am alone with a still-cooling corpse, the ecstasy passes and the grief blooms briefly. I flee, aching, swearing that it would be better to die forever than to go through it all again.

But then that passionate regret is smothered by the growing weariness, the torpor; I find somewhere I can hide and rest, and it all begins again.

I cannot stop myself.

But I can warn you. I can give you a chance. I can't fight my nature, but perhaps *you* can.

One part of the vampire legends is true—I cannot enter a home until I have been invited.

Another part, as well—the sun can destroy me.

So when I come to your door at midnight, wearing that silk dress you admire so, with my hunger radiating from me as an almost-visible aura of overheated sensuality, my scent reaching into your heart, don't let me in.

If you let me in, I'll kill you.

If you can keep me outside until dawn, I'll flee, I'll seek shelter from the burning sun, and you'll be able to build defenses, to keep me out. I'll go elsewhere, seek other prey—perhaps little Brandon, or that Ashley we saw at the theater. If I retain enough control, I'll even warn them, as I am warning you. If you can keep me outside until dawn, you'll be safe.

I love you, Jim—I love you for your warmth and your beating heart, for your smile and your rich, deep voice. I don't want to kill you. I want you to live and be free and happy. I don't want to hurt anyone.

That's why I'm warning you. That's why I've warned the others, time after time, for more than a century. I've told them all to keep me out, to forbid me entrance, to hold out until dawn.

How hard can it be? It's not forever; it's just until dawn.

I may beg. I may weep. I may scream with anger, shout bitter threats, tell you I hate you. Don't let me in.

The others did. All of them. They all *died,* Jim, snuffed out to appease my hunger for a few more weeks. No one has ever believed me strongly enough, or loved his own life enough, to keep me out.

Maybe you'll be the first. I hope so. Or part of me does.

Believe this, Jim. Really believe it. Don't let me in.

If you let me in, I'll kill you.

Feeding the Mouth That Bites Us

L. Jagi Lamplighter

The cold winds blew down Fifth Avenue. Hannah shivered but could not find the energy to zip up her coat as she plodded along the sidewalk towards her apartment. It puzzled her that such small actions, such zipping her coat or adjusting her hat, seemed to require such Herculean efforts. It had not used to be that way. Only a year ago, she could recall running across Central Park, laughing as the kite she was trailing behind her became entangled with a bicyclist instead of taking flight. Had it really been only a year ago? . . . Seemed like an eternity.

Hannah blinked quickly, hoping to moisten her eyes, but they remained uncomfortably dry. Her mouth was dry, as well. She would have liked to believe that the winter wind caused this unpleasant sensation, but it had been with her for months now, even in the most balmy weather of the early fall. Her doctor said it was extreme dehydration, for all the good that information did her. He could not come up with a single explanation of why a recently healthy girl like Hannah would suddenly suffer such symptoms.

She had been tested for every popular disease, chronic, contagious, or sexual, and some less popular ones, as well. She drank huge bottles of Evian and popped iron pills like M&M's. Yet, neither the dry eyes, nor the nausea, nor the anemia improved. Recently, she had become so tired, so drained, that she was beginning to contemplate telling her doctor the truth. But, how did one explain to a modern Jewish doctor that your boyfriend was a vampire?

Having a vampire for a boyfriend had its good points. The night life was always interesting, for instance. On the other hand, it also had its downside, such as having to put up with him always necking with other girls. Okay, he called it dining. Furthermore, it gave a whole new meaning to the fear that "he just wanted her for her body."

Some people, she mused, might think her a jerk for allowing someone to suck her blood and then wondering why she felt like shit. Yet, it just did not make sense that the small amount of blood she let Ambroise take could be making her feel so bad. The Red Cross was willing to take a pint every fifty-six days. Hannah gave Ambroise a half a cup every other week, which, over fifty-six days, came to a pint. So, why should she feel so much worse than other donors? It had to be something else that was making her feel so bad; maybe her doctor had missed some important clue.

As she passed Central Park, she wondered if there was still snow on the branches, but could not find the strength for even so simple a task as raising her head. Frightened by her own weakness, Hannah started to cry, only no tears came. Her body was racked by the force of her sobs, but her eyes remained dry. What was happening to her? When had things become so bad?

Ahead a group of nuns handed out bright yellow flyers. The sight of them in their traditional black robes and white wimples calmed Hannah's spirits. She examined them with more interest. Each nun wore a pin, in the shape of a gold cross surrounded by a sun, over her left breast. It was not a denominational logo Hannah recognized, but then she knew very little about Christian denominations.

One of the nuns spotted Hannah, where she leaned against the stone wall separating the park from the busy street, her face in her hands, her shoulders shaking with self-pity. The nun came forward, smiling kindly. Hannah raised her head and revealed her face, dry-eyed with no trace of tears. The nun's smile died. She thrust a yellow flyer into Hannah's hand and muttered something about how help sometimes comes from unexpected places.

Arriving at her apartment, Hannah sat motionlessly in her living room, unable to find the energy to move. Her eyes trailed about the cluttered room. Her cello stood in the corner by the fireplace collecting dust. She had not played it in weeks, maybe months. On her bookshelf, the newest books by three of her favorite authors languished unread. The scarf she had started last summer as a Christmas present for her mother lay on the coffee table, still a pile of knitting needles and yarn. The scarf for Ambroise, however, she had finished. It sat on the mantel wrapped in shiny red paper, awaiting his visit later that week.

It bothered her that they had so little time together. Once every two weeks hardly seemed like enough, and how empty and lonely were the hours that stretched between his visits. Yet, it could not be helped. Apparently foraging for food in this modern age took so much of Ambroise's time, not to mention holding down a night job to pay the rent, that he could spare only one day out of fourteen for himself. Sometimes he could not even spare a whole night and would come just for an hour, before hurrying off to work. During the long hours she spent alone, too morose and tired to do more than stare blindly at the droning television, she sometimes dreamed that a time would come when they moved in together. Then, she could see him every night and guard him during the day while he slept. Sometimes, she even imagined that she might bring home guests, so that he would not need to go out to forage. Though, she often wondered if such dreams were disloyal to the friends and coworkers she pictured in the role of the guests.

She would have felt more comfortable if Ambroise had been more forthcoming about exactly what he did with the rest of his time. She understood his desire to shield her from the more gruesome aspects of his life. Yet, secretly she felt he should have recognized that she was enough of a modern woman to face the graphic truth without flinching . . . or at least she had been before her malaise began. And why did he shy away from certain restaurants or areas of town? She understood why he would not go to the Full Moon Café—the place was wall-to-wall mirrors. But, what did he have against the Golden Bull or Formicidae's?

Yet, when he was with her, all her doubts and fears evaporated. He was so handsome and carefree, with his auburn curls and porcelain skin. When they were alone together, he whispered such sweet caressing words. She recalled his strong arms, his musky smell, his infectious laugh. Sinking deeper into the couch, she contemplated the feel of his hands pinning her down as he bent his head to kiss her bare stomach. Hannah sighed. No other man made her feel so good. How empty her life would be without him.

Ambroise.

She wet her dry lips.

Ambroise.

Half an hour later, she found the strength to make it to the kitchen and open a can of soup. As she sat waiting for the soup to warm, she noticed the yellow flyer lying facedown on the kitchen table. She pushed lackadaisically at it until it flipped over and exposed its print, wondering vaguely what it might be. Most likely, it was an ad for a charity or a church. Hannah did not go to temple very often, but she had no interest in become a Christian. Still, she felt a mild curiosity as to what brand of poison the nuns had been pushing.

The flyer read,

> *Do you suffer from the following symptoms?*
> > *Dry eyes*
> > *Bouts of depression*
> > *Exhaustion*
> > *Anemia*
> > *Back or stomach pains*
> > *Numbness*
> > *Troubling Dreams*
> *If so, there is hope! Come to the Order of Saint George's Clinic*

At the bottom was an address in Westchester, a phone
number, and an e-mail address.

Hannah pushed back her long black hair, which had always been unruly but which was even worse now that she
seldom washed it, and read the flyer again. It listed her
symptoms exactly. Not one at a time, as the medical books
did, but all together—as if their presence was significant in
conjunction with each other! If she suffered from symptoms others suffered as well, then her condition could not
have anything to do with Ambroise after all! With a feeling
of buoyancy she had not felt in months, Hannah rose and
made toast to go with her soup.

It took her three days to get up the energy to actually visit
the clinic. The only reason she finally went was that Ambroise was coming the next day. Hannah lived in fear that
her lethargy might become so overwhelming that she would
be unable to enjoy their time together. Ambroise's biweekly
visits were the high point of her otherwise dreary life. So
far, she had managed to perk up whenever he arrived. As
the effort it took to stir herself to action grew, however, she
began to fear that even his presence would soon fail to
cheer her. If she was no longer fun to be with, would Ambroise stick around?

The clinic was situated in an old church that was connected by a hall of black glass to a stone rectory. Since the
flyer had boasted of night hours, Hannah had considered
waiting for Ambroise and asking him to take her. Now she
was glad she had not. Ambroise would have been out of
there already. He hated walking on holy ground.

Tentatively, she pushed open the heavy oak door and
found herself in a mirrored corridor. Compounded reflection of the hall lamps in the many mirrors produced a dazzling glare of lights. Hannah hurried through the hallway
and escaped with relief into the large sunny waiting room
beyond.

The soft noise of rushing water greeted her. A tall three-
tiered marble fountain stood in the center of the room. As

Hannah entered, a nurse in white nun's robes was filling a pitcher from the fountain waters, which she then poured into a silver samovar that sat on its rolling stand near an inner door. The blue flames heating the samovar were reflected against the silver wallpaper dancing among its gold foil flowers. Hannah, still cold from the street, found a seat near the samovar. However, the lure of the reflected flames proved false. They offered no warmth.

The spicy hot tea and the braided herbs hung about the windows gave the clinic a very pleasant aroma. A small garden, which circled one side of the waiting room, provided additional pungent scents. Mint and Saint-John's-wort grew in the soft dark earth, along with other herbs Hannah did not recognize. Every few feet, a tall wooden cross rose above the greenery.

That the clinic was run by a Christian order was obvious. In addition to crosses in the garden, a golden crucifix topped the fountain, and silver crosses hung on the walls. Crosses also marked the burning candles and the leather golf bags containing croquet sets that sat in every corner. Hannah thought of the simplicity of her synagogue and felt out of place. She wondered bleakly if the nuns would expect her to convert.

As the chill of the outside air left her, Hannah examined the other prospective patients. They sat on the benches sipping tea from delicate china cups or filling out paperwork. Their faces were uniformly drawn and exhausted. Hannah shivered. What ailment did this clinic treat? Did she have it, too? If so, would she end up as bad off as that sunken-eyed man sitting by the hat rack?

In the shiny surface of the wallpaper Hannah could see her reflection. Was that her? So pale and drawn, with such a mop of unkempt hair? What had become of the pretty Jewish American Princess she had been such a short time ago? Hannah thought of her adoring father seeing her like this, so wan, with dark circles under her eyes, and nearly began to cry.

A nun brought Hannah a questionnaire, which she proceeded to fill out immediately. Yes, her eyes and mouth were often dry. Yes, she often found herself crying. Yes, she often suffered from depressing thoughts and troubling dreams. No, she did not use recreational drugs. No, she did not make regular use of opiates or Pepto-Bismol.

The questions comforted her, despite her fear that she might turn out to have some incurable disease. It was reassuring to know that others experienced what she experienced. Especially as, if these symptoms were common to some ailment, it meant her problems had nothing to do with Ambroise.

The next question gave her pause, and her hand stole unconsciously to her neck. "Have you ever noticed a lump or bug bite about the size of quarter? If so, were there two such lumps very close together? Did any numbness or tingling you might have experienced seem to originate from the location of the lumps?"

Hannah glanced around surreptitiously. Previously innocent aspects of the decorum began to take on ominous implications, such as the herbs which she now recognized as braids of garlic, or the polished wood spikes and flatheaded mallets she had taken for croquet sets. Her eyes flew quickly over the walls, but found none of the medical posters usually found in free health clinics. If the Order of Saint George helped the sufferers of an accepted disease, why didn't the name of the illness appear on any of the wall hangings or literature?

Upon finishing her questionnaire, Hannah was led into a private counseling room. It was small and comfortable, with firm leather seats and a wide window looking out on the church grounds. A TV and VCR on a wheeled cart sat in one corner, next to a small refrigerator. On the other side, near the window, was a large oak desk. Behind the desk sat a young man in black with a head of blond curls. He was so youthful that it was not until Hannah took in his calm beneficent expression that she recognized him for a priest.

"Welcome. Come, sit down. I'm Father Joseph," he said

kindly, rising to help her with her chair. Hannah handed him her finished questionnaire, then sat mutely as Father Joseph read it over.

"You wrote here that you have found lumps such as the ones described." He glanced quickly down at the questionnaire. ". . . Hannah. Do you have any now?"

Hannah wanted to lie, but felt obscurely uncomfortable since he was a priest. She really did not know much about priests, except for what appeared in movies. But in movies, people were always confessing their innermost thoughts to them. Reluctantly, she nodded.

"Can you show me?"

Trembling, Hannah stood and unbuttoned the top of her shirt, exposing the bites on her neck. The priest glanced briefly at her throat and nodded. Touching an intercom button on his phone, he called for a nurse. A young nurse in white with a white wimple came bustling in, carrying a silver pitcher, much like the one Hannah had seen when she first arrived. Father Joseph gestured towards Hannah, commanding.

"Hannah, show the nurse."

Hannah did so. The bites were nearly two weeks old and had faded to bruised lumps faintly resembling old mosquito bites. The nurse took a swab of cotton from the pocket of her white smock and dipped it into the pitcher.

"Holy water. From the fountain," the nurse explained brightly. Swabbing the cotton over Hannah's neck, she added, "Hold still—this may sting a bit."

The cool water felt good against the numbness in her shoulder. Then, the burning began. Hannah screamed as molten lead ran through her neck and down her veins. The searing pain rapidly approached her heart. She was going to die, Hannah thought, trying to push the nurse's hand away. Behind her, the priest moved deftly to catch her arms, holding her immobile. As the pain entered her heart, like the heat of a blowtorch, she prayed that her death might be quick.

Then, just as quickly, the pain was gone, and she felt . . .

better. The priest released her, and she stood a moment, ro-
tating her shoulder and lifting her arm. The numbness that
had troubled her for months was gone. As the priest returned to his seat, she gave him a shaky smile.

"Thanks . . . I guess."

The nurse had left. She returned now with a cup of tea.
From the pleasant smell, Hannah recognized it as the tea
from the samovar. She recalled that it, too, had been made
with fountain water.

"I-is it going to burn?" she asked.

The nurse smiled and shook her head. "No, that's all over
now, ma'am." She handed Hannah a bottle of some kind of
vitamins. "You'll be wanting to take one of these every day
for a month. They'll have you feeling better in no time."

"Will . . . will I get better?" Hannah asked. She felt a
sudden stab of hope.

"Most certainly." The priest gave her a reassuring smile.

Hannah sat down, and the nurse left the room. Carefully
at first, she sipped her tea, but it tasted wonderful and produced no strange side affects. Examining the vitamins, she
read the ingredients: Iron, garlic extract, mandrake root,
pennyroyal, wolfsbane, belladonna. And underneath, MADE
WITH HOLY WATER. Hannah shrugged and put the bottle in
her purse. She did not believe that blessing water made it
holy, of course. But, hey, if it worked, why fight it? After
all, this was the first time she had been able to breathe
properly in months!

The priest leaned forward. "From what you say here, I
don't believe it's a serious case. However, I still have some
questions I must ask you. It is very important that you answer as best you can. Your own health and the health of
others depends on your honesty. Please tell me everything
you remember about how you received these marks."

Hannah raised her teacup to hide her blush. "Like what?"

"Do you know what is causing them?"

After a pause, she nodded.

"Can you tell me who it is? A name? A description? An
address?"

Hannah hesitated, afraid. Eventually, she mumbled. "If I tell you, what will you do?"

"Come, I'll show you."

He took her through the old church into the dark glass hallway that connected the church to the rectory. The windows were black, making the corridor dark and gloomy. When they had gone about halfway down the corridor, Father Joseph touched a switch on the wall. Instantly, the glass cleared. The light of day streamed through the windows, and Hannah felt the sun's soothing warmth touch her face.

"This is all we'll do," Father Joseph said. His blue eyes sparkling kindly. "It's not so bad, is it?"

At first, Hannah returned his smile cheerfully. Then, understanding came and she blurted out. "But won't the sunlight kill him?"

The sparkle in Father Joseph's eyes died. "So, you do know."

Back in the counseling room, the priest and Hannah sipped their tea in momentary silence.

"So, you know about vampires," Hannah said finally, breaking the silence. It felt good to have someone she could discuss the subject with, even if the priest was technically a member of "the enemy." "Basically, the Order of Saint George runs . . . what?"

"A vampire victim crisis center," Father Joseph said with a flicker of amusement.

"There are really so many vampire victims?" asked Hannah.

"The number grows every day," replied Father Joseph. He put his teacup down. "You may have heard of the increased incidents of clinical depression over the last decade or so? Most people blame our modern lifestyle, but much of this is actually caused by vampires. Most of the victims are not like you, Hannah. They don't know. They are hypnotized at the time of feeding and are not aware of how they received the marks. Usually, as their condition grows worse, they are treated by psychiatrists, who give them Prozac or Paxil and send them on their way."

"What causes the depression? The lack of blood?"

"The toxin the vampire imparts in his victim in order to draw blood painlessly. It is similar to the poison used by mosquitoes. Only, a vampire deposits a great deal more into the nervous system than the average mosquito."

"I don't understand. Are we talking about a real chemical? Something science can study?" asked Hannah, who had expected some mystical mumbo-jumbo explanation.

"Certainly. When we have patients who are less sure of the cause of their troubles, we often draw blood and test for traces of this toxin. It breaks down slowly in the human body. Traces can be found in the bloodstream for two to three weeks after the initial bite."

"So, after three weeks, a person would be fine?" asked Hannah.

"Theoretically. In reality, it depends on the length of exposure. The toxin works by overstimulating the pleasure receptors in the brain, which is why their victims find vampires so enticing. Over time, traces of the toxin build up on these receptors, damaging them and causing a chemical depression. Eventually, if left unchecked, the receptors burn out all together. We have a few such patients in our inhouse care program back in the rectory."

Hannah shivered, inwardly seething at Ambroise for causing her such misery. But, then, he probably had no idea what he was doing. After all, vampires could hardly be expected to visit such crisis centers on fact-finding missions. Besides, she had done everything possible to hide her condition from him. She would not hold her love responsible, she decided. He could not help what he was.

"Now, I must ask you again. Can you give us anything to go on?" asked Father Joseph, and he pushed a card across the table which had places for Vampire's Name and Address.

Hannah thought of the hall and the sunlight. She tried to imagine Ambroise dead, his beautiful face marred or his perfect breast pierced. The image upset her so she nearly started crying in front of the priest. Silently, she vowed that she would rather die herself than let such a thing happen to Ambroise.

"But, Am—he hasn't done anything wrong! I consented," she cried hastily.

Father Joseph looked at his hands and sighed. His face looked careworn and sad, as if he had been through this scene a hundred times before. Hannah wondered why she had thought he was so young.

"I did not want to have to show you this. I spare all those who I can," he said, rising and moving to put a videotape in the VCR. "You will excuse me if I don't stay and watch it again myself. Watch the whole thing—to the end. Just press the intercom button when you're done."

The videotape showed a real vampire initiation. The hidden camera gave the scene an odd warped look, but she could still see the vampires converging on the initiate like vultures on roadkill. The initiate, now pale and trembling, then approached an old man, who had been bound to a stake and gagged. The old man wept as he awaited his fate. Hannah felt a stab of envy at his watery tears. Then, the initiate slit the old man's throat with a ceremonial knife and began sucking up mouthfuls of his spurting blood.

"All vampires are murderers," explained the announcer. "Their power to sustain their existence beyond the grave is granted to them by an unholy power. This power will accept only initiates who have proved their loyalty by sullying their soul with the murder of an innocent. All vampires have murdered before and will most likely murder again."

Hannah dismissed some of the explanation as Christian claptrap. Yet, she did believe that what she was seeing was real. The old man's death was not like any special effect she had ever seen. For one thing, there was much more blood than they showed in the movies. Hannah had never seen a real person die before, and the experience rattled her. She tried to console herself with the thought that the sacrificial victim was very old and probably would have died soon anyway, but she could not quite believe it. Her dear father, who adored her so faithfully, was not much younger than that man. The thought of her father perishing so ignominiously filled her with fury.

But, if she ratted on Ambroise, wouldn't that make her a murderer, too?

Unexpectedly, she remembered the night she and Ambroise broke into the Central Park Zoo and toured the menagerie together. It was never open during the hours they saw each other. She remembered the raucous monkeys and the sleeping lions. She remembered the cotton candy machine Ambroise had found. How he had laughed when she got the sticky stuff all over her nose. How he had bent his head to lick it off. No. She could not kill him. She loved him.

And yet . . . much as she loved him, she wanted to play the cello again and to enjoy a good book. She wanted to be able to take a shower or call her mother without weeping at the terrible effort it took. She wanted to live her life.

Shakily, Hannah acknowledged that her relationship with Ambroise must end. She would go home and explain to him the harm he was causing her. She would explain that under the circumstance it would be wrong for them to continue to see each other. She imagined herself, an old lady, unmarried and alone, still pining in her heart for her one true love. Perhaps, they would meet on the street—her old and withered, him still young. Perhaps they would exchanged a brief smile or a fond word. The thought made her cry, but no tears flowed. She hid her head and left the priest to face her shaking shoulders.

"I . . . I can't help you," she said finally.

"Hannah . . ."

"I love him. I would rather die myself than be party to his murder," Hannah declared valiantly.

The priest frowned. "What about his other victims?"

If she left Ambroise, would it push him into the arms of other women? An image came to her of Ambroise embracing various young women of her acquaintance, whispering to them. She pushed it angrily from her thoughts. No, no one who said the wonderful things Ambroise said would ever hurt her as her no-good, son-of-a-gun ex-fiancé had. Ambroise was a one-woman man, just as she was a one-man woman. He might feed off other women to stave his incurable hunger, but he would never love them as he loved her.

Now, if someone had offered to kill Eddie, her two-timing ex, that might have been a different matter!

"I feel sorry for his other victims," Hannah began, "but—"

"But not sorry enough." Father Joseph cut her off. He thrust the card at her again. "Here, carry this. Come. There is someone I would like you to meet."

Father Joseph led her through the glass hallway to the rectory, where patients with more serious aliments were treated. The rectory, or the infirmary, as the priest called it, was a long chamber with thick white walls and tall arched windows. Beds extended from the walls, each bed draped about the head with soft white fabric, forming a short canopy. The room was airy and bright, but smelled heavily of disinfectant.

From each canopied cot, pallid, drawn, and tired faces stared back at Hannah from behind the thick green goggles that kept their eyes moist. Many were on IVs. The nun who had swabbed Hannah's shoulder sat beside one of the patients, wetting his lips with a pink mouth sponge-stick. She smiled at Hannah and the priest as they passed.

From the last bed on the left, a shrunken wrinkled woman in a white hospital gown watched the newcomers with a malevolent glare. Hannah recoiled, shocked by the woman's horribly withered appearance.

The shrunken woman's dry eyes fixed on Hannah. Her voice was a rasp of scorn. "How old do you think I am?"

"Me? I—I don't know," Hannah stuttered. The woman must be at least in her nineties. Hannah prayed she would never get that old! She decided to flatter the old hag and guess young. ". . . seventy-six?"

The deadened eyes watched her, unblinking. "I am thirty-eight. . . . Surprised you, didn't I?"

Hannah turned to Father Joseph and whispered conspiratorially. "How old is she really?"

The young priest's face was grave. "Clarissa is thirty-eight, my child. She is one of our most difficult cases."

The shrunken woman spoke, her voice scornful. "I thought myself so fancy with my vampire lover. I looked down on my friends because I was going to live forever. After all, he loved me sooo much. He so often said so." She scowled angrily. "Where in Anne Rice does it say that you have to murder someone to become a vampire? I . . . I couldn't do it." Her eyes drifted, as if her thoughts moved far away.

"Time for your transfusion, ma'am," said a pretty nun, coming up beside Clarissa. The woman scowled.

Father Joseph inclined his head towards Hannah and said quietly, "Clarissa was seduced into participating in a vampire initiation. However, when it came time to kill the victim, she refused. She can no longer produce her own blood, but at least her soul is her own."

"That's small comfort when the pains start," the shrunken patient rasped moodily, wincing as the nurse turned her to prepare for her transfusion. "Sometimes, when the pain is very bad at night, I curse myself for not having gone through with it. I could have been deathless. I could have been immortal . . . but, then I wake to the sunlight and know I've been fooling myself. I could never have withstood that life. Most vampires fade away within the first five years. Did you know that? It's only the rare initiate who actually grows hardened enough to survive that depraved life."

Her eyes focused on Hannah and she added, "None of them would survive if we did not make it easy for them. We criticize the stupidity of dogs who bite the hand that feeds them. But, how much stupider we women are when we continue to feed the mouth that bites us."

Hannah shifted uncomfortably, tugging at her unruly hair.

Father Joseph said gently. "Hannah has not yet decided whether or not to help us."

"So you brought her back here to show her the likes of me, hoping to shock her into feeling pity for her lover's other victims?" Clarissa laughed, a short uncomfortable sound. "Priests! They know shit about women. But, don't worry, Father Joe. I'll fix things for you."

She fixed her baleful gaze on Hannah. "Let me ask you a question, honey. When you first met lover boy, did you see him every day?"

"Yes."

"But now, you see him once every two weeks, right?"

". . . Yes."

"Even then, there are places or parts of town where he doesn't want to be seen with you. Am I right?"

Hannah nodded reluctantly. Her heart skipped a beat. It made sense that the clinic had been able to identify a pattern to her symptoms. But, how could someone else know the pattern of Ambroise's behavior?

"You want know why, sweetheart? I bet you don't. But I'm going to tell you, nonetheless. Because the damn bloodsuckers have a feeding cycle. They can't sip from one 'cup' more than once every two weeks. Otherwise, they weaken their victims beyond their usefulness. The average fanghead has between twelve and twenty-five victims, and that's not counting their constant supply of one-time supplements. And, since most of their victims experience the toxic-induced euphoria as sexual pleasure, they usually oblige them."

"I don't understand. . . ."

"Oh, yes, you do! Your lover has between twelve and twenty other squeezes he visits the other nights when he's not with you. He has places he goes with you and places he avoids, because that's where he takes his other girls. He's got it all worked out. They all do. Face it, sweetie. To him, you're just a glorified ham sandwich."

"I don't believe it! Ambroise is different!" Hannah said stoutly.

"Ambroise? What, him again?" Clarissa raised a faint scornful eyebrow. "Didn't we have two other girls babbling about Ambroise just this week?" When Father Joseph nodded, she snorted. "Seems this Ambroise is quite the ladies' man. If I remember correctly, one of them vowed to die before anyone laid a hand on her true love."

"You mean, he's cheating on me?"

"My, how sharp you are." Clarissa's thin lips settled into a malicious grin.

"That bastard!"

Hannah felt as if she had been punched in the solar plexus. She allowed Father Joseph to help her to a chair, where she sat rocking back and forth, as a thousand pleasant memories shattered like tempered glass. After all she had done for him! All she had given up. Her very life's blood! And all the time, Ambroise had been using her like so much cotton candy!

Father Joseph offered her his pen. Hannah stared at it blankly. Then, snatching it, she wrote out the card, describing exactly where Ambroise would be the following evening, and thrust it at the priest, who accepted it gravely. Wiping an honest-to-goodness wet tear from her cheek, she sniffed and said, "Sunlight's too good for him. Can't they use a stake?"

Emptiness

BRIAN STABLEFORD

It was five o'clock on Tuesday morning, with an hour still to go before dawn, when Ruth found the abandoned baby. The plaintively mewling infant—who was less than a week old, if appearances could be trusted—had been laid in a cardboard box in a skip outside a former newsagent's in Saint Stephen's Road. The skip was there because the shop was in the process of being refitted as an Indian takeaway. Ruth was coming home from the offices of an insurance company in Queen Street, where she'd been sent to work the graveyard shift by the contract cleaning firm that employed her. She was all washed out, drained of all reserves of strength and momentum.

Ruth knew that she ought to call the police so that they could deliver the baby to social services, and that was what she vaguely intended to do when she plucked the child's makeshift crib out of the skip. The first thing she did thereafter, obviously, was to stick an experimental finger into the baby's open mouth. When she felt the nip of the newborn's tiny teeth the vague intention ought to have hardened into perfect certainty, but it didn't. She was adrift on the tide of her own indolence, rudderless on the sea of circumstance.

The baby sucked furiously at the futile finger, desperate to assuage a building hunger. In order to get it out of the infant's mouth Ruth had to tear the finger free, but the ripped flesh on either side of the nail didn't bleed. The pain quickly faded to a numbness that was not unwelcome.

The baby had thrashed around vigorously enough to work free of the shit-stained sheet in which it had been wrapped, and Ruth took note of the fact that he was a boy before wrapping him up as best she could in the cleaner part of the sheet. Her own kids were both girls. Frank had done a bunk while they were supposedly still trying for a boy; if they had succeeded in time, she would have stood exactly the same chance as everybody else of giving birth to a vampire—the publicly quoted odds had been as short as one in fifty even then, fourteen years ago.

The nearest pay phone was a quarter-mile up the road, practically on the doorstep of the estate. By the time Ruth drew level with the booth she had not brought her resolve to do the sensible thing into clearer focus. The baby had stopped crying long enough to look into her eyes while she rearranged the sheet by the glare of a sodium streetlight, but it had been only a glimpse. Temptation had not closed any kind of grip upon her—but fear, duty and common sense were equally impotent. When she reached the phone booth she paused to rest and consider her options.

If she did as she was supposed to do, the baby would be fitted with a temporary mask and whisked away to one of the special orphanages that were springing up all over. Once there he would be fitted with a permanent eyeshield, stuck in a dormitory with a dozen others and fed on animal blood laced with synthetic supplements. He would go straight into a study programme and would remain in it for life.

The primary objective of the study programmes was to find a cure for the mutant condition, enabling its victims to survive on other nourishment than blood. Their secondary objective was to find a way of helping the afflicted to survive longer than was currently normal. Nobody thought the scientists were knocking themselves out to obtain the latter achievement while the former remained tantalisingly out of reach. There was a certain social convenience in the fact that real vampires, unlike the legendary undead, rarely survived to adulthood. The average life expectancy of an orphanage baby was no more than thirteen years; the figure was probably three or four years higher for babies raised at home, but they were in a minority even in the better parts of town. The best reason why so many vampire babies were abandoned was that they were direly unsafe companions for young siblings; the more common one was that the neighbours would not tolerate those who harboured them.

In theory, Ruth's younger daughter was still living with her in the flat, but in practise fifteen-year-old Cassie spent at least five nights a week with her boyfriend in a ground-floor squat. Even if she were unwise or unlucky enough to become fixated on the child, sharing donations with her mother wouldn't do her any harm. In any case, Cassie's blood was probably too polluted by various illegal substances to offer good nourishment to a fortnight-old vampire. All in all, Ruth thought, there was no very powerful reason why she shouldn't look after the baby herself for a little while, if she wanted to.

Carefully, she counted reasons why she might want to hesitate over the matter of handing the baby over to the proper authorities.

Firstly, the flat had been feeling empty ever since Judy had moved to Cornwall with the travellers, even before Cassie took up with Robert. No matter how much she hated the work itself, Ruth simply didn't know what to do with herself anymore when she wasn't working.

Secondly, she'd put on a lot of weight lately, and everyone knew that nursing a vampire baby, if only for a couple of weeks, was one hell of a slimming aid.

There wasn't a thirdly; Ruth wasn't the kind of person to take any notice of those middle-class apologists for the "new humankind" who were fond of arguing that vampire children were the most loving, devoted and grateful children that anyone could wish for and ought not to be discriminated against on account of unfortunate tendencies they couldn't help. She didn't have any expectations of that kind—her own children hadn't given her any reason to.

In the end, Ruth decided that there was no hurry to make the call. Surely nobody would care if she waited for a little while, provided that she didn't hang on too long. If it were only for three or four days, she could probably keep the baby's presence secret from the Defenders of Humanity, and if she couldn't, she could hand the baby over as soon as she had to. It was no big deal. It was just something to do that might even do her a tiny bit of good. Just because she was pushing forty, there was no reason to let go of the hope that she might still be worth something to someone.

Unfortunately, Cassie made one of her increasingly rare raids on her wardrobe later that morning, before Ruth had had time to get her head down for a couple of hours. The baby was asleep but Ruth hadn't taken him into her bedroom. The dirty sheet had been swapped for a clean one but he was still in the old cardboard box—which was anything but unobtrusive, sat as it was on the living-room table.

"Why aren't you in school?" Ruth demanded, hoping to distract her daughter's attention and ensure that she didn't linger.

"Free period," Cassie replied, ritualistically. "What's that?"

"None of your business," said Ruth, defiantly.

"Whose is it? Is baby-minding a step up from office cleaning or a step down? Can't its mum find anything better to keep it in than a cardboard box?"

Cassie peered into the makeshift cot as she spoke, but the baby's eyes and lips were closed, and there was nothing to betray its true nature.

"Shh!" said Ruth, fiercely. "You'll wake him up." There was, of course, little chance of that, given that the sun was shining so brightly, but Ruth figured that there was no need to let Cassie in on her secret yet if she could possibly avoid it. Her tacit arrangement with the baby was, after all, strictly temporary.

Fortunately, Cassie showed no inclination to inspect the visitor more carefully. Sexual activity hadn't made her broody. In fact, when Ruth had first tackled her on the subject of contraception, Cassie had sworn that if ever she fell pregnant and couldn't face an abortion she'd jump off a top-floor balcony. Most people who said things like that didn't mean them, but Cassie was short for Cassandra, and ever since Robert had told her what the name signified in mythology, Cassie had taken the view that whenever it was time for one of her gloomy prophecies to come true she'd have to make bloody sure that it did.

When Cassie had gone Ruth unearthed an old cot from the junk cupboard under the stairs. Two baby blankets and a couple of Baby Gros were still folded neatly within it, although she had to run the vacuum over them to get rid of the dust. She left the baby asleep with the bedroom curtains drawn while she hiked over to Tescos in search of Pampers, red meat, Lucozade, iron tablets and various other items that now had to be reckoned essentials. Luckily, she'd been off-shift on Friday and Saturday and hadn't been able to collect her pay until Monday, so she was as flush as she ever was.

By the time she got back the sun was at its zenith and she was twice as exhausted as before, but the baby was awake and whimpering and she knew that she'd have to feed him again before getting some sleep on her own account.

The thought of putting the vampire to her breast again made her hesitate over the wisdom of her decision not to call Social Services, but as soon as she looked down into the child's tear-filled eyes her squeamishness vanished, as it had the first time when the child had been terrified and starving. His gaze had filled up once again with tangible need. He was thin and pale and empty, and the pressure of his eyes renewed Ruth's awareness of her own contrasting fullness: her too-substantial flesh, her still-extending life, her superabundant blood.

It did hurt when the teeth clamped down for the second time on the tenderised rim of the nipple, but once they were lodged the anaesthetic effect of the baby's saliva soothed the ache away.

Ruth couldn't feel or see the flow of blood as the child took his nourishment. Vampires used their teeth only for holding on—they took the blood by some kind of suction process that drew it through the skin without breaking it. When he released her again, already falling back to sleep, there was no leakage from the residual wounds. The control that vampires exercised over the flesh of their donors was ingenious enough to forbid any waste.

When she had put a clean disposable on the baby and put him down again, Ruth fought off her tiredness for the fourth time and made herself a meal. She knew that she had to eat regularly and well if she were to be adequate to the baby's needs, even for a fortnight. She had a second cup of tea in order to maintain her fluid balance but she left the Lucozade for later. Before she finally went to bed she phoned the agency to say that she had flu and that she would have to come off the roster for at least a week, until further notice. Her supervisor didn't protest; Ruth's attendance record was better than average and there was no shortage of night-cleaners in the area.

She slept very soundly, as was only to be expected. She didn't dream—not, at any rate, that she could remember.

Cassie didn't figure out what kind the baby was until Thursday evening, at which time she threw an entirely predictable tantrum.

"Are you completely crazy?" she demanded of her mother. "It's kidnapping, for God's sake—and the thing will bleed you to death if you let it. It's a monster!"

"He's a human being," Ruth assured her. "His mother obviously couldn't cope—but she didn't turn him over to the authorities either. She'd be grateful to me if she knew. It's only temporary, anyhow. It's kindness, not kidnapping."

"It's suicide!"

"No, it's not. They're not dangerous to adults, even in the long run. A couple of weeks will only make me leaner and fitter. I need to be fitter to do that bloody job five and six nights a week. It'd be different if there was a child in the house, but there isn't, is there?"

"They're cuckoos," Cassie blustered. "They're aliens, programmed to eliminate all rivals for their victims' affections. Why do you think they keep them masked in the homes? That's where he belongs, and you know it—in a home."

"He is in a home," Ruth pointed out. "A real home, not a lab where they'll weigh and measure and monitor him like some kind of white rat. He's entitled to that, for a little while at least. There's no need to tell anyone—it's my business, not yours or anyone else's."

"It is so my business," Cassie retorted, hotly. "I live here, too—I'm the rival that the cuckoo is programmed to squeeze out while he squeezes you dry and leaves you a shrivelled wreck."

"I thought you had decided that this place is just a hotel," Ruth came back, valiantly. "A place to keep your stuff, where you can get the occasional meal and take a very occasional bath whenever you happen to feel like it."

"Don't be ridiculous, Mum. I want that thing out of here—now, not next week or next month."

"Well, it's not what I want," Ruth informed her, firmly. "It's just for a few more days. Stay away if you want to. You usually do. Don't interfere."

Cassie told her boyfriend straight away, of course, but it turned out that she didn't get the response she expected. If he'd been the kind of Robert who condescended to be called Rob or Bob he'd have run true to form, but even on the estate there were kids with intellectual pretensions. Robert hadn't left school until he was eighteen and he would tell anyone who cared to listen that he could have gone to university if it hadn't been for the fact that the teachers all hated him and consistently marked down the continuously assessed work he had to do for his A levels.

* * *

Robert came up to inspect the infant at eleven o'clock on Friday morning. Ruth had had a busy night but her nipples had now adapted themselves to the baby's needs and the flow of her blood had become wonderfully smooth and efficient. The numbness left behind when the child withdrew wasn't in the least like sexual excitement but it was delicious nonetheless. She was tired, certainly, but she wasn't dishrag limp, the way she had been after finishing a long night session in some glass-sided tower. Although she was keen to get to bed she knew that she could stay awake if she had to, and she knew that she had to persuade Robert not to do anything reckless. It was a pleasant surprise to find that he was a potential ally.

"Do you know whose he is?" Robert wanted to know, as he stared down into the cot with rapt fascination. The baby's eyes were closed, so the fascination was spontaneous.

"No," said Ruth. "I've kept my ears open, but I didn't want to ask around. The neighbours haven't cottoned on yet—Mrs. Hagerty next door's as deaf as a post, and if the Gledhills on the other side have heard him whimpering they haven't put two and two together. He doesn't scream like ordinary babies, no matter how distressed he gets—not that he gets distressed, now that he's safe. He's a very sensible baby."

"I could probably find out who dumped him," Robert bragged. "It must be one of the slags on the estate—it's easy enough to do a disappearing bump census when you've got connections."

Robert didn't have connections, in any meaningful sense of the word. He was a small-time user, not a dealer. He didn't even have any friends, except Cassie—who would presumably dump him as soon as she found someone willing to take her on who was slightly less of an outcast.

"It doesn't matter where he came from," Ruth said. "The important thing is to make sure that he doesn't come to any harm. You have to stop Cassie shooting her mouth off to the Defenders."

"She wouldn't do that," Robert assured her with valiant optimism. "She's with me—she knows that all the scare stories are rubbish. We don't believe in demons or alien abductions or divine punishment. We know that it's natural, just a kind of mutation—probably caused by the hormones they feed to beef cattle or pesticide seepage into the aquifers."

Ruth knew that Robert probably hadn't a clue what an aquifer was, but she didn't either and she wasn't about to give him the opportunity to run a bluff.

"He needs me, for now," she said. "That's all that matters. It's only temporary. When he's strong enough, I'll hand him over."

"Does it hurt?" he wanted to know. Ruth didn't have to ask him what he meant by it.

"No," she said. "And it isn't like a drug either. Not pot, not ecstasy. He isn't even particularly lovable. Little, helpless, grateful . . . but no cuter than any ordinary baby, no more beautiful. Alive, hungry, maybe even greedy . . . but it's my choice and it's my business. I don't need saving from him—and I certainly don't need saving from myself."

"They must always have existed, mustn't they?" Robert said, following his own train of thought rather than trying to keep up with hers. "Much rarer than nowadays, of course—maybe one in a million. Intolerable, in a pre-scientific age. Automatic demonization. The idea that the dead come back as adult vampires must be an odd sort of displacement. Guilt, I guess. Never seen one close up before. Quite safe, I suppose, while the sun's up. Safe anyway, of course, if you're sensible. Adaptation makes sure that they don't kill off their primary hosts. What's good for the host is good for the parasite."

"He still needs to feed during the day," Ruth pointed out. "He wakes up from time to time. But it's perfectly safe. He doesn't intend to hurt anyone. He doesn't hurt anyone."

She smiled faintly as Robert took a reflexive step backwards, mildly alarmed by the thought that the child might open its eyes and captivate him on the instant—but Robert regained his equilibrium as she finished the last sentence.

"What do you call him?" Robert asked. He was being pedantic. He hadn't asked what the baby's name was because he knew that Ruth couldn't know what name the child's real mother had given him, and wouldn't feel entitled to give him a name herself when she knew that she would have to hand him over in a matter of days.

"I don't call him anything," Ruth lied, before adding, slightly more truthfully, "Just the usual things. What you'd call terms of endearment."

Cassie's boyfriend nodded, as if he knew all about terms of endearment because of all the things he said to Cassie while subjecting her exceedingly willing flesh to statutory rape.

The boy was long gone by the time the baby bared his teeth again and searched for his anxious provider with his pleading and commanding eyes. Ruth was certain that Robert had had nothing to worry about; the infant knew by now who his primary host was, and he only had eyes for her.

It was Ruth's rapid weight-loss that finally tipped off Mrs. Hagerty, and it was Mrs. Hagerty—despite the fact that her own kids were in their thirties and long gone—who passed the word along to the Gledhills so that the Gledhills could make sure it got back to the local chapter of the Defenders of Humanity.

Fortunately, the conclusion to which the stupid old bat had jumped was only half-correct, and the rumour that actually took wing was that the child was Cassie's and that Ruth had decided to take him on in her daughter's stead. This error qualified as fortunate, in Ruth's reckoning, because it persuaded the Defenders of Humanity that shopping her as a kidnapper would be a waste of time. If the baby had been Cassie's, the whole thing would have been a family matter, much more complicated than it really was.

When she knew that the secret was out, Ruth expected

shit and worse through the letter-box and a flood of anonymous letters in green crayon, but the Defenders of Humanity were canny enough to try other gambits for starters. The first warning shot fired across her bow was a visit from the vicar of Saint Stephen's. She could hardly refuse entry to her flat to an unarmed and unaccompanied wimp in a dog collar, although she wasn't about to make him a cup of tea.

"You must put your mind at rest, my dear," said the vicar, hazarding an altogether unwarranted and faintly absurd familiarity. "It is not because it was conceived in sin that the child is abnormal."

"No," said Ruth, as noncommittally as she could.

"There is no need for shame," the vicar ploughed on. "It is not your duty to accept this burden. There is no reason at all why you should not deliver the infant into the hands of the proper authorities, and every reason why you should."

"That's what God wants, is it?" Ruth asked.

"It is the reasonable and responsible thing to do," the vicar assured her. "Your first duty in this matter is to your daughter, your second is to your neighbours, and your third is to yourself. For everyone's sake, it is better to have the child removed to a place of safety. While it remains on the estate it is bound to be seen as an increasing danger, not merely to your own family but the families of others. I do not ask you to concede that the child is an imp of Satan, but I do ask you to consider, as carefully as you can, that even if it is not actively evil it is an unnatural thing whose depredations pollute the temple of your body. It is a bloodsucker, my dear, which only mimics the forms of humanity and innocence in order to have its wicked way with you—and I use that phrase advisedly, for what it does is a kind of violation equally comparable to vile seduction and violent rape."

"Suffer the little children to come unto me," Ruth quoted, endeavouring to quench the fire of zealotry with a dash of holy water—but to no avail.

"It is not a child, my dear," the vicar insisted, all the while keeping his eyes averted from the cot. "It is a leech, an unclean instrument of temptation and torment. If you would be truly merciful, you must give it up to those who would keep it safely captive."

"Well," said Ruth, "I'm grateful for the lesson in Christian charity, but I think he's about to wake up. I'm sure that modesty forbids . . ."

Modesty did forbid—and the first note didn't arrive until the following day, when the vicar had washed his hands of the matter.

GET RID OF IT, the note said. IF YOU DON'T WE WILL. Apart from the lack of punctuation it was error-free, but given that the longest word it contained was only four letters long it was hardly a victory for modern educational standards.

The notes that followed were mostly more ambitious, and the fact that the longer words tended to be misspelled didn't detract from the force of their suggestion that if Ruth wanted to spill her blood for vampires, there were plenty of people living nearby who would be glad to lend her a helping blade.

Cassie was incandescent with rage when she heard what was being said about her. "How dare you?" she yelled at her hapless mother. "How dare you let them believe that it's mine?"

"I never said so," Ruth pointed out.

"But you didn't bloody deny it, did you? You let that shit the vicar blether on without ever once telling him that you found the little fucker in a rubbish skip. Mud sticks, you know. Some round here will remember this forever, and God help me if I ever have a kid of my own. Well, I'm done protecting you. Robert wouldn't let me phone 999 myself, but I've put the word out that you have no claim at all on the cuckoo, and that the fastest way to get it off the block is in a police van. Expect it tonight."

That was on the second Saturday, by which time Ruth had had the child in her care for twelve days. She had not really intended to keep him so long, and his tender care had already turned nine-tenths of her spare fat into good healthy muscle, so one of her reasons for keeping him had melted away. As for the other, she was almost out of cash and she really needed to get back to work. The fact that she would have nothing to do when she wasn't working was no longer a significant issue, given that if she couldn't feed herself properly she'd soon be no use at all to the baby.

For once, reason stood fair and square with bigotry. Both asserted that she must not keep the baby any longer—but their treaty had been made too late. Ruth's devotion to blood donation had passed beyond the bounds of reason, and whatever failed intellectuals like Robert might think about the cleverness of the adaptive strategies of vampires, baby bloodsuckers had no means of dispossessing themselves of primary hosts that were no longer adequate to their needs. The baby was just a bundle of appetites, a personification of need. He had learned to lust after Ruth's breast, and he could not help the instinct that guided his tiny teeth. He could not let her go—and his incapacity echoed in her own empty heart.

Despite what Cassie had said, the police did not put in an appearance on Saturday night; they had their own cautious rules about picking up vampire babies after sunset. Ruth contemplated doing a runner, but she hadn't got anywhere to run to so she decided to front it out. When the WPC turned up on her doorstep on Sunday morning Ruth wouldn't take the chain off to let her in.

"There's no baby here, and if there was he wouldn't be a vampire, and if he was he'd be mine and I wouldn't be interested in giving him up," Ruth said, breathlessly. "Don't come back without a warrant, and even then I won't believe that it gives you any right."

"It's not my problem if you don't care to cooperate, love," said the WPC, shaking her head censoriously. "Just don't come crying to me when your hall carpet goes up in flames."

Ruth had taken the child to the supermarket a couple of times before the word got out, but she didn't dare do it once

the local Defenders knew the score and she certainly didn't
dare to go out and leave the poor little mite alone while she
spent the last vestiges of her meagre capital. She wasn't
surprised when Cassie refused point blank to fetch groceries for her—but she was pleasantly astonished when
Robert not only said that he would but that he would also
chip in what he could spare to help her out.

"We shouldn't give in to ignorance," he declared. "We
have to stand up for our right to take our own decisions for
our own reasons in our own time according to our own per-
ceptions of nature and need." The false-ringing speech
didn't mean much, so far as Ruth could see, and even if it
had, it wouldn't have been applicable to her situation, but
she figured that Robert's muddy principles would buy her a
few extra days before she finally had to let go. Even though
she'd always intended to let go in the end, she thought that
she was damned if she'd give the so-called Defenders of
so-called Humanity the satisfaction of seeing her do it one
bloody minute before she had to.

There were no more notes, and nothing repulsive came
through the letter-box in their stead. The Defenders of Humanity knew that the message had been delivered, and they
also knew that they only had to wait before it took effect.
They knew that as long as they were vigilant—and they
were—there was no danger to any human life they counted
precious. Besides which, they simply weren't angry enough
to march up the concrete stairs like peasants storming Cas-
tle Frankenstein, demanding that the child be handed over
to them for immediate ritual dismemberment. Things like
that had happened twenty years before, but even the most
murderous of mobs had lost the capacity to take the inva-
sion personally once the numbers of vampire babies ran
into the thousands. Even the most extreme religious mani-
acs lacked the kind of drive that was necessary to sustain a
diet of stakes through the heart, lopped-off heads, and bon-
fires, night after night after night without any end in sight.
By now, even the dickheads on the estate couldn't summon
up energy enough to do much more than write a few notes

and wait for inevitability and the law to take their natural course.

In a way, Ruth regretted the lack of strident enmity. There was something strangely horrible in the isolation that was visited upon her as she eked out her last supplies and went by slow degrees from slim but robust to thin and tired. It was, she thought, as much the loneliness of her predicament as the baby's ceaseless demands that made her so utterly and absolutely tired. She had not realised before how much it meant to her to be able to shout good morning at Mrs. Hagerty or glean the available gossip from Mrs. Gledhill's semi-articulate ramblings.

The baby was a continuous source of comfort, of course, and that would have been enough in slightly kinder circumstances, but his powers of communication were limited to moaning and staring, and they just weren't enough to sustain a person of Ruth's intellectual capacity. He loved her with the kind of unconditional ardour that only the helpless could contrive, and she was glad of it, but it simply wasn't the answer to all her needs.

She knew that the end of the adventure was coming, so she made every attempt to milk it for all it was worth. She became vampiric herself in her desire to extract every last drop of comfort from her hostage. She had never been subject to a desire so strong and yet so meek, a hunger so avid and yet so polite. She had never been looked at with such manifest affection, such obvious recognition or such accurate appraisal.

She flattered herself by wondering whether even a vampire would ever be able to look at any other host with as true a regard as her temporary son now looked at her. She took what perverse comfort she could from the fact that nothing the orphanage would or could provide for him would ever displace her as an authentic mother. For as long as the baby lived, it would know that she was the only human being who had ever really loved it, the only one who had ever tended unconditionally to its real needs.

But it wasn't enough, and not just because there wasn't enough time.

By the time she had had the baby for nineteen days Ruth was at the end of her tether. Cassie had not come near her for a week, and had somehow contrived sufficient emotional blackmail to keep Robert away, too. The wallpaper had begun to crawl along the walls. She was out of Pampers, out of Lucozade, and out of tinned soup.

She decided, in the end, that she would rather die than hand the baby over, although she knew as she decided it that she was being absurd as well as insincere. She tried with all her might to persuade him to feed more and more often, but he would not take from her more than he needed or more than she could give, and she had always known that this was the way that things would finally work out. She grew weaker and weaker while she could not bring herself to bite the bullet, but she was never drained to the dregs.

In the end, she didn't need to contrive any kind of melodramatic gesture. She only had to make her way next door and ask the Gledhills to call an ambulance, not for her but for the child. It would not take him to a hospital, but that wasn't the point. It was far, far better—or so it seemed—to surrender him into the arms of a qualified paramedic than to let him be snatched away by a blinkered policewoman or a so-called social worker.

She cried as she handed him over. Her tears dried up for a while but when night fell and the time of his usual awakening arrived she began to cry again. Her breasts ached with frustration, and the waiting blood turned the areolae crimson. She knew that the hurt would fade, but she also knew that the nipples would be permanently sensitised. She would never recover the lovely numbness that she had learned so rapidly to treasure. She would never see eyes like his again. No one would ever understand her as he had. No one would ever think her the most delicious thing in the world.

She wondered whether they used contract cleaners at the orphanages. She wondered whether it would be possible, in spite of her lack of formal qualifications, to retrain as a nurse or a laboratory assistant, or any other kind of worker that might be considered essential by the scientists for whom vampires were merely an interesting problem. She made resolutions and sketchy plans, but in the end she went to sleep and did not dream—at least so far as she could remember.

She went back to work the next night. It was hell, but she survived.

The labour left her desperately devitalised for the first couple of weeks, but she soon began to put on weight again and her desolation turned first to commonplace debilitation and eventually to everyday enervation. Mrs. Hagerty began to respond to her shouted good mornings and Mrs. Gledhill began filling her in on the gossip. Cassie resumed regular expeditions to her wardrobe, and slightly-less-frequent ones to the bathroom. Robert dropped in more often than before, stayed longer, and talked nonsense to her for hours on end.

It wasn't great, but it was normal. Ruth had learned the value of normality—but that wasn't why she remembered the baby so fondly, and sometimes cried at night.

Things had been back to normal for nearly three months when Cassie, still three weeks short of her sixteenth birthday, found out that she was pregnant, panicked, and jumped off a top-floor balcony.

The autopsy showed that the child would have been a vampire, but Ruth knew that that didn't even begin to justify Cassie's panic, or even to reinforce the ironic significance of her name. She would have been able to get an abortion. She would have been able to hand the baby over to Social Services. She would have been all right. She would have been able to resume normal life. There was no reason to kill herself but stupidity and sheer blind panic. It wasn't Ruth's fault. It wasn't anybody's fault. It was just one of those things. It would have happened anyway—and it wouldn't have happened at all if Cassie had only had the sense to talk to somebody, and let her terror be soothed away.

Robert was heartbroken. He moved out of the squat into Cassie's old room, but the consolation with which he and Ruth provided one another was asexual as well as short-lived. Within a month he was gone again, just like Frank, along with the intensity of his grief and the pressure of his need.

Once Robert had gone, Ruth never did figure out what to do with herself during the day, or during the long and lonely nights when she wasn't on shift cleaning up the debris of other people's work and other people's lives—but every time she went past a rubbish-skip while walking the empty streets in the early hours of the morning she kept her eyes firmly fixed on her fast-striding feet, exactly as any sensible person would have done.

Home Visitor

ANN K. SCHWADER

Today I can hear him waiting for me even before I've pulled the keycard out of the loft's security door. Not a good sign. Soft whisper of Egyptian cotton sheets across skin and pajamas, fidgety creaking of bedsprings, straining lungs . . . all the sickroom noises I barely heard standing by his bed six months ago, now perfectly clear as I set down my two IV bags and slide the door open. The bags slosh a little as I pull them inside. I catch my breath, hoping against hope that Robert hasn't heard.

But he has, of course.

"Jan-ice!" His motorized bed whines in the next room, propping him up to greet me. "I thought you'd never get here this afternoon. What kept you?"

Expedited funeral call for my two o'clock, but I'm not about to say so. Waiting alone with that wasted body for nearly an hour was bad enough. Exped funeral teams don't want their clients left unattended, though they're quick enough to kick you out once they've arrived. I wish I didn't know why.

"Screwed-up traffic," I fib, trying not to notice the sun sinking fast beyond the darkening privacy tint of a floor-to-ceiling window.

Hefting both IV bags again, I start across the great room's collection of antique Turkish carpets. Their mellowed colors and soft textures under my cross-trainers tempt me to dawdle—until I hear Robert's breathing quicken. No sense risking him getting impatient. He's probably too weak right now to even stand, let alone do any damage, but there's always a first time.

Pasting my patented Home Visitor smile across unsteady lips, I try not to react as I step into his bedroom suite. Full-blown CRS isn't pretty. Robert's pale, blue-veined arms on top of the down coverlet look noticeably thinner than they did last week. Their surgical shunts jut out near the bend of each elbow. The sunken planes of his face make it hard to remember that he's only forty-nine . . . forty-nine not likely to make fifty.

And you're expecting to? Setting down the IV bags and injection kit, I struggle with my own fears. Yes, I'm CR-positive, but I sure as hell don't have CRS yet, and maybe by the time I do there'll be a cure.

Probably the same way the Bangkok vaccine "cured" AIDS thirty years ago. Nobody gets it anymore—at least, nobody newsworthy does—and we're all just supposed to forget how long it took the last cases to die.

At least AIDS got a little sympathy in this country, endless feel-good charity benefits with celebs eulogizing dead friends and relatives. CRS never made it that far. About six years ago, when the first full-blown cases hit, one CR-positive Hollywood actor did the liberal thing and admitted his status. Forty-eight hours after that interview hit the Net tabloids, the guy's body turned up in an L.A. back alley. In pieces.

Even the tabloids wouldn't touch that one.

"You don't look so good," says Robert, though his yellowed hazel eyes still target my IV bags. "Was the elevator out?"

We both know his building's elevator never goes out for more than five minutes. Downtown luxury loft complexes can't afford problems like that. Robert used to own, maybe still does own, the hottest and wildest nonvirtual nightclub in this city. I used to think it was no wonder he caught CRS, but life's gotten too short for blame games. After all, it wasn't my fault I got jumped behind the gallery two years ago, sneaking a breath of fresh air during my first solo show's evening opening.

"Nothing to worry about," I finally tell him. "I was just up a little late last night."

Last night and every night. As I pick my way through the teetering piles of books surrounding his bed, I try to remember the last time I slept for more than an hour before dawn. Or really woke up before noon without popping caff tablets.

A knowing smile knifes across Robert's face, but the craving in his eyes doesn't ease. I move to the left-hand IV stand and change its bag. The empty sags on the floor like a small drained animal. Robert's gaze follows its replacement as I put it up. By the time I've repeated the process on the right side of his bed, one skinny hand is snaking out for the needle tube.

"Uh-uh." I grab the tube and hang it over its stand. "You know the rules. Injection first."

He lunges for the left-hand needle tube instead, knocking a book off his coverlet onto the floor. I loop back the tempting tube before retrieving his reading material: *Dylan Thomas Collected*. It's a real hardback, cloth covers polished with wear.

"Always knew you had good taste," I murmur.

Robert's not in the mood for literary discussions. Snatching the book from my hand, he collapses onto his pillows with a nasty wheeze, sounding far too much like my two o'clock client had last week. I turn away quickly for my injection kit.

"Haven't been taking your pills today, have you?"

He glares up at me, then shrugs. We both know he'd be flat on his back and nearly comatose if he had been. Sometimes I suspect that's the whole point of CRS chemo.

"Do you take yours?" he demands in a painful whisper.

I hesitate. "Most of the time." But I haven't for nearly a week, and something in those discolored eyes knows. Something in them has watched me choke and run for the toilet at the merest whiff of those pills, never mind getting one down my throat.

My prescription isn't the same as his, but it's close enough. Very pure essential oil—expensively pure, unaffordable without my Home Visitors program discount.

With it, the cost is ridiculously low, probably heavily subsidized. The feds need us Visitors just the way we are: CR-positive and holding. Any sicker, and we'd be useless. Any improvement (sweet dream!), and we'd be outta here, baby. The program's stipend for our one day a week couldn't possibly justify the risks.

But nobody holds at CR-positive forever.

"Having allergy problems?" Robert's thin smile turns momentarily vicious. "I remember mine. Quit taking the damn pills for nearly a month, felt marvelous."

His smile fades. "Then the craving started."

The craving. There's only one with CRS, and this little former vegetarian doesn't feel like discussing it. I fish Robert's preloaded sprayhype out of my kit, take a deep breath, and reach for his arm.

Something between a curse and a growl emerges from his cracking lips. Both arms disappear under the coverlet.

"A neck vein will work just as well, you know." The black joke dies in my mouth. "It's your choice. One way or another, I've got to give you this. . . ."

"Poison."

"I'm not here to poison you, Robert. I'm here to help you." I glance away from the damn sprayhype, trying to focus his attention on those two plump IV bags. "The sooner you get your shot, the sooner I can hook you back up."

But his attention won't refocus. Those jaundiced eyes burn into mine like a dying wolf's, with a predator's absolute truth.

"Tell you what," he rasps, lungs straining again. "Take a whiff of it first—then try telling me how much it's going to help." The room falls hospital silent as he struggles for breath. "See if either of us believes it."

My gorge rises just thinking about his suggestion, but I step back from his bed and unsnap the sprayhype's drug chamber. Raising the open cylinder slowly toward my nose, I fan its scent upward.

Then snap the chamber closed with a curse of my own.

It's lucky that Robert's bathroom is only a few steps away. Afterwards, I scrub my hands with Lady Macbeth thoroughness, fine-milled sandalwood soap exorcising the last lingering hint of garlic.

When I emerge from the bathroom, I do not say any more about helping. Robert's arms are lying outside the coverlet again. Their twin shunts quiver with each breath he takes, but he hasn't tried another grab for the IV tubes. Maybe our brief argument wore him out too much.

Or maybe he's decided to trust me. Cursing us both for idiots, I pick his sprayhype off the polished hardwood floor with two fingers and drop it back into the kit.

Then I reach for the looped-back needle tubes and start hooking him up.

"Thank you," he whispers as his left-hand shunt opens for business. Trapped by the bitter truth of the moment, I wonder what the hell he's thanking me for. These bags I've hung are our program's largest, the legal limit, and Robert's been doing two a day for the past month or so. They're always drained when I arrive. I'm afraid to compare notes with his other Home Visitors to see if they've noticed anything different.

Very soon now—maybe tomorrow—the maximum ration won't be enough. Carpathian Retroviral Syndrome is a uniquely demanding progressive disease.

I start connecting the right-hand shunt, but Robert's hand snaps up to intercept the IV tube. His burst of energy startles me—until I realize how long I took recovering from that whiff of chemo. It's undoubtedly full sundown outside. Releasing the tube, I back off slowly, spreading my hands to show them empty and harmless.

Then I realize that Robert's not even focused on me.

More for my sake than his, I look away as he disconnects the needle plug to put the tube in his mouth.

One-one hundred, two-one hundred, three . . . After checking out the floor's hand-pegging for a full minute, I look up to see both needle tubes properly shunted and the right-hand IV bag a quarter low. The scent of whole natural blood curls through the room like incense. Swallowing a mouthful of my own saliva, I wonder what this week's mandatory donors would think.

Most probably assume they bled for the rich. After all, blood substitute works fine for almost everything from surgical transfusions to trauma. Too bad CRS knows the difference between the real stuff and synth—or animal blood, for that matter.

As it is, some of our cities are bleeding themselves dry. Since NIH pushed the Medical Emergency Act through Congress two years ago, any state that deems it "essential" can call up each qualified donor once per three months, without explaining the actual nature of the emergency. California's increased that to once per two, and I hear they're still not keeping up. So much for CRS therapy in America.

China's using bullets.

"I wouldn't do that again," I finally tell him, weaving my way back through the stacks of books. "Won't last you nearly long enough that way."

Robert shrugs and picks up the Dylan Thomas. His hands tremble a little, but his color is improving rapidly. Flipping the book's cover open across his lap, he leafs through its worn pages, almost without looking.

Then taps one finger against a poem until I move closer.

My stomach clenches. "'Do Not Go Gentle Into That Good—'? Holy shit, Robert; don't do this to me. Not now."

Not this week, I mean—not after calling the exped funeral team for my two o'clock. Remembering the muffled thwack of a mallet behind an apartment door—and other, uglier noises—I know I can't call those people again just yet. Not even if it means leaving a CRS casualty alone overnight.

But he keeps tapping the page until I have to look again.

"This," he whispers faintly, painfully; "this is what they want. Bastards want us all to go gentle." The whisper turns to a gasp. "Rage, rage . . ."

He sinks back then, pulse fluttering under my trained fingers, heightened color from the blood fading fast. I reach for his right-hand shunt and work the tube free, then the needle plug. A little blood smears my fingertips. Pushing those fingertips between his lips, I feel the tiger rasp of his tongue while I'm trying to poke the tube into place.

"Easy," I murmur. "You'll be getting enough soon."

Sharp enamel threatens to replace the sandpaper, but I pull my fingers out just in time. The fluid level of the right-hand IV bag drops abruptly. Robert's eyelids close. Watching his desiccated lips sucking at that tube, I wish certain EastEuro nuclear inspectors could be here with me.

They had their warning way back in '86, with those mutating voles around Chernobyl. Supervoles, biologists called them ten years later—before Ukraine started losing their wheat crop to the furry plague. Before said plague developed a taste for live protein. By the turn of the century, outlying farmers were sleeping with their AKs and yelling for chemical warfare.

There aren't any Chernobyl voles now—one season of gene-tailored bubonic saw to that—but the lesson didn't stick. When Romania's substandard plant in the Carpathians went critical later that year, even the Black Death couldn't save us from what crawled out.

Robert's eyelids finally flicker back open. His right-hand IV bag sags almost empty. If he gets agitated again, he'll probably drain the other, as well, so I try reading that damn poem to him softly. Aside from its blunt defiance of death, I can't see why he's chosen it. It's not even about death, really—more about the poet's beloved father slipping away and him hating every minute.

Beloved father. Yeah, right.

But Robert's fingertip moves down the page, stabbing at the last stanza. "Curse, bless, me now with your fierce tears, I pray . . ." I look at the moisture forming in his yellow wolf eyes, filling papyrus creases at their corners, and the poem evaporates on my tongue.

A few weeks after I got attacked—and about five minutes after I finally told my folks I was CR-positive—my dad asked for the keycard they'd let me keep when I moved out. Last conversation he and I ever had. Mom called me next morning, voice-only, and tried to explain. All I could hear were fresh bruises: Dad doesn't hit her often (or hard, she claims), but he's a binge abuser like some guys are binge drinkers.

Mom still won't leave him, and I've got a kid sister living at home.

Which is why I started signing my paintings janICE, trying to believe it. Trying to stay cold enough.

Almost unwillingly, I touch the pinkish tears on Robert's cheek. He doesn't move. Maybe this last, cursed blessing took too much out of him. My own wet fingertips smell faintly of blood and pain and garlic. Government-approved poison. The same stuff I've gulped down for months now, fighting to hold off the inevitable—to keep CRS from making me over.

But now Robert is doing his damnedest to show me where that fight leads.

Rage, rage against the dying of the light.

Technically, I guess, his light won't be dead very long. Funny thing about CRS . . . which is where exped funeral teams come in. I've heard lots of rumors about how and where NIH recruits these, but I sleep better if I don't remember. And I won't sleep at all tonight if I leave Robert to them.

The right-hand IV bag hangs like a collapsed lung now. Working quickly, I free his left-hand tube from its shunt and press it to his searching lips.

Then I start sifting the mess on his bedside table. As I dig through months' worth of nightclub schedules, unfilled prescriptions, and less identifiable things, Robert's eyes slit open. "What? . . ." he asks, with all the force of a kitten's sneeze. "What the hell are you? . . ."

"Found it."

I hold the object out to him. It's a loft keycard: his personal one, not the copy I've got to turn in tonight. Shadowy gold holographs writhe across its surface. Some are just pretties, upscale flash to impress the girls he used to bring up here. Others work as code to disarm the loft's security system—or a thief's better judgment. I smile at the sparkling bait and slip it into my pocket.

The ghost of a smile haunts Robert's face, as well, though his last IV bag is already shriveling.

"Don't worry," I whisper, for CR-sharpened ears only. "I'll send something up for you later."

Given the early dark of late autumn, the tempting proximity of this complex to less choice real estate, it shouldn't take long. The only risk might be another CRS victim. One who couldn't afford "therapy," or had the street sense to refuse it. There are worse things to be in this world than a faster, stronger, nastier predator.

"Thanks," he says around the tube in his mouth.

Not a kitten sneeze now, but the cough of a waking tiger. He's already sliding his feet out of bed. I start backing away, small hairs prickling the nape of my neck, heightened senses on alert. Whoever or whatever tries that keycard, my gut says Robert won't be the loser.

Halfway across his Turkish carpets, I realize he's still just sitting there on the bed in his PJs, watching me leave. The retrovirus shines in his eyes like a benediction.

Or a father's last blessing.

"See you later, Janice," he says, very quietly. "Look me up whenever you're ready, but I wouldn't wait too long if I were you."

I let myself out as always, making certain my keycard resets all the loft's alarms. An elevator waits at the end of the wide plush hallway. This early in the evening, in a haven for hyperachievers and go-getters, it's still empty. I slip inside and savor the richness of privacy.

Then, for the first time in almost two years, I let myself smile with my teeth showing.

Even the sharp ones.

A Dance with Darkness

JOSEPHA SHERMAN

Chattering and giggling like so many cheerful birds, by midday they'd gathered enough flowers for more than a dozen wreaths. Now the girls of Dyrevnya, their village in the midst of Russia's wilderness, sat in the dappled forest sunlight this warm midsummer's day, sharing their bread and cheese, weaving their flowers together, gossiping of the village boys and the night of dancing to come.

Marusia studied them—plump Sasha with her long blond braids; slight, dark-eyed Anna, frail as a new fawn; plain, cheerful Sophia who was already betrothed to Semyon the butcher's son—and felt a hundred years and a thousand *versts* away from their lightness. All this day, despite the bright sky and the lush greens of the forest about her, despite all the laughter and chatter, she'd felt a strange darkness pressing in on her till she almost could have wept.

She came back to herself with a jolt as the other girls pounced on her, pulling her to her feet, draping the finished garlands over her.

"What are you doing? I'm not in the mood—I don't *want* to be *kupaljo*!"

Maybe nobody really believed in the old ways, not in these so-very-modern days when steam locomotives crossed the country and it was a few years into the bright new century. Maybe nobody off in royal Moscow or Saint Petersburg had ever even heard of the Feast of Kupalo. But out here in the ancient forest, where most folks still found horses more useful for travel, roads were few and villages stood where they'd always stood—well, their local priest might have scolded them for playing these pagan games, but not all that severely.

The girls were already blindfolding Marusia with her own woolen scarf, the fringes tickling her face, and spinning her around as they sang. They stopped. There was an expectant silence. Dizzy and resigned, Marusia blindly handed out the floral wreaths, one by one, to the silly girls. As if flowers could predict—

A gasp of horror made her toss the scarf aside. Anna, face ashen, stood staring down at the sadly wilted wreath she held, and the terror in her eyes made Marusia exclaim impatiently, "Oh, Anna! How could a bunch of flowers possibly tell your future?"

"My grandmother said her cousin's wreath fell apart in her hands." Sasha's voice was hushed. "And she died the very next year."

"That's ridiculous!" Marusia snapped. "Anna, you got the flowers we picked earliest, that's all. They had more time to wilt." She glanced about at the already shadowy forest, which was darkening rapidly even though the sky overhead remained stubbornly blue. "It's growing late. Let me just find my scarf." Why had she tossed the thing away so fiercely? "Akh, now I've lost it."

Sophia made a face. "Maybe one of Them stole your scarf," she teased. "Maybe a *leshy* took it for his wife."

"Don't joke about Them!" Sasha insisted.

"Why not? Have you ever even *seen* a *leshy*?"

Marusia bit her lip and kept still. Once, when she'd been gathering firewood, two bright green eyes, fierce with an intelligence very alien to humanity, had stared out at her from the branches of a tree, eyes that just might have belonged to a *leshy*, one of the mischievous, perilous, nonhuman lords of the forest. Good Christian folks, *modern* folks, weren't supposed to still believe in such pagan things. But here in the middle of that forest, it was difficult *not* to believe!

The other girls were more than making up for Marusia's silence. "No, no," Sophia whispered dramatically, "it wasn't a *leshy* who took the scarf. It was an outlaw."

"Sophia!" begged Anna. "Don't!"

Ah, here's the scarf, Marusia thought in triumph, ignoring them, *caught on a bush.*

"A fierce, lean, *mean* outlaw," Sophia continued, "who hates everybody! He has *no ears,* because the Law cut them off, and he's carrying a dozen sharp knives, and he's just looking for a nice, plump girl to *eat!*"

She pounced on Sasha. But Sasha's squeal was drowned by Marusia's startled scream. Instead of the scarf, she'd touched someone's arm!

"Forgive me," a man's cool, low voice murmured before she could run. "I didn't mean to frighten you."

"C-come out here where we can see you," Marusia commanded.

There was a deep chuckle. "I hear and obey."

The stranger stepped into the open. Marusia heard the other girls gasp, and nearly gasped herself. Oh, he was fair, tall and young, slender and elegant as a lord in his elegant traveling suit. His fine-boned face was as elegant as the rest of him, his hair glinted bright gold even in the twilight dimness, and his eyes were large and so dark a blue they seemed almost black. With a great effort, Marusia tore her gaze away from their amazing depths as bold Sophia asked defiantly, "Who are you? What are you doing here?"

"Call me . . . Vasilko." Marusia wondered at that faintest of hesitations. "And, well now, ladies, what do you think I'm doing here, dressed like this?" His sweep of hand took in the elegant suit and fine leather boots, but his glance remained on Marusia.

"Robbers," gasped Sasha. "They stole your horse or—or maybe your motorcar—" She stumbled over that unfamiliar word and hurried on. "And they stole your goods, too, didn't they? Oh, are you hurt?"

"Only in my pride," Vasilko said with a chuckle, as though inviting Marusia to join in some private joke. "But the night will be here shortly. Is your village nearby, ladies?"

Marusia couldn't find her voice. She stood, staring, as the other girls chattered, almost as one, "Oh, of course! Forgive us. Come, follow us, it's not far!"

"Lady?"

Vasilko held out his arm to Marusia. After a moment she realized what he wanted. Blushing fiercely, she put her hand on his arm, and they walked on together. He stopped as they reached the old-fashioned wooden palisade surrounding Dyrevnya, and Marusia, noticing for the first time how some of the poles sagged and others were actually broken, felt a new flush of embarrassment, realizing how provincial all this must seem to a nobleman.

Herself included. All at once she could almost have hated Vasilko for being what he was. "The others will see that you're properly welcomed," Marusia said shortly. "I—I must go. My parents will be waiting."

But he caught her hand. "Why this sudden urgency? And what are all those ribbons on the houses? Is today some feast day?"

She felt herself blushing all over again. Now he really would think them all hopelessly provincial! "It—it's midsummer."

"Ah, of course. Which makes it a holy saint's day. How could I have forgotten? And how do you celebrate out here so far from everyone?"

"With prayers and feasting, of course, and after that, song and—"

"And dance?"

"Yes, in the village square, but—"

"You'll be there, I take it?" At her nod, Vasilko bowed low over her hand, then released it. "Till then, my dear."

The night air was chill for midsummer eve, and a sudden breeze made Marusia shiver and pull her fringed woolen shawl more tightly about herself and her brightly embroidered sarafan. The dark mood of the day hadn't left her, not even after the arrival of Vasilko, and now . . . She glanced nervously about, wishing just for a moment that her parents had come with her. But though they'd dutifully prayed beside her in their home, kneeling before the family shrine, they'd insisted midsummer night was a time for the young to celebrate.

Besides, what was there to fear? Even if the palisade did sag a bit, it still formed a reassuring ring around Dyrevnya, hugging the log houses safe within its circle. Beyond, the forest loomed like some dark, brooding beast, but she was hardly afraid of that! Sophia had been right: If there was anything for a young woman to fear about the forest, it was the purely human menace of the ragged outlaws who preyed on their own kind. They were out there, she was safe in here, and wasting precious dance time! Marusia shook her fringed shawl into more attractive folds and hurried on her way.

The village square was bright with firelight and music. There was Vanya the baker and his fiddle, the twins, Gleb and Bori, playing their flutes with flying fingers, and old Simeon tootling away on the trumpet he'd brought back ages ago from fighting in the Tzar's wars, and if the music was a little thin and wavery, no one really minded. Marusia let herself be drawn into swirling spirals of dance, young women facing young men, flirting, not quite daring to touch. But all the while she found herself hunting one tall, blue-eyed figure.

And then she froze. He was standing half in shadow, chatting with the men, but where the torchlight struck, it etched the sharp, fine bones of his face and turned his hair to richest gold. Marusia stared, watching him move, transfixed by the careless grace in the turn of a leg, the wave of a hand.

Plump little Sasha giggled. "Isn't he *handsome*? He has to be someone fine, some merchant's son maybe, come all the way from Moscow. I mean, *look* at the cut of that caftan!"

Marusia was no longer listening. Vasilko had turned her way, and those deep, deep blue eyes were drinking her in. Dazed, Marusia was hardly aware that he was moving smoothly to her side.

"Forgive me." His soft voice brought little shivers to her spine. "I didn't mean to gawk at you, Lady Marusia."

"I'm n-no lady," she stammered, but he silenced her with a light flip of the hand.

"Lady you are, by grace if not by birth. Come, lovely lady, will you dance with me?"

She would. She did. Lost in wonder, Marusia danced with him till the moon faded, hardly aware of the scandalized whisperings of the elders and her friends' gigglings, seeing only his face, feeling only the strength of his arms about her.

"This is how nobility dances," he told her, smiling. "Since we are both noble tonight, we can do as we will."

Only when he drew her aside into shadow and began to lower his fair face to hers did Marusia come back to her senses. "No! I-I mean, you know my name by now, you know all about me, but I don't know who you are, not really, or where you come from."

"Why, what do you think I am?"

The mockery hinting in that elegant voice angered her. "Some rich man's son," she said, more sharply than she'd intended, "come from a grand estate to play among the peasants. Then you'll go home, tell everyone how quaint we were, and forget all about us."

"Forget you? Never. Marusia, ah sweet Marusia, do you believe in first sight, first love?"

"What are you—?"

"I cannot stay. I have . . . obligations. Will you come with me, Marusia, my Maruiska?"

His eyes were boundlessly blue, deep and dark, fathomless as a forest lake. She was losing herself in those eyes, drowning ... drowning forever ... *Yes, oh yes, I'd go with you to the ends of creation ... yes ...*

"No!" It was a cry of pure panic. It took all her will, but Marusia managed to tear her glance away and snapped, "This is ridiculous! I certainly won't run off with you, you—stranger!"

"Ah." If he was disappointed, he didn't show it. "Then I shall, perhaps, stay just a short while longer to court and win you."

Mockery was so plain behind the smooth words that Marusia turned and all but fled, not sure if she was angry at him or afraid of herself. By the time she'd reached her home, though, she'd managed to compose herself enough so that when her smiling mother asked how the dancing had gone, Marusia was able to smile and answer, "Well enough."

But her dreams were dark, troubled things in which Vasilko's smiling face turned, again and again, to a cold, demonic mask. At last Marusia sat bolt upright, staring into blackness, her inner time sense telling her this was the darkest hour of the night, somewhere after moonset, before sunrise. She should surely try to go back to sleep till morning. And yet, and yet ...

There is something you must do, something you must see.

No. That was ridiculous. She must still be half-asleep, dreaming.

There is something ... something you must see.

She *was* asleep. This was a dream, and the only way she was going to wake out of it was to follow it along.

Quietly Marusia dressed and slipped out of the house, closing the door behind her, wincing as it creaked on its leather hinges, then stood for a time, shawl wrapped tightly about herself against the cold. All around her, Dyrevnya slept, silent and unreal in the darkness as a village enchanted.

A dream. Surely a dream.

And so, she couldn't really wonder that despite only the faintest glimmering of starlight, she could see as clearly as though the village was still flooded by moonlight. Lapped round with silence, Marusia waited.

A flicker of motion: Vasilko, moving with silent grace through the night. There was nothing alarming about him, save for that almost unnatural grace, yet Marusia felt her heart all at once pound with nameless fright. She watched in tense, terrified silence as he reached the wooden palisade—and swarmed up and over it as smoothly as a wild thing.

No man could do that.

She should shout, wake her parents, wake somebody. But this was only a dream, and so Marusia found herself instead moving to the palisade's gate. Misha, whose turn it was to stand guard, was asleep at his post. After all, who would expect danger on such a peaceful night?

I don't want to go on! It was a childish wail, deep in Marusia's mind. *I want to go home and hide in bed.*

Instead, she helplessly slid the gate open just enough to let her slip out into the night and the forest, stumbling along deer trails, blindly following Vasilko.

He was standing in the clearing where they'd first met. Pinned in his arms, as helplessly as a child, was a second man, and Marusia felt a little thrill of horror as her strange, moonlit sight showed her the ugly scar where an ear had been cropped away. Here was the desperate outlaw of Sophia's story, and yet now she could feel nothing but numb pity for him for his impotent terror. Vasilko bent over him, as tenderly as a lover, bright hair falling forward to hide his face. Marusia saw the captive tense, then struggle wildly, yet Vasilko held him fast.

The struggles faded, stopped altogether. A lifeless body sagged in Vasilko's arms as he straightened, blood staining his elegant mouth.

Deep blue eyes met hers: eyes warm and sated and thoroughly inhuman. Never taking his glance from her, Vasilko wiped his lips fastidiously with a scrap of cloth and smiled. Deep within her, Marusia shrieked with horror, but she could only stand frozen, staring.

"I see." Vasilko's voice was as calm as though they'd been politely conversing all this while. He opened his arms, letting the limp body drop. "I wasn't quite careful enough, was I?"

At last Marusia could speak. "You aren't human. *Vampyr.*"

"If you wish. Oh, this shell is—or was—human. I, of course, am not. Come, my dear, why the look of horror? I've done your little village a service, rid it of this vermin." A boot delicately spurned the corpse. Vasilko smiled lazily. "What, no gratitude?"

"You brought me here."

A bonelessly graceful shrug. "Not by design. I would have had you as my prey this night at the dance, but you resisted me so strongly I was intrigued. And so I stared too long into your eyes and mind, and in the staring quite accidentally bound us together. Interesting, isn't it? And possibly useful to us both. You'll always be aware of me. And you have night-sight now, don't you? Not that it matters. My dear, I've found rich hunting here, and I will not let you interfere."

"You can't—"

"Can't I? Listen to me, child." He glanced down at his late prey with a frown of distaste, spurned the body with an elegant foot. "Not here. Come."

He strolled away, and Marusia, helpless to resist, followed. "I was a nobleman, yes," Vasilko continued lazily, "but one thoroughly bored with my lot, ever seeking a goal, a purpose in being. And so I traveled far, spoke with many strange folk. It was during those travels that I became the guest of an ancient count—or rather, one for whom all time had stopped. I shall not name him here; I suspect the outside world will someday know that name quite well if, indeed, it does not already do so."

Vasilko paused, the tips of his sharp teeth glinting as he smiled. "Ah, the long hours we spent comparing our nations' histories! He was a fascinating being, that one, the greatest hero of his people as well as their greatest Darkness, and it was he who taught me . . . many things. Including, little provincial child, the love of power on a grander stage."

"Wh-what do you mean?"

His glance was contemptuous. "Word of the outside world must have penetrated even this backwoods site. What, do none of the Tzar's tax collectors wend their way here?"

"Sometimes, yes, but—"

"Do none of them gossip of the royal court, of our glittering Nicholas and his Alexandra? Don't you know of their sad little Tzarevitch? Poor little Aleksei, the crown prince for whom even the slightest cut means such a terrible loss of blood?"

"Th-they have someone to treat him. That's what people whisper. The Tzarina's councilor. A—a powerful magician."

"Who, that self-named Rasputin? A loud-mouthed, ambitious, filthy charlatan! I could cure that child."

"Y-you'd kill him, you mean. You'd kill the Tzarevitch."

"Why, no, dear Marusia." Vasilko's smile was radiant. "Translate him, rather. Translate the heir to the throne into someone . . . better. Someone strong and lacking in the foolish weaknesses of his parents. Someone quite fitting to rule in these new, darker, much more interesting days."

"And what would you be? Ruler of the ruler?"

"Why not? Don't glower at me, girl. Think. There's unrest out there in the civilized realm, a foolish tzar on the throne, a sickly heir—if not me, someone else will rule. I, at least, will keep the throne in Romanov hands. Someone else—bah, who knows? Come, child, you may be a peasant, but I doubt you're stupid. Why should I not protect our land from foreign rule? Why, for that matter, should I not bring Rus out of its stagnation? Make it a true power in the world game?"

"No!" Marusia clung frantically to what she knew. Her village in peril, and the Tzarevitch—Vasilko was right, she wasn't stupid, and she could see nothing in his eyes but a cold and total self-interest that probably had been there even when he was—when he was still human. "No! I will not let you!"

The deep blue stare seemed suddenly to pierce her skull, no longer warm or at all gentle. Marusia staggered and fell, unable to scream or breath or think, engulfed in cold blue fire, in chill, chill Power far beyond anything she could ever understand. Dimly she heard Vasilko's words:

"You amuse me, child, with your little human will and your little human courage. I plan to stay here for a time and gather strength for my, shall we say, mission. But you shall not be my prey, not yet. Not till I am finished with your village. Live, Marusia. Live with the knowledge I have enslaved you. You will remember who and what I am—but you will be able to tell not one human soul about me! Now, go!"

Marusia woke with a start of sheer horror—in her own bed. For a long time, she simply looked up at the painted wooden ceiling of the closet bed, too shaken with relief to move.

A dream. It really was only a dream.

But when she at last mustered the strength to climb out of bed, Marusia realized she was still fully clad.

Sleepwalking. She must have been sleepwalking. Anything else was just too unthinkable. Struggling not to think, Marusia went through the morning as normally as she could, desperately pretending to her parents and herself that the only thing wrong with her was weariness from all the dancing.

But her mother took her aside. "Marusia, Maruiska, I think I know what's bothering you."

"You—can't!"

"My dear, I know who you were dancing with. That young stranger may be handsome, but—he is who he is. Be wary."

"Wh-what—?"

"There never can be anything honorable between a man of his rank and a woman of ours."

"Oh, *that!*" Marusia could have laughed in relief. "Is that all? Mother, believe me, I don't intend to have anything to do with him!"

Yet when Marusia went to fetch water from the communal well, bucket in hand, there he was, blatant as a trumpet call, perched on the lip of the well, flirting lightly with the women, jesting with the warily respectful men, his manner so charming and urbane that she wanted to scream.

There, her mind crowed, *he* can't *be* Vampyr, *all the stories swear that evil things can't bear the daylight.*

Or maybe it was the sunlight that was fatal. For one terrified moment, Marusia saw herself pushing him boldly into that sunlight to see if he'd burn to ash. She even took a step forward. But then Vasilko glanced up from his jesting, his stare transfixing her. The deep blue eyes were all at once empty and cruel as endless night, and in that terrible moment, Marusia could no longer deny the truth. *"You see?"* that cold stare told her. *"There are benefits to our linking. Thanks to it, I can walk in daylight, even as you. I can do as I will, and you can say nothing to stop me."*

Marusia bolted for home, nearly colliding with her mother.

"Why, Marusia, what is it?"

"Mother, I . . ." But nothing more would come. No matter how frantically she struggled, she couldn't even mention Vasilko's name, as though a cold, dark fog was shrouding her mind, drowning her thoughts. "It was nothing," Marusia murmured helplessly.

"Are you feeling ill, dear?" Her mother felt her brow with a gentle hand. "You don't seem fevered. Tsk, too much excitement last night, I think."

"Oh, yes," Marusia agreed with weary humor.

The rest of the day was a slow, endless nightmare. As Vasilko had promised, Marusia soon found she could tell the truth about him to no one, not priest, not friends. She could not even find the words for prayer. Head aching from the struggle, sick with the weight of horror, she could do nothing but wait, dreading the night, dreading the hunt to come.

With the night, Marusia found herself once more outside the village, helplessly following Vasilko, numb with dread because she'd found the palisade's gate already ajar: This time the prey wasn't going to be some nameless outlaw but someone from Dyrevnya.

She saw who struggled feebly in Vasilko's arms, and looked frantically about for a rock, a log, anything she could use as a weapon—nothing! But Vasilko was already lowering his head to feed—

"No! D-damn you, no!" Still shrieking, Marusia hurled herself at him.

"Enough." Vasilko's voice was harsh and thick with hunger. He pulled her from him without effort, holding her dangling from his half-raised hand, and Marusia froze, stunned at his strength. "You shall not attack me again," Vasilko whispered. "You *cannot* attack me again, I so command!" For a long moment he held her at arm's length, her feet barely brushing the ground, and Marusia held her breath, terrified by the nearness of death.

Then, casually as a man brushing away a fly, Vasilko hurled her away. "Live for now. Sleep," he ordered brusquely.

And Marusia, lying crumpled on the ground, helplessly slept.

She woke once more in her own bed, with no memory at all of how she'd gotten there. She woke feeling a thousand years old, and dragged herself out of the house before her parents could ask her questions Marusia literally couldn't answer.

And so she was one of the first to see a crowd entering the village. Anna's father was in their midst, his face gaunt and white with shock. In his arms sagged his daughter's lifeless body, bloody and torn, eyes still wide and glazed with horror.

Anna, oh God, Anna. The light Kupalo games, the wilted wreath . . . *It really did foretell your death.*

Screaming, Anna's mother rushed forward to embrace her daughter's body, only to be pulled away by Misha. "No," Marusia heard him murmur, "don't. She must have gone out to—to meet someone."

"She wouldn't! She was a *good* girl!"

"She was out there," Misha continued reluctantly. "And . . . wolves must have . . ."

Of course, Marusia thought numbly. How clever of Vasilko to rend his prey so that it seemed only an animal kill.

"No, that's impossible!" Anna's mother sobbed. "Wolves have never attacked anyone, not in the summer!"

Not wolves, Marusia corrected savagely. *Only one wolf.*

Suddenly Vasilko was rushing forward to join them, his face so horrified, his voice so solicitous that Marusia felt her stomach heave. She hurried blindly away, ending up huddled against a wooden wall, retching dryly, choking on sobs. Oh God, oh God, what was she going to do? She couldn't let him go unpunished, she couldn't let him kill anyone else!

I can't attack him myself, I can't tell anybody else about him—

No . . . what had he said, really? *"You will be able to tell not one human soul about me!"*

Human. Marusia straightened, remembering fierce green eyes, grimly wondering.

That day she managed to steal away from the others amid all the grief and confusion and wandered deep within the forest, farther than she'd ever gone alone before, for once unafraid of bears or outlaws; mortal perils right now were too trivial for notice. At last she stood in a small clearing, huge oaks towering over her, and listened to the forest slowly accepting her human presence with renewed rustlings and chirpings. Marusia took a deep breath and called out, *"Leshy! My lord leshy!"*

The forest fell silent for a startled moment. Then the normal stirrings started up again. There was nothing else.

This is ridiculous. No one heard me. There's no one to hear me and if the priest should learn . . .

But what else was left for her to do? Marusia called again, "My lord *leshy,* please! I must speak with you!" What did the old stories all say? That *leshiye* adored games and gambling? "I have a bargain to make with you!"

"Human child. Silly child."

Had she actually heard that, or had it been only the whisper of leaves in wind?

There was no wind. "My—my lord *leshy*—?"

"Silly child, human child, woman-human-child."

This time the wind-whisper had come from somewhere behind her. Marusia whirled, fighting down a shriek, fighting down the urge to cross herself. "Oh, please, I haven't come here to play!"

"Play, not-play," mocked the wind. "Here, not-here."

The whisper was all around her, making the leaves tremble without wind. Marusia swallowed dryly, suddenly very much aware of the forest as one vast, indifferent, powerful thing.

A living thing. "Your life is being challenged!" she called out.

Utter silence followed her words. Then, very softly, very coldly, the wind-whisper asked, "What challenge? From humankind?"

"From—from Unlife," Marusia gasped, stumbling over the words in her haste to get them out. "Please, you must have sensed him—it—the—the *Vampyr.*"

All at once the forest seemed to press in about her, alien, hating. "Unlife," the soft voice hissed. "Yes."

"I'm not . . . uh . . . that one's friend!" Marusia protested. "All I want to do is stop him!"

"Go to your humans."

"I *can't*! There's a spell on me, I can't tell anyone human! But you have the forest's Power, you can help me. Can't you?"

There was a long, long pause. Marusia waited, feeling her heart pounding painfully. And then she saw a flicker of motion, something that might have been fur, horns, leaf-green skin. "What will you give me?" the *leshy* asked, so close to her now she fought not to flinch. "What in exchange?"

"Uh, this brooch." It was Marusia's finest treasure, the only gold she owned. But to her disappointment, the *leshy* only laughed, a whispery, mocking sound.

"What have I to do with human trinkets? Come, you are asking no small thing! You would have my aid, the forest's Power, Power from the Very Beginning of Things! Would you try to buy *that* with silly gold?"

Marusia flushed. "No. Forgive me."

Leaves shook. "Enough, enough!" the leshy snapped. "Hurry! What would you offer in exchange?"

All at once Marusia was aware of the wild, sharp, not-quite-animal scent of the *leshy*, primal and terrifying and bewilderingly intriguing. Marusia felt a sudden warmth in her breasts, her belly and, horrified at her body's confusing reaction, fought down the cowardly urge to hug her arms protectively about herself. Oh, he couldn't be hinting—it was impossible! Even if he was human, she couldn't—how could she ever hope to make a good marriage if her reputation were lost?

But Anna hadn't had a chance to choose. Anna's life had been brutally raped away against her will. Marusia thought of those ravaged, terror-stricken eyes and nearly sobbed aloud. Oh, God, how could she be worrying about anything as—trivial as her reputation now? If Vasilko wasn't stopped here, now, others would die, bold Sophia, or plump little Sasha, or—

"All right," Marusia said softly. "You know what I offer."

Hands trembling so badly she could hardly untie laces, she stripped, blushing feverishly, and lay down on a bed of moss, cool and plush beneath bare skin, closing her eyes because she just couldn't bear to watch, praying that what-

ever happened would be quick and not too painful. She felt
warm breath on her cheek and bit back a sob. Surprisingly
gentle hands (not human hands! she realized with a new
thrill of panic) touched her body, *here,* and *here,* and Marusia almost opened her eyes in surprise, because in that caress was nothing brutal, only . . . reverence. To the *leshy,*
she realized suddenly, what she was offering was something wonderful. Something holy. Despite herself, Marusia
felt fire start up within her in response, a new, amazing fire
she'd never known before, surging through every vein, de-
stroying fear. All at once she stopped being merely *Marusia,* stopped being something small and merely human. She
was the forest, leaf and twig and tree, she was everything
within it, she was wild green birth and growth and Life, and
Marusia opened herself to all of it, crying out in wild, wild
joy. . . .

Shivering, Marusia woke to find herself alone amid twilight, and snatched up her clothing. Catching the faint chatter of rushing water, she hunted out a stream, wincing at her
body's soreness, and scrubbed herself as clean as she could,
trying not to think about . . . down there, teeth chattering as
loudly as the water, then practically threw on her clothes,
welcoming the warmth. Somewhat to her relief, she could
remember only the vaguest details of . . . that; she was still
human. Odd, she felt no shame, either. What had happened
had had nothing of human shame about it.

But where was the *leshy*? Marusia stiffened. Everyone
knew the *leshiye* were tricksters. Maybe all this had been
only a prank pulled on the gullible human! Maybe he was
off somewhere laughing at her right now!

"My lord *leshy*!" she shouted in sudden fury.

"No need to shout." Though she saw nothing, Marusia
sensed that the being stood beside her, hidden in shadow.
The faintest tinge of respect colored the whispery voice.
"You have kept your bargain, little human-girl, brave Forest
Friend. I keep mine."

A small stone vial was pushed into her hand, words murmured in her ear. Marusia gave a fierce shout of a laugh. "Oh, what lovely, lovely irony!"

The *leshy*'s chuckle answered, filling the forest about her, then fading away. Alone, Marusia went in search of Vasilko, the spell he'd cast pulling her back to the clearing where he'd killed the outlaw and poor Anna.

He was there. And it was plump Sasha who hung, half fainting, in his arms.

"Vasilko," Marusia said, and he stared, nostrils flaring.

"So," he said with distaste. "You have coupled with Other."

"With Life, Vasilko. Even as you have with Death." Marusia's hand tightened about the vial. "And Life will destroy you."

"You can't attack me, child. Or had you forgotten? Go away, little fool. Go wail your ruined reputation."

Scornfully he lowered his head to Sasha's neck.

"No," Marusia said quietly. "I'm not attacking you, Vasilko. I'm offering you Life."

She darted forward and hurled the contents of the vial right into Vasilko's face. He stared at her for the barest instant, eyes wide with sheer, disbelieving horror. And then he began to scream, shriek after shriek of agony ripping the night. As Marusia watched, numb with shock and the breaking of the spell binding her, she saw that which had been so fine and handsome fall into a lifeless heap, so many shards of bone caught in rags.

Marusia glanced down at the empty vial. The vial that had contained no poison, no acid, nothing but the forest's own Power condensed into the purest Water of Life. Life had indeed destroyed Unlife.

"There's unrest out there in the civilized realm, a foolish tsar, a sickly heir—if not me, someone else will rule. I, at least, will keep the throne in Romanov hands."

Had she done the right thing? Had she stopped a lesser evil only to make room for a greater one?

Just then, Sasha began to stir, moaning, and Marusia bent

to comfort her, pushing her doubts back into the corners of her mind. At least Sasha was safe. Dyrevnya was safe.

For now.

"Marusia—?" Sasha blinked, looking around, then sat up with alarm. "What am I doing out here? I was dreaming about Vasilko, that he was a—a—demon." Her voice trembled with terror. "I was dreaming, wasn't I? Dreaming and walking in my sleep." Sasha's eyes pleaded with Marusia. "It was only a dream, wasn't it?"

Time enough to tell her the truth when they were both back safely in Dyrevnya. "Yes," Marusia soothed. "It was only a dream. Come, let's go home."

But when she looked back once into the forest, still wondering, she caught the quickest flash of bright green eyes and heard the faintest echo of a chuckle whisper through the leaves. The land would survive. Come what may, Rus would survive.

The Sun Knows My Name

Vickie T. Shouse

Glittering skyscrapers lined the horizon like jeweled fingers reaching toward the sky in hopes of snatching the stars from the heavens for their adornment. Headlights blinked along the expansion bridges, casting twinkling reflections in the dark waters of the Hudson, giving the city a clean, crisp look.

To the uninitiated.

Beneath the glitz and glamour was another, darker world, ruled by things most humans refused to believe in. They also didn't realize the city was split into hundreds of territories whose borders were guarded, fang and claw, by these very creatures.

The gangs ruled the inner city, maintaining their turf with cold indifference to the human populations within their borders. A curtain of desolation hung between the abandoned warehouses and vacant storefronts, blocking out hope. Dimly lit tenements glowered over the darkened streets, affording little protection for those inside against the ravages of the night.

Ren was oblivious of the dark poetry of the moment as she slunk through the shadows. She was too busy avoiding the werewolf pack on her trail.

An alley opened to her left and she veered into its litter-strewn recesses, hoping to find a way out of the mess she had gotten herself into. That hope died quickly when her foot met something squishy and foul, sending her headlong into a solid brick wall.

Shit, shit, shit! she ranted, shaking the stars from her eyes.

An unearthly howl split the air. Even if Ren hadn't been fluent in 'shifter, she still would have known the pack was close, way too close.

She raced along the walls, frantically trying each door only to find them all locked. Sure, she could break through one of them, but if the racket didn't draw the pack straight to her, the busted door would be just as clear a trail.

But where can I hide from something with a nose as sharp as a bloodhound's and eyes made for hunting in the night?

A hiss from an agitated cat caused Ren to nearly jump out of her skin. She glared up into its blazing yellow eyes as it perched atop a rusty fire escape, starting to hiss back when a partially boarded-up window behind it gave her an idea. It'd be a tight fit, but it would have to do. Anything was better than becoming a midnight snack.

Her eyes glittered with determination as she scampered through piles of garbage, hoping as she did that the confusing scent trail would throw off her pursuers. Once done, she tiptoed to the street, cautiously peeking around the corner. Good, the coast was still clear.

A slight breeze lifted a wisp of dirty blond hair to tangle in her lashes. Impatiently brushing it aside, a rush of cool air hit her exposed ribs. Ren grimaced at the pale, bluish flesh and pink welts visible through the gaping holes in her leather jacket, vivid reminders of the close call she'd had earlier with the 'shifters.

Slipping out of the jacket, Ren bit back the bitterness as she heaved it down the street. Although a mere hand-me-down, the worn jacket had belonged to Runt. Throwing it away was like losing the last piece of her soul to the darkness.

Hot tears stung her eyes. At times she'd been able to delude herself into believing his scent still clung to the frayed lining.

"*Ren . . . Ren . . .*" A soft, insistent voice wormed its way past her defenses, trying to take center stage in her mind.

No, she screamed silently. Her clawed fingers viciously yanked hanks of greasy hair loose from her scalp. Ren welcomed the pain, as it forced the voice to retreat. The sun would have to wait its turn.

Running back into the alley, she studied the fire escape. It was a good five feet over her head, but that wasn't a problem. Like the 'shifters, Ren wasn't exactly human.

Wiry leg muscles propelled her upward, but she misjudged the distance. Almost missing the railing, she dangled by one hand before managing to awkwardly swing herself onto the rickety apparatus. She winced as the stressed metal shrieked in protest. Surely the pack would hear all the racket.

As if on cue, the Devil's Blades roiled into the alley, snapping and growling at each other. This deep in their own territory the pack brazenly prowled the night in all degrees of wolf form, relying on fear and disbelief to shield them from prying humans.

Ren barely wriggled behind the warped plywood before the seething mass of fur and claws came to a halt. Several raised their scruffy, matted heads, their snouts quivering, trying to divine her presence.

There was a crashing of trash cans and a melodious string of curses as they haphazardly rooted through the trash. When the noise grew closer, Ren squeezed deeper into the tiny cubbyhole, but stopped as a shard of glass jabbed her in the ribs.

She froze. One drop of her blood would end this little dance. Even if they couldn't reach her, all the Blades had to do was wait for sunrise. The results would be the same.

Holding her breath, Ren waited, wondering what was taking them so long. Surely those big ears could hear the jackhammer pounding of her heart.

A sharp cramp in her stomach doubled her discomfort. *Cripes! Why didn't I grab that cat?*

It had been a long time since she'd fed, so the smell of the 'shifters' blood, even under all that grungy fur, made her mouth water uncontrollably. Ren ground her teeth into the soft flesh of her jaw, sucking down the meager trickle of blood, hoping it would keep her stomach quiet.

"Chops! Where is she?" she heard the alpha male, Gaffer, demand of his second.

"Nuthin' here but garbage, boss!" Apparently Gaffer didn't like that answer, because there was the sound of more musical trash cans.

"Yow! Take it easy, Gaffer!"

"Shut up, you moron! I want that bloodsucking bitch! Now!"

Even though she couldn't see him, Gaffer's craggy face and red-rimmed eyes, eyes full of hatred and death, *her* death, were permanently etched into her memory.

It was her own fault, really. She'd refused to leave the lair after becoming a vamp, so she had no experience in avoiding the patrolling 'shifter packs. As she bumbled through their turf, it hadn't taken them long to find her. She'd fought as best she could, but there had simply been too many of them.

Paralyzed by terror, Ren had watched Gaffer morph into full 'shifter mode, his putrid breath making her gag. Yellow teeth had flashed as his jaws extended toward her throat, then, as if it had a mind of its own, a scrawny leg had whipped out and a slender foot had made contact with his exposed groin. By the time Gaffer's cronies had stopped howling in laughter, Ren was long gone.

Now, shades of déjà vu.

"It came this way, boss. I smell its stink all over," Chops muttered.

"You reckon she turned into a bat and flew off?" an anonymous voice asked.

Gaffer's response was quick and brutal. There was the sound of a meaty paw connecting with the unfortunate idiot's head and Gaffer's triumphant blood-howl followed by an uncomfortable silence.

"Any more of you brain-dead fuckers gonna ask me stupid questions?" His mounting anger at being denied bloody revenge for his earlier embarrassment was a tangible thing, squeezing at Ren's heart. Cold sweat ran down between her shoulder blades as she waited, knowing beyond a shadow of a doubt she wouldn't survive if he got his paws on her again.

She was nearly insane from the tension when an excited yip drew Gaffer's attention.

"Let's go. She ain't here." Growls of delight filled the air as the pack pulled together and bound out of the alley, eager for the resumed hunt.

As the pack's noise faded into the distance, Ren carefully maneuvered around the jagged glass. Once free, she spent several precious moments resting on the cool metal, waiting for her nerves to calm down and for the feeling to return to her legs.

When the tingling stopped, she climbed over the railing and hopped nimbly down, or at least she tried to. Misjudging the distance, *again,* it felt like her kneecaps exploded as she hit the ground, hard. Ren nearly bit through her tongue to avoid crying out in pain.

She hadn't practiced any of this stuff, so graceful she wasn't.

Limping out of the alley, Ren headed out in the direction opposite that of the pack. Despite the urgency knotting her guts, she forced herself to casually work her way through the few pedestrians insane enough to be out in this neighborhood at this hour.

She smiled grimly. This she could do, this using of the shadows to blend into the woodwork. She'd perfected the technique over the past year by avoiding Malik's attentions.

A chill shook her at the thought of Malik, but she convinced herself it was only the cold air whistling through her ripped T-shirt. Trembling hands stuffed the troublesome garment into her jeans, giving her time to marshal her thoughts back to the matter at hand.

Besides, a naked chest, even one this pathetic, draws too much attention, and I don't have the time to deal with any more delays.

Thanks to Malik, the 'shifter packs had pulled together in a surprising show of solidarity. Instead of the usual pissing contests, they'd overlapped borders, trying to catch vamps too arrogant for their own good.

She'd been "lucky" enough to see the remains of one such vamp. The poor sucker'd been gutted, his entrails scattered about the deserted railroad yard just inside clan turf. From the ashy outlines, he'd been staked spread-eagle, his decapitated head jammed into his crotch.

Knowing how 'shifters despised vamps, Ren could just imagine the glee with which they'd staged this gruesome little scene, could hear their hysterical howls of laughter filling the morning air as the sun scorched their victim to dust. Yet, she didn't pity the dead sucker. In fact, very little moved her at all anymore.

What *had* tweaked her heart was the charred note tacked to the center stake. Bearing a single phrase, THE SUN KNEW HIS NAME, it was simple and to the point, putting words to her own personal torment.

As overlord of the Blood-n-Gutters, Malik had insisted the entire clan take a good, long look at the filet o' vamp. While he claimed he wanted them to learn from the fool's mistake, Ren hadn't missed the glint in his dark, bottomless eyes.

Feigning resigned acceptance of her fate, she began to investigate the clan's sudden burst of clandestine activities. Night after night she wandered casually through the rambling warehouse which served as their lair, trying to put the pieces together.

Ren's snooping paid off. Stashed in a carefully guarded storeroom was an entire arsenal of mundane weaponry pilfered from heists over the past year. Everything from AK-47s to simple crossbows was piled to the rafters.

Her curiosity bloomed into outright dread when she

found the mountain of silver in another storeroom. All this, plus the "recruitment" of several gunsmiths and mercenaries, added up to only one thing. Malik was planning a campaign of monumental proportions against the 'shifters.

A 'shifter's formidable claws, teeth and strength plus its enviable ability to move freely during the day gave it an advantage over the vamps. But it had an Achilles' heel—silver.

While fatal only in massive quantities, Malik wouldn't have to waste this precious commodity. Only a short barrage of silver bullets would be required to take the 'shifters down. Then, while they writhed in agony from silver shock, something as simple as a chain saw would effectively finish the job.

Such wholesale slaughter would satisfy Malik's blood lust, but he couldn't blatantly start a war either. Unlike him, the other overlords enjoyed the benefits of the uneasy truce between the two species. All-out hostilities resulted in corpses, which brought too many humans around asking too many questions. Their precious, bloodless hides and personal empires were far more important than any ancient feud.

So, to cover his own jugular, Malik would rely on the less intelligent of his subordinates. Young and hotheaded, they'd take matters into their own hands if sufficiently riled. Naturally the 'shifters would retaliate. He could then intervene without serious repercussions to his own person.

This elaborate plan confirmed what Ren had known all along—Malik was certifiable. Not gibbering-in-the-corner insane, but the scary kind of nuts coupled with way too much intelligence. He wouldn't stop until the entire clan was killed.

Which wouldn't be so bad, except it would begin with Runt and his father's pack, the Night Slashers. Malik had never forgiven the indomitable Bloodhunter for wresting the old neighborhood from his bloodless grasp. Malik wouldn't rest until Bloodhunter and his entire pack were a dim memory.

Which is why I'm out here avoiding critters who'd just as soon tear me to dogshit as look at me. I can't let that happen. I owe them too much.

Once she knew what Malik was up to, Ren left the warehouse. After spending a few uncomfortable days camped out in smelly Dumpsters, she managed to slip out of vamp-held territory and to set up a meeting with Runt.

Whether or not Runt would show up was a whole other question.

While her thoughts meandered, Ren's feet had automatically carried her to the site she'd picked for the meeting. Now, staring up at the defunct dry-cleaning business, she was beginning to have second thoughts. The dilapidated building was full of too many bittersweet memories.

The Night Slashers, like all 'shifter packs, were notoriously soft-hearted when it came to children. Therefore, it came as no big shock when they adopted a scrawny, homeless human; these things happened from time to time.

With the open mind only the young possess, Ren accepted her new family and its unique way of life without question or judgment. Her only regret was that she couldn't shed her own humanity to run wild and free in the night with them.

Runt had been her best friend. He was the smallest in the pack, and it was inevitable that the pair's physical limitations would draw them together. They had spent endless hours on the gritty rooftop, playing games and soaking up the warmth of the afternoon sun.

It was where they escaped punishment, shared secrets and planned for the future. And, most important of all, it was where they declared their undying love on the eve of Ren's sixteenth birthday. Tears ran down Ren's cheeks again, but she wiped them *and* the memories away with the back of a grubby hand. There wasn't time now to dwell on all she'd lost.

With a bony shoulder, she pushed through the disintegrating rear door. Creeping over debris left by bums and junkies, she carefully avoided the pitfalls so common in condemned buildings. It helped keep her mind focused.

After nearly being gutted by Gaffer, she couldn't risk another serious injury. Despite the constant hunger that plagued her, Ren refused to hunt humans. Having resorted to a steady diet of rat's blood, her system was so weak she doubted even a scraped knee would heal.

Climbing up to the roof, Ren picked a shadowy corner with a clear view of all access points and settled down to wait. Hopefully, Runt would come soon; judging from the moon's position, morning was only a few short hours away.

There *was* the distinct possibly Runt wouldn't show up. *Either way, I'm not leaving this roof,* she thought, her mouth set in a grim line. The sun knows my name.

"*Ren . . . Ren . . .*" That annoying voice tried again.

Digging her knuckles into tightly clenched eyes, Ren watched the fireworks displayed on her eyelids, ignoring both the sun and the constant hunger pangs. It worked until an hour later when a faint noise echoed through empty building, snapping her to back to reality.

A year ago she wouldn't have heard the stealthy movements. Nor could she have smelled the intruder; the sharp musky odor definitely belonged to a 'shifter. But, was it Runt? Until she was sure, she'd have to remain hidden from the 'shifter's own finely tuned senses *and* his claws.

When the 'shifter finally made it to the rooftop, Ren nearly swooned in shock. Not only was it Runt, but anyone with eyes could see his childhood nickname no longer fit. At seventeen, he stood six feet tall, and from what she remembered of his pack, it was a good bet he'd max out somewhere around six feet five inches.

Gone was the scrawny build; muscles rippled under rich, golden fur she knew to be soft as velvet, as his fists flexed open and closed. Ren ached for those arms, wanting to feel their strength once more, but knew it could never happen.

Eyes the color of a gray winter's day flashed as they swept the shadows for any sign of threat, his muzzle twitching as he deciphered the smells filling the night air. A faint growl rumbled deep in his chest, and lethal claws flashed in the moonlight.

"All right, leech! You wanted a meeting, so get to it," Runt growled. Ren winced. She'd unreasonably hoped he'd fail to notice her scent, hoping this meeting would go more smoothly.

"Patience was never one of your strong suits, was it?"

"Ren?" he said, cocking his head to one side in utter confusion.

"Yeah."

"It can't be. They said you were dead."

Ren's heart wrenched at his words. Malik had taunted her with the lie being perpetrated by the pack to explain her disappearance, hoping to get a reaction, but it hadn't worked. She knew it to be best for all concerned if Runt believed the lie.

Knowing hadn't stopped it from hurting. Still didn't.

"Well, I'm not, but that's not the issue right now," she plunged ahead. "I've got something important to tell you."

"More important than telling me where you've been?" he roared.

"Yes! I mean no. . . . Oh . . . just hush!" she sputtered. "It's Malik. He's planning something big."

"Malik's always planning something big. We'll handle it like we always do."

"Not this time. He's got too much silver, too much firepower," she explained. "You've got to warn Bloodhunter. I've brought the plans to the lair with all the secret entrances marked, plus the number of guards and such."

"How do you know so much about Malik's lair?" he said, eyeing the tattered piece of paper she held out to him suspiciously. "Unless . . . It's true, isn't it? I'd heard the rumors, but I told everybody they were lies. . . . Lies! Oh, Ren . . . why?" Her heart twisted at the anguished accusation in his voice, but a small part of her was angry.

"You think I chose this?" she shouted. It took all her self-control to rein in her raging emotions. How could he?

"We should have listened to Bloodhunter," she said, all the weariness in her soul in her voice. "Malik may be crazy, but he isn't stupid. He thought by grabbing me, he'd get first you, then Bloodhunter. Your father tried to warn us, but we wouldn't listen, so . . . here I am."

"Why didn't you let me know?" he repeated.

"What good would it have done? I'm a vamp now, a fucking bloodsucker, your sworn enemy." Her words dripped with bitter what-could-have-beens.

"Where do we go from here?" he asked.

"You take this information to your father. Stop Malik!"

"What about you?"

"What about me?"

"You can't go back. Malik will kill you."

"So? Malik has to destroy me anyway. This'll just give him a chance to get it over with."

Ren knew Malik had broken the vamps' most important edict by taking her: Never convert anyone younger than eighteen. Children, denied the chance to fully mature, always went insane.

"Ren, let me see you!" he begged.

"No!"

"Ren, I swear I won't let you leave until I've seen you!"

She ached with indecision, torn between wanting to flee into the night and wanting to race into his arms. She wanted him to make everything right.

But, Runt and his world was lost to her, had been from the moment she'd been yanked into that dark alley so long ago. Malik's hateful laughter had tormented her every day, would continue to haunt her until the sun called her name one last time.

She must have been quiet for a long time, lost to the pain, because a shuffling brought her back to the present.

"Ren? You still there?"

"Yeah," she rasped.

"Ren, I promise I won't hurt you. Just let me see you."

She listened carefully, hoping the truth she thought she heard in his voice was actually there. But, did it really matter whether Runt tore her to pieces or if the sun got her?

"All right, if that's what you really want."

Taking a deep breath, she stepped into the moonlight, praying it would be kind. She focused on a point above his head, not wanting to see the revulsion on his face.

A quick mental image of her appearance flitted through her mind. Tiny blood vessels tracing delicate patterns under translucent skin stretching over prominent cheekbones. Dark eyes filled with despair staring from their sunken orbits. Matted, shoulder-length hair and tattered, unwashed clothing completed the unappetizing picture.

An anguished whimper tore through her defenses, forcing her to look at Runt. The pain in those beautiful eyes nearly killed her.

"Oh, Ren," he choked.

She tried to turn away, finding pity more hurtful than disgust, but a powerful paw grabbed her arm, pulling her into a strong embrace. She wanted to resist, but the need, the yearning was too powerful to defy.

So she gave up, burying her face in his chest to shed the tears she'd refused to cry for Malik. Great racking sobs shook her slight frame as Runt's arms tightened around her, his deep voice murmuring in her ear.

At last, there were no more tears, just a dull ache where her heart had once been. Reluctantly, she pulled away from Runt's warmth and peered once more into his eyes. Faint shadows of hope danced there. For a fleeting moment, she almost believed.

But, even if *they* worked beyond her "condition," the pack would never stand for it. Taking a step back, she shook her head, regretfully crushing that fragile hope.

"Ren, what are we going to do?" he tried again.

"We? There is no *we* anymore," she insisted, thrusting the map into his hand. "Take this to your father. End this once and for all."

"Ren, you can't go back," he repeated.

"I never planned to."

"What?"

"Runt, I love you, but I can't go another night like this. It's time."

"No!"

"Don't, Runt. The sun knows my name."

Ren stood her ground as his steely gaze drilled into her,

watching his teeth grind impotently as he tried to come up with an argument to change her mind.

All at once, the fight went out of him as the inevitable finally sank into his brain. His shoulders slumped and his body shimmered out of focus. Ren blinked and Runt's features solidified, presenting a human face much too young for the pained expression it wore.

"All right," he grudgingly agreed. "But I'm staying, okay?"

She almost said no, but found she couldn't be so cruel. If the past year had been half as hard for him as it had for her, he'd been through enough hell. The least she could do was help him close the final chapter of this sorry little tale. Besides, a small part of her selfishly wanted his company.

"Are you sure?"

"Yes."

"Then, come, let's watch the sunrise like we used to do," she said.

Runt took her hand, and they walked to their favorite spot. Peace warmed her as he opened his arms, allowing her to snuggle close. Oh, God, how she'd missed the feel of him, the warm, rich smell of him.

They were silent, lost in pleasant memories, refusing to mar this precious time with idle small talk. It wouldn't be long now; a faint fingernail of light peeped shyly over the horizon. Ren squeezed his fingers tightly before releasing them. Her skin was already tingling as she stood up.

"Shh, now." She smiled at him, gently touching the dampness on his cheeks.

"Ren . . . Ren . . ."

Ren turned to face her old foe, drifting toward the light she'd missed, welcoming the heat building in her flesh. Funny, there was no fear now, only contentment, knowing that Runt and his pack would survive and that Malik would pay for all the pain he'd caused.

And the sun really did know her name.

"Ren . . . Ren . . ."

"Yes," she whispered as the flames blinded her. "I'm here."

Under the Tangible Myrrh of the Resonant Stars

CHARLEE JACOB

It was almost like the night used to be. When it glittered and so did we. Under the incandescent guise of neon and flash with the shadows glowing like effigies of phantoms, we had been so animated in the dark. But the heat gave the disguise up as people panted like dogs in the Dallas street.

An old woman on a bus stop bench wore red lipstick. In the gasping hot air it had streaked down her receding chin. She appeared first to have hemorrhaged. People blinked as they went by, trying to determine if she'd been coughing up blood or drinking it.

Someone stared a moment too long. The old lady swiveled, stared back viciously, and then hissed.

"What are you lookin' at? I ain't no sucker!" she yelled. She sprang to her feet and wrenched open her blouse, exposing her sunken chest, pale empty sacs of breasts. "See? The light ain't burnin' *me* up!"

She huffed and peeled all the clothes from her scrawny body, folded them neatly, and then sat down again, stark naked. The sun showed only sweat, which proved she wasn't a vampire. The sun didn't harm her.

God, it wouldn't come down to this finally, would it?

Our little family shivered as we hurried past, hoping the idea wouldn't catch hold with everyone suddenly stripping to prove their humanity.

We tried not to cling to one another. Clinging was a sign

of desperation and it brought attention. Of course, most people were desperate these days. Since the sun began its assault on the earth through the damaged atmosphere, one supercharged bolt finding a crack in the ozone could torch everything in sight. So far rains of fire had done little damage to Dallas, unlike other places we had been. But everyone waited tensely, one eye on the sky and the other on the lookout for creatures like us.

If the crowd went ballistic and folks had to strip, we'd never hide our vulnerability. Only pre–sun alert self-tanning creams with plenty of SPF helped us to get through the days. We covered up in clothes but stuck to pastels. Dark colors, especially black, accentuated the bloodlessness and could get us killed in a heartbeat. We wore just enough rouge and lipstick to give us normal color. Ours didn't melt since we didn't perspire.

A teenager went by. Without warning he began slapping his arms and staring up at the murky sky. Everyone else jittered and looked up. It had only been a firefly, alive past its season. It was December now but it was always August with fireflies, mosquitoes and chirping crickets all through Christmas. The kid blushed and walked past, fresh mosquito bites leaking dots of blood. Our small son, Matt, squeezed his eyes shut, firmly pressing his lips together so he wouldn't be seen licking them. So no one would see the inside of his mouth. I was proud of him and touched his curly head lovingly.

"Dad?" Matt asked Martin. "Can we find something to eat?"

Martin and I exchanged sighs: We knew it was hard for the boy, walking among the crowd and smelling them, salty and scarlet-fine.

An officer in an Aurora uniform stepped out of a restaurant and gave us the lean stare, fingering the ostentatious crucifix that publicly proclaimed him a dayperson. But we wore ours, too, over our clothes so that the emblem didn't touch our skin. How long would it be before the commission wised up to that ruse and required people to have crosses tattooed on their foreheads?

Seeing him, I thought of all those I had seen butchered by these bastards. I lowered my eyes so he wouldn't see the hatred in them. He swaggered away, whistling the Aurora theme. I waited till he was out of earshot before I said to my husband, "Martin, maybe they still have exchange stores in Dallas."

Martin looked at me sadly and a bit reproachfully. I felt like an idiot for even saying it, especially in front of Matt. As if plasmic groceries were still possible and we could belly up to the bar.

"Yeah?" Matt lisped hopefully. "Think so, Dad?"

Martin shook his head, replying, "We should find a park. Or a good alley. We have to be careful, son."

We squinted at the sight of an Aurora callbox on the corner.

"There's a parking garage," I suggested, pointing to the end of the street where the garage went under a bank.

"Most of those are under camera surveillance," Martin said. "I don't want to chance it."

A pretty woman came out of Neiman's. (So strange to see a department store still doing business as if tomorrow couldn't bring a solar storm that would wipe it all away.) She strode swiftly up the sidewalk. Her skin was a radiant peaches and cream. She kept her eyes down as she looked furtively up and down the walk. She briefly glanced at us, sniffing the air like a cat. She smiled before hurrying by. Then a gust of wind came through the canyon of high-rises. It tossed her skirts up and her white legs flashed.

"Sucker!" someone screamed.

Why hadn't she made up her legs, too? I wondered if she'd been finicky about the color rubbing off on her clothes.

"Sucker!"
"Sucker!"
"Sucker!"

She dropped her shopping bag to run. Martin snatched us

back protectively against the granite of a law building as she turned in the direction she'd come from, back to the other end of the street. Her eyes were wild and her lips stretched in an involuntary grimace as she cried out, a scream that was more of temple bells than banshees. I saw how pale her gums had become, almost indistinguishable from her teeth.

People shouted as they pursued her down the block. Someone hit the callbox and the alarm was deafening. There was nothing we could do but watch as she tried pitifully to shift, her outline fluttering unevenly as she attempted to fly. Her shifting was at best only partial and grotesque. She could barely even run without recent blood for nourishment. Bound to the land, she was no faster than the mob behind her.

The van screeched smoking tires around the corner, the sunrise logo of the Aurora Commission emblazoned on the door. The man we'd seen coming out of the restaurant was driving it. I heard his rebel yell through the windshield and could barely suppress the growl in my throat.

They cornered her in underground parking. Her chimes echoed on the same wind that had blown up her skirts to give her away. As they hammered their pitiless thorns into her heart, her screams were a solemn nocturne.

"Momma?" Matt buried his face in my lap.

Martin held us while the commission's wagon blared out its anthem on pumped-up speakers.

You are my sunshine, my only sunshine.
You make me happy when skies are gray.
You'll never know dear, how much I love you.
Please don't take my sunshine away.

The war cry had been a joke at first. Sunshine. Nightpeople. As if the slaughterers whistled while they worked. Heigh ho, heigh ho.

I trembled, trying hard not to do so as the van toodled by

a bit later. Everyone on the street was singing along joyfully. "You are my sunshine. . . ."

As if this were just an old ice cream truck with popsicles. Martin forced himself to sing, too, through tight lips.

"It's okay, lady." Some redneck nudged me. "They got the sucker. Devil lost hisself another 'un."

I stared down at the spilled contents of her bag. Several pairs of beige pantyhose, expensive and rare since nylon was no longer being manufactured. Too bad she hadn't slipped into a Neiman's dressing room to pull a pair on. Had she feared the rooms were monitored, studying customers for glimpses of outlawed bloodless flesh?

The bag also contained numerous pots of medium complexion makeup base, rouges, lipsticks. Featherweight gloves. All to conceal her natural pale. And a personal caprice: a violet bottle of Passion perfume. This had broken and the furnace wind smelled so sweet.

"We have such secrets to share," the first vampires to be interviewed whispered seductively. Ten years ago. The networks clubbed each other for the rights to their stories. Books were written. A *wunderkind* director made a very classy movie. There were a couple of vampire sitcoms. The public was delighted to find that the people of the night were splendid. And immortal. They had been around for thousands of years. They were history itself.

And they didn't have to kill to exist, just meet an evening's requirement of a pint or so. It was all very sexy, oral, stimulating. *New.* They were so handsome and compelling.

Martin and I were still in college when the undead were discovered, understood, popularized. Hits. Soon there were more bite-groupies around than even the vampires themselves could have foreseen. Many people wanted to experience the orgasmic thrill of being bitten, not to mention the fashionable hickeys. Others wanted to cross over entirely into the latest in-crowd. The ranks swelled until there were vampires in nearly every walk of life, no pun intended.

Vampire actors rehearsed only after sunset; vampire teachers held classes between 9 P.M. and 4 A.M.; vampire philanthropists set up nutrition programs for the homeless, exchanging food for small quantities of blood. Vampire businessmen worked alongside mortal ones to expand business hours to accommodate the rising numbers of affluent nightlife. Vampire politicians nibbled obligingly on proffered babies instead of kissing them.

It was nouveau and profitable. It was a revelation to a worn-out populace that had been drowsing in dissipation and cynicism. The nights glittered like never before. Superstition was dead. Long live the night.

Vampire scientists finally cured cancer in all its forms because by understanding blood they knew how to purify it. Vampire leaders steered potential conflicts away from eventual wars because they respected blood too much to approve of slaughter. Vampire poets comprehended total union and the emotions that made the blood pound so they made us weep and sing. It was a precious time. No more hunger or racism or murder. Only an incredible sense of sharing as more discovered the style beyond the fashion, experiencing the invigoration in shadows and the sacramental healing of starlight.

I crossed because I wanted to write and felt I needed the knowledge to take me past the mere artifice of words. Martin was an architect who wanted to design sun-proof homes. We married at one minute past midnight as a slowly creeping fog curled at the edges of the garden where our wedding party stood. Pledging all of time, the "till death do us part" deleted from the vows. We had Matt and settled into always being there, wondering how the human race could have remained ignorant for so many centuries, fleeing from rapture.

"We have such secrets to share."

The secrets weren't horror or damnation after all.

But they were an exchange of losses. First of daylight and sunny pleasures, the flavor of Mrs. Fields cookies, spaghetti sauce and milk shakes. Not so bad considering what these were replaced with. Glory, marvels, physical in-corruption in a luster of spotlights. Then that, also, was lost. When it began to rain fire.

Ten years compared with the rest of forever was nothing more than a single crimson moment.

It came down in glossy pellets no bigger than flaming matches and no smaller than tears. Bolts of solar corona zigzagged like lightning but were far more incendiary. It went off like nitro when it struck and burned like phospho-rous. It cremated everything utterly. For miles. Everything and everyone—but us. Firefighters stood helplessly with hoses gushing at impenetrable edges, watching us emerge from conflagrations unscathed, only our clothes burned off. We bore the ashes of the dead on our bodies, cupped hand-fuls of it from those mortals we had attempted to rescue. We came out naked, unhurt, carrying cinders. We opened our mouths to cry and black smoke puffed out.

This was providing it was night. We slept through daystorms unknowing, unharmed as our beds burned away beneath us and our houses fell down, disintegrated. Those who poked through ruins after the fires had burned out found us lying whole on blackened earth, opening our eyes with innocent yawns, looking at the burned dusk in amaze-ment, and at the ashes that had shielded us from the sun.

Yes, we could be burned. But only after our souls had been pinned to the earth with a stake of hawthorn or pure iron. And even then we had to be beheaded before we could be set ablaze.

Naturally, people became terrified of the threat of fiery rains. And they resented it deeply that we were immune. A rumor started among suddenly pious fools that the old leg-ends were true. Vampires really were the devil's minions. Sure to follow was the associated gossip that the fire was God's punishment for making us popular, creating a golden calf out of heretical Night. God was smiting the many who had left the sphere of ordinary woundable flesh to become glittery Liliths and brash young Draculas. For partaking of Eden's truly forbidden fruit: life's blood. Those who hadn't crossed had done nothing to stop us. They had been entertained, amused, and had willingly given us that fruit and incense besides. These were the last days. It was Judgement. So far, we minions hadn't suffered so it lacked a certain logic.

The scientific community was more pragmatic. The sun was heating up, a gradual process as it swelled over thousands or millions of years before it died into a cool dwarf. It would only be making temperatures noticeably warmer at that stage. It wouldn't engulf Mercury and Venus for a very long time nor would it burn away our oceans. But that would occur eventually so perhaps in that respect it was the beginning of the last days. The scientists were puzzled since this wasn't supposed to start for another five million years. How could their careful calculations have been wrong? Well, they had also sworn that such things as vampires did not exist. Perhaps the universe really was more magic than measure.

If only they hadn't damaged the ozone layer, rupturing it like a series of bad hernias. Solar wind poured through until even the longest night at winter solstice was uncomfortably sultry. There were volcanic eruptions, earthquakes, tidal waves. And as always vampires came out of the molten lava rivers, out of the rubble and steaming fissure, swimming up from newly submerged Atlantises to be alive when all others perished.

You would think they might seek us out, bending forward with breasts exposed, begging to be bitten and brought into the immortal fold. You would think they might find what we offered to be that much more precious. It didn't happen that way; it never does.

The first thing that did happen was that furious fundamentalists broke into the blood exchanges and ruined all the equipment, dumping the plasma down sinks and into gutters. With our food supplies closed, vampires got hungry. Unable to solicit donors, they grew starved enough to attack people. Now we hadn't only brought down God's wrath but we had become a clear and present danger. The Aurora Commission was born.

We had been living our lives, clinging to what we had. It could never happen in our city. That vestige of human hope is a frailty. We knew others had fled, had been driven out to wander the country, or had been destroyed. In those nights we lived in Massachusetts: sane New Englanders, ivy walls and the cold Atlantic Ocean and dependable Yankees.

Until the soldiers came onto our street. They had been storming every residence in town all during the day, searching for sleeping vampires. If they had come to us before sunset, we would have died. But there had been so many that the dispatching in every neighborhood stole the hours away. It was sunset by the time they made it to our block. We awoke to chimes in the wind, the dying screams of friends pierced and beheaded, rendered into poignant final notes. I got up in a rush and took Matt from his bed.

"Momma, I had a bad dream," he said, rubbing his sleepy eyes.

"What's that? Music?" Martin asked as he tilted his head and listened.

The Aurora trucks and vans rolled up nearby avenues, tinny speakers blaring *You are my sunshine, my only sunshine.* . . . The symbol of human righteousness in a rising solar disk was ironic since this is coincidentally what would destroy the planet. Well, we could have told them that.

Please don't take my sunshine away.

"Momma, is that the ice cream man?" Matt clung to me as Martin hustled us into the attic, it being too late to run from the front or back doors. They were in the yard, trampling all my carefully chosen night-blooming flowers underfoot. Those that hadn't already been scorched by the awful heat.

"It's a pogrom, son," Martin told him.

"What's that?" Matt asked.

"It means we're no longer the beautiful people," Martin replied grimly.

I shook my head. "It's just too easy to blame us, isn't it?"

"They have to blame someone. You remember what it was like to be mortal, don't you? To be that vulnerable?" Martin reminded me.

"I'm feeling pretty vulnerable right now," I said, trembling as we heard the first-floor doors splinter from the force of axes wielded by soldiers who would also use them to decapitate us. We heard all of our lovely things being smashed as they went from room to room and then moved upstairs looking for us.

Martin had to use a crowbar to pry open the attic window that had been nailed shut for years. Normally he could have opened it with a gentle shove of his fingers but we'd been forced to ration our blood from what little we still had in the refrigerator. We'd grown enervated. He helped me climb onto the roof. I pulled Matt after me. The soldiers were trying to yank the ladder down to get access to the attic. They pounded on the other side of the hatch. Matt began to cry.

"What do they want, Daddy?"

Martin climbed out last and we stood briefly on the roof with our son between us. Neither one of us was strong enough now to carry him alone so we lifted him together as we flew into the sky. The soldiers ran to the window and cursed, but could do nothing.

Our son was not a flier. Only those who had changed flew. Those born into the dark could not. Matt had never been mortal. He'd been conceived after both Martin and I had given ourselves to the night. Odd, you might think it would be the other way around, that those born with twilight native to their genes would have the inherent ability for wingshifting. This was a misconception on the part of the populace who opted for remaining human, that the fact that our children couldn't fly was somehow a degenerative characteristic. Ah, but they could race as superwolves and spread themselves into spectral smoke. Bats weren't noble creatures but wolves were fine, the consummate beasts. To be able to become smoke was profoundly mystic. Matt was such a little master before starvation made him too weak to shift. We'd been so proud of our son.

Once, I wanted to be a writer, but I never had much success. Maybe if we'd had more time. As we flew with Matt between us—hunted animals now—I composed out loud into the air. Unless we were too weak to fly. On those nights we ran, on all fours through the dark, down the eastern coast from a burned-out Boston to the monuments of D.C. that melted like fragile images in a wax museum.

There were many refugees, some like us fleeing at night and seeking the next shelter before daybreak. Others were mortals whom we easily trapped, taking only what we needed and then letting them go, reluctant to harm them because we used to be like them. We went over mountains, simpler to find cover from the sun but harder to find people. We grew feeble until even running was sluggish, humanly slow.

Finally we were sick, locating just before one midnight a farm in the heartland that hadn't been abandoned. It was alone in a quadrant of cornfields. We dragged ourselves through rows of scorched and useless crops, thinking we saw moonlight along the path to the house. Heart. Land. How inviting. The words when spoken were meaty. We could almost swallow them and feel satiated.

"I love thee as I love the night," I whispered into Martin's ear as we crouched in stuffy shadows from farm buildings. Matt was gasping. "One and the same, darkness and you. Come seal me in your evening arms and make us a bed upon the wings of nightbirds."

My husband nuzzled my shoulder affectionately, excitement barely suppressed because we could sense the living warmth glowing within the walls. We were nearly fainting from hunger, smelling the rusty odor of the blood of those inside.

"The infinite lingers in your breath," I sighed as we crept

to windows, prepared to launch ourselves through them, "and there is the taste of twilight on your tongue. The world is a dreaming tomb tonight where death is not an end but the genesis of a long graceful running under the tangible myrrh of the resonant stars."

We weren't strong enough to beat down the door. So sick. The metallic red odor was narcotic.

The windows shattered inward as we threw our bodies through them. The glass cut the family sitting by a radio in their living room. But it didn't cut them so much that they couldn't jump to their collective feet and scream. I breathed in their wonderful scent, murmuring as I squeezed Martin's hand before grabbing a pulsing throat, "I do love thee as I love the night, inhaling the musk that never fades."

We didn't want to kill them. We really didn't intend that it go that far. We couldn't help ourselves once we started. We were so hungry. It can make even the most honorable into hunters.

From that first time it became easier to drain what solitaries we tracked down. They were so few and far between that every drop that flowed through them might be what stood between paralysis and the ability to run to one more shadow and one more straggler. When I first crossed, I did it for poetry, never dreaming I would eventually kill or that the compulsion for the elixir could escalate into a fever in which I became a butcher.

We saw scarlet glowing on purple horizons. Corona bolts dancing that far away seemed elemental and elegant. We watched the distant storms in awe, as the solar wind blew back to us the stench of ruined meat.

We ran along the coast of Louisiana, splashing through fetid bayou, scores of water moccasins rising up, deadly mouths sprung open and as cottony white as ours. We came up under a boat of Cajun fishermen, biting them to discover that their flesh tasted of crawfish. But their blood had been rich so we managed to fly for a while, lifting Matt who giggled when taken high enough to see the lights below twinkle in sequins. When we descended at last to find a safe place to sleep, I had trouble losing the wings. I shifted back painfully, bowed into an arc, shoulder blades jutting monstrously. It frightened me but it was finally gone two sunsets later as we ran across northeast Texas and into Dallas.

Going down the sidewalk under the illuminated dandelion of Reunion Tower, we were shaken by the swift work of the Aurora Commission. We hadn't seen that much of them since we'd been driven from our home in Massachusetts. They were easier to dodge in the outlying areas. Sticking to routes that included no roads, it was possible to be missed by them entirely. Of course, it was also easier to starve since refugees kept to the roads.

We didn't attempt to feast the first night. We had been scared off from hunting after the woman was killed in the underground parking. So it had been three nights since we'd had anything at all. Matt was stumbling. People were staring at our haggardness suspiciously. They used to say you couldn't be too rich or too thin. But when the gauntness began to resemble the feral, mortals might recognize the animal you carried. We had to leave the compact crowds of downtown for the privacy of the parks at White Rock Lake. We hoped to find some succulent bag lady asleep amid the heat-wilted willows.

There were swans on the silent water, gliding rhetorical question marks in ghostly white feathers. Matt scampered ahead of us and into the water, splashing up to his chin the way a frisky dog would. He caught a swan not too far from the bank and dragged it to shore with its wings beating furiously. There he broke its delicate neck to drink deeply. It wasn't nearly enough to fill a starving hollow but it took a fraction off the edge of the boy's hunger.

Martin and I sniffed the air. There was the scent of rust somewhere to the left, slight, pulsing only one set of coronary rhythms. It was gliding gradually closer. It glowed like a ripe strawberry in the dark. Matt smelled it, too, and trembled with excitement, the swan's blood still damp on his tongue. He whimpered and ran in the direction of that glowing strawberry.

"Matt," Martin said sharply, trying to warn him to show caution. "Wait, boy. We'll check it out first."

But Matt had already leapt onto the man slowly pedaling up the old bike path. He knocked him off the ten speed and the two of them rolled into the dried grass. The man didn't yell much, hearing the growl from the half-pint who had tackled him. He groped for a device clipped to his belt and managed to set it off. Latest gadget on the market, similar in intent to the rape whistle. It was a vampire alarm, tattling a noise that was a high-pitched oscillating birdcall. Matt didn't care. He easily soaked in—grunting with each—the few punches the mortal managed to connect and then leaned in for the soft throbbing artery that beckoned so deliciously.

We arrived to see the shock in the man's eyes of being murdered by a wispy seven-year-old with the tender face of a poster child. He blinked his confusion, limply flailing one more fist as Matt tore into him.

"I don't know if anybody heard that or not," Martin said, worried, as I ran forward.

I was helpless to resist the richness of that odor. Our faces were close, Matt's and mine, brushing brows as I bent to lap up greedily. He winked at me. I got no more than a few swallows when I heard Martin shriek in dying bells.

We bolted upright in the grass, startled, confused in starving blood lust. And saw a soldier deliver another blow to the spike gleaming through my husband's chest.

Aurora had arrived speedily, silently. We had just been too preoccupied and enthralled, filling ourselves on what emptied from the dying man into us to hear the commission's park patrol pull up. I stood and charged, screaming at them hysterically as the soldier swung the axe and my Martin's handsome head parted a gaping rictus deeper in the neck than what Matt had done to the man on the bike. That damnable tape switched on then and their anthem warbled out a slaughtering vaudeville. *You are my sunshine, my only sunshine. You make me happy when skies are gray. . . .* Another swing and the head rolled free. Martin's chiming song echoed off, backdropped by *You'll never know, dear, how much I love you. Please don't take my sunshine away.*

I howled, feeling my heart doing a nearly mortal twist. I wanted to rush at them, kill them. Which I wasn't strong enough to do but the fury and grief could easily have made me try it anyway. There was Matt to consider. I tried to turn in time to grab my boy and flee, praying I had enough blood in me to wingshift and that I'd be strong enough to carry him up. I knew I didn't. It was pointless anyway because the soldiers had come around the side of us and now scooped him up where he still hunched over his kill. He opened his mouth in terror and cried, *"Mommie,"* the mortal's gore spilling out onto his T-shirt, a sparkling gobbet of it clinging to his chin.

I attacked in rage, biting and clawing any part of anyone I could get hold of, but I'd been sick and starved too long. A soldier turned casually and clubbed me with the blunt end of a hatchet, again and again until I fell away weakly. It never could have happened had I been well nourished. He and another held me down.

"Do it to the kid while this bitch watches, Frank," he shouted to one of his companions throwing Matt onto his back. He'd fed well by the time they grabbed him and it took four of them to hold down this one small boy. He beat his arms and legs in frenzy, almost jerking free of them. Pink foam ran freely from his lips. He began to vaporize, fingers and hair turning into smoke.

"Get him fast. He's shifting. Don't want to lose the little bastard," the soldiers were shouting.

I heard Matt cry out for me as someone pulled Matt's own crucifix up over his T-shirt and pressed it against one baby blue eye. The boy shrieked as skin bubbled and the optic tissue popped as if probed with a hot poker. His misting stopped, hair and fingers reforming.

"So, Momma, do you just suck necks or could we interest you in something streamlined?" one of the soldiers remarked as he hit me in the crotch with the axe's blunt end several times.

I doubled up, coughing up what few bloody mouthfuls I'd swallowed only minutes before.

You are my sunshine, my only sunshine, babbled that inane tape. The soldiers hocked out the words roughly as they pinned Matt's soul to the earth.

"Sucker's full," joked the man with the pure iron as blood fountained up into his face. "Not hard to find the heart on this one. That other one was so dry he didn't even spurt."

They laughed as I struggled, weaker, no more violently than a toss in troubled sleep would produce. I wept as I watched them behead my little boy.

"Are you getting all this down, sucker?" one of the soldiers pinning me asked.

Once in the shimmering night of richer moments, even these men would have admired my beauty and sought out the sweetness offered in my shadow. Their sweaty faces leered now, and sour perspiration dripped from them into my eyes. Matt's voice thinned away like the spectral smoke he once did well, into the solar wind a scream that was a dying flute playing "Greensleeves."

You'll never know dear, how much I love you. . . . The tape whined on, sappy, bemused on saccharine.

"Please don't take my sunshine a-way!" the soldiers sang lustily, whooping it up as if at a drunken wake.

"Your turn, baby. How do you like your stake? Slow and easy or hard and fast?"

A soldier produced another hearty splinter of iron, ready-made by a foundry for the commission and the material of choice since hawthorn wasn't plentiful. I was too weak to fight at all. I looked up at the ring of oily mortal faces prepared to launch me from the night's musky eternity into another dark's unconscious impotence. Ten years we possessed the forever. Now it seemed we were past our season, like the fireflies. I could see them, winking in the night sky as the soldiers ripped off my blouse to expose my pale breasts.

"X marks the spot," old mallet-man chuckled.

One of them screamed. Not bells nor chimes but the raucous grating human version that clattered with a rattle in the wind. A firefly had landed in his hair and he went up like a torch.

It was raining fire, pellets of it striking the lake and fizzing. The soldiers jumped to their feet, forgetting about me, and began to run for cover. Only there was no cover from this storm.

Corona bolts flashed over the water and high-rises were exploding on the visible silhouette of downtown. All the Aurora men were on fire before they could even make it to their van—which was useless anyway.

I stood up wearily in the shower of sparks and flames, seeing the bodies of my husband and son ablaze. Staked and decapitated, their flesh dissolved into spilled ether, whispering steam as it glossed, then slid off in graying layers from unraveling limbs to cloying bits of sizzling organs in an ashening pool.

The humans fried differently, more brightly. I stumbled to the nearest and grabbed his shriveling body. I took him, and then I helped myself to another. More, feasting quickly before their juices could boil away. It was like sucking the juices from whole carcasses roasting on spits, trying to catch the glimmering red that spouted from the cracks before it could run as grease into the flames. I held their crackling bodies to me and couldn't burn myself as they blackened into husks, then fell apart in my hands. I fed well. Deeply. Until my veins glowed and my own skin shone all rosy in hell.

I brought out my wings easily and ascended through the walls of incredible heat. My shifting was arch, leathery, and I knew that I would never be able to shift back. The wings were mine forever. As were the talons and the harsh rustle of skin as stiff and lustrous as taffeta.

My back angled under the coarsening ridge of deformed spine that supported the wings. On the ground I scuttled crookedly, warped and graceless when not in the air. Only my face was still beautiful, my eyes bright as moonlight and my lips full, able to sing chimes and sweet high bells to lure travelers into my nest of stings. Happy little tunes to catch them off-guard.

You are my sunshine, my only sunshine. . . .

But when alone I remembered the true music, while the sun swelled like a sore on the other side of the world until even the dark became too hot to bear. And I would shed lilith tears over that lost dusk that had glittered so. I love thee as I love the night.

CONTRIBUTORS' BIOGRAPHIES

Sharon Lee has been writing speculative fiction for twenty years. "Passionato" is her first vampire story. She is co-author, with Steve Miller, of the popular Liaden Universe; visit their Web page at www.korval.com.

Diana Pharaoh Francis has a Ph.D. in Victorian Women's literature and has sold stories to markets including *Glyph, Medusa's Hairdo, Romance and Beyond, Shadow Sword, and Shadow Sword Presents.* She writes science fiction, fantasy and dark humor. On the personal side, she is married with dogs, and has discovered that remodeling the house isn't as easy as everyone makes it look on TV.

Warren Lapine is the publisher of DNA Publications and the editor of *Absolute Magnitude,* and has had more than forty stories and poems published in such magazines as *Dreams of Decadence, Pirate Writings,* and *Fantastic Collectibles,* as well as several anthologies. Warren has also edited an anthology of stories from *Absolute Magnitude,* available from Tor Books. He has been nominated for a Chesley Award and a World Fantasy Award. Visit the DNA Publications Web site at www.dnapublications.com.

Tippi N. Blevins has been writing for as long as she can remember. Originally from Taiwan and living in Texas, Tippi has written stories and poems that have appeared in dozens of magazines, anthologies, and Web sites, including *Dreams and Nightmares, Epitaph, Pirate Writings, Prisoners of the Night, Star*Line, Talebones, Zero Gravity Freefall,* and BookFace.com, plus numerous anthologies. In her spare time, she pursues her interests in anthropology, history, marine biology, and very loud industrial music.

Robin Simonds Fitch's first short story, "Prima Facie," won first place for fiction in the 1997 edition of Southern Connecticut State University's *Folio Art and Literary Magazine.* She graduated from SCSU in 1997 with Honors in English and credits Professor Tim Parrish and her fellow writers (and friends) with helping her develop her talent and her voice. "After the Fire" is part of the novel *Venom,* on which Robin is currently working.

Laura Anne Gilman's fiction has appeared in over a dozen magazines and anthologies, and she is the author of several novels, including two *Buffy the Vampire Slayer* novels, *Visitors,* and *Deep Water,* as well as the Executive Editor of Roc Books.

Siobhan Burke is a lifetime student of English history, and a member of the Richard III Society. She enjoys re-creating period food and feasts, and has worked professionally re-creating period costume. She lives in Maine with her husband, a literal ton of books and an odd assortment of houseplants.

Steve Patten breeds exotic reptiles, and shares his apartment with "a seventeen-foot-long python named Doc who likes to read over my shoulder, fourteen other snakes of various breeds, four cats, six leopard geckos, a fish, and several turtles and tortoises" as well as his roommate. His work has appeared in *Bloodsongs, Black Lotus, Shadowdance, The Cosmic Unicorn,* and the anthology *Dominion of the Ghosts.*

Sarah A. Hoyt has published over two dozen short stories, a substantial portion of those in DNA Publications magazines *Absolute Magnitude, Weird Tales, Fantastic,* and *Dreams of Decadence.* She has also been published by other magazines including *Analog* and *Dark Regions* and the anthology *Apprentice Fantastic.* Her first novel, *Ill Met by Moonlight*—a Shakespearean fantasy—was published by Ace in 2001. She has sold two other novels in the same series.

Angela Kessler is the editor of *Dreams of Decadence* magazine and assistant publisher of DNA Publications. Her poetry has appeared in magazines such as *Pirate Writings, Shadowdance,* and *Haunts,* among others. Visit the *Dreams of Decadence* Web site at www.dnapublications.com/dreams.

Alexandra Elizabeth Honigsberg is known for her darkly numinous, romantic-gothic poetry and fiction. Anthologies such as White Wolf's *Dark Destiny* series, *Dante's Disciples,* and *Pawn of Chaos,* as well as *New Altars* (Angelus Press), *On Crusade* (Warner/Aspect), *Blood Muse* (Donald I. Fine Publishing), and *Angels of Darkness* (SFBC) have included her work. She is a professional musician, a scholar of comparative religions, and lives with her husband and two cats in Upper Manhattan, land of forests, fjords, and the Unicorn Tapestries. She is a regular guest artist with the Don't Quit Your Day Job Players and appears on their first CD, *TKB.*

Angelique de Terre writes that she lives in a garret with a gilded ceiling located on soil with a history of bloody rebellion. A tiny trust fund enables her to lie around all day fantasizing, mostly about vampires. Every so often one of her fantasies manifests a beginning, a middle, and an end, so she gets up, switches on one of the ancient pieces of digital circuitry that litter the place, and taps it out. At night she consorts with transsexual witches and has been known to perform the occasional supernatural act herself. She hopes that all you story-eaters out there find this one especially tasty.

Tanith Lee is a British author well-known in both the U.K. and the U.S. for her many novels and for her excellent short fiction. Her stories have appeared in magazines such as *Asimov's, Interzone,* and *Weird Tales.* She is a World Fantasy Award winner and a Nebula nominee.

Mike Watt is a semi-successful, Pittsburgh-based screenwriter, playwright, and novelist. His first play, "Pfc Everyman" swept the awards at the 1994 Pittsburgh New Works Festival. His fiction and essays have appeared both electronically and in print, including in David Silva's "Hellnotes."

Lyda Morehouse has been writing science fiction/fantasy professionally for over seven years. A proud, card-carrying member of the National Writers Union, her short stories have appeared in such intriguing publications as *Dark Moon Sisters, QRD,* and *Nocturnal Ecstasy Vampire Coven.* She lives in Saint Paul with her partner and works at the Minnesota Historical Society. Her novel *Archangel Protocol* is available from Roc Books.

Lawrence Watt-Evans the Hugo Award–winning author of more than two dozen novels and around a hundred short stories, as well as innumerable articles, comic scripts, poems, and other miscellany. Visit his Web site at www.sff.net/people/lwe.

L. Jagi Lamplighter is a graduate of St. John's College in Annapolis. She lives in Northern Virginia with her husband, writer John C. Wright, and their sons, Orville and Wilbur. "Feeding the Mouth That Bites Us" was her third published story.

Brian Stableford lives in England. His short fiction has appeared in *Asimov's, Interzone,* and *SF Age,* among others; he is the author of dozens of science fiction novels and nonfiction books.

Ann K. Schwader's poems have recently appeared in *Weird Tales,* Chaosium's *The Innsmouth Cycle* and *The Nyarlathotep Cycle,* and elsewhere. Some have earned Honorable Mentions in past volumes of *Year's Best Fantasy and Horror.* Her fiction credits include *Aboriginal SF, Prisoners of the Night,* and Chaosium's second "Deep Ones" anthology. She lives and writes in Westminster, Colorado.

Josepha Sherman is a fantasy, science fiction, and *Star Trek* novelist, as well as a folklorist and storyteller, with over two dozen novels and over 125 short stories and articles. Her work has received a Compton Crook Award. She's an active member of The Authors Guild, SFWA, the American Folklore Society, and the SCBWI, as well as a fan of all things SF, equine, computer-oriented, aviation, and of the long-suffering New York Mets. Visit her Web site at www.sff.net/people/Josepha.Sherman.

Vickie T. Shouse is a typist and bookkeeper in an insurance office by day and spends her evenings feverishly pecking away at the computer keyboard between quick trips to the library to do research. She says she is learning how to deal with the strange looks that she gets when she asks for books on such subjects as bombs and neurotoxins. Her credits include *Dreams of Decadence* and *The Vampire's Crypt.*

Charlee Jacob's first novel, *This Symbiotic Fascination,* was published by Necro in 1998 and was nominated for both the Bram Stoker Award and the International Horror Guild Award for best first novel; it has been reissued in paperback by Leisure Books. Her first fiction collection, *Dread in the Beast,* was released by Necro in 1999 and the title novella was nominated for the Bram Stoker Award. Her second collection, *Up, Out of Cities That Blow Hot and Cold,* was published by Delirium Books in 2000 and was also nominated for the Bram Stoker Award. Leisure is also publishing her second novel, *Soma.* Another fiction collection, *Guises,* is scheduled to be published by Delirium Books in 2003. Her recent poetry collection, *Flowers from a Dark Star,* has been nominated for the Bram Stoker Award for Best Poetry Collection. Her poetry and short fiction have been published in magazines including *Aberrations, Deathrealm, Galaxy, Keen Science Fiction, Midnight Zoo, Star*Line, Stygian Articles, Tales of the Unanticipated,* and *Terminal Fright.*

COPYRIGHT NOTICES

See what's coming in April...